DATE DUE			
MAY 24 2022			

The Sky Worshipers

F.M. Deemyad

ISBNs: 978-1-73295-086-3 (pb); 978-1-73295-088-7 (hc); 978-1-73295-087-0 (eBook)

Front cover artwork: Cameleers and sky background courtesy of Dmitry Rukhlenko / Shutterstock.com; Desert foreground courtesy of Anton Petrus / Shutterstock.com
Cover and book design by Mayfly Design
Map illustration courtesy of Narges and Chris Thayer

Library of Congress Control Number: 2020938813
First Printing: 2020
Printed in the United States of America

Publisher's Cataloging-In-Publication Data
(Prepared by The Donohue Group, Inc.)
Names: Deemyad, F. M., author.
Title: The sky worshipers : a novel / by F.M. Deemyad.
Description: Minneapolis, Minnesota : History Through Fiction, [2021] | Includes bibliographical references.
Identifiers: ISBN 9781732950863 (pb) | ISBN 9781732950887 (hc) | ISBN 9781732950870 (eBook)
Subjects: LCSH: Mongols—History—13th century—Fiction. | Genghis Khan, 1162-1227—Fiction. | Princesses—13th century—Fiction. | Karakorum (Extinct city)—Fiction. | Man-woman relationships—Fiction. | LCGFT: Historical fiction.
Classification: LCC PS3604.E299 S59 2021 (print) | LCC PS3604.E299 (ebook) | DDC 813/.6—dc23

In the Name of the Almighty

This is a fact-based work of fiction infused with elements of fantasy covering the Mongol invasions of Asia, Middle East, and Eastern Europe during the thirteenth century and beyond. The episodes detailed in this story are inspired by real events that took place centuries ago. Imaginative changes that are consonant with the reality of the time have been made and details added to bring the events of that era to life.

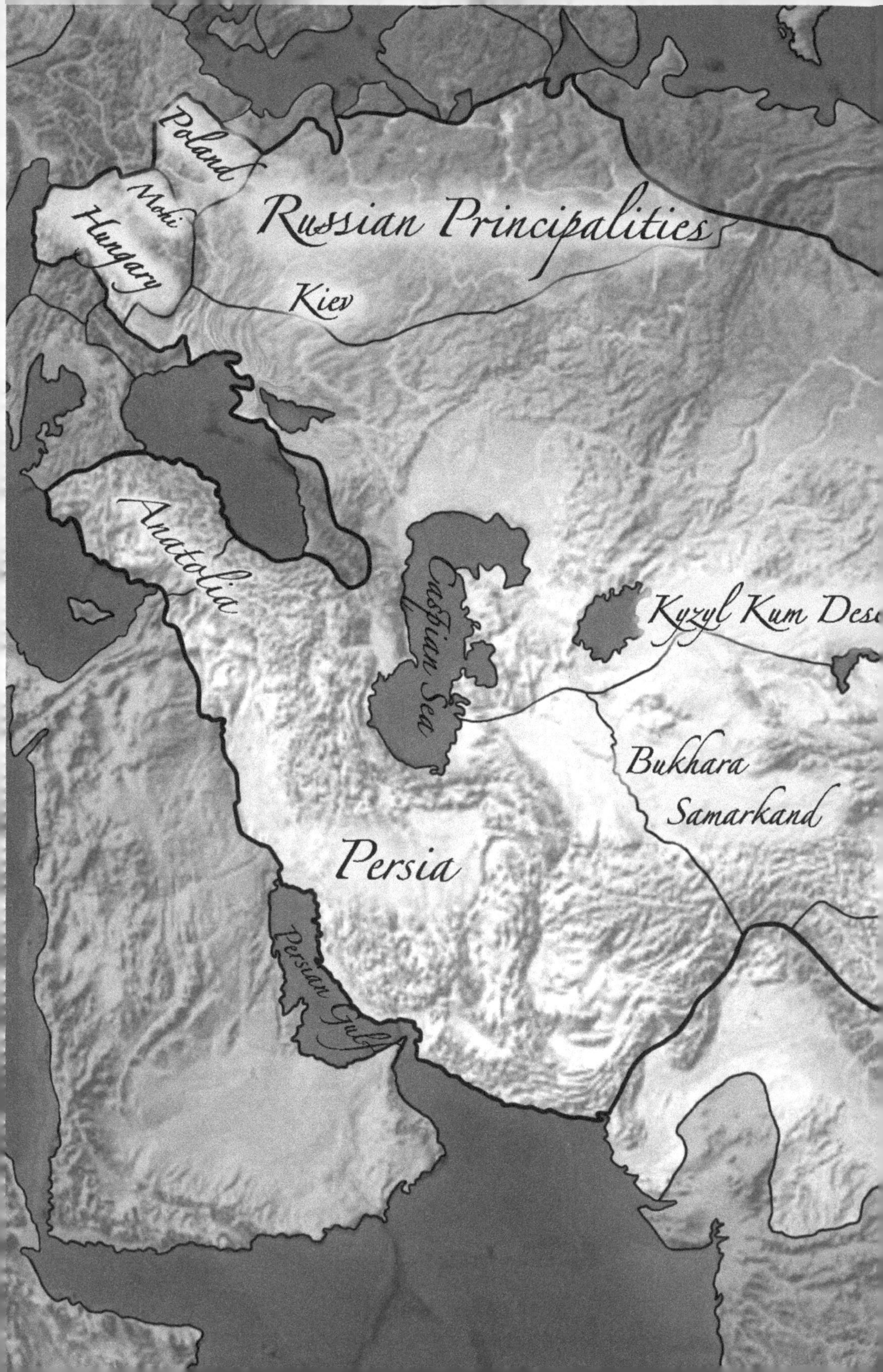
Poland
Mohi
Hungary
Russian Principalities
Kiev
Anatolia
Caspian Sea
Kyzyl Kum Des
Bukhara
Samarkand
Persia
Persian Gulf

Mongolia
Karakorum
Gobi Desert
Tangut Kingdom
Chinese Territories

Power decrees the norms by which people live. When power changes hands dramatically, all equilibriums, calculations, and norms turn upside down. When the sky-worshiping Mongols began ruling large portions of the earth in the early years of the thirteenth century, they vanquished or annihilated any power that stood in their way. The Mongols spared the lives of those who submitted to their rule, but those nations had to forgo their previous notions of living in order to survive in this new world.

Introduction

THE 13TH CENTURY IS AN EPISODE IN HISTORY THAT, TO this day, remains in the minds of many people whose countries were affected by the Mongol invasions as an unforgettable era. Documentaries based on this tumultuous period attract tens of thousands of viewers, and generations of people have read with great fascination the many books and articles written about Genghis Khan and his legacy.

The swift and mindboggling manner in which the Mongols were able to conquer much of the world, subduing magnificent civilizations of the time despite their relative naïveté and lack of a huge army is quite impressive. One can easily argue that Genghis Khan was among the most striking personalities of the 13th century, although most people in the United States know little about him. His dramatic rise to power from humble beginnings, the fact that not only he united the country that came to be known as Mongolia but conquered a large stretch of the world, has indeed fascinated historians and students of military strategy.

Genghis Khan promoted his officers for their talents and skills, regardless of their tribal affiliations. Such promotions were contrary to the prevalent Mongol culture; yet, at times, he even allowed his former enemies to reach high ranks in his army if they proved their loyalty to him. He displayed great tolerance for foreign religions, although he could hardly distinguish one from the other. Muslims, Jews, Christians, and Buddhists practiced their faith freely in Karakorum, the Mongol capital.

He offered a chance for peaceful submission to the Mongol rule, and nations that did not resist Mongol invasions were spared. However, he showed no mercy to those who defied him. Like lightning, the

Mongols conquered lands from Transoxiana to Persia and China, from Russia to Hungary and Poland, from Vietnam to Japan and Korea. No power could stand in the face of Mongol onslaught as they raped and plundered the fruits of the earth with an insatiable hunger. It is hard to imagine how moats were filled with prisoners of war, as Mongol siege engines constructed on-site by captured Chinese prisoners allowed these warriors of the Steppes to reach deep into the heart of the most magnificent cities of their time.

James Chambers, a contemporary historian, describes Samarkand, the capital of Persia during the pre-Mongol era, with these words: "Huge suburbs shaded by poplar trees and decorated with fountains and canals surrounded a city so rich that even within its walls every house had a garden. In the factories the citizens wove silk, cotton and silver lamé, the Persian craftsmen worked saddles, harnesses and decorated copper, and the workshops of the Chinese quarter produced the rag paper that was used throughout the Middle East. From the fields beyond the suburbs, the farmers exported melons and aubergines wrapped in snow and packed in lead boxes." Ata Malek Juvayni, one of the greatest Persian historians of the Mongol era, wrote the following account of the invasion: "They came, they reaped, they burnt, they killed, they plundered, they left."

According to some accounts, during the Mongol conquests that lasted through generations and left a large portion of the earth empty of its inhabitants, nearly 40 million people lost their lives, and great civilizations of that time were brought to their knees. Hungarians, to this day, mourn the horrors of the Mongol offensive. Modern historians, scientists, and archeologists have disputed some of these records. Their experiments and excavations show that the numbers actually killed by the Mongols in conquered lands were intentionally exaggerated to strike fear in the hearts of those who dared to resist.

Studies on the types of tools used by the Mongols indicate their ingenuity in utilizing military equipment. Their agility on horseback, and the fact that they trained children at a very young age to ride horses, gave them superiority in combat. Not only did they hire or force into labor scientists and engineers, chemists, and craftsmen of conquered lands, but they also resorted to fantastic strategies and maneuvers that to this day are taught at military schools around the world.

As a child growing up in Iran, I wondered why people named their children after Genghis despite the destruction and pillaging of the country by his hordes. My father, son of a scholar who taught English literature in India's universities, came to Iran when he was 29 years old and there he met and married my mother. I still recall my father's nighttime stories about his adventures, hunting in the jungles of India. He became an animal lover later in life and let me keep pets as wild and varying as my imagination would allow. He also introduced me to the beauty and eloquence of classic English literature. I recall how I would memorize passages I hardly understood as a preschooler and relate them with great animation to an audience of relatives who had no knowledge of the language, although they admired the fact that I could speak in a foreign tongue.

I was sent by my Muslim parents to a Christian school for the first two years of my education, and then to a primarily Jewish one until ninth grade, for they offered English courses. The last two years of high school before obtaining my diploma and heading to the U.S. for graduate studies, I attended a public school in Iran. After decades of living away from the Middle East, however, when the politics of the region leave me confused, I find it rather refreshing to place my focus on life during the 13th century.

My research on the Mongol era began during my studies at Johns Hopkins University, and I recall that for a long time I felt overwhelmed not only by the magnitude and complexity of the information regarding the Mongols but also by the contradictions that existed between the different narratives.

I knew that the Mongols had hired Persian, Chinese, and Armenian historians to chronicle their victories and legacy in a manner that pleased them. Having knowledge of the Persian language had enabled me to study the impressive works of Persian historians. Reading the writings of Juvayni and translated works of other historians, I noticed how at times, truth emerged cloaked within words that the Mongols did not find offensive.

I remember complaining to my professors at school that I felt as if I had swum to the middle of the ocean where there was no turning back and no going forward. The era seemed just as dark and deep. Eyewitnesses to the events who were hired by the Mongols to chronicle their victories were probably too fearful of their vengeful masters to give true accounts. In some areas, I could not even find consensus among modern historians, such as Morris Rossabi, Jack Weatherford, James Chambers, Rene Grousset, and the works of Charles River Editors. Reading countless articles and online sources about the era failed to give me the clarity I sought.

I decided to try seeing the world through the eyes of both the Mongol rulers and the inhabitants of the areas they conquered as Genghis Khan and his sons trampled rich and poor under the hooves of their horses all the way to the gates of Vienna. Visualizing life in the 13th century was difficult. Roads and transportation, dwellings, palaces, lifestyles, and even the flowers that grew in different parts had to be meticulously researched. I felt hindered and frustrated, but I had invested so much time and energy that I could not set the work aside and begin another. Finally, one sleepless night, for the first time after months of confusion, I began to see the world of the 13th century as diverse and magnificent, from the colorful turbans of the Muslim caliphs to the metal attire of the knights and the leather garments of Mongol warriors.

My new outlook toward the era allowed me to put the pieces of this complicated puzzle together, although many a time rewriting some sections became necessary. For example, the reason why Genghis Khan decided to choose an heir while he was still living had puzzled some historians. After all, this went against the Mongol tradition. But then reading about Genghis's childhood and how unexpectedly his father was killed, leaving him and his mother and siblings at the mercy of nature, made me realize that he had every motive to select an heir while still powerful and of sound mind.

Also, the accounts of Genghis's death varied as did his place of burial. Originally, based on one account, I wrote that he was buried in a region of China, where he was struck by an arrow and died. However,

I was not comfortable with that account. His followers revered him and would not leave his body at the disposal of his enemies. Whatever it took, they would most certainly carry his remains back to Mongolia for proper burial, very possibly to the area near the holy Burkhan Khaldun Mountain where he was born.

I found the innovating tactics of war used by the Mongols fascinating, but my intention was not to write a book of horror but one resembling "One Thousand and One Nights" that would be enjoyable to read. The question was how to tell a tale filled with brutality in a way that places the focus on the humanity of the heroes and heroines who allowed life to continue under the most taxing conditions? Tolstoy came to my rescue, and after re-reading "War and Peace," I learned how to fade the accounts of war, leaving the blood and gore of the era in the background, while bringing to the fore the interactions of the characters in the story. I avoided direct references to the carnage and placed true accounts beneath a veneer of storytelling focused on survival.

A major issue that has baffled historians of the Mongol era is the profound transformation the Mongol rulers underwent in a relatively short period of time with each generation becoming much more sophisticated. I have reached the conclusion that the children of Genghis and his sons were probably reared or were influenced by the well-educated women from other civilizations who were kidnapped or taken as prisoners of war and brought to the Mongol court.

The existence of a secret history of the Mongols is at times mentioned in the works that I have studied. Research shows, however, that such a secret history exists but has been dismissed for being too pro-Mongol. I wondered if, among the many women taken as captives by the Mongols, there were those who actually wrote a secret history to be found by future generations.

The first personality I studied in this regard was Chaka, a Tangut Princess, about whom I found a few lines of information online. I also knew that women, probably high ranking ones, were taken from Persia. Thus the personality of Reyhan, granddaughter of the last Seljuk King, was shaped. I also learned, during the course of more than five years as I researched the Mongols, that two princesses of European origin were held captive within the Mongol court. The only information I had about them was that they were both called Mary and that the European courts disowned them once they were taken. The children of royal families of the time in Hungary and Poland were accounted for, but then I learned that the brother of Henry II had died. It was quite possible that the king had taken his brother's children under his wings, and it was also possible that the two kidnapped from Poland were personalities like Krisztina and Zofia mentioned in my novel. Princess Sokhokhtani is a well known Mongol personality, and Lady Goharshad is a much revered historical figure, both of whom take on center stage in the novel.

One can only imagine how difficult it must have been for women, let alone princesses belonging to sophisticated courts, to be kidnapped and forced into conformity with the Mongol society and culture at the time. Most writings about this era depict the women taken by the Mongols as victims; however, my idea was to avoid such generalizations and show how women influenced the Mongols from within. I also wanted to portray the entire era of Mongol invasions in one book, and to this end, I am thankful to my professors at Johns Hopkins University who suggested that I place the focus on the main female characters and use the secret chronicle they shared as a medium that bond them.

Growing up, reading the original works of writers like Oscar Wilde and Sir Walter Scott, filled my pastime. A passion for reading has continued throughout my life. Books have been my mentors in hardship, my companions whenever I have felt lonely, and my advisors when I needed help. It is my hope that my novels would one day do for others as they have done for me, being the best friends one could ever have.

On a dark winter night in 1162 AD, a nomad woman gave birth to a male child on a hillside near the Khentii Mountains. She called him Temujin, but history remembers him as Genghis Khan. In a period of less than a century, Genghis Khan not only united his own people but also conquered numerous lands on the Asian and European continents. Among the many women who were taken by force or as prisoners of war, there were a few princesses who came of age in the palaces of conquered lands. This is their story.

Book I

The Sharp Dagger

Prologue

Karakorum [1398 C.E.]

"BURIED? HOW LONG?" LADY GOHARSHAD PEERED CLOSELY at the manuscript as she stood beneath a torch among the ruins of Karakorum, her silk gown thc same soft amethyst as the evening sky above.

"More than a century," King Shahrokh traced the lines with his finger. Leather worn with age covered numerous sheaves of papyrus. Tiny specks of dust illuminated by light rose from time-worn pages.

"And we discovered it?" Lady Goharshad watched as her husband, Shahrokh Mirza, the ruler of Persia and Transoxiana, examined the voluminous cord-bound manuscript. She could hear sounds of tapping and knocking as laborers placed tiles on newly repaired walls and floors, and guilders worked their fine brushes over candelabra.

"*We* did not discover it. The workmen did during the renovations I ordered. It was buried in a hidden compartment under a layer of tiles that covered the floor of the atrium."

The queen's curiosity piqued, but she would not touch the book, caked in dust. Her husband ventured his hand and randomly opened a page. "It is in some foreign language. Let us get away from all this noise."

She followed her husband past the stupas that bordered the vast enclosure. Before her stood palatial buildings of an era gone by; candles squatted in every niche and torches flickered between the ramparts.

"Do you believe history repeats itself?" she asked, looking around at the ancient structures.

"Yes, I believe that is true. Here," Shahrokh walked toward an archway of masonry that led into a courtyard and the rusted iron base of a fountain. They entered the main auditorium and stood before a tall brick fireplace. Perforations here and there in the walls allowed one to view the flames in the fire pit when lit. They stepped onto the bare dirt floor with only a few blue tiles visible upon it, remnants of flooring that had been pilfered piece by piece over time. The light of a nearby torch illuminated one brick on the arch-shaped panel above the fireplace that had moved out of place.

"Time may have caused the brick to come loose!" Shahrokh said, and then quickly added, "No, it is not time that has caused this. No mortar was used in the first place to attach it to other bricks." He gestured to an attendant accompanying them, and the young lad quickly placed one foot on the raised hearth, the other on the mantel shelf and pulled his body up by holding on to the crown molding. He then removed the loose brick, disclosing a vacant spot in the wall. Dust rose as he reached inside and excavated a small silver box, lined in red velvet. He handed the box to the king.

Shahrokh took out a turquoise talisman attached to a thin leather cord. He set aside the box and began re-examining the manuscript he was still holding, carefully turning the frayed pages. "Looks like a chronicle written in several different languages. It is mostly in some Latin script that I cannot decipher. There are segments in Chinese as well. I have no time to read this but I can have this translated if you are interested," he said, addressing his wife.

"I certainly am. It would keep me busy while you visit the coastal towns of the Persian Gulf."

"Wait," he said as he walked closer to a nearby torch for a better look. "This very first page bears a line in Persian."

"What does it say?"

"It is written as if by someone with poor knowledge of Persian calligraphy, but it is still legible."

My name is Krisztina, but they call me Dounia which means "the world," and my story begins years before my birth with a princess by the name of Chaka in a land that is today called China.

Chapter One

Dragon Dance

1209 C.E.

PRINCESS CHAKA'S HAIR, OFTEN COMPARED TO A SEA OF pearls, rolled over her right shoulder as she peered down from the palace balcony for a closer look at the procession. She knew her carnelian hanfu accentuated her natural pallor and cherished her time in front of the mirror as changes in her appearance indicated the blossoming of womanhood. The performers looked close enough to touch. She gazed back at the crowd and caught the rhythmic, sinuous movements of the dragon. The artificial creature, made of bamboo and cloth, undulated and lurched in a frightening way. Chaka stood motionless as the bulging eyes of the dragon looked straight at her.

As the youngest daughter of Emperor Xiangzong, Princess Chaka stood beside the other members of the royal family on the wooden lower balcony of the palace engraved with depictions of coiled dragons. She greeted with a wave of her hand the people of Tangut celebrating the anniversary of her father's ascent to the throne. The balcony allowed a degree of intimacy between the royal family and the subjects. Behind her rose the king's summer palace of carved teak wood with its pagoda roofing covered in a layer of gold.

The traditional dragon dance had commenced on that warm summer night and this year's dragon was the biggest ever constructed. Rumor had it that the head of the beast rivaled the height of a tall slave, and the length of his tongue was twice the said slave's arm. Close encounter proved the enormity of the monster.

Emperor Xiangzong wore his ceremonial attire embellished with rubies, sapphires and other precious gems sewn onto its shimmering fabric. A short white cape with black ribbon trim covered his shoulders, and a long necklace of large white pearls hung from his neck. As usual, his countenance displayed no emotion, yet his severe gaze held the enormity of his authority. The Empress smiled. A golden bouquet for a crown trembled upon her head as she turned from side to side to acknowledge the crowd. Birds and flowers embroidered in yellow and orange covered her hanfu.

One hundred members of the king's special guards had received the honor of animating the artificial reptile in the streets of the capital as crowds of young and old looked on in amazement. They manipulated wooden poles under the dragon to create rhythm. Cries of jubilation rose as "the black-hats," the elites, and "the red-faced people," the peasants, followed a team of acrobats dancing around the yellow beast. Chaka waved to the crowd, fighting back an urge to scream with excitement. Never had they built a dragon so big and so life-like.

The moon had refused to put her silvery face on display that night, and the stars were nowhere to be seen. Instead, the lantern holders, with their incredible acrobatic movements, lit up the darkness as they held the attention of the dazed audience. The performers put on quite a show, moving swiftly around the dragon and between each other's arms and legs before the flames could burn their limbs. Incense clung to the air in their wake.

The dark night obscured the figures of most dancers, dressed as mythical creatures like vermilion birds, black turtles, and white tigers. Their masked faces became visible only when they stood near the lighted torches set up for the occasion. Among the performers, some faces glistened with sweat. Chaka wondered. *They must be strangers to these parts for it seems as if they cannot stand the hot and humid air. Is it possible they are spies?*

She tried to convey her concerns to her mother by tugging at her hanfu and whispering in her ear. But the queen quickly dismissed

Chaka's complaints, calling it her mere imagination. Her two older sisters, who stood to the left of the king, could not have heard her. They always made sure to stand next to their royal father.

With her outstretched finger, Chaka pointed to the shadow of a horseman who appeared out of nowhere. At that very instant, the dragon's head turned toward her in a manner that hid her from all eyes. Moving with extreme dexterity and swiftness, the rider, dressed in black, face covered except for his searching eyes, grabbed her hand and pulled her off the balcony. He mounted her right onto his horse and rode away toward a dark alley behind the palace.

Before being carried away from the scene, Chaka could see that all heads had turned toward the nimble figure of a young female acrobat who jumped over the body of the dragon. Members of the royal family and the other spectators would not notice that she was missing until the dragon's head moved, and the vacant spot where she once stood became visible.

Chaka wiggled and tore with her teeth and fingernails at the rough arm holding her. The foul-smelling brute who had grabbed her reacted by tightening his grip. She screamed as loud as she could for as long as she could. But the noises of the procession of imposters who carried the manmade dragon muffled her ceaseless cries for help.

Princess Chaka had never felt so vulnerable. She had roamed the palaces of the kingdom like a proud peacock, ordering her servants and chambermaids to tend to her every need. Now as fear took hold of her, she knew she must retain her wits to survive. She wondered who her captor was and what objective he had in mind.

The kidnapper turned into another alley. Riding bareback, he lashed his horse so hard that it flew like a Pegasus, its hooves sliding at times as it trotted full speed on the cobblestone pavement worn smooth. Suddenly he came to a stop and waited a few moments at a crossroads until another horseman carrying a large creel approached them. Before Chaka realized the extent of her predicament, the second horseman, moving with great alacrity, lifted her like a weightless plume and shoved her, body and head, into the creel.

Chaka had to squat in the woven seagrass cage used for carrying vegetables as the second rider fastened the ropes that kept the lid of the creel tightly closed. Perforations allowed her to breathe. The kidnappers must have planned this in advance and wanted her alive, maybe to exchange her for ransom. That idea made her hopeful of deliverance.

Back at the festivities, the euphoria gave way to screams of agony when it became clear that the princess was missing. The performers unmasked, showing themselves as foreign warriors from the Steppes. Arrayed as palace guards they had earlier murdered, the alien soldiers pounced on the stunned crowd. They struck the spectators, using the poles with which they had kept the dragon upright as lances to pierce their victims.

A few palace aides quickly moved the royal family to a hiding place within the palace walls; an enclosure constructed years ago to ensure their safety in the event of an ambush. Between confusion and chaos, restoring order or calling for help became difficult. The few peasants who single-handedly confronted the enemy were slaughtered.

The "performers" dispersed as quickly as they had appeared. They used their lit lanterns to set nearby buildings and farms and animals on fire. Soon every tree near the palace was ablaze. Little bursts of fire jumped from one location to another, a destructive jubilee of light.

Chapter Two

The Mongol Khan

CHAKA KNEW THAT BY NOW HER FAMILY HAD NOTICED her absence, yet hope remained elusive as the second rider handed her over to a third man whose horse, well-rested and agile, carried her still trapped in the creel a long distance with ease. He finally stopped after riding for another hour or two and unburdened his load. Chaka burst out like a serpent emerging from a snake charmer's basket and found herself within a tent-like structure.

The scent of dung burning in a fire pit placed in the middle of the tent made her nauseous. She looked up and saw a hole in the roof through which the smoke from the fire escaped. A latticework of bamboo formed the walls of the rather large makeshift enclosure, taller than the height of two men. A group of about forty warriors squatted in a circle around the fire pit. Dressed in leather suits of armor that looked far more impressive than the ragged outfits of the brutes who had dragged her there, she gathered that the men were high-ranking officers.

Chaka stood, held her arms akimbo, and stared intimidatingly at the man sitting next to the fire on a tall hassock who seemed to be their leader as if to say, *what right have you?*

"Ha ha," he laughed and set in motion roars of laughter coming from all sides. The leader of the gang of kidnappers, a tall and handsome man, appeared impressed by Chaka's defiant spirit. Her hair disheveled, she must have looked like a trapped animal. His wide grin showed that the flash of anger in her eyes had made him admire her even more.

One of the officers pointed to the man sitting on the hassock as being "Genghis Khan." The other officers chanted "Urra" three times.

Chaka had been taught several ethnic languages and could understand the exchange. Quite absorbed in thought when she heard the officer's words, she almost spilled the goat milk offered to her by a slave. Without thinking, she looked up to see the reaction of the man identified as Genghis Khan. The latter smiled confidently.

Genghis had rough but princely features. His piercing eyes, in a unique shade of grayish brown, were almond-shaped and looked larger than that of her countrymen. Red streaks accentuated long black hair tied with a leather cord behind his neck. Unlike the other warriors squatting around the tent, Chaka did not fear this warlord. Quite the contrary, he had a likable aura about him that reminded her of a young army commander she had once idolized as a little girl. Still, she feared she might be forced into the arms of this stranger.

Chaka felt somewhat relieved when one of the officers led her to a nearby tent after a signal from Genghis. It was rather spacious, and it provided a degree of warmth and privacy. The officer assured her that the tent remained her private abode for the time being. For that, she was thankful.

Emperor Xiangzong paced up and down in the royal chamber. Of the three dynasties that ruled different territories in China, the Tangut Kingdom in the northwest was militarily the weakest and therefore vulnerable to attacks by the more powerful Jin and Song Dynasties. The kidnapping of Princess Chaka had shattered the tranquility of the Tangut Kingdom, known as a land of seasonal rains and warm sunshine; of colored parasols and beautiful maidens. The hardworking women of the region, their feet submerged knee-deep in water and their conical hats bobbing up and down in the air, harvested fresh ears of rice from these fertile lands. The Yellow River moved its amber body languidly through the territories like a tamed snake; poets recited tributes by its side and musicians paid homage to it as if it were a golden-haired maiden. Painters depicted its movements in the most complimentary manner and tried to outdo one another in showing its graceful waves. The presence of foreign forces, however, threatened to jar this tranquil image.

Jianjun, a Tangut master spy who had spent most of his nearly fifty years of life pursuing the enemies of the kingdom, had requested a private audience with the emperor. Jianjun informed the emperor that the combatants who had penetrated the kingdom of Tangut were sent there by their leader, a man called Genghis Khan. "Genghis has managed to bring the tribes of the Steppes that roamed the landlocked area between Manchuria and Altay Mountains under a united rule, calling their new country Mongolia."

"They are a bunch of nomads. The number of our warriors far exceeds theirs," the emperor interjected.

"That is true, but they use every trick imaginable to win against larger armies and well-trained cavalries," Jianjun countered. "Some are children of the wilderness. Growing up in a fierce environment and flourishing among wild beasts has taught them to embrace nature in its most dramatic expression. Freezing temperatures bring joy to their hearts. Torrential rains are music to their ears. They use the rivers of the Steppes as bathing grounds and see the sky above as their deity."

"Are you suggesting that we cannot defeat them?"

"No. But I am concerned. Strains of day-to-day hunting give the body of a Mongol warrior greater flexibility and strength than any civilized fighter, and no daily exercises of sophisticated armies could match the level of exertions the Mongols undergo in uncultivated grasslands. Strong and robust, they are not easily overcome by ordinary soldiers. With a keen awareness of their surroundings, they sense every little twig's movement and can see far away, detecting hidden creatures among branches," the spy warned.

Emperor Xiangzong's long figure bent over as he sat behind his desk of black lacquered wood. Its shiny surface reflected his image like a mirror. His needle-like slanted eyebrows moved closer together as he furrowed his brow in contemplation, staring at his reflection. If it weren't for his long, thin mustaches, the doughy pallor of his face and his small red lips would give him a child-like appearance.

Since Chaka's kidnapping, the Mongols had placed the capital, Yinchuan, under siege and food was running out. Palace spies had followed the trail of the three horsemen to the Khan's tent. They had informed the emperor that the Mongols had earlier attempted to flood the capital by changing the course of the Yellow River. Failing miserably at this attempt, the Mongols had ended up submerging their own base instead, a temporary setback.

Emperor Xiangzong spoke after a few minutes of contemplation. "I have heard about the Mongol attacks on our foes, and I am considering turning these warriors into allies to use against our more potent enemies."

The spy agreed.

The dilemma had occupied the emperor's mind for days. The kidnapping of the princess, although a heart-wrenching matter, provided an opportunity for negotiations. Now that the emperor knew where his daughter was, he could stage a rescue mission. But being a cunning statesman who placed the well-being of his kingdom before all other considerations, he always kept in mind the result of any action. Therefore, he decided to send an envoy carrying a communiqué for Genghis Khan which read:

> *"You can have my daughter's hand in marriage, provided that you honor our traditions and allow for a formal wedding at the capital. In return, we hope to become allies of the great Mongolian warriors to fend both nations against external foes."*

Chapter Three

The Talisman

TEARY-EYED, THE TANGUT QUEEN RAN DOWN THE STAIRS from her private chamber to the king's consultation room the moment she heard the news. To those uninitiated in the field of warfare, the rapid pace of deterioration of civilizations that had succumbed to Mongol aggression seemed incredible. She had heard that prosperous lands reverted to wilderness when the Mongols annihilated the inhabitants, leaving dense new woodlands and underbrush that made them unsuitable for cultivation. She could not comprehend the fact that the Tangut nation faced a similar destiny. The most pressing issue for the Tangut Queen was the fate of her daughter, Chaka.

"You want to sacrifice the life and happiness of our daughter to prevent war with the Mongols. Is that true?" she blurted without preliminaries as soon as she saw the calm face of her husband. Her normally genteel voice turned high-pitched.

"It is for her own good that I do this. Do you think it is easy to free her from the hands of those brutes? This way at least she will earn their respect and will be honored as their queen. I have already forwarded a communiqué to Genghis."

The rest of their conversation blurred. *It is not too late, you can save her*, she said or thought she did. *I care for Chaka, she is my daughter, but I have an entire nation's responsibility on my hands*, he said. *I cannot bear it*, she said. *She would be fine*, he said, *honorably married to a man of royalty*. *Not all marriages are happy ones*, he said. Her loud protestation having had no effect, the matter settled as it always did, with him having the last word as she curled away in silence, her face tear-streaked.

Poor Chaka, torn between her desire to flee her strange fate and her deep-rooted sense of obedience toward her father, finally succumbed to the latter compulsion. The two sides agreed to a date for the wedding, and soon after the agreement, the embargo ended. The gates of the capital opened to arriving merchants, and convoys of camels carrying loads of food entered the kingdom.

The wedding took place amid prodigious week-long celebrations with all the pomp and ceremony required to make it a royal event. Baskets of flowers hung by poles adorned the streets near the palace during daytime while paper lanterns lit the way at night. Crowds gathered outside as palace guests watched Chaka's marriage to Genghis Khan. The Tangut guards looked stunned, as the author of the king's downfall received the honor of becoming His Majesty's son-in-law.

The hungry inhabitants feasted on trays of food while the foreign warriors ate their meals with the voracity of the famished, though they had not experienced any shortages. The Mongols took copious mouthfuls of the flesh of slain beasts. Chaka watched them with revulsion during the wedding ceremony as they stared at her with yearning in their eyes. She turned to her father who hid his face by starting a conversation with one of his ministers. Her sisters also looked away when she searched for sympathy in their faces. They probably felt lucky that they were not the ones forced to marry their kidnapper. Even her mother avoided her questioning eyes by keeping her head down during the entire ceremony.

Little did Chaka imagine that she would be led by foreign warriors to this strange, unfathomable circumstance. This past year she had entertained the idea of marriage. How girls, barely older than she, were literally placed upon a pedestal, all dressed up in impeccable attires with their virtues sung by every mouth. How with their faces painted in the richest colors but their eyes cast down, smiling demurely, they were led to new lives. How exquisitely beautiful they looked, ready to be carried away by a chivalrous, handsome prince to the fairytale land of marriage where they would live in eternal bliss, no longer a child of their folks but the wife of a man.

Trepidation filled Chaka's heart. Who would have thought she would be forced to marry her captor, a man who lacked higher sensibilities? She had an urge to flee, to run away from that place before Genghis took possession of her at nightfall. She did not know what to expect from a Mongol husband, one with such authority and ambition as Genghis. But despite her fear and the droplets of sweat that had formed on her forehead, realizing that no means for escape existed, she tried to appear impassive and accept her fate.

Overwhelmed by the idea of captivity and life in a strange land, Chaka did not respond to Genghis's kind words. No intimation on his part or his gifts of jewelry and fine fur during the week of wedding festivities could win Chaka's heart. He directly addressed the matter on the very night of their wedding.

"You are the wife of a Mongol Khan, so you better behave like one," he said, sternly.

"Why? What have I done?" she asked, surprised at his temper.

"In your mind, you still consider yourself a captive and behave accordingly," he said. "You do so in front of my warriors and army commanders. That is an insult. It degrades me before them. You stand next to me, meek and unresponsive as if I am some sort of monster. I do not intend to treat you like a prisoner, so stop acting like one."

"Well it pains me to know that I was taken against my will away from my family!" she exclaimed without thinking.

Genghis looked away as if to study the painted panel that separated their canopy bed from the rest of the room. Dark wood covered the walls of the luxurious chamber. Chaka wondered what effect the grandeur of the palace had on this warrior who had lived all his life in the rough environment of the Steppes.

"You don't even know what pain is," he said irritably and walked out of their wedding chamber. He did not come back until several hours later, leaving Chaka in a state of continuous apprehension for she did not know what would become of her. When he did return, he held her in his arms for a long time. The warmth of his body near her made her shudder, not due to a sense of repulsion, quite the contrary, she felt drawn to him. She felt secure in his embrace, and her fears began to melt away. He pulled an oval-shaped talisman of turquoise out of a small silver box. It hung on a thin leather cord, and he tied it around her neck.

"This belonged to my mother, and she wore it to ward off evil," he said, staring into her eyes with such tenderness that it almost made her forgive him. "I want you to keep this for your protection so no harm will come to you." He then told her about his childhood, of his father, Yesukai, a great warrior in his time and a leader of their tribe.

"After his death, when the tribesmen found me, his eldest, too weak and young to lead, they abandoned us. My mother, my siblings and I became easy prey for the enemies of my father and had to be constantly on the run. Many a night I slept on ice-covered grounds and scavenged for food, relying on the meat and skin of rodents. Thus, poverty became my habitat and hunger my sustenance. This life of luxury that you lead is alien to my people and to me.

"For me, my love" he added, pain visible in his face from the remembrance of his childhood, "success and failure are potions to drink with equal zeal. I have learned early on that suffering is just a fact of life. Neither victory nor defeat, temper my spirit, you see. When I fall, I lift myself up, work relentlessly to regain my strength and start over as if nothing has happened. I then continue my struggle to achieve my goals. Those goals, I believe, were ordained by the Mighty Sky."

Tears welled up in Chaka's eyes, not only because she sympathized with him but also because of the relief from the trepidation she had felt earlier, not knowing what would happen if Genghis refused her as a mate. She now felt secure, protected. He kissed her quivering lips, then her eyes, allowing her tears to fall freely down her cheeks.

From that moment on, Chaka began to see him as that lost child who had grown up under the most insufferable circumstances, rather than the ferocious commander that he had become. She would be fooling herself if she thought she was not attracted to him. She found the aura about him, an aura of power and determination, admirable. She wanted to tame the heart of this man who claimed that the skies above had ordained him to rule the earth and subjugate all mankind. She placed her head on his chest as a gesture of consent. From then on, she called him by his childhood name, Temujin.

The following morning, maids and housekeepers of the palace prepared the best breakfast that the king and queen of the Tangut people had seen in months. A long walnut dining table displayed copper containers filled with hot and cold morsels. The aroma of pastries filled the air, complementing the scent of fresh flowers arranged in tall vases at every corner. But the newlywed couple, Genghis and Chaka, attracted the greatest attention. They came down from their upper story wedding chamber, holding hands and frequently exchanging loving glances and smiles.

Chapter Four

Mongolia

CHAKA SOON LEARNED TO ADJUST TO HER NEW LIFE. From the very moment of her encounter with the Mongolian warlord, she had realized that her fate had been sealed; she quickly recognized that her only means of survival lay in keeping the appearance of total submission. She longed to see her family but Genghis had forbidden this.

The thrill of being attached to a man of such power, and play a part in history, had allowed Chaka to overcome the trials of captivity. At times, when she reached her utmost limit, her imagination filled the void in her heart. This happened often during episodes of war, particularly when Genghis readied his army for an attack on the Jin Dynasty.

Although her father was a foe to the Jin, Chaka knew many innocent civilians would be killed during the skirmishes. Instead of worrying about the fighting, she tried to imagine her family happy and her sisters married off to proper suitors. She wanted to believe that they would be bearing children of their own, and they would tell those children stories of her bravery. She also envisaged her nation safe because of her sacrifice. Maybe unlike her two sisters, she had what it took to endure the challenges of life in the new country.

Contrary to the densely packed houses that surrounded the palatial structure where Chaka grew up, in Mongolia no permanent structures existed. Mongols lived in numerous tent-like homes they called *ger* that looked as fluid as their surroundings. A turquoise line on the horizon separated the vast blue skies from an equally vast green prairie. In the distance, hills and mountains marked the boundary of the grassland. A cobblestone pathway that led to the Grand Ger and a garden nearby with two rows of trees, recently planted, broke the monotony of the scene.

Time lost its meaning in such an environment, and events were marked by thunderstorms and other natural phenomena that shaped local history. The Mongols revered their horses and learned to ride them at a very young age. From the herds that roamed the land to the distant rivers, all were constantly moving in slow motion. Once in a while, the men engaged in wrestling, momentarily halting this continuous floating, and crowds gathered to watch the hand-to-hand combat.

Genghis showed no tolerance for disobedience of any kind. Chaka had to fully contemplate the meaning of every word she used before speaking. She could never interrupt him and never expressed outward anger, resentment or pain, for fear of his reaction. Her opinions she kept mostly to herself and wrote about them at every chance.

One night, as plans were being hatched for an imminent attack on the territories of the Jin Dynasty, Genghis addressed his commanders in the main ger. Chaka was standing in a corner listening. A young commander, who seemed to have found it an opportune moment to address the Khan, rose and said, "I am of the opinion that we should postpone the attack until the heat in that region subsides a bit. That way, we would have a better chance at success."

"I despise you and your opinions," the Khan hissed. "I disregarded tribal affiliations, I did away with Mongol traditions and rose the likes of you to high ranks based on merit, merit," he repeated that last word louder.

His jaw twitched as he continued, "And you expect Mongol warriors to scurry off like rodents in acclimate weather and find refuge in some hole? A little rain, a little heat, and off they go. What kind of message do we send to our enemies when we behave in such a way?

"Take him," he commanded two of his guards. "Strech him over a scaffold, and leave him under the sun until both his body and his tongue dry up in its heat. Let this serve as a lesson to those who assume their worthless opinions can impact my decisions."

Chaka was grateful for the red hue she had chosen earlier for her cheeks and lips and hoped no one noticed as she felt the color drain from her face.

Despite Chaka's struggles to adapt to life in the Mongol court, confinement had taken its toll on her. One morning as she opened the felt door to her ger, allowing the sunlight to illuminate her image in the mirror, she noticed the many strands of hair that had come loose, clinging to her comb. In her reflection she could see fine lines developing at the corners of her eyes. What would become of her, she thought, if Genghis no longer found her appealing? What would happen to her if her husband passed away, leaving her at the mercy of other Mongol rulers? What if she said something, did something wrong that Genghis would not forgive? She felt a choking sensation for which she could find no relief. The frustration and anger that she could neither express nor swallow led to a sense of utter dejection and gloom.

An attendant, apparently surprised to see the door to Chaka's ger ajar, peered in and asked permission to enter. "A soldier is bitten by a cobra and is rolling in pain in the Grand Ger," he announced abruptly.

"Will it kill him?" Chaka asked.

"They have brought in a shaman who has knowledge of healing herbs and poisons."

"Can I come and watch?"

"I am sure that will not be a problem, my lady."

When they entered the Grand Ger, Genghis greeted Chaka with a frown, as if questioning why she had rushed in on an occasion where her presence was neither necessary nor appropriate. The emptiness and sense of uselessness Chaka had felt earlier, intensified. She felt as if she was slipping off the edge of a precipice.

"The remedy worked, and the fellow will recover soon," Genghis said rather coldly, addressing no one in particular.

The shaman began to show the Khan the variety of healing herbs as well as potent poisons that he had in his wooden medicine box. As the two were speaking with their backs to Chaka and the box of medicines, she quickly removed a small vial that the shaman had mentioned its content as dangerous and fatal if swallowed.

"The person drinking only a small amount of this will die instantly," he had explained.

The vial was too small for its vacant spot to be noticed immediately, and when the shaman turned to close the box, he did so abruptly without checking the contents.

Chaka, who had placed the vial in the folds of her sash, returned to her ger immediately. She examined her pale face in the mirror again, contemplating the life she was now leading and whether putting an end to it would be far less painful than the excruciatingly slow one she had to endure, living with her enemies and under their command.

She had heard of the tortures disobedient women of the court suffered before being killed and wondered which action of hers, purposefully or inadvertently, would lead her to such an unfortunate destiny. Maybe if she would end her life now, she would be reincarnated as a bird soaring in the skies or a doe, free to roam the earth. She was sure this action would not negatively affect her homeland. Her death would probably be a cause of sorrow and sympathy, not anger and revenge.

Chaka took one last look in the mirror, envisioning herself lying peacefully in the morgue. She tried to steady her trembling hand as she brought the poison to her lips. This would be a far better ending than the bleak future that awaited her. She would thus still the hands of time and leave the world before greater harm comes to her.

"May I come in," said a voice outside her ger. It sounded like Borte, the woman Genghis had married when they were both very young.

Chaka quickly hid the vial in a box on her dresser and rolled aside the felt curtain. "Pray come in," she said.

"I saw what you did," Borte exclaimed bluntly as soon as she entered. "You did not notice me standing in the corner of the Grand Ger, but I saw how you swiftly removed a vial out of the shaman's box. I can only guess it was his most potent poison."

Chaka felt color draining from her face. "I mean to do no harm to anyone."

"No harm to anyone but yourself," Borte said with the severity of a mother admonishing a child.

"Where did you hide it?"

Chaka, feeling utterly embarrassed and miserable, pointed to where she hid the vial, and Borte quickly removed and tucked it in her silk purse.

Borte's eyes emanated wisdom and maturity. Chaka had an uncontrollable urge to pour out the contents of her heart. The humiliation of being captured, the politically arranged marriage, the frustration of having to adapt to an alien culture, and the constant fear of taking one wrong step or uttering one wrong word, knowing that even the smallest misunderstanding could lead to catastrophe came to the surface like bile.

Borte made a gesture with her hand to silence her. After all, they could be overheard. Borte's knowing look and her motherly motion as she embraced Chaka proved that she understood everything without her having to explain years of sorrow and anguish. Borte drew Chaka near and the poor Chinese Princess hid her face in the folds of Borte's gown and wept. She hadn't been hugged by her mother for so long, and Borte's motherly embrace soothed her. Her sobs eventually stopped, and as Borte wiped away Chaka's tears with her handkerchief, she told her about her own marriage at a very young age to Genghis.

Borte caressed the silky strands of Chaka's hair away from her face. "You are not alone," she said. "I am old now but I was a young girl when I married Temujin. We lived through difficult times for the Mongols, particularly for women. We had to do with very little. Things are different now. We have more wealth today than any other nation. Yet, some things have not changed. Patience is the key to survival in the Mongol court. Remember that and try to be patient."

"Here," she said, removing a carved wooden comb from her own hair. "Temujin gave this to me as a wedding present. You keep it, and remember what I told you on this day."

Chaka took the comb, and holding it to her chest with both hands, bowed gratefully.

Genghis seemed to marvel at Chaka's calligraphic skills even though he said he did not understand the meaning of the strange lines she drew with the sharpened tip of a hawk's feather. Mongols had no written language, and this he admitted was the weakness of the young nation he had founded. Without the knowledge of writing, they could never reach the level of sophistication of other civilizations.

Genghis's excitement over the new art had prompted him to bring rolls of looted paper from his foreign adventures, and he had them piled up in a corner of Chaka's ger. She liked the smell of papyrus and didn't mind giving up a portion of her living quarters. Particles of ash mixed with animal fat formed the ink she used for writing.

Genghis approached her on the issue of illiteracy and lack of a written language in Mongolia one morning saying, "I am of the firm belief that my people too can develop these mysterious arts like other cultures."

"I do not doubt this," Chaka replied. "But what exactly do you have in mind?"

"I wish you could teach my commanders," he replied with that look in his eyes that always made Chaka remember his childhood trauma, and she most happily obliged. She considered this vocation as her opportunity to prove her worth. It not only filled her days but also gave her a chance to learn about Mongol strategy and techniques of warfare should the right moment come for her to express her views. And express she did. On multiple occasions, she reasoned that by avoiding war and seeking trade with other nations, the Mongols could reap material rewards without risking their lives and shedding the blood of others.

Chaka kept reminding herself daily that she had many things to be thankful for. She was still a member of royalty, albeit in a foreign land. She had gained the trust of the Khan and most of all, she was his chronicler. Knowing the power of the pen, she had noted down events upon arrival in Mongolia. This segment of her writing she kept hidden.

On one occasion, when Temujin walked into her ger unannounced, she quickly put aside the ink bottle and papers and rose to greet him.

Although Genghis was illiterate, she knew that he would have the material translated immediately.

He walked toward her, apparently noticing a droplet of ink on her embroidered sleeve. She laughed nervously and said that she planned to surprise him with this portrait of his she had been working on relentlessly.

"I would like to see that," he said.

"Oh, no, don't ask me that. Not yet. Let me finish first," she pleaded, and her sweet feminine charm won Temujin's heart. She quickly painted a portrait of him later that day to erase any hint of suspicion from his mind.

Genghis was a very powerful man, but in a way, she knew she possessed power over him. After all, she would be the one to decide how history would judge him, and she had resolved to be fair in her assessments. And thus, her journal entries began in a loose-leafed cord-bound notebook with a brown leather cover, pillaged by the Mongols from distant territories.

First Entry by Chaka:

> *As spring turns over its command of the world to summer, then summer surrenders its reign to autumn and autumn to winter, I watch the change of seasons, lamenting each day for separating me from my family. Temujin forbids me from having any contact with them for fear that they will influence him through me.*
>
> *I wonder where my sisters are and how my parents are doing. I felt resentful at first that my father had given me away so cavalierly. But I now realize that he had no choice. The only thing that puts my mind at ease is the fact that through my marriage to Temujin and the ensuing peace treaty between my nation and his, the Tangut people are safe from Mongol attacks and atrocities.*
>
> *For Temujin who was forty-six-years-old when we married, taking on another wife was not a complicated matter, for the Mongols marry multiple wives during their lifetimes. His first love, Borte, only a few*

years younger than him when they first met, would always retain her much-respected status among the clan.

When I first arrived in Mongolia, adapting to life in this punishing environment was difficult to do. The cold weather, the recurrent thunderstorms, the long stretch of grassland in which rarely any other vegetation grows, make one rather melancholy. There are hills and mountains beyond that I dare not venture toward. Though my bones are delicate, my stubborn soul refuses to succumb to despair.

Civilizations are far away. The Mongols do not understand the rules of other nations or their own limitations, and because of that, they display outstanding courage. They hunt humans as they hunt beasts. To them, the objective justifies the means as they seek victory at all costs.

Ignorance can be an advantage, while knowledge at times is an impediment. For these warriors, ignorance means greater self-confidence; with their aggrandized self-praise, they see no limit to their ambitions. If they can slaughter a bear, if they can kill a lion, they can certainly overcome foreign warriors.

The Mongols abhor the feeling of being inferior to others, and they want to get even. If the other nations have superior literature and poetry, if they possess artisans and capable architects, the Mongols have enough brutality to win wars, and by gaining power through violence, they can capture those artisans and engineers. No civilized mind could resist such brute force.

Men wear long robes they called deel and flat boots of leather with fur lining that reach up to their knees. Fur-lined pointed hats cover the backs of warriors' necks as well as their ears while the commanders wear metal helmets. The clothing of women looks much more colorful, and their headwear is more elaborate than that of men. I like their attire, especially the embroidered fabrics of lighter weight women wear during warmer months.

Life lacks permanency here, and I find the transience difficult to bear. Being the wife of Genghis Khan, I live in one of the fancier gers. The entire felt structure is rolled away at times, placed on oxen and carried off to where the whim of the Khan decrees.

The routines established in sedentary civilizations and considered the norm there, such as public welfare and taxation, are lacking here. Also lacking, are codes, regulations, and guidelines that bring order to society. I have spoken to Temujin on several occasions about this. That one must establish a society on some form of structure and devise rules for it. I mentioned that Mongolia needs overseers of activities such as building of roads and bridges within the different jurisdictions. Each overseer must then be held accountable by higher ranking officials who in turn must report regularly to the Mongol court.

At first, he would feel offended that a woman was trying to teach him things, but when scholars from the territories of the Jin and Song Dynasties captured by the Mongols gave him the same advice, he relented. Make no mistake; he is indeed a genius in military matters. But he grew up in the wilderness. He is now considering devising a statute of some sort, a body of laws he calls Yassa that would be implemented in all the territories where the Mongols rule.

I must add that one of the best souvenirs the Mongols brought with them from conquered territories is this manuscript upon which I am writing my first entry. The moment I laid eyes on it, I knew it was meant for me to fill its pages. Temujin has some foreign historians at his service and does not permit any other writing about the Mongols. This manuscript must remain hidden or my life will be at risk.

Temujin has left for the warfront; therefore, I feel safe that he would not suddenly walk in and see this. The fire in the pit has died out, and it is getting cold in my ger. I will have to cut short my writing, but I will return to it at every chance.

Chapter Five

The Rage

1219 C.E.

IT WAS AN AUTUMN DAY IN THE YEAR OF THE RABBIT. THE early morning sun had spread a shimmering carpet across the landscape. The cobblestone path that led to the Grand Ger gleamed in the sunshine. The light shadows of the trees looked like the haphazard drawings of a child on a blank canvas. Standing next to the Khan, Chaka began reminiscing about the day when her destiny changed. These recollections she had gone over a thousand times, the disappearance of life as she knew it, slithering before her mind's eye like a dark snake at night, how incredibly fast her fortune changed, not only hers but that of her nation. Her father had shown weakness. Caught between two enemies, he had decided to side with one against the other. Thus, the Tangut people had become hand in glove with the Mongols.

Time had healed some wounds, but those remained for which there was no healing. Chaka had not seen her family since her wedding day. She blamed herself for not missing home as much as she should. With the passage of years, fresh vivid colors of the life she was leading had replaced her faded memories of childhood. At the same time, she knew that she must find a way to reach out to her father.

Initially, she felt entrapped by the Mongol Khan, because she was given no choice and never actually gave her consent to the wedding. Yet, her ambitious soul kept her striving to overcome many a predicament, to swim through uncharted waters, and to reach the highest status the land had to offer a woman.

In time, a sense of mutual trust and compassion had developed between Chaka and Genghis. It was not quite the passionate love that draws young couples toward one another but a more subtle form of mutual admiration. Chaka admired Genghis's charisma and how his former enemies revered him and joined his growing army. Individual capabilities rather than family connections mattered to him, and he promoted his warriors to the rank of officer and commander, regardless of their ancestral background, thus contradicting the norms of the people of the Steppes. She had also seen the fervor with which his men spoke of him and wondered how he had risen from his humble beginnings to such a lofty status.

Genghis appeared equally drawn to Chaka. She knew her youth, graceful manners, and sophisticated elegance set her apart from the multitudes of women he had come across during his military campaigns. Chaka's well-calculated and timely remarks had won the respect of the Khan. Genghis never concealed the fact that he still cared for his first wife Borte, and only her children, four sons by now, would inherit the kingdom one day. Yet, with the passage of years, Chaka knew she had earned his respect. Borte was only a few years younger than Genghis and no rival to her.

The matter had come to surface all of a sudden, a few months earlier when Genghis stepped inside Chaka's ger and saw Borte's comb on a small table. The comb had a peony drawn on it, and Genghis said that he remembered it as a wedding gift he had given to Borte.

"I have special feelings for Borte that will always be a part of me, and she will remain my most respected companion. She is a part of my soul that can never be separated from me, although we are no longer physically close. She was the glimmer of hope when I had none. I met her when misfortune still had its grip upon our family, and she gave me the strength to go on. But you, Chaka, you are the love of my life. It is you who bring meaning to my existence, and I cannot envision life without you."

"Then you need to start treating me not like a child but as the intelligent woman that I am," she had replied fearlessly. "At a young age, I learned the art of diplomacy, and I know how to treat the dignitaries of other nations; when to engage in war and when to avert one to promote one's interests. Such capabilities could be of use to the Mongol nation."

"What exactly are you suggesting?" Genghis asked, pensively.

"To be not just your wife but your advisor, a counselor in matters of state, and to play a role in the political arena," Chaka replied.

"A woman?" he said, raising his eyebrows.

"My gender does not matter. It is my abilities that count."

He grinned approvingly, and she knew at that moment that he had learned to trust her in matters of administration. From then on, she allowed the bond between them to grow stronger, both to secure her own well-being and to retain her influential role in the arena of Mongol politics. Thus, she could exert influence when necessary to prevent greater carnage and thwart any attempt by the Mongols to infiltrate or attack her homeland.

As Genghis's perception of Chaka changed, so did his attitude toward her. Chaka noticed that he no longer saw her as a child he toyed with, but a caring friend to whom he could turn to at times of trouble. She even suggested what he should wear to appear more presentable before foreign dignitaries.

Chaka knew the rules of the court established by Genghis. His advisors never expressed their views in his presence unless he asked for their opinion. Although well-informed of the affairs of the land through the women of the court, Chaka kept her opinions to herself. This increased Genghis's trust and admiration for her. She always waited patiently for the right time to express her concerns, and the right time was when he asked her for advice.

At twenty-eight, she had reached the peak of her beauty and femininity and the Khan, almost three decades her senior, had attained the summit of his mental maturity. As the grandmaster of all the tribes and nations of the Steppes, Genghis's status had certainly changed. His robe-like attire, still displaying the Mongol taste, was no longer made of rawhide or coarse cloth; instead, he wore intricately embroidered silk. Most of the low-ranking warriors, though, kept their seamless coat of rough material that reached below their knees.

On that autumn morning, the Khan and Chaka walked hand-in-hand in the garden toward a small hill of flowers. Chaka recalled the tender buds that bloomed throughout spring and summer in her father's garden. Chrysanthemums in every color brought from the territories of the Song Dynasty sidled up to the two sides of the pathway that led to the Grand Ger. The flowers held their heads up high, flaunting their petals. Every time Chaka glanced at them, she remembered the homeland she had left behind.

Signs of age could be seen on Genghis's countenance, but his resolve to wage war had not diminished in any way. He had mentioned more than once that he considered himself an instrument of divine retribution, but she saw in him a lost child who had never known his true calling in this world. Struggle for survival and being victorious to the detriment of others was a code he had learned at a young age, and that knowledge had formed the foundation of his philosophy. She had committed herself to reforming him, and through him, the newly formed Mongolian nation. Yet, she knew the limit of her power and the narrow chances of her success.

"Temujin, my love," Chaka said, calling the Mongol Emperor affectionately as she always did since their wedding night, "do you not enjoy the beauty of the garden?"

Genghis looked pensive. His eyes, peering through almond-shaped lids, stared thoughtfully at a bright red chrysanthemum bush brimming with blooms in a corner of the garden. Chaka had learned to admire his grayish brown eyes when they cast their tender rays upon her, warmer than the mid-day sun. Today, however, their piercing beams reflected the Khan's inner turmoil.

"Twice now I have sent emissaries to Khwarazm territories. They harassed and ridiculed my first group of messengers who may have appeared unusual in their Mongolian outfits. They arrested a second convoy I dispatched that was carrying precious goods, killing members of my trade delegation and confiscating their merchandise. A governor in the border region of Otrar ordered this last atrocity."

Chaka made no reply, just listened. Genghis added that he knew that man to be a nephew of the king's mother, a woman of great influence, and that was why the Shah of Khwarazm, the Turkic ruler of Persia and Transoxiana, had refused his request to hand over the culprit.

Since the Buddhist lands bordering Transoxiana fell to the Mongols, Mohammad Shah, the king of Khwarazm, and Genghis Khan had become neighbors. And as a neighborly gesture, Genghis had made an offer of mutually beneficial trade to the powerful Shah; an offer that he had hoped would not be refused.

Gardeners were busy pulling weeds and clearing the garden for planting spring bulbs. Suddenly Genghis approached an elderly landscaper whose face turned yellowish white as if he had seen a wolf. He had been leaving the roots in the ground and pulling on the stems and leaves. The Mongol Khan knelt in a manner that stunned Chaka as well. He plucked out a bunch of weeds with such ferocity that the roots came out, dirt still attached.

"Weeds need to be pulled by the roots, so they will never have a chance to grow again," he said. He continued after an uneasy pause as if talking to himself. "There are people who, not unlike weeds, need to be obliterated. And there are those for whom a mere chastisement will suffice."

Chaka stole a glance at the gardener and saw him cringe as these words were spoken.

"I sought trade with them," Genghis continued, appearing insensible to his surroundings. Only a slightly noticeable twitch in his jaw muscles indicated the intensity of his frustration. "I dispatched a trade convoy carrying camel loads of gold and silver that we had plundered in China after suffering massive casualties, hoping for commerce and trade with the Khwarazm Empire, but they ended up slaughtering my men and confiscating their goods." His voice rose, "They have robbed me. Robbed me! Just as our own clan robbed my mother and me of our only means of livelihood when I was merely a child, leaving us in the wilderness to die."

"Temujin," Chaka said meekly, "you remember your mother's words that became your inspiration to survive. She told you that you were born clutching a lump of blood in your closed fist. She believed that this was a sign from heaven, meaning that you would become a great warrior, a legend. Do not destroy what Providence has ordained for you."

Genghis remained quiet. Chaka knew he despised being subordinate to others; a sense that had prompted him in his earlier life to resort to fatal vengeance against his older half-brother for his abusive behavior toward younger siblings. There and then he must have felt the power of the killer over the killed, of the conqueror over the vanquished.

Although Chaka had not personally witnessed any acts of aggression by Genghis, but the words he had uttered and the fear she saw in the eyes of captured prisoners who would prostrate, trembling before the Khan, told her how brutal a Mongol ruler could be. At times, he showed such a sweet temper that she could not even imagine him hurting the tiniest of creatures. But she knew there was another side to her husband's character. Tales she had heard about the rape and slaughter of women and children terrified her, and she wondered about the impact of Mongol aggression on the minds of the subjugated nations. She had seen scars on the bodies of prisoners that indicated whippings, and the horror-stricken faces of female captives told her of the emotional scars they bore.

Genghis stood up, shaking the dirt off his hands, and added in a calmer manner, "This time I have sent one small delegation to make sure the king himself did not order the killings, and it was just a misstep by one individual, the governor of Otrar, who accused my messengers." He then continued almost in a whisper, "They thought my envoys were spies. I will show them spies."

"A great leader," Chaka said, wanting to nurture in him the values that dignified a world power, "must understand the cultural differences that can lead to misinterpretations and improper reactions in others."

"I have dispatched a small group of my emissaries to the very court of the Khwarazm King," he repeated, collecting himself and sounding more confident. "I have been informed that he disagrees with his mother on this issue. I am hoping, this time, my envoys will be received with great respect. I have requested that they hand over the governor of Otrar to us and in return, their land will remain immune to our strikes."

Genghis had mentioned to Chaka before that he had long been impressed by the Persian civilization. Their advancement in all fields of science and medicine, as well as their methods of governance, fascinated him. However, the mistreatment of his emissaries had deeply hurt and infuriated him. Despite this, Chaka knew he was wise enough to be understanding and would give the great nation whose boundaries once extended beyond imagination, another chance, especially when making such a concession would be to his advantage. After all, Genghis had other concerns.

The Mongols controlled parts of the Silk Road, but some parts remained in the hands of the Shah. This resplendent route linked China to the European and African continents and through it, tons of magnificent handcrafted merchandise, spices, and minerals were traded each year. Commercial relations with the Khwarazm Kingdom would certainly give Mongolia a greater part in such lucrative exchange. Chaka knew Genghis still found the idea of an invasion tempting. Conquering Khwarazm would place the entire Silk Route, albeit by force, under Mongolian control, and at last this thought seemed to have flowered in his mind. This way, the Mongols would gain access not only to the opportunities in trade that the route offered, but they would also have a convenient means of controlling the territories that came under their command.

Chapter Six

Baako

DURING THE YEARS OF RAMPAGING AND BLOOD-LETTING by Genghis Khan and his hordes that Chaka chronicled in secret, she had an accomplice, an African eunuch by the name of Baako whom she had learned to trust. She had no other friend with whom she could share her concerns and sorrows.

Baako, whose name meant "first-born," had been castrated by the Mongols, and she knew deep in his heart he abhorred them for what they did. Every time their eyes met, volumes of unspoken words were exchanged between them, and she saw him as a dependable confidant when the outer limits of her patience were tested, and her soul could no longer contain the pain of confinement in Mongolia.

Baako was a nimble sort of fellow who had worked for many years at the court. Chaka would ask about the battle every time they dispatched him to help out at the front, but she never shared her entries. She would only tell him that out of female curiosity, she wanted to know what happened on the battlefield, and he would come back with stories that would make her lose sleep at night.

"Are there historians who are chronicling these events?" she asked Baako one afternoon.

"There are some foreign scholars hired by the Mongols, my lady," Baako replied. "But they are all forced to write what pleases the Mongol Khan. Rarely do they undertake any effort beyond the permissible lines."

It was there and then that Chaka's journal turned into a chronicle of wars. She realized the importance of the responsibility she had toward future generations. The lessons of Mongol wars should not be lost to them. In writing her journal, she took the side of the victorious and the vanquished alike. As the advisor of the Mongol Khan, she sometimes accompanied the great commander in his foreign military adventures. Although staying at make-shift camps far from the battleground, she learned the news of the devastation through Baako. Secretly, she recorded the stories of the victims and kept her writings, so often spattered with tears, hidden from unwanted curiosity.

Chaka recalled one time, during an attack on the Jin Dynasty, how Baako came to her in a rush of excitement saying, "My lady! My lady! You don't know what happened today. There was this man who had learned a few words in Mongolian. He fell to his knees before the Khan and asked to be spared for he had five children and a young wife to support. But he, being weak in the language, did not use the proper terms to address the conqueror. The Mongol Khan said that he would spare his life, but not that of his family. He ordered the entire family beheaded right before the man's eyes. The poor man ended up begging the Khan to be killed as well, for he could not bear to live any longer. They left him there, mournful and wretched, probably in hopes that he would carry the news to other regions and instill in them the fear of Mongols."

Chaka felt wretched too. But every time she recorded the events, she felt better. On one occasion, Baako told her the following account of Genghis's war against the Jin Dynasty: "From the Chinese who had joined the Mongol Army or were taken as prisoners, the Mongols have learned how to build battering rams, siege towers, and catapults. They surrounded the walls that the Jin Emperor had constructed to protect his territories."

"How tall were these walls?" Chaka asked.

"The walls were taller than the height of seven men, my lady, yet the Mongols could climb the barricades. They set up camps in the outskirts, placing the people under siege for a long time and preventing merchants from carrying food and supplies to them. A massacre ensued when they finally attacked and overcame the starving population."

"I knew Temujin would be particularly merciless toward the Jin Dynasty," Chaka said. "The envoy they had dispatched to the Mongol court before the war had the audacity to face the Khan and demand his submission, saying that their empire was a glorious civilization and that the Mongols lived on sand and dirt. Temujin had spat on the ground and sworn vengeance."

Weeks later, when Temujin returned from the fronts, he looked as if wrath had consumed his soul. Blood-soaked to his knees, he stared at Chaka with lifeless eyes. She feared him a bit but believed that he loved her too much to ever harm her. She was, after all, considered a Mongol queen.

Once he bathed and changed into his white nightgown, Chaka decided to reach for her tea set. She had learned to soothe him during periods of contention by making tea, a choreographic art she had mastered in China, and a skill she had developed to perfection. She measured the tea, poured it into a pot to brew, and moving the teacups dexterously, she filled the containers in quick succession with the green brew. This ritual infused their surroundings with such a sensation of tranquility that the Khan looked mesmerized and the lines of frustration on his forehead faded away.

Chaka had used her time in the court wisely to acquire everything needed for her to become the favorite companion of Genghis. Other than the exquisite art of making tea, she had learned the poetry of the lands they had conquered and had found the means of translating them into the Mongolian language. She recited a poem every night, dramatizing it in the most delightful fashion for the Mongol Khan who melted in her loving presence. Her life in Mongolia became almost pleasant during those moments which did not last.

She had learned the rules and protocols of a palace in childhood and having come from a more genteel culture, she had the upper hand when it came to diplomacy and engagement with other nations. She displayed the honor and dignity of her upbringing and roamed among royalty like a beautiful swan. The resentment she felt in her heart for being ripped away from her family had to be buried under the ashes of memory. She had to show a calm face and an agreeable manner to become a constant companion to the Khan in matters of state and in official gatherings.

One night as a meeting adjourned with visiting Uyghur officials who had voluntarily submitted to Genghis's authority and therefore were to remain safe, the Khan, apparently impressed by Chaka's quiet but elegant presence, followed her to her ger. Chaka, who had not anticipated the Khan's visit to her private space because they spent their time togbether in his magnificent pavilion, hoped that she had not left the place untidy.

As they walked in, to her shock and surprise, she saw in the light of the firepit a young Mongolian servant girl trying on her turquoise talisman in front of a small mirror placed on her black lacquered table. The girl, obviously daydreaming, initially did not realize that the Khan and his wife had entered the enclosure, and when she finally saw their reflection in the mirror, she froze, holding the talisman in mid-air. Her mouth left half-open, she appeared unable to speak.

Chaka quickly turned toward the Khan and lied, saying, "I often ask the girl to clean my place and have told her that she could play with my jewelry."

Genghis looked fiercely at Chaka as if he knew she was lying to save the life of the poor girl. "You asked a servant girl to play with my mother's heirloom?" he hissed.

"I am sorry. In our culture, we do allow children to play with the jewels inherited from those who have passed away. We believe it brings peace to the souls of the departed," she lied again.

Genghis stared at her for a moment or two with a look that said he knew the baselessness of her claims. With a gesture, he dismissed the girl, and she sprinted out of the ger like a flash of lightning, dropping the talisman on the dressing table.

"I know you made up all those stories to protect the girl. Never test my resolve in punishing liers again. I ignored the matter this time because I see you are showing devotion to your Mongol subjects."

Later that night, when the Khan left, she reached for her quill pen.

Entry by Chaka:

It is sometimes a struggle to keep up my writing. Many a time my inkwell fell, spilling its content, and my quill repeatedly broke as I rushed to inscribe every detail about the wars. The feeling that these incidences must be documented spurs me to stay up so late. These climactic moments in human history cannot just fade into oblivion. I will not let them.

The tales of Temujin's charisma and his power to bring the warring tribes of the steppes under one command mesmerize me, as does his fierce bravery. As a young lad, he was taken captive by a rival clan that enslaved and pilloried him. Yet he managed to escape when one clansman, impressed by Temujin's character, helped him.

There is an aura of authority about him that overwhelms people. His veracity and determination allow him to attract followers. And then there is this compassion and empathy that he shows toward those he trusts. He rescued his first wife Borte early in their marriage from a rival clan that had kidnapped her. Borte had become pregnant during captivity. This only increased his compassion toward her, and he called the baby she gave birth to, Jochi or "lodger," never mentioning the fact that another man may have sired the child.

I am impressed by all this; yet, his reputation for ruthlessness terrifies me. I share the pride of the conquerors; but I know that many atrocities have taken place, atrocities that I have to record for the sake of the victims.

I have far more authority now than when I first came here. I demand to wear the best of clothing made with material that Turkish and Arab merchants bring with them from their lands and from China and Persia after their long journey through the Silk Road. My ger is now decorated with Chinese furnishings and a red dragon tapestry. I also use spices like ginger and cloves that the purveyors bring, instructing the cooks to prepare foods that are more to my taste.

Of all the things that the Mongols have plundered during their skirmishes with the Jin Dynasty, it is those parasols that I cherish the most. I carry them elegantly but guiltily, knowing that by flaunting them before the Mongol crowds, I share in the loot they have pillaged from my part of the world.

What concerns me the most is the war that is taking place within me; whether my cooperation with the Mongols has made me hand in glove with them, and whether I am sharing their atrocities. But what choice do I have?

Chapter Seven

The Fragile Ewer

THE TREES PLANTED AROUND THE GRAND GER HAD shed all their summer clothes even before the gusts of late autumn winds stripped them. Dried up shreds of leaves blanketed the landscape. As the sun's rays began to warm the cold surface of the earth, Baako, breathless from running, asked to enter Chaka's ger. He had been sent by Chaka to her father for news of the family. She had taken the risk of disobeying Genghis, hoping she could keep Baako's mission secret. Once alone with her, he parted his black curls to disclose an encrypted message written with henna on his scalp, enciphered codes with which Chaka had been familiar since childhood. She had learned the figures along with her alphabets, like all the other members of the Tangut Royal Family.

Asha, the military commander of Emperor Xiangzong, Chaka's father and leader of the Tangut nation, had written the note stating in clear, concise terms that he absolutely refused to join any military campaigns against the Khwarazm Kingdom. Although the Tangut had earlier joined forces with the Mongols to confront the Jin Dynasty in China, this attack he would not support. Adding that Chaka's father shared his sentiments, Asha had urged her to do her utmost to convince the Mongol Leader not to attack the Khwarazm Empire.

Chaka agreed, telling Baako, "The people of the Khwarazm Empire are a sophisticated nation. The Tangut people cannot be party to such carnage. Our people will only end up defeated and destroyed. I will try to convince the Mongol Khan that nothing will come out of this bloodshed, save for the destruction of the Tangut people and the Mongol nation as well."

Chaka knew that Genghis was a proud man, a well-trained warrior, and a shrewd strategist. But his forces consisting of two hundred thousand cavalrymen were no match for Khwarazm Empire's well-trained and sophisticated army, twice as great in numbers as the Mongol cavalry. Realizing the gravity of the situation, she felt compelled to confront her husband before he undertook this rash act. Trepidations shattered her nerves. Her mind, however, remained focused, determined. The importance of her mission gave her strength.

Without seeking permission, she walked into Genghis's private ger, where he stayed when he needed time to contemplate. No one dared to disrupt him there, and Chaka had never done so before. But this was no ordinary moment: the fate of her nation, nay two nations, both the Tangut and the Khwarazm Empires lay in her hands.

To her surprise, the warlord received her calmly as he held in his hand an intricate shiny vessel that looked to her like melted stars.

"They call it crystal," he said. "It is the work of Persian artisans."

She had seen crystal before in China, but never in such luminous form. "They don't just create artwork; they create miracles of art," she exclaimed, jumping on the opportunity his words provided. "Such a nation you do not conquer and subjugate."

His jaw muscle twitched, but he kept gazing at the ewer as if marveling at the intricacy of the instrument. A fragile loop forming the handle stretched from the mouth to a turquoise-blue sphere that held the clear top and bottom of the pot-bellied container together.

"The emissaries that I had dispatched to the court of Khwarazm Shah returned to us this morning, beard shaven, humiliated and beaten up, carrying with them the severed head of the lead envoy. This time, the only message I have for them is *war*. No one humiliates me and my people repeatedly." He said this in a surprisingly calm tone and added, "I have been to the holy mountain of Burkhan Khaldun to seek wisdom from the sky above, and I have made up my mind to attack Khwarazm territories. If they have no respect for us, we have none for them."

Chaka, her lips quivering, began first inaudibly, then more clearly, "I beg of you to refrain from attacking the Khwarazm Kingdom. They have sophisticated armies and have dispatched them in the past to lands as far away as Rome. My people have been your faithful allies up until now, but an attack on Khwarazm territories could leave them exposed to retaliatory measures by their vengeful king."

Many a time Chaka would open her fan and hold it in front of her face to hide her expression when agitated. But this time, she did not do so, exposing the concern in her countenance. She had learned to charm her way in and out of difficult situations, her beauty being an asset that helped her in this regard. Now things were different, however, and matters far more serious. Her mind restless, Chaka tried to maintain her composure.

"*Your people*, your people," Genghis said as if fury like fire consumed his soul. "After all this time, are the Mongols not *your* people?" He was quiet for a moment, turning away from her. She felt miserable. At length he spoke, his face distorted with contemplations that were obviously bothersome to him. "You have been communicating with the Tangut Court, haven't you? You have somehow managed to contact them despite my clear command that you refrain from doing so. Otherwise, you would not have known their position on this matter."

Not daring to show any sign of fear, Chaka felt like a fawn left alone with a hungry lion. She had sometimes wondered what her master of a spouse was capable of when he felt betrayed. Something in the intensity of his gaze told her to remain perfectly still.

Rage seemed to have consumed Temujin's soul. She sensed a tremor in her backbone. Her self-confidence was threadbare in the face of this unfolding calamity. Temujin had told her that Hoelun's necklace that she wore had warded off danger from his mother in many instances. Chaka put her hand over the talisman and hoped that it would protect her now in her hour of need.

The gravity of the situation made Chaka's earlier suggestion seem all the more impudent. She knew he would not tolerate it. Minutes went by as they both stood still. The lapse of response exacerbated Chaka's horror, unleashing the seething emotions within her.

Revulsion against a fate not chosen but imposed came to surface in an instant; a revolt that had surged through her veins like the tides of an uneasy ocean, threatening the veneer of her pretended calm. Her soul could no longer endure it. Her body shook uncontrollably. Strong ethics and a solid upbringing had helped her maintain the pretense of civility and submissiveness to this point but now, her voice reaching fever pitch, she found herself confronting the Khan brazenly.

"You say the King of Khwarazm has robbed you. You have robbed me of my life. You have deceived my family and trampled upon my happiness for too many years," she said, uttering the words without restraint.

"I have lived," he said, his voice quivering with the intensity of his rage, "through great turmoil, through hunger and thirst. We lived on the flesh of rodents and used their skin as our garb when our tribe betrayed us. I had no one to help me. I bore the shame, the pain for years. I waited. But today, I do not want to wait. I can't stand it. I want to put an end to this right now."

He then added as if talking to himself, "It teaches me to trust a woman. I gave you all the beautiful things that you had ever wanted. I shared with you my wealth and glory and power, and you . . . you have betrayed me!"

"I *had* wealth and glory and power as a Tangut Princess," she retorted far more angrily than she intended, "before I was dragged like a beast to your tent."

"I will give you a choice," he said, hissing his words through his teeth like a snake, "either a quick, honorable death without anyone knowing of your deceit or full disclosure of it in the Khuriltai."

The Khuriltai was the assembly of elders where Mongol chiefs engaged in all essential consultations and made crucial decisions. Chaka could not stand such humiliation. With a gesture toward his dagger, she conveyed her preference.

"I give my life gladly rather than be party to this never-ending carnage," she said and felt a sharp pain in her stomach as the dagger tore through her. His once loving hands stabbed her with such ferocity that it took her breath away. The piercing edge of the dagger cut deeper than her delicate skin and flesh; it severed forever the ties of the Tangut and Mongolian nations.

Blood stained her attire until it was the color of the hanfu she wore on the day of the kidnapping. He tore off her necklace, avoiding her gaze, her questioning eyes, and the tears that rolled down her cheeks as life began to drain slowly out of her body. *You never take back a gift you have granted someone. Those who do so are less than a thief. For a thief steals out of necessity, but a wealthy person who does so is dishonorable.* Those were her mother's words told to her often when she was but a child.

As she rolled down onto the floor, bleeding but still alive, the Khan walked out into the open air swearing loudly, "The sky is my witness, I will bring the Khwarazm Dynasty to its knees through all means at my disposal, be it violence or deceit."

With what little strength she had left, Chaka dragged herself to the adjacent ger where she did her writing. There, she lifted herself onto a large cedar chest where she kept her manuscript, hidden underneath a pile of clothes, and etched the final words of the journal with an ink that had mixed with her blood.

Baako had rushed to her side. She turned to him saying, "I have honored my promise to serve my nation. I have done my utmost to save the lives of others in faraway lands, and I have bravely confronted a warmongering ruler when even the bravest of men did not dare do so."

Uttering her last words with difficulty, she handed the manuscript to Baako. "I trust you with its safekeeping," she said and closed her eyes forever.

Genghis remembered the first time he hunted a wolf cub at twelve years of age. They had stared into each other's eyes, deep into each other's souls, and each one knew what their fate would be. When he thrust his spear into the animal's throat, he felt the thrill of the kill, although the blood that spilled repulsed him. He had the same sensation when he aimed his arrow at his own half-brother and watched him succumb to death. He had endured his abuses far too long and the time had come to end them.

He now had to take on his powerful foe, the Shah. The method had to be an unconventional one to ensure victory. He chose a venue for the attack that no other army had threaded before, the barren desert of Kyzyl Kum. An attack from that region was unprecedented, for no living army had ever crossed such treacherous terrain.

Genghis had brought order and discipline to the ranks of his army and had them divided into units of ten, with ten being the smallest component and ten thousand or a *Tumen* being the largest corps in the army. He had then placed each interdependent unit under one command. A unit of ten Mongolian soldiers under one commander he dispatched to Kyzyl Kum, seeking a desert dweller who could guide the army through the desert in a frontal assault on Bukhara. Over the course of several days, they had quietly kept watch from a distance, monitoring a lonc desert dweller's every move, in order to approach him at the right moment.

Book II

The Persian Invasion

Chapter One

The Jackal

Winter of 1220 C.E.

THE SYR RIVER QUENCHED THE THIRST OF THE INHABITANTS of the busy region of Otrar. An abundance of fish swam in its waters as its currents sang a note of tranquility for those dwelling nearby. Otrar was strategically located along the Silk Road. Caravans roaming the trade route that extended from the East to the West frequently stopped there for supplies. Local businessmen traded woven baskets or clay pots for the silk and cotton fabrics of China. Silk was expensive, but a small scarf could win a woman's heart.

From this oasis Jamsheed was banished. He had to spend the rest of his days in Kyzyl Kum desert, a no man's land of some fifteen thousand square leagues. He was now a fugitive who passed his time sitting on top of a high hill; the sturdiest sand dune in the entire desert. It was also home to a magnificent palm tree that had become his shelter and source of sustenance when he could find no other.

On a few occasions, when he dared set foot in a town or village near the borders of Kyzyl Kum, he used a fake name and tried not to get any attention. He stole goods when he could and engaged in honest labor when robbery was not an option. People called Jamsheed "Shoaghol" meaning "the Jackal."

Life in the desert wasn't so terribly bad after all. Things could have been worse, he thought. They might have hanged him. He could have been married, with a wife now crying over him. He had a camel for a companion and camels don't cry, thank God. The camel was an old one and older in camels, as in humans, means wiser.

Jamsheed's aging dromedary knew every nook and cranny in the desert. By instinct, she helped him find every water hole and desert route during his three years of intermittent exile. Intermittent that is, because he broke the rules occasionally by seeking provisions in the city and escaping before they discovered him. The animal provided companionship and served as a means of survival to the poor robber. From the tree would fall a date or two on lucky days. A water hole nearby that the camel had first spotted sustained them through the hot days.

Unlike the backstabbing characters Jamsheed had known throughout his life, the camel was a harmless creature and a very good listener indeed. So he had developed a habit of telling the overgrown mammal tales of his childhood experiences, often adding imaginative details to which any human would have raised an eyebrow. But the camel moved her tail in seemingly great satisfaction, for the sound of a master is sweeter than a lullaby to a pet.

Jamsheed's beard, that at times he had tried to cut short with sharp stones, reached his collar bone. His hair, once a lustrous brown, had turned the color of desert sands. His skin, scorched by the hot sun, fared no better than that of his camel. The passing of occasional caravans, lonely camel herders, or a rider on horseback became his sole source of entertainment at night. Tradesmen preferred to cross the desert on moonlit nights to escape the sweltering daytime heat and use the stars as tools of navigation.

Jamsheed wondered what would become of him if his luck ran out, if the water in the hole depleted, if he could no longer find a prey, or if the palm tree dried out. But at night the breathtakingly beautiful desert sky put its spectacular stars on display and melted away his worries.

He embraced the barren environment, and nature in turn welcomed this out-of-place creature, displaying before him a kaleidoscope of colors and contours. During the day, his companion would munch on thorny desert vegetation, and Jamsheed would hunt desert animals of all sorts, sharing the camel's food when no other means of sustenance was available.

Barely twenty-nine-years-old, he had already gained infamy for his robberies. Yes, he had robbed a place or two in his younger days, but what really got him into trouble and branded him with his nickname was the fact that he had dared to raid the treasury of the municipality of Otrar.

The governor of Otrar had placed a bounty of five hundred dinars on the Jackal, captured alive or dead. But the caravans that passed through the desert needed the knowledge of the fugitive for safe passage through the rough terrain, so no one bothered to turn him in for the money. Preserving life in that barren land meant more than getting one's hands on gold coins. In time, he had turned into a sort of hero. People despised the governor and knew him as a greedy, devious fellow who would never meet his end of the bargain. No one wanted to deal with him for he had a reputation of hanging subjects for petty reasons.

The governor occasionally boasted that he was of royal blood. After all, being a relative of Khwarazm Shah who now ruled the territories of Persia and Transoxiana had its advantages. Greedy like the rest of that clan, the governor had his eyes on a recently arriving caravan from Mongolia to pillage its bounty.

One evening at sunset, the sands took on a scarlet hue. Dust rose in plumes of yellow and orange and descended in red upon the ever-changing landscape of the desert. The fugitive, sitting on a hill like a king upon his throne, pierced the tender skin of the heavenly fruit with his overgrown fingernail. It was a ripe pomegranate which among other things he had gained days ago as a reward for hard labor at a blacksmith shop.

Jamsheed imagined the fruit to be the forbidden one from the Garden of Eden, for it tasted too sweet to be considered the produce of the arid lands surrounding him. And like the one bitten by Adam, he believed it would change the circumstances of his existence. Jamsheed tried to entertain his idle mind with this idea. As he licked the juices dribbling from his mouth, for a second or two the enormity of exile and constant deprivation placed its heavy footprint upon his lonely heart.

As the sky above darkened, Jamsheed remained seated under the night sky's shimmering blanket of stars and an incredibly bright moon. He suddenly heard the ringing of camel bells, a sign that a caravan was passing by. He could distinguish silhouettes of riders in the moonlight. Treasures of silver and gold were also visible on the backs of camels that moved in their graceful ways, carrying an enormous fortune fit for a king. From a distance, it had looked as if the stars of heaven were visiting the earth. Gems of every color blinked at him from under what seemed to be layers of rugs and furs.

He had robbed lone desert travelers before but seeing the multitude of riders and the length of the caravan that stretched to the horizon, he decided that the dagger he had as his only weapon would not suffice to trap and loot the travelers. Sweet temptation came and went in a blink of an eye as it usually did.

The fact is that he was no longer considered a threat. So much so, that travelers had learned to seek his aid in finding the safest routes out of the desert and in return, they shared their meals and provisions with him. Traders knew he lacked the means to rob them, and they formed a sort of kinship with him over the years. Jamsheed the Jackal, now completely subdued, had in time turned into a road sign, a monument by the lonely tree, for traders who sought him during their long journey from scorching lands into prosperity.

The trader, who had features Jamsheed had never seen before and obviously came from an alien land, approached him. In broken Persian, he announced his intention of finding Otrar and a safe passage through the desert. Apparently aware of the Jackal's desert vocation, he then offered Jamsheed a plate of dried beef jerky. Jamsheed happily obliged his request for information, beef jerky being a rare treat.

What seemed like a mirage, Jamsheed later learned was actually the ill-fated trade delegation from Mongolia that had moved at the speed of a tortoise through the rough terrain, in hopes of reaching Otrar. The leader of the caravan, known as "caravansalar," was a Mongolian Muslim who had been intentionally dispatched by Genghis Khan to soften the heart of the Shah and encourage him to agree to mutually beneficial trade.

This benevolent act of the Jackal, meaning the assistance he provided to the Mongol convoy, was related to Genghis Khan by the spies he had dispatched to find desert dwellers willing to cooperate with the Mongol army. The Mongols had chosen the desert for their venue of attack, and the man of the desert to guide them was no other than the Jackal. He could lead the Mongols to their destination safely, and the armies of the Shah would be taken by surprise. The Shah had already made the fatal mistake of dividing his army in two, dispatching one division to Bukhara and keeping the other to defend Samarkand. He must not have been anticipating an attack through the barren desert, leaving that frontier unguarded.

Chapter Two

The Beast

UNAWARE THAT HE WAS BEING WATCHED, THE JACKAL waited in hopes of finding prey as hours turned into days. Occasionally, he had been able to hunt a hare or gerbil but luck was not on his side this time. The endless sea of caramel-colored sand kept changing shape before his eyes, and he had an urge to raid a nearby town or village again. Even a few hours away from the tiring landscape would have been enough to renew his spirits. The endless silence of the barren land weighed heavily upon his ears. His eyes were tired of staring at the ever-moving sand dunes. Of course, he still had the luxury of imagination, as if his mind had found a blank canvas to write on. Hallucinations became real and he had to pinch himself back to reality each time he thought he saw a horseman, a beautiful desert dwelling girl or a child carrying a basket of fruit above his head.

He had eaten no food for at least three days now. He shook the palm tree with all his might, hoping for its sweet fruit to fall before his feet but to no avail. The tree was too tall for him to climb. Solitude and hunger had already worn him down. He knew he had to wait until the break of dawn to find something to eat and gain enough strength to put his plan into action.

Soon a blanket of gray silk covered the creamy dunes of the desert in darkness. Then, like magic, the desert gradually turned black and the sky, lit with the light of the crescent moon, became a slightly paler color than the earth. Everything above the ground, although still distinguishable, appeared as black specters. Pangs of hunger made sleep an impossible exercise.

Dawn was near, and silence filled the air. Suddenly behind him, Jamsheed heard a beastly cry. He reached for his dagger. Swiftly turning, he plunged it into the apparition before him, using all his remaining strength. Sheer terror filled his heart as the beast breathed down his neck. The smell of fresh blood filled Jamsheed's nostrils, warm liquid splashing across his face. The beast's claws scraped down his chest as it slowly succumbed to death, rolling to the ground.

Jamsheed could hear the pounding of his heart. He had come within inches of death. From what he could distinguish, the beast before him was large and ferocious. It lunged and bit his foot but failed to clamp down as life was drawn out of it before it could carry out this final act. The break of dawn revealed it to be a hyena.

Jamsheed's face and body felt wet with the blood of the animal. He stared, stunned to see a group of foreigners approaching him. They threaded the sandy path toward him. A warrior who appeared to be the commander of the group began to speak with the aid of a translator who accompanied them, "We are Mongolians, here to rid your nation of an evil Shah. Are you not Jamsheed, a fugitive sought by the armies of the Shah?" the alien officer asked. Jamsheed noticed the officer's dust-covered boots; a dagger hung by the belt of the leather outfit he wore. His rugged features were proof that he was indeed from a faraway land.

"Let's say I am. What good would that do for you?" the Jackal replied, realizing that these soldiers, whoever they were, were not spies of the Shah.

"You are a man of great bravery and competence," the officer said, adding that he had been surveying the desert and had seen and admired Jamsheed's heroic earlier performance. The slain beast, barely visible in the dark, lay still as blood flowed from its wound. The rays of the sun painted the scene in vivid colors.

"Well, I have heard such praise of my talents more than once," he replied boastfully.

"How would you like to govern the municipality of Otrar?"

"I don't quite understand," Jamsheed said, flabbergasted.

"You have earned the right to lead the people of Otrar, for they have suffered long under the brutality of Inalcheq, the governor."

"I am a fugitive, as you may very well know, and I have but little knowledge of governance," the desert dweller, feeling giddy, divulged information he would have ordinarily withheld from strangers.

"You will be granted advisors who will ensure the success of your mission. Administration of a municipality is not as difficult as you may think when you have counselors assigned to you from our country. The Mongolian civilization is a very powerful one, and we have proven our capabilities in managing the affairs of many lands."

"I have no financial resources," Jamsheed said, smiling sheepishly.

"We plan to place Otrar under siege," the commander replied sternly. "We will then depose the governor and place the treasury of the province in your capable hands."

Jamsheed saw no choice but to concur with the foreign commander. After all, things couldn't get any worse than this current dismal condition, plus the idea of such a quick ascent to power didn't sound so bad. He also feared that they might put an end to his life if he refused.

"What would I have to do in return for such a great favor?" The shrewd robber asked.

"You would serve as a guide to the Mongol army in a conquest that would change the trajectory of the world."

Chapter Three

The Grand Bazaar of Samarkand

THE NEWLY BUILT GRAND BAZAAR OF SAMARKAND, A source of pride and pleasure for the inhabitants of the city, stretched like a dragon from the main gate of the metropolis to its very heart and center. Passersby had to tilt their heads all the way toward the sky at the entry to the bazaar to take in a measure of its lofty splendor.

Fine masonry covered vaulted ceilings with multiple pointed arches, too numerous to count. Elaborate honeycomb windows installed in the walls and ceilings allowed sunlight to penetrate the enclosure in spots which placed certain precious items in the public eye. The shade and the sun outwitted one another as they played a game of light and dark on the colorful merchandise of the bazaar. Even on a cold and snowy day, a series of small fire pits of stone provided warmth.

Massive metal containers of dried fruit and scented herbs and spices filled the enclosure with enticing aromas. Other than the copper and silver containers of all types that sparkled in the shops, jewels made with precious metals and stones twinkled in the goldsmith's corner. The sounds of merchants and shoppers haggling over the prices rose in a cacophony, sometimes in unison. There were also bakeries and tea shops with young lads holding trays, running around to serve tired customers.

When members of the royal family planned a visit to the marketplace, the bazaar remained closed to its regular customers, and a sign stating "Ghorogh," meaning "Special Guests Only" warded off commoners at the entrance.

Persians celebrated the longest night in winter known as the night of Yalda since time immemorial in festivities that kept most people awake until dawn. On the morning following the night of Yalda, a thin layer of snow covering the paved and unpaved roads of Samarkand had frozen over the thick layer of earlier accumulations. As pedestrians stepped on the smooth, icy surface, deep holes formed under their heavy footwear.

The dark gray winter sky indicated more snow to come. The air was crisp but mixed with a thousand tiny particles of ice. Chunks of white snow, stuck to leafless treetops like balls of cotton, imitating blossoms of spring. A few early risers roamed the streets of the sleepy city. Shoppers carried empty baskets made of ropes, in hopes of purchasing the freshest produce before the market filled with bargaining customers, and laborers trudged through the slush and snow to begin their daily toils.

Layers of grayish cloth covered everyone, replacing colorful clothing in warmer days, and making the rich indistinguishable from the poor. Among the specter-like bulges of human form that were plodding through the frozen landscape, were two men for whom remaining inconspicuous meant more than retaining body warmth. Few dared to stare anyhow, for the spears of cold air could blind their watery eyes.

Dressed as beggars, faces wrinkled and red with misery and hardship, the pair dragged their tired bodies toward the promise of warmth and kindness. They had lately shown up in the streets of Samarkand as the deaf and dumb pair who were denied the blessing of speech and hearing since birth.

Every morning, in the luminescent dawn, the two beggars made their way to the bazaar. At times, they held out their hands for coins and begged for a morsel to eat by making sounds and gestures. They would make grunting noises, gesticulating with their fingers to show both the fact that they could not speak and that they were hungry.

A branch from an old tree, overburdened by snow, broke off and fell before the feet of one of the mendicants. With a swift motion, very uncharacteristic of one who is hard of hearing, he jumped backward to avoid being struck by the broken limb. Luckily, the usual ramblers roaming the city took no notice of him.

Most passersby ignored them as droplets of snow fell upon their ragged clothes. No one knew that underneath their beggarly outfits, layers of fine fur protected their bodies from the intense weather. Yet, it was easy for them to feign shivering, for they had extensively trained for the mission in Mongolia.

The two walked at equal pace for some distance. Then they stopped abruptly before the entrance of the bazaar. As the first rays of the sun began to warm the frozen earth, the sleepy shopkeepers opened their doors to early bargain hunters. For it is a common belief in Persia, that if the first person to enter a shop purchases an item, it is a good omen and the merchant will have a successful day.

The deaf and dumb pair had become a familiar sight in the marketplace, and the shopkeepers apparently found their odd gestures amusing. They had been coming to the bazaar for several months now, and like the first purchasers of goods, they had come to be known as good omens as well. No one wondered why there were two of them, and why their features looked so unfamiliar? People attributed their odd looks to the circumstances of their birth. They would beg for enough coins to be able to eat a breakfast of cooked whole beets offered by vendors, hot upon a small stove. The pair also carried with them congealed horse blood that they sucked on inconspicuously. It was quite a treat, for the people they encountered in other civilizations did not drink blood. The pair did so when their appetite got the better of them, and they feared that they would expose their identity and mission out of sheer hunger as they stood among such large stashes of delicious food.

As they lingered—now here, now there—their sharp ears picked up information about the events in the kingdom, including among others, the price of commodities, scarcity of certain goods and occasional complaints about the local administration. Sometimes they heard discussions among the merchants that gave hints about brewing tensions between rival communities. They listened out especially for gossip from the palace guards. Rumor had it that relations between mother and son in the palace of the king had soured. They already knew of the Shah's mother, Turkan Khatun's extravagance and the fact that on occasion she overstepped the limits of her authority as the mother of the Shah. They knew the king was not happy with his mother's influence peddling that at times had led to the execution of one major personality or the other. Such information gave the spies cause to smile with secret triumph.

A lone Central Asian trader who frequented the bazaar carried this information back with him to the Mongol ruler. Thus, the stage was carefully and meticulously set for an invasion that would result in the fall of Bukhara and Samarkand, the two cherished cities in the Kingdom of Khwarazm. The Khan's horsemen, being fewer than half the numbers of Khwarazm Empire's army, planned to overcome their powerful foe in less than a fortnight.

With the pain of Chaka's loss burning in his heart, Genghis Khan became more determined than ever to punish those he deemed responsible for the circumstances that led to her death. Genghis had told Baako to bury her in accordance with the rules for unwanted bodies. The poor slave had no choice but to abide by his master's command, burying Princess Chaka in the graveyard of prisoners. In Genghis's mind, Chaka had lost her life trying to prevent war with the Khwarazm Kingdom, and thus their happy life together was destroyed. He saw the inhabitants of Khwarazm territories not as subjects of Khwarazm Shah's whims, but as villains who had destroyed his personal life.

On the morning of the attack, he gave a simple order to the Mongol cavalry as they stood facing their leader in a makeshift camp outside of Bukhara. His voice thundering, he addressed his army prior to the invasion. "Exterminate any town, city or village that shows resistance. They tried to outdo me with guile and used their wits to get their hands on what they had not earned. I shall use every machination on earth to unravel their plans, to make widows of their wives and to orphan their children, leaving them at the mercy of my servitude.

"We do not possess the sophisticated armies of other nations," he continued. "Our numbers are few, but our determination is solid. We must use every means available to us and if necessary, resort to deception and trickery. We will strike terror in their hearts. We will create the illusion of being greater in number by lighting numerous torches at night to give the impression that a huge army is about to attack. We will pretend to be defeated, leave our weaponry behind, then attack from unexpected quarters. Thus, we will keep the enemy unhinged, unsure of where we are, and from which corner the next ambush will take place. We will be their worst nightmare. We will spare the cities that submit and annihilate those that resist. We will make such examples of those who defy us that our foes would think twice before attacking us."

His men stood in silence as if taking every word he spoke to heart. Soon war would be underway the likes of which they had never experienced before. They would have to face their formidable foes, knowing that there would be no turning back because a Mongol soldier who deserted the army was a good as dead.

Chapter Four

The Year of the Dragon

AS THE HORSEMEN OF GENGHIS REACHED THE BORDERS of Persia, rays of a barely warm sunshine flooded the main hall in the stately palace of Khwarazm. Molten silver had given the one large dome and two smaller ones that topped the upper floors of the gigantic structure a glitter that could be seen from a distance. Gray marble covered the exterior, and intricately carved wood frames accentuated the numerous windows. Within, Sultan Alaeddin Mohammad known as Khwarazm Shah was having a bitter conversation with his mother over some equally bitter Turkish coffee, void of its ordinary sweetness as recommended by the palace physician.

Khwarazm Shah's grandfather had wrested power from the last Seljuk King and established his own dynasty. Now during the 12th year of the Shah's rule, the people of Persia and Transoxiana had no choice but to submit to his leadership. At times, however, they showed their dissatisfaction.

Just like his grandfather, The Shah was a thin man of medium stature with olive skin and dark hair. But that was where the resemblance ended. He had rather delicate features and a full beard that covered most of his face. His sunken eyes and downturned lips gave him a countenance that appeared gloomy rather than resolute. A tall rimless red hat embellished with a black feather covered his head. A bejeweled silver sword hung by a belt of similar quality adorned his robe-like brown attire. Thin strands of pearl were sewn onto his neckline. Although lacking in sound action, he still had intellect, and perception.

The King's mother, Turkan Khatun, whose social gatherings and lavish parties had brought both fame and shame to the palace, had donned the most exquisite dress sewn with threads of gold and silver. Her influence over the affairs of the kingdom had become legendary, though few could claim that she possessed any wisdom. Exerting authority not vested upon her, she appointed members of her clan to positions of power. Among those appointees was a greedy nephew of hers who had become the governor of the province of Otrar. It was this very governor who had confiscated the treasures of the Mongolian convoy out of sheer avarice and had asked the Shah's permission to arrest, prosecute and hang members of that trade mission for espionage. The Shah had granted this permission under pressure from his mother.

"My nephew, your cousin," the Shah's mother said, her makeup overdone as usual, "is the genius in our family. He is the most perceptive, insightful and discerning fellow that I have ever known. When he identifies somebody as a spy, you can be sure of it. He has a nose for trickery."

"Well, based on those assumptions, mother, I allowed him to execute the entire Mongolian delegation. They were seeking trade with us for God's sake. Now they intend to exterminate us. We don't need barbarians at our borders."

"*You* said it. They are barbarians indeed," Turkan Khatun replied, swallowing her anger, "they are just a bunch of nomads coming from a no man's land. We have over four hundred thousand fighting men in our kingdom, and they can slaughter those ruffians in no time. Plus, it will give our people a much-needed victory to celebrate during Nowruz festivities. That will certainly increase your popularity among the subjects." She smiled gently as if trying to be the portrait of a loving mother without adding to the number of wrinkles on her face.

"The army? The army you keep referring to consists of a bunch of soldiers who have been trained in recent years to keep an eye on the subjects, making sure that they do not revolt against my rule. They lack the training needed to fight foreign cavalry." He then lowered his voice a bit and added contemplatively; "Besides, wars are unpredictable. It is easy to start one, but sometimes like wildfires, they are hard to extinguish. One never knows where they will lead."

Turkan Khatun merely stared at her numerous rings.

"It is my belief that the better path would be for us to apologize to the Mongolians," the Shah continued pensively, realizing the danger to the territories. "What we did was a mistake. It was more than a mistake. I call it a blunder, and I am going to punish my cousin by turning him over to the Mongols."

"You will do no such a thing," she retorted. "He is your flesh and blood. No one kills their own kin in order to satisfy a bunch of vengeful savages. They are no match for our army."

After a moment of silence, during which the Shah kept staring out the palace window, he went on to say, "I am brave enough to fight any force which threatens my people, and I will do so even in this case. At the same time, I am not so conceited that I would ignore the facts on the ground."

"War is necessary. The barbarians have placed us in this situation. They are the ones who have asked for war, and we cannot show weakness. This is the seat of the Persian Empire that you are now ruling. We will fight the Mongols as we would our most vicious enemy," Turkan Khatun stated with the conviction of an army commander. Her thin head veil adorned with a crown glittering with diamonds did not cover the tips of her dark curls that poked their heads out like serpents.

The monarch replied, "I have news from our ambassador in India that they have gone all the way to China attacking the Jin Dynasty, causing great havoc in that region. We do not need such chaos inside Khwarazm territories. I shall send an envoy to the Mongol King."

"The Mongols did send another small delegation," she said. "I had them beaten and humiliated and ordered that they behead the lead envoy."

"You did what?"

"That envoy had the audacity to ask for the capitulation of my nephew again," she replied, now shaking with anger. "Can you imagine that! The ruffian, dressed in rags and looking like the beast that he was, insulting the royal family of Khwarazm."

"And you did not even notify me?" he asked flabbergasted. "Sometimes I wonder who runs this country, you or I." The king then grabbed a tall wine-colored hookah impatiently and began inhaling the smoke out of its hose and blowing the fumes toward the ornate ceiling of the palace.

The Amir, the army commander, asked permission to brief the king about the latest news from the fronts. Sporadic attacks had already occurred to the east and west of Bukhara. The Mongol marksmen, famed for their agility on horseback, would attack then pretend to retreat. Such moves would lead to hubristic vanity in their enemies until the next bewildering surprise attack would occur. They would appear like specters, ghosts from an unholy graveyard, terrorizing civilians and soldiers alike. Thus, security, like an invisible veil, was slowly lifted off the land.

"May I sacrifice my life for thee, sire," the commander announced as he entered. "The Mongols are defeated for sure this time. They have left their ammunition all over the battlefield in their rush to leave the arena. This is cause for celebration indeed."

The king and his mother, both smiling now, welcomed the good news and rewarded the Amir with more gold coins than he had ever received before from His Majesty. Khwarazm Shah still had his doubts about the unfolding scenario and ordered the commander to position his well-armed troops along the southern flanks of Bukhara. "Upon my eyes, I will do it, sire," the Amir replied, bowed and left.

During the journey toward Persia, Genghis's high spirit and vigor gave courage to every warrior as they sang their triumphant songs of unity and fraternity. The warriors, their commander and even their horses moved like one unit, a tornado of energy and fire ready to consume the world. Battle-hardened and fearless they could almost smell victory from afar. Ambition, thirst for power and glory, and the longing for recognition mixed with vanity blinded them as their horses' hooves trampled upon lands and souls, their shining swords splattering the blood of young and old. Indiscriminate in their fury and proud of their newfound nation, they roamed the earth, ready to take on the Khwarazm Empire.

Chapter Five

The Bride of Baghdad

If that maiden from Shiraz wins my heart
I will grant her the lands of Samarkand and Bukhara
Just to reward
The beauty mark on her sweet complexion

~Hafez (14th Century Persian Poet)

PRIOR TO THE ASCENSION OF THE KHAWARAZM DYNASTY to the throne, the Seljuks ruled Persia and Transoxiana. Unlike the current rulers, the old dynasty, also a Turkic one, was known for its benevolence toward the subjects and appreciation for the Persian language and culture. An ancient palace in the suburbs of Samarkand had now become the former royals' abode. Persian subjects of Khwarazm Shah would have revolted if he had granted the Seljuk family a less than honorable place to stay.

The ancient structure, although run down, still retained a portion of its former grandeur. Images of flowers and birds depicted on a mosaic frieze adorned its exterior. Tiny mirror tiles embellished the white interior of the multistory pavilion. White marble steps that led to marmoreal flooring still maintained their luster.

Its carpets, some over one hundred years old, looked threadbare, but the servants and chambermaids, who had tended to the needs of the Seljuk family for generations, made sure that the palace remained in presentable condition, and that the garden continued to brim with roses in spring.

The family was sidelined though and remained outside political and social circles. Although the former king had passed away long ago, just about everyone in Samarkand still called his family by their royal names; and sentries known as "gharavols" provided security services when called upon.

Princess Reyhan, the witty granddaughter of the last Seljuk King had reached the peak of her beauty, for further attainment in that area did not seem possible to her admirers who grew in numbers by the day. Reyhan's beauty was of the kind that commanded respect. When she shyly lifted her long, curled lashes, her large hazel eyes were like round cut amber upon her porcelain face. She looked fragile as she carried herself with the poise and grace of members of royalty.

Tensions were running high between Khwarazm Shah and the Caliph of Baghdad. Mistrust had grown between the two leaders especially since rumors had begun to circulate that the Caliph had secretly encouraged the Mongols to attack Persia. The Caliph, motivated both by the desire to mitigate tensions with the Persian subjects of the Shah and the stories he had heard about Reyhan, made her a proposal of marriage on behalf of his son. Such a match would win the hearts and minds of the citizens who had admired the Seljuk kings and despised Khwarazm Shah. At the same time, it was meant as a snub to the Shah who did not want members of a former dynasty finding a lofty status in society.

It was a time known to Europeans as the Ides of March in the year 1220 AD. Persian astronomers had calculated the precise timing of each month, based on earth's rotation around the sun. In less than a week, at the exact moment of the commencement of spring, Nowruz or "new day festivities" that lasted for thirteen days would begin.

As nature augured the season of hope with the melting snow and the warming earth, the family decided that the wedding should take place on the very first day of the ancient festivities. The news of the wedding had placed fresh focus on the family of the former king. The word "former" was dropped from all conversations, however, as residents of Samarkand shared the joy of young Princess Reyhan.

Reyhan and her family used the private pool of the palace for bathing. Only on special occasions, like the upcoming wedding of Princess Reyhan, did they venture out to the main bathhouse of Samarkand which would then be closed to all commoners. A sign stating so, as well as the presence of gharavols outside the bathhouse, warded off inquisitive passersby.

The bathhouse had wide steps that led to a deep green door with two small windows at each side. Hours before the arrival of the princess, ten gharavols had stood at considerable distances from one another in front of the bathhouse, each almost invisible to the other at dawn. No pedestrians or vendors lingered nearby, for all had heeded the morning call to prayers.

A unit of ten Mongol warriors dressed as bathhouse workers approached the gharavols from behind. The Mongols had covered their faces in the red checkered cloth used as towels in such public places. Before the Persian gharavols realized the presence of encroaching enemy and before fear could settle into their hearts, their throats were slit one by one. They made no noise as they succumbed to death. In the eerie quiet of dawn, the Mongols dragged the bodies of their victims into the empty bathhouse and dumped them where they would not be discovered for days to come.

By the time Princess Reyhan and her companions arrived, the sun had squeezed through the branches and left its trace on the pavement, shedding light on a bright red drop of blood, too small to be noticeable. The former crime scene appeared innocent, and nothing was out of the ordinary. The Mongols, wearing the outfits of the slain gharavols with blood rinsed out of them, performed guard duty as expected. The fact that they held their heads down was merely attributed to their piety and reluctance to stare at the ladies entering the premises.

The special preparations made for Reyhan's arrival surprised the Persian Princess and her chambermaids who had accompanied her. A reflection pool shaped like a flower and edged with mud bricks greeted them at the entrance. Water flowing from a fountain splashed onto the deep green tiles of the pool which stood in the middle of a large space. A vaulted ceiling, painted the color of fresh-made butter, met halfway down the walls with tiles of like color, studded with emerald green pieces of marble. The entry led to a larger space of similar design that contained an enormous pool of water. Tile-covered seat walls encircled the pool.

The workers had scrubbed the entire bathhouse or Hammam until its tiles gleamed in the candlelight at every corner. Hammam workers had filled the warmed pool with fresh shimmering waters before leaving the premises to allow the ladies complete privacy. The male attendants, as well as the regular female bathhouse workers, were given a day off so that Reyhan's trusted chambermaids would tend to her needs.

Petals of rose, a flower grown and revered for centuries in Persia, filled the surface of the pool, and the scent of rose oil added to the water, infused the bathhouse with an intoxicating aroma. After all, few were the times when the old royal family visited the place. Princess Reyhan's chambermaids washed her hair with an aromatic potion of green lotus powder called *sedr*, which made it the color of ripe dates. Thus, she got prepared for the next day's ceremony of applying henna paste to her hands and feet in elaborate designs as required by tradition.

Eager to get to the Grand Bazaar after luxuriating in an early morning bath, Reyhan felt an inexpressible sense of elation as she got dressed in an antechamber in the bathhouse. After wearing a long-sleeved silk dress, the color of the palest pink roses, she donned a short-sleeved black brocade topcoat with pink embroidery. A triangular scarf of yellow silk tied at her chin with a bejeweled ornament kept her long braids from the eyes of strangers. The ornament, covered in precious stones, was among the few pieces of jewelry the family still possessed. As she stepped out of the antechamber, her companions began to sing an old Persian bridal song in unison:

The roads are narrow, oh yay
Our bride a beauty, oh yay
Hands off her tassels strewn with pearls
Oh yay, oh yay, oh yay

Looking fresh and renewed, the party left for the bazaar in several covered horse-drawn carriages which had been arranged to spirit them away at the appointed time. The Mongols dressed as gharavols followed them in their own coaches, maintaining a distance. The intruders wouldn't attack the women at such a public locus, for the entire city would begin pursuing them within minutes.

The barely visible strands of cloud soon began to give way to dark ones and a heavy rain shower ensued. Incessant rains of the past few days had already washed off any residue of snow. Little blades of grass poked their heads out of the previously frozen earth. Early blooms of white crocuses dotted the landscape. Tall cypress trees that had lived more than a century rose like columns toward the sky, and fields of red poppies adorned the sides of stone-paved roads.

As Princess Reyhan entered the Bazaar, an elderly woman, who appeared to be the wife of an even older shopkeeper with a snow-white head called out to her, *Shazdeh Khanoom* (Lady Princess)! She brought out an incense-burner to ward off evil from the bride-to-be, and as the smoke of dried rue seeds in it rose, she prayed for the princess's health. "May the angels protect you, my dear Khanoom," she said with sincerity. Reyhan gave her a coin as a small token of appreciation. Funds had been tight, for their limited allowance approved by the court of Khwarazm was dwindling further and further each year. Thanks to the marriage proposal, however, she could shop to her heart's desire, courtesy of the Caliph of Baghdad. There were dresses to be selected, shoes to decide on and of course perfumes and jewelry.

The numerous customers of the bazaar had still not quite worn the cobblestone pathway that ran through its length. In the virtually empty marketplace, the sounds of shop owners resonated as they called out, "Shazdeh Khanoom look at this fabric . . . Shazdeh Khanoom see this beautiful gem . . ." It had been a while since Reyhan had come to the Grand Bazaar. Her fellow countrymen had to go through so much trouble for her to maintain security that she shied away from the place and sent her chambermaids instead.

The two Mongolian spies dressed as beggars waited patiently in the bazaar until finally, the opportunity they were expecting presented itself. They had informed their superiors in advance that the youngest daughter of the king who intended to marry the son of the Caliph of Baghdad on the very first day of Nowruz, just a few days away, would arrive with her entourage to make her purchases for the occasion. Thus, they had planned for the abduction of the princess. The act would strike terror in the hearts of the inhabitants and leave them vulnerable during the ensuing invasion.

On that Sunday, a sign bearing the Persian word *Ghorogh*, meaning reserved, was placed at the entry to the bazaar, assuring the two spies of the timing of the royal visit. One of the fake beggars, hiding underneath a table displaying rolls of exquisite fabric, could see the hem of the princess's pink silk skirt dancing in the breeze. At times, the soft fabric caressed the fingers of the ruffian, tempting him to touch the polished leather of the princess's pointed toe boots. Her boots were a far cry from the rugged footwear he had seen back home. He pulled away his fingers though, resisting the temptation, knowing that if caught he would certainly be hanged.

The other imposter had the inconvenience of being stationed outside on the bazaar's roof near a peeping hole, right above the goldsmith's shop. Despite the heavy rain that had soaked his clothes, he must have hoped to at least catch a glimpse of the fair ladies' faces, for surely, they would stop at the Jewelers' Corner. Luck was on his side. Not only did they come in, but were in his full view as they closely examined the fine craftsmanship of the flawless marvels of gold and silver. Delight sparkled in his eyes as he watched the fair maidens try on a number of rings and bracelets. Knowing that the Mongol warriors would soon arrive, however, he left his post and ran toward the entrance of the marketplace to await further orders. He did not have to wait long, because the famous falcon of a Mongol prince flew above his head and perched on the roof of the bazaar.

Chapter Six

Two Pools of Honey

IN THE MONGOL ENCAMPMENT ERECTED NEAR SAMARkand, Genghis Khan addressed his sons with his distinct aura of authority. Looking toward the makeshift ger's entrance with his jaw muscles twitching he said, "The sky has ordained me to rule the earth and impose my will upon the nations of the world. I have brought emperors to their knees and taken their women as prisoners of war."

Genghis's four sons, all off-spring of Borte, his first love, and most respected wife, stood apart from one another, as their father addressed them. The Great Khan intended to choose the heir to the Mongol throne, the Khaqan or the leader of the Khans.

"What I have achieved," Genghis continued, "has not been easy. Many of our people, including some of our kin, lost their lives to establish this empire. What is being handed to you is a responsibility above all, to maintain the cohesion of our nation, to sustain our supremacy and to ensure that the Mongols are never humiliated again."

Although each one of his sons would be granted the status of Khan with his own dominion to rule, Genghis intended to select only one as Khaqan, to the will of whom all others would have to submit.

At the same time, Genghis had finally come face to face with a lie he had lived with all his life. He noticed how Chaghatai, the second in line of succession, stared with contempt and hatred at Jochi, the heir apparent. Their contentious attitude had infuriated the Khan and forewarned of a crisis that threatened the unity of his empire. Family problems had come to surface like an old festering wound that was now impossible to heal, making him face a specter he had wished never to witness.

Jochi, the eldest, a stout forty-year-old, was the natural choice, save for the fact that his mother Borte, while Khan's wife had been kidnapped by a rival clan exactly nine months before his birth. Genghis eventually rescued her, and the matter was forgotten. No one had brought the issue up until that very moment when the Khan intended to announce that Jochi would be his successor. What had so far been mere insinuations to Jochi's questionable birth and circumstances of conception exploded into open confrontation. Chagatai viciously questioned the legitimacy of his elder brother's lineage, calling him the spawn of the enemy. Thus, the meeting ended abruptly.

Tolui, the youngest son, had repeatedly called himself a warrior and not a statesman. He spent most of his days on the battlefield and during his short stays at home sharpened his military skills. Politics, statesmanship and the machinations needed to run vast territories did not seem to be what he looked forward to or cared much about.

Ogodei, five years younger than Jochi and third in line of succession, possessed a disposition that distinguished him from his three brothers. He had a relatively mild temperament and enjoyed the bountiful beauty of nature and riding his favorite black stallion.

Ogodei left the ger and its tense environment the very moment circumstances permitted him to do so and rode his horse far from the squabbling that had opened an old painful wound. Thankfully, no other soul was present in that meeting, save for Genghis's most trusted advisor, a Chinese sage by the name of Ye Liu Chutsai.

As he rode away, Ogodei recalled the determined, stern look on his father's face. Hardships of youth and a lifetime of struggle had left their mark upon Genghis's forehead. He tried to erase from his mind the image of the Great Khan pleading with his two eldest sons and how he failed, leaving him with no choice but to dismiss both as his possible successors. What made it all sound so ludicrous, was the fact that the Khan was still alive and well and needed no help in running his kingdom's affairs. Ogodei had no idea what had possessed his father and made him decide to choose a successor at this pass. He did not want to even think about the fact that he might be the chosen one.

He rode his horse through the wilderness without stopping, hoping to reach the unit of ten commandoes on a mission to kidnap the Persian Princess. The location was not too far from the Mongol encampment, and the adventure would surely ease this gut-wrenching feeling he had had all morning. Once he mounted his horse, his falcon tethered to his wrist; he felt free from the rules and regulations imposed by the Mongol court.

Ogodei loved the wilderness and hunted beasts with the same agility as his ancestors. Alone, his fury at the way his brothers had treated each other in the presence of their father and their lack of respect for the Khan slowly subsided as the wind blew in his face, and he felt the sweat of the horse on the skin of his hand. He beat his feet against the sides of his stallion so many times, enticing it to ride faster that he feared he might have broken the poor animal's ribcage.

The earlier rain showers had left the fields smelling fresh. The scent of wet earth mingled with that of green grass. He loved the smell of the wilderness and knew he belonged to it. Trusted steed, rider and the wind together formed one instrument, the strumming of which became the music that satiated his soul. From all the territories that the Mongols had captured, the one he sought was indeed the tranquility of the meadow.

The aromatic scent of wild hyacinths filled the air. Blades of grass turned translucent in the sunlight raised their spiky heads toward the sky. Ogodei imagined them to be sword-wielding enemy armies and lifted his sword in an illusory combat with them. He heard his falcon, now untethered, hovering above his head and laughed. The sound of his laughter mingled with the shrill cry of the bird. He took this as a good omen and thought of the adventure ahead. The bird was trained to lead him to the commander of the unit of ten Mongol warriors dispatched earlier to the Grand Bazaar of Samarkand.

He arrived breathless in time to join them, as they entered the bazaar. Being the son of the Mongol Khan had its privileges. He took on the mission of capturing the princess without complaints from the others, who were left with the task of kidnapping the remaining members of her entourage.

Ogodei longed to see the look of surprise on the faces of the women they were about to capture, as he liked staring into the eyes of the animals he hunted when he entrapped them. It thrilled him to see the realization in their faces that there would be no escape. He anticipated a similar look of surprise on the faces of these women. But even from a distance, he felt overwhelmed when he laid eyes on Reyhan. He was about to pick the most beautiful flower in the land. The princess's eyes, like two pools of honey that would have melted any man's heart, remained focused on him.

Chapter Seven

The Rug Handlers

TIRED BY THE ENDLESS SHOPPING, THE PRINCESS RESTED upon the soft, colorful cushions of a hookah shop and along with her companions began drinking sweet tea while they awaited a lunch specially prepared for them. Reyhan was the first to notice that the gharavols approaching them had features that belonged to some faraway land; high cheekbones, slanted eyebrows, almond shaped eyes and long thin mustaches. As they came close, they drew their daggers. Before she could open her mouth to scream, they began their ambush. Nearby shop owners and merchants immediately hid behind their counters in fear.

The dark figure that had appeared before Reyhan had his face covered. His features were not visible, save for his eyes. Those eyes almost looked innocent, even apologetic. "I do not wish to harm you," he said in broken Persian, his words washing over her like the sweet waters of the Caspian Sea; he was her enemy, yet his voice sounded so calming, even reassuring.

"I have to carry you far away from here, but I will not harm you." He paused, then added, "I beg of you to come with me."

Beg of me? Reyhan wondered.

His hand caressed her face when he tied a piece of cloth over her mouth, making her shiver slightly at the unfamiliar touch, but it did not feel unpleasant. Although the why in her gaze and the frown on her brow must have made him feel like the villain that he was, the magical allure to their encounter left Reyhan confused. She did not feel fear, but something else entirely. Every impulse that should have made her run away melted into a form of submissiveness one feels toward a protector.

The princess and the women accompanying her were each gagged and rolled into a stolen rug. The Mongol spy, hiding under the table, jumped out and used the opportunity to pull off one of Reyhan's boots as a souvenir to be cherished later.

The fake gharavols held a roll of rug each on their right shoulders, secured with their left hands, thus partially covering their faces. In such manner, they left through the back exit of the bazaar in broad daylight. They mounted horses that were awaiting their arrival. From these, Ogodei claimed his black stallion. They left the scene calmly as if ordered to carry the rugs purchased by the princess for her future home.

The other shopkeepers throughout the length of the bazaar had not seen the spectacle or heard the noise, persumably under the impression that the lovely princess and her companions were shopping elsewhere. No one, not even some sentries stationed at the proximity of the bazaar, reported anything out of the ordinary. The few merchants who had been witness to the spectacle looked too frightened to speak, and by the time they did so it was already too late.

The Mongols carried the fragile bundles with ease to the Mongol camp in the outskirts of the city. Later, however, as the story was told a thousand times by a thousand tongues and the news traveled far and wide, people shook their heads in regret remarking, "if only the guards had been more alert."

When the rug handlers finally brought forth their precious cargo, Ogodei expressed his hope that the presence of the Persian fairies would help Genghis Khan forget the memory of the earlier incident that had left him in a sour mood. They unrolled the rugs before the Mongol warlord, and the chambermaids stood trembling. The princess, however, remained a portrait of propriety.

She rose gracefully, taking time to smooth out her skirt like a flower unfolding its petals. The layers of fine silk that covered her body moved like a dream with each motion. One of the guards who spoke some Persian asked her to bow before Genghis Khan, leader of the Mongols, pointing to where the Great Khan sat. She only made a slight bow with her head to acknowledge the Khan.

Curiosity made her look up to find a muscular man of commanding stature and handsome features before her. His intense gaze conveyed power, resilience and remorselessness, or maybe her imagination made her think so.

They were in a tent-like structure with a fire glowing in the center. She watched the ruby-colored late afternoon sun through an opening as it melted into the horizon. About two dozen alien warriors sat around the tent talking. Despite the torn shoulder of her topcoat, with one boot missing and her long braids fallen out in disarray, Reyhan's radiant beauty appeared to have left those present awestruck. The Mongol Khan looked angry; however, ready to crumble her beauty under his feet.

"Princess," Genghis said, his tone formal but bitter, "your father, Khwarazm Shah, has murdered and mutilated my envoys who were only seeking trade with him. On more than one occasion, I sent emissaries to your land, hoping for trade relations. But each time my ambassadors were treated like game. What do you have to say for your family?"

Reyhan was about to flinch when she heard the name of Khwarazm Shah but tried to remain impassive, the safety of her loyal companions on her mind. They were girls about her own age who had served her earnestly through joys and sorrows, and she wished no harm to come to them. She maintained her calm for their sake. Within her heart, however, fear took root, but like most members of royalty, she had been taught how to place a firm lid on her emotions. She turned to him and spoke.

"Sir," she said her voice calm and steady, "I do not know you and do not understand why you have brought me here."

"Be careful not to address me inappropriately," Genghis Khan's voice thundered, "for you are but a captive, royal or not. And I am the ruler of Mongolia, and I shall stand no insult."

The tranquil ocean was not disturbed by the roaring of the lion standing before her.

"Your Majesty," Reyhan rephrased her words after a short pause, her tone gentle, "I do not know why I was brought here. I believe you have been misinformed, for I am no kin of the Khwarazm King. Quite the contrary, we are despised by him."

"Are you not a princess?" he raised his voice a pitch higher as he spoke. Her serene complexion underwent no change.

"Yes," she replied, oblivious to the outburst, "I belong to the Seljuk Dynasty. My grandfather had ruled the land before power was wrested out of his hands by his own servant, the predecessor of the man we know today as Khwarazm Shah."

Genghis Khan surveyed his men. The warriors who had squatted around the tent kept grinning for they must have assumed the Khan was going to take revenge on the trembling girls. They did not understand the language being spoken but could surely see gestures or emotional outbursts. Some of them he had earlier dispatched to the bazaar. After the disclosure by the princess, however, the attitude of the Khan changed. The stern rays of his gaze made all the men wipe the humor off their faces immediately and sit more attentively and respectfully.

Further explanation was unnecessary because the Khan noticed how faded and timeworn the princess's beautiful outfit looked. He became pensive since he could not fathom what it was about this fragile girl that he found so disconcerting. Reyhan used the back of two fingers to tuck behind her pink shell of an ear, brown silken strands that had strayed onto her delicate face. The princess had merely pulled her hair away from her face, but that very feminine motion just like the way Temujin's mother used to brush away her hair, affected the Khan deeply. Hoelun, as lovely as she was in her younger days, did not have Reyhan's enchanting beauty, but so much about this princess's calm demeanor and soft voice reminded him of her.

The Mongol Khan spoke at length, his voice much calmer, "My spies have informed me that you were treated like a princess in the Grand Bazaar when in fact your family no longer rules Persia."

"One attains royal status by noble birth, not by taking over lands and territories," Reyhan replied with a noticeable hint of sarcasm in her voice. In the battle of minds and spirits, she had won and in the battle of hearts even more so.

The exchange between Genghis and the Persian Princess had clearly attracted the attention of those present. There was complete silence within the ger, save for two fellow officers quietly conversing in a corner. In the silence, the voice of one of them, who had obviously found the Khan's weakness before women of beauty risible, was heard by all when he said, "Looks like we have another Chaka here." The Khan's stern gaze lingered on him for more than a few seconds, an indication that this intrusion of his would not go unpunished.

Chapter Eight

The Heir to the Mongol Throne

REYHAN FELT THE INTENSITY OF SOMEONE'S GAZE FROM the right corner of the tent. She turned to find the brown eyes of her kidnapper, a man in his mid-thirties, with handsome features, long black hair, and thin mustache that curled under his chin. Another look confirmed that she was not mistaken, for he had the same stature as the masked man who had brought her there. He smiled at her, apparently noticing the lingering stare. Transfixed by the encounter, she lowered her gaze demurely. He stood not far from where she was, smiling mirthfully as if he challenged her and yet found her amusing.

The shrewd Khan must have noticed this exchange, for his eyes moved from one to the other, indicating that he realized the special attention his son was giving to the young captive. After all, the emotional attachment of two young people is sometimes difficult to conceal because of the curious way they regard one another and the sensitivity they show to each other's presence. An experienced eye discerns such attachments.

The Mongol Khan ordered the maidens to be transported to Mongolia, as his soldiers readied themselves for an all-out invasion of Khwarazm territories. Upon howdahs mounted on camels, the group left the outskirts of Samarkand for Karakorum, the tent city which was slowly becoming the seat of Mongol power. Workers quickly disassembled the makeshift tents and rolled them away with all their contents, leaving no sign of their former existence.

As Reyhan and her chambermaids were carried off to Mongolia, the Mongol army successfully traveled through the desert of Kyzyl Kum stunning the population of the legendary city of Bukhara with a frontal attack that paralyzed their resistance and burned the lush oasis to the ground.

On their way to Mongolia, Reyhan could feel that they were approaching a much colder climate. The frequency of thunderstorms and showers of hail that she witnessed made clear the reason for the Mongols' obsessive fear of the sky, an issue she learned about during the journey. Their land appeared bare and exposed to the elements. A flash of lightning seemed far more dramatic in Mongolia than in the cities where she had lived.

The Steppes, centuries after the birth of Christ, had remained unchanged since that auspicious day. Unlike the rivers Onon and Kerulon that border it, the prairie in between rolled like the sands encased in an hourglass, returning with the seasons to the very spot where it all started. Throughout the journey, Reyhan had noticed the barren landscape. *Their quest for conquering fertile lands may have been borne out of necessity, rather than from the thirst for power and glory. Even Genghis's cunning ways and machinations could be a cover for his basic instinct to survive.*

Reyhan was assigned a ger as soon as they arrived in Karakorum. Her maids all shared a spacious one next to hers. This provided her with some degree of privacy while the girls were at her service whenever she needed them. Not long after Reyhan settled down, an African eunuch who introduced himself as Baako and knew enough Persian to communicate with her, brought a large bowl and a pitcher of warm water and asked permission to wash her tired feet. Reyhan saw so much compassion in the eyes of the eunuch that as he knelt before her, she involuntarily uttered the question that had been on her mind throughout the long journey.

"Who is this Chaka?"

"Oh' my lady," he pleaded as tears welled up in his eyes, "do not mention her name if you value your life. She was the apple of everyone's eyes, particularly that of the Khan."

"What happened to her?"

"There was a yearning in her to speak her mind, and she willingly laid down her life in hopes that others could live."

He then relayed the story of Chaka and added, "The extreme weather in this God forsaken land, the frequent thunderstorms, and the winter blizzard they call *zud*, leave people vulnerable to natural phenomena. Life is difficult in these parts and that has hardened the hearts of the Mongols. Many have become their victims, including Chaka."

Reyhan shivered as she heard this.

"She was killed for she spoke her mind," Baako said. "As a wise man once said, in this place, one's teeth must serve as the prison bars for one's tongue."

The Seljuk Princess enjoyed the company of Baako who had entrusted her with Chaka's manuscript in the hope that the recording of Mongol history would continue. The eunuch translated parts of the manuscript for her, and Reyhan quickly realized the importance of Chaka's writing and vowed to continue in the same tradition.

As Reyhan held the manuscript in her hands for the first time, she felt a sense of mission. Her life here in Mongolia would not be in vain. She now had a duty to fulfill what Chaka had left unfinished. Baako used every opportunity to inform Reyhan about the character of the Mongols, lest she suffered a similar fate to that of Chaka.

On one occasion Baako told her, "Genghis experienced great calamities as a child. But having had to live in the wild throughout his younger days has allowed him to possess a superb sense of his surroundings. He can almost smell a traitor. He trusts only a small circle of his close kin and like a wolf is merciless to his foes. One might even say that he has taken on the characteristics of the wild beasts he grew up with, for he is cunning like a fox, sharp like a serpent and wise like a lion. How much of that he has passed on to his four sons with Borte, remains to be seen."

Reyhan had learned from Baako that when the Mongol warriors finally arrive after weeks of battle in Persia, a gathering would be held to announce the appointment of the new heir to the throne. Upon the arrival of the warriors, a celebration took place in the large white ger of Genghis that could easily encompass hundreds of guests under its magnificent dome. The ger was decorated with a lining of bright yellow silk. Outside, the dome of the sky looked magnificent too. Fixed constellations twinkled, and shooting stars waged war against one another, drawing glittering lines upon the dark blue domain.

A long stretch of white felt, unrolled on the floor, displayed cooked meats of horses and oxen placed in large ornamented tureens. For drink, they served the fermented milk of the mare they called *airaq*. A large bowl of pomegranates, a rare imported commodity brought there from Persia took center stage at the feast.

Genghis sat cross-legged upon a richly embroidered cushion next to the fire, the most honorable seat under the dome of the tent. Broad shouldered, long dark hair tied at the nape of his neck, his skin tanned by the sun, Genghis's stature certainly appeared impressive, despite the signs of age. Ogodei, chosen by the emperor as Reyhan's betrothed sat next to his father. He clearly had a good sense of humor, because he laughed quite a bit and appeared to be an affable sort of character.

Although the story of Chaka told by Baako left Reyhan with much anxiety, in some ways, she felt lucky that she was not to wed one of Ogodei's two older brothers. She cared little for her bethroted in Baghdad as well, never having laid eyes on him. Sitting far from one another on the right side of the ger, Genghis's two older sons eyed each other spitefully and stared begrudgingly at Ogodei. After all, he had not only endeared himself to their father but had also found a Persian beauty for a mate.

Reyhan did not know exactly where to sit. She noticed all the women huddled in the left corner from the door and took a seat next to them. The meat on the bone served to her in a wooden bowl smelled half-cooked, and when she forced herself to take a bite, tasted bland as if no spices were used. If it weren't for the smell of smoke that rose from the food, an indication that it was seared over fire, she would not have been able to hold it down. No bowls and pitchers of water for washing hands were to be seen, so she felt grateful she had held on to her handkerchief from Samarkand.

Smoke from the fire escaped through the opening at the top of the ger. Animal skins, drawings of birds and fish that appeared to be Chinese, pieces of handmade artifacts shaped like various animals, and carpets that Reyhan recognized as being Persian-made hung from the walls. Noticing that the other Mongolian women of stature were paying full attention to her every gesture and reaction, Reyhan nodded and smiled approvingly at the haphazard decorations.

Through the heat wave that radiated from the fire pit, Reyhan could see the blurred faces of Mongol warriors sitting around the ger. In the dead silence before Genghis Khan announced his heir and successor, everyone seemed to be contemplating the impact the announcement would have on their nation and subsequently the world's future.

"I realize," Genghis began, his voice booming through the enclosure, "that like my father, death may come to me unexpectedly. Therefore, I feel it incumbent upon me to choose a successor while I am still of sound body and mind."

He kept his eyes for a moment on Subutai Bahadur and Chepe Noyon, his most cherished army commanders and added, "I have contemplated long and hard before reaching the decision of which I am about to inform you. I do not want our young nation to fall into disarray as my family became after my father's demise. Upon my departure from this world, all who are present, particularly the lead commanders of the Mongol Army, Subutai Bahadur and Chepe Noyon, must heed the orders of Ogodei as you have heeded my commands. I have found him in possession of a solid character, and I have chosen him as my heir and successor to lead the Mongol nation in the event of my death."

Chapter Nine

The Khaqan

OGODEI NOTICED THAT HIS FATHER LEFT UNSAID THE earlier quarrel between his older brothers and did not bring up the cause of tensions that had led him to choose the third in succession as his heir. For a moment there was complete silence as everyone was probably expecting to hear the name of Jochi. Then all rose to chants of *urra* as both Jochi and Chaghatai, left with no alternative but to abide by their father's command, humbly bowed before the future leader; an act that appeared to have pleased Genghis greatly.

With Jochi's birthright impugned and Chaghatai's malicious self-interest exposed, the even-tempered Ogodei had ultimately won the coveted position. Ogodei, initially overwhelmed by the unexpected change in his status, soon began to smile broadly, exposing two rows of pearl white teeth. He lifted his goblet of wine and drank to his father's health and long life.

Following the announcement, a group of shamans began singing praises to the eternal sky. The soft, melodic tune of the two-stringed Mongolian lute accompanied the singing. After a while, Genghis Khan lifted his hand in a gesture that instantly quelled the noise. He took up his goblet of Shiraz wine and proclaimed, "There is another cause for celebration tonight. Ogodei is to marry the former princess of Persia, Reyhan of the Seljuk Dynasty, on this very night."

Reyhan blushed as what seemed like a thousand eyes suddenly turned toward her. The enormity of the situation, the marriage that she was being led to, left her mind racing. Golden embroidery covered the red bridal gown she was given. A tall, bejeweled headdress framed her face with strings of pearls. The headdress was a bit loose, and thus she had to avoid tilting her head too much, worried that it could easily fall. At least the material she wore, a mixture of lamb's wool and silk, felt soft.

From the way the Mongol officers stared at the bowl of pomegranates, she almost felt like her looks were competing with that of the bowl of fruit for the group's attention. The harsh environment to which they belonged was not conducive to growing vegetation, she concluded.

Borte, the Mongol Empress sitting next to Reyhan, spoke little. When Reyhan was offered pomegranates, she politely accepted her share and then turned and presented it to Borte, to the latter's delight. Baako had told Reyhan that Borte was younger than Genghis when they married, but she looked older than him now. Reyhan pitied her and hoped to gradually gain her trust and to count on her support as Ogodei's mother.

An assortment of weapons, some of them recognizable as swords and daggers and other ominous-looking sharp objects quite unfamiliar to her hung from the walls. She tried not to stare, fearing that it would only arouse suspicion.

Genghis looked happy, telling jokes and laughing heartily. He frequently looked at Ogodei sitting to his right and at Reyhan sitting at the far-left corner of the ger. The meal being over, Genghis Khan lifted his silver goblet of wine. As he drank the intoxicating liquid, holding the goblet with his right hand and placing his left hand on his knee, his gaze remained on his new daughter-in-law, so conveniently captured. He looked so approvingly at her in this moment, yet she wondered how at other times those eyes could be void of all human emotions. How else could one kill a man or maim fellow human beings, merely because they stood in one's way?

"So, tell me," Genghis asked. "What form of communication have the wise kings of Persia devised for their armies? Although their late monarch, Khwarazm Shah, I must admit, was no favorite of mine."

Sounds of laughter echoed through the ger as those who knew the language explained to the others what the Khan had just said. Reyhan hesitated. She did not want to give away any clues that would help this warmonger in his military expeditions but quickly inferred that the Mongol Khan, although fully aware of Persia's Chapar courier system, intended to test her forthrightness and honesty.

Genghis appeared enthralled by Reyhan's resourcefulness, as she tried to charm more than just the khan with her smile. She then began to speak describing in great detail the Chapar system devised by Cyrus the Great.

"Couriers ride agile horses, carrying mail from one station to another, placed at regular intervals to be reached within one day on horseback," she said, animating the explanation with her fingers. "Well-rested men on fresh horses then continue the journey to the next station to expedite the delivery of written messages. These stations are furnished with accommodations and are considered resting places for the mail carriers of the Shah. Refreshments of all sorts are provided for the relief of the courier who has arrived, and fresh horses are kept ready for the departure of those who are to continue the journey."

While she spoke, Reyhan registered the reactions of those present, particularly when she mentioned the name of the late Persian Monarch. For even those among them who were unfamiliar with the language, could identify the name of King Cyrus. She fancied she could perceive potential enemies and possible allies in their expressions. Reyhan hoped that by enlightening the emperor regarding the ingenuity of the Persian people, she could somehow gain his trust, winning her survival and the protection of her companions.

"Ingenious indeed," the Mongol Khan replied. His meaningful smile seemed to express both his approval of the girl's tact upon this invisible chessboard and his awareness of her diplomacy. He mentioned to Ogodei that he would need exactly such a mate to rule over the empire and added, addressing the princess, "We shall follow suit. I will establish the same system throughout Mongol territories." He paused for a moment then asked, "And what is the characteristic of the Seljuk that has made them so popular in Persia?"

Reyhan explained that her family's popularity stemmed from the fact that although Turkic in their origins, they promoted Persian language and culture. "My grandfather even encouraged us to speak Persian at home." Reyhan knew she was crossing the line when she added, "A leader should never attempt to destroy the culture of the lands he invades."

A frown appeared on Genghis's forehead as color ran to her cheeks, and she felt herself blush. She pledged to herself to be more careful next time, for she was jeopardizing more than her own life.

Ogodei intervened in an obvious attempt to alleviate the situation. "What she means is that among the inhabitants of the lands we conquer, we should save the cultured people. Like the artisans and engineers, for they can enhance the greatness of our own civilization."

No one spoke their mind in Genghis's presence unless invited to do so by the Great Khan, let alone lecturing him about the proper manner of treating his subjects. Fire flashed for a moment in Genghis's eyes, but reason soon returned, allowing the wedding ceremony to take place. Shamans blessed the newlyweds, and a Muslim clergy recited the words that united Ogodei and Reyhan in accordance with the bride's wishes.

Chapter Ten

A Treasure Chest

A WEDDING GER IN ACCORDANCE WITH MONGOL TRADITION was set up for Reyhan. She passed from among two large lit torches at the entrance of the ger. Flames from the torches almost touched the felt fabric of the enclosure and Reyhan feared she would be burned alive in it. The Mongol guards must have noticed her look of concern, for they quickly removed the torches as soon as she stepped inside. The smell of wood and musk coming from a fire pit greeted her upon entrance. Candles burned on small metal tables set up at different corners of the ger. Embroidered tapestries depicting the animals of the Steppes hung from the walls and a bedspread of red velvet covered a feather mattress in a corner. Ogodei was nowhere to be seen and Reyhan felt her heart beat in anticipation of the unknown.

When Ogodei finally arrived, he was carrying a large wooden chest as a gift for his bride. He unlocked and laid open the heavy container. He then walked out of the ger abruptly, allowing Reyhan a chance to hunt for treasures in the chest. Reyhan surveyed the contents and found numerous pieces of Persian style silk garments and bejeweled pointed leather shoes of the best quality. The pieces shimmered in the light of candles, revealing the hand-woven fabrics made with gold and silver thread. There were also embroidered outfits in shades of sapphire, emerald, and ruby.

Reyhan pulled the pieces out of the chest like jewelry and examined with great astonishment the two-piece garments with long flowing skirts and intricately sewn tops that had pleats at their lower edges. When she finally looked up, she noticed that Ogodei had only pretended to have left. He stood at the entry to the ger, wearing a mischievous smile.

"You bought these for me?" she asked, embarrassed that she had shown so much interest in them without knowing he was watching her every move.

"Plundered," he replied bluntly without mincing words.

"Plundered? Where from?" He never failed to surprise her.

"Right out of the palace of the Shah!" Ogodei proclaimed triumphantly.

Reyhan immediately dropped the deep violet skirt she was holding and rose in protest, but when Ogodei suggested that Mongol ladies would appreciate such garments, she pulled the chest toward herself defiantly, to her husband's great amusement.

He laughed as he grabbed her by the waist and pulled her toward him. His loving embrace melted any resistance left in Reyhan as she succumbed to the joys of marriage.

The next morning Ogodei left for the fronts. Not long after his departure, Reyhan asked for tea and Baako brought in a tray. She excitedly told Baako about Ogodei's gift and went through the entire contents of the chest, holding each piece out for Baako's opinion. The latter's mind, however, seemed preoccupied with distressful thoughts.

"I hate to upset you at this time of joy, my lady, but I fear that you will learn about the devastation in your homeland by those who might disclose such accounts in much harsher ways."

Reyhan dropped the dress and suddenly felt submerged in a pool of icy water.

"They showed no mercy. I wish I had better news, my lady. Many died, young and old, homes left in ruin, places of worship faring no better. One can hardly recognize Samarkand today."

The news instantly made Reyhan melancholy, and it was obvious that Baako regretted his minimal disclosure that very moment. Days of tears followed with chambermaids asking Reyhan what was wrong, while she refused to disclose the mountain of pain she felt weighing upon her soul. Even after Ogodei returned, her husband's loving attention did little to soothe her and only made the burden of guilt heavier upon her young heart. Ogodei had not taken part in the raids on Persia, but even if he had, he would have considered it the right of the Mongols to destroy all that stood in their way.

Reyhan knew that Baako had been holding back the most gruesome parts, and her imagination ran wild. Baako had told her how Chaka's countenance turned white as death when news of Mongol atrocities against Chinese territories reached her. He must have feared a repeat of those moments. He had said that from that point onward Chaka's communication with Genghis often turned into bitter arguments. Baako certainly wanted to discourage an outburst, like the one which ended Chaka's life. But she was bound to hear about the horrors inflicted upon her nation through palace gossip anyway. When she asked for details, Baako clothed cruel facts with heartwarming stories of survival in an obvious attempt not to further disturb her troubled mind.

After days of living with visions of the devastation of her country, Reyhan finally took to the pen and dipped the sharpened tip of a feather in a pot of black ink. Making sure not to waste the precious space on the paper, she began to write her version of events, taking Baako's hopeful slant as her own. Always reluctant to divulge her true feelings and disinclined to further explore the massive destruction and loss of life in her homeland, Reyhan penned fables, half-truths. The whole truth was more than she could bear, let alone describe, and she hoped others would discern the deeper reality of destruction between the lines.

Entry by Reyhan:

The Coppersmith's Tale

The village of Behesht, meaning heaven, was located in the outskirts of the city of Marv, one of the most magnificent cities in Persia. But while the latter boasted impressive buildings, cultural centers, white brick walls, rose gardens, and a great library filled with numerous volumes of handwritten manuscripts, the former didn't have much to show for it. In fact, it had little resemblance to the paradise described in holy books and looked quite commonplace indeed. The population fared a little worse, one might say, than those of neighboring areas. Poverty was rampant and the well-off, if you could call them that, could only claim that they owned a domestic animal or two.

"Try to find a better heaven," was the common expression the locals used to ward off any potential newcomer to the village, for what little they had could not be shared.

Life in the village did indeed have some advantages. In the lazy afternoons, freshly watered roses in their tiny gardens became home to singing nightingales. Benches covered in thick carpets, as brightly colored as the flowers would be set up in backyards. Men smoked hookahs, enjoying the scenery as women chatted over hot tea and bits of caramelized sugar.

Majeed, the coppersmith, owned the smallest house in the village. He had built a shelter for himself and his wife next to a small hill and almost as an extension of it. Although it had a rather sizeable room, it appeared more like a basement of a house with no top floors. The roof, covered with a compact mixture of mud and straw, was at a level with the adjacent road, making the dwelling nearly invisible to outsiders. It was also located at a considerable distance from the nearest collection of dwellings, which were equally dilapidated. Majeed considered himself a happy man though, until something horrible happened one day.

The coppersmith always took pride in his small suburban shop, despite the long commute from home to work. In his shop, he displayed a collection of his artwork which included embossed trays, pots, and jars covered in animal shapes, floral designs and human figures. The sight always brought a smile to his face. One day he would open his shop in Marv, he had told his wife on more than one occasion, where he might attract wealthier customers.

It was almost noon on that spring day. Majeed picked up the copper tray that he had finished engraving and took a final look at it. A frequent customer to his shop would receive the tray the following day. He had embossed intricate designs of birds and beasts onto its shiny surface.

He tilted the tray toward the light for a closer inspection. As he did so, his eyes drifted from the flawless artwork to the dark trousers of a man standing before him, apparently admiring Majeed's skill. But when his eyes settled on the stranger's penetrating gaze, he realized the predicament he was in. That sinister half-smile brought back memories he had fought hard to forget. He got up, almost shaking. "What are you doing here?" he asked, stuttering a bit.

"I have been pursuing you for the past several years," the man said with a thick Arabic accent, "I have not forgotten what you did."

The coppersmith looked up. The sun, like an ever-watchful eye, stood in the middle of the sky. The call for prayer was heard. "It is time for noon prayers. I have to close shop and go to the mosque," he said as fast as he could before shoving the finished copper tray into the man's hands. He then threw aside the piece of cloth meant for wiping his instruments, locked up his shop and ran as fast as he could toward his humble dwelling.

"You have to go to the mosque," the stranger repeated sarcastically, as he watched the coppersmith run, "make sure you don't murder anybody on your way there!"

This encounter happened when Majeed was at the peak of his career and had grown from being a mere apprentice to be the master. He had married the prettiest girl in the neighborhood, Golnaar which means pomegranate flower, and now when all was going well for him, disaster had struck from the most unlikely quarter.

The next morning and the one after, he stayed in bed. Golnaar was hesitant at first to bring up the matter, for she must have noticed the utterly dejected look on her husband's face. Finally, on the third day, she served him some tea from a coal-burning samovar and then asked, "What happened the day before yesterday that troubles you so? What is it that ails you? Pray tell me."

Reluctantly he began, "I lived in Baghdad before I married you. You remember?"

"Yes, I know that," Golnaar replied, filling her glass as well.

"There was a Persian metalwork master in Baghdad that I worked for as an apprentice. Early one morning I went to his workshop to begin my work. I found my master stabbed to death with his body resting on the very table where he did his craft. The shop appeared emptied of its treasures, which included containers made of copper, silver, and gold. Thus, it occurred to me that the murderer must have been a thief. Knowing that I would probably be the one to be accused of murder, I tried to flee the scene. Only one man, a former customer of the shop, saw me. 'I am innocent,' I told him, but the sinister smile on his face told me that he did not believe me, nor cared to think otherwise."

Golnaar's pretty eyes widened in disbelief but her hands were visibly shaking when she picked up her glass of tea.

"The wicked man even accused me of having plotted this in advance," Majeed went on to say. "He concocted this tale that he had seen me the other day, quarreling with the shop owner over money. I was left with no choice but to point the finger of accusation back at him. This enraged him further, and he made up tales about my character that began to sound fearfully convincing. That vulture then tried to blackmail me. I refused payment, of course, but he said he would testify against me in the Mahkameh. Before he could take the case to the authorities, and before they could arrest me, I left Baghdad."

Here he stopped and began staring blankly, his dark past recurring anew before his eyes.

"What grief, what shame, how could I ever face my family again?" she said. "If this is disclosed, we will be castigated, blamed for deceiving the people; your business would be in ruins. We have to flee. We can go to Damascus and start anew."

"But I have no means to leave the city and set up business elsewhere," Majeed said. They had only been married for a year and all he had saved was used up for the wedding and the dwelling they now shared. They would have to devise a plan, a means of escape, and an explanation that would satisfy everyone.

Hope had earlier crept up in him, like the seedlings shooting out of the earth, that they too would have a bright future at last. Now all their hopes were dashed. He did not want to leave his bedchamber, though he knew they needed to move on.

Golnaar poured more tea for the two of them. She often ignored reality when things became too complicated and listened as if she was hearing a bedtime tale.

Majeed felt a degree of relief after having unburdened himself and noticing that Golnaar was not about to walk out on him, continued with a greater degree of ease. "Later, I sought shelter among a group of highwaymen who took pity on me, and seeing that I had nothing they could steal, they helped me find my way back home to Persia. Here I began a new life, married you and settled down. I thought I had put all that behind me."

"So, what happened the day before yesterday that has distressed you so?" Golnaar asked.

"The other day, while working in the shop, I saw that same wicked man with the sinister smile. It had been five years since the last time I laid eyes on him. The expression on his face told me that he would betray me the first chance he gets. Like an apparition out of my worst nightmares, he stood before me. Now I dare not step outside and face the fate that might be awaiting me there. And neither should you."

Days passed and Majeed did not leave his house. "Why me Allah?" he lamented, raising his tearful eyes toward the low ceiling of their small house that badly needed fresh paint. He knew he was the talk of the town and waited for something to fall from the sky, to either put an end to his miserable life or change the subject of conversation in the neighborhood. Unbeknown to them, something had indeed happened. The Mongols had raided the village, wiping out the inhabitants.

Like many families in those days, Majeed and his wife used to place a pot on top of mud bricks laid outdoors and made fire underneath for cooking. But now there was little to cook with, so the poor wife had not attempted to light a fire outdoors for days. Instead, Golnaar brought bits of dried bread out of a copper bin he had made for her as a wedding gift, upon which they munched to keep themselves going day after day.

Thus, their house bearing no sign of life did not attract the attention of the invaders and kept the coppersmith and his wife unaware of the mayhem. Being situated rather far from the arena of battle, and absorbed in their own troubles, they never heard the rhythmic sound of the Mongol army drums that shattered nerves and foretold the imminent death of so many residents. Neither did they hear the screams that were eventually silenced as the hooves of horses trampled bodies.

A week passed. Golnaar finally wrapped herself in her floral print chador, determined to go fetch some food before they starved to death. By then, the Mongols had left to invade other towns and villages.

As she walked out, she noticed the stench in the air and the eerie silence. She could not even hear birds, cats or dogs. And then . . . she saw it, the first corpse. Is there a murderer on the loose? She swallowed hard. And then there were others. An injured man who looked more dead than alive began dragging himself toward her.

"Help me," he begged. She shrieked back.

"What happened?" she asked, gasping.

"We were under attack by enemy invaders. They spared no one. How come you weren't hurt?"

"I can't explain it," she said, inwardly thanking God for having been out of danger. "Stay here. I will get some help."

Shocked at the scenes of horror, Golnaar returned pale-faced and shivering to the house. She informed her husband that they were no longer the talk of the village. The village no longer existed. Then the idea slowly took shape in her mind that the wicked man who was probably killed by the Mongols may have inadvertently saved their lives.

Chapter Eleven

The War

THE WAR DRAMA THAT UNFOLDED FAR SURPASSED REY-han's descriptions. In Persia as in China, Genghis resorted to every atrocity imaginable. He threw living prisoners of war into moats to build human bridges for his army and used them as shields of flesh and bone against enemy attacks.

Upon reaching Bukhara, the Mongols cut down the trees near the city to build siege engines and heavy war equipment. Under the light of torches, Chinese engineers and carpenters taken captive by the Mongols supervised the process overnight. A newfound tool called the trebuchet as well as mangonels threw giant boulders to break down the barriers. Within hours, Mongol horsemen entered the metropolis as the long reaching fiery arrows of their archers, standing high atop the city walls, bombarded the defenders of Bukhara.

Despite a heavy downpour that ensued, the Mongols in their rain-saturated outfits with their horses soaked to their very hooves started to plunder. People ran for their lives to escape the horror raining upon them. Swords slashed skins and limbs, beheading some and disemboweling others. Blood formed small rivers and soon there was a sea of dread and destruction, but no one cried. The pale skins of amputated limbs and headless bodies left an eerie scene that contrasted with the tranquil beauty and the fresh breeze of early spring as if body parts had bloomed in the land in lieu of flowers.

Some defenders like Jalaluddin, the son of Khwarazm Shah, fought gallantly, but others submitted without resistance. No fortifications remained immune for long as the determined Steppe warriors climbed, dug tunnels, and used every means at their disposal to seek and kill their foes. Bukhara crumbled almost overnight and Samarkand fared no better.

Khwarazmshah's magnificent war elephants became the first casualties of war. The Mongol warriors, who had never seen such giant creatures before, targeted the hefty legs of the animals with their arrows, sending them, half-crazed with fear into enemy lines. The elephants ended up trampling the Persians rather than destroying their foes. Seeing the extent of Mongol brutality, the Shah fled toward the Caspian Sea.

Entry by Reyhan:

The Birth of Hope

The city of Neyshabur took pride in its magnificent orchards, shady woods and green hilltops. Its meadows, filled with corn poppies in spring and its rivers and fountains added further charm to the land. Its mines of turquoise gemstones attracted merchants from China and other parts of Asia. Its temperatures remained quite mild in the summer, and spring always appeared everlasting there for it lingered longer in Neyshabur than any other part of the known world. But the greener the land, the lusher its fields and orchards, the more swiftly the Mongols were attracted to it.

Shereen, the young wife of Nauder, had ventured out early in the morning to buy fresh-baked bread. The cool air that still had bits of winter in it embraced her. She felt like screaming with joy. She felt so full of love, of life; a child, a miracle growing within her would be in her arms in just a few days. She could hardly wait.

The aroma of the blossoms had mingled with the scent of wet earth. Months ago, scents of any kind would make Shereen nauseous, but not today. Almost nine months into her pregnancy, she was completely over that part.

Hassan, the baker, busy preparing his dough, boasted that he was always the first at his job, never neglecting his duty as the main source of nourishment for the inhabitants. A bee buzzed around his white apron but his hands being submerged in the concoction had become too sticky to be used for shooing off the insect. Shereen watched and laughed inwardly at the spectacle.

An unusual sound of drums could be heard in the distance. It appeared to be from out of town. It aroused little curiosity though, for at times groups of entertainers came to town from nearby villages to gain a few coins off their tiny circus of odd acts.

Shereen purchased her bread and after walking a short distance, rested on a large boulder near her house. She did so every time she returned from the baker, breaking a piece of her Barbary bread into tiny morsels for the doves. She wrapped her white shawl twice around her belly to keep it warm in the chilly morning air. The birds walked around the hem of her long skirt as they always did, but something erratic in their behavior left her puzzled. They took quick bites and flew away. She wondered if there was going to be a thunderstorm and got up from the rock to hurry home.

A watermelon vendor with his horse cart carrying a load of large melons passed her by. The vendor had drawn out his knife, ready to cut up the melon and prove the sweetness of his produce upon demand. With one hand already tied up with the large piece of bread, Shereen reluctantly decided to forgo the treat.

Tumbling down the road like a duckling, she finally reached her home. Nauder, her husband of three years, protested as soon as he opened the door. "Why did you do that? I would have gone for the bread. You shouldn't be out there in such condition."

Shereen laid her tired body on the piles of cushions that served as furnishings and allowed her shawl to roll off her rounded frame. She stared lovingly at her husband with her large brown eyes. Nauder placed his hand on her belly. The baby kicked. They both laughed.

Shereen, like her name which meant 'sweet,' was a kind-hearted woman who belonged to the higher echelons of Zoroastrian families. Nauder felt lucky to have wed her. His own family consisted of farmers whose income barely sustained them. Nauder had inherited a small apple orchard, and they lived off the sale of its produce.

"It's going to be a boy," he said, proudly. "He is already pushing me aside."

"We should call him Farhod," he suggested.

"I hate that name," she said, making a funny face. "Farhod is the folkloric hero always struggling to win the heart of his beloved. It's such a sad name for our first child."

"Let's call him Roestam then," Nauder suggested, smiling.

She laughed again, "What if he is a puny little child? His name would sound ludicrous."

"Wait, I hear something. It feels like the ocean is moving toward our home."

The voice of the town caller echoed in the street. The couple ended their conversation and rushed toward an open window. He was screaming, "Moghoal, Moghoal!"

They both rose to look out the window. No ocean, just horses; thousands of them.

"Chie shodeh? Chie shodeh?" People in the streets were asking what happened.

"We are under Mongolian attack. Hide. Hide wherever you can," the caller urged.

Shereen wanted Nauder to investigate the matter further but a glass of water set on the table that had begun to tremble told them there was no time to lose. "Come, come, come, come, come, come," he began shouting, his eyes searching for a different place to hide each time he repeated the word.

They ran into a spandrel under the staircase in the basement. It barely had enough room for the two of them. It had a door visible from the outside and could not be considered a safe hiding place, but no other option remained. Nauder pushed his way to the farthest corner of the interior, sweeping nails and bits of wood with his hands. He pulled Shereen in front of him and closed the door. This gave her more room to breathe. She hoped that this would be a short episode and soon pass.

Shereen could not see the horrors, she could only imagine them. Blood mingled with soil and the skies thundered in anger and shed tears of rain, as the city of Neyshabur succumbed to the barbarians. The pulse *of nature skipped a beat, and the heavens gasped in horror. The angels held their heads down in shame at man's atrocity against man and his violation of the sacred life on earth.*

Shereen heard screams, some were her own, some coming from people being slaughtered above. She could not distinguish one from the other. Tears came rolling down her cheeks. The labor pains were coming rather quickly.

A gap between the hinge leaves of the door to the spandrel allowed Nauder a peek into the basement. He noticed the presence of a young warrior searching the house. Nauder had placed his hand firmly on Shereen's mouth, silencing her cries, his own heart beating with fear for her and their unborn child. Shereen's tears, mingled with sweat, rolled down his fingers and his heart ached with pity. He could hear the door to the house being yanked open. Moments passed excruciatingly slow. The soldier turned toward the door of the spandrel. Nauder could see his rough looking boot. But then the voice of an enemy fighter in the street, uttering cries in an unfamiliar language got the soldier's attention. He ran out in an attempt to help his comrade but never returned. When the sounds outside dimmed to an earie silence, Nauder moved slowly from behind Shereen and opened the door. He gently pulled her out of the tight enclosure, allowing the baby to be born with greater ease. His mother who lived in the south had taught him how to act as a midwife if one could not make it there in time for the baby's birth. The tiny underweight baby girl could not be called Roestam, but he was thankful that they were alive.

When she finally settled with the baby, Nauder walked out of the house, closing the door behind him. The extent of the devastation was unbearable to see. Human remains—an arm here a leg there—could be seen everywhere. Nauder felt the crushing weight of guilt upon his shoulders. He had not been there to help his fellow townsfolk. He could not even bury them. Drained and numbed by the awful experience, he walked towards a neatly stacked pile that appeared to be a mound of cannon balls, newly introduced items in the arena of war. Upon closer examination, however, he realized he was looking at a mound of severed heads.

Nauder returned, too stunned to speak. The Mongolian whirlwind had come and gone, razing their land, killing their people. Only a few had survived. He looked at Shereen whose face showed no sign of the pain, fear, and horror they had just experienced. The little miracle she held in her arms opened her eyes.

"What shall we call it?" she asked, looking at Nauder.

"Call what?"

"Our baby, what shall we call her?" she asked again.

"I . . . I don't know. I can't think," he said, "We seem to be among the few who were left alive."

"We have to think. We must live. I haven't been outside, but I can imagine the devastation. We know what happened to Bukhara when they attacked."

"We have nothing. No city, no inhabitants," he replied, shaking with fatigue and fear.

"We should call her Oameed (Hope) then. Hope is all that we have left."

Oameed's cry shattered the eerie silence of the city in the early hours of the morning, a week after the Mongol tsunami wiped away the inhabitants of Neyshabur. The sky shed tears of rain for days and since there were no undertakers for the enormous task of burying the dead, merciful earth gave the city a helping hand. Mud formed and piled high on roads, as nature supplied a morgue.

When the sun came up after a fortnight of downpour and dried the accumulated mud, it was as if the earth had swallowed the inhabitants, for no sign of them remained. Men and women, young and old, suckling babies, horses, and goats all lay beneath newly formed earth. Soon grass would grow, tulips would bloom and when their baby girl would turn into a lady, all would be forgotten.

Chapter Twelve

The Ebony Prison

DESPITE REYHAN'S REPEATED ATTEMPTS AT BEFRIENDing the Mongol chatelaines, they shied away from conversing with her and limited their communication to a polite smile or a word or two, usually just complementing her good taste in clothing. She even tried to strike a conversation with Borte. But the latter kept to her ger and spoke little with anyone, let alone Reyhan who by now knew only the basics of the Mongolian language.

The one time they did speak as friends was when Reyhan found Borte teary-eyed after a conversation she had with Genghis. Reyhan felt sorry for the wrinkled-faced woman. "What bothers you so, pray tell me," she pleaded. Borte, who seemed reluctant at first, confided that Genghis planned to wage war against the Tangut nation again. "I told him that he had punished them enough. Plus, I fear for his life," she added and began sobbing uncontrollably. As Reyhan tried to console Borte, she recalled the fire she had seen in Genghis's eyes long ago on the night of the ger celebration. The destruction of Khwarazm territories did not satiate his thirst for revenge.

Days later, a messenger from the fronts informed them that Genghis Khan had died. When the news reached Reyhan, she recalled Baako's words about the Mongol leader. As if the connection between Chaka and her homeland in China could not be forgiven. He must have considered the people of Tangut as the ones who ultimately played a role in her demise. Against all rationality upon which rules of strategy are devised, and against the recommendations of his advisors and his own sense of logic, Genghis had decided to make the annexation of Tangut territories his last conquest.

Reyhan later learned that an old Tangut palace guard who had long prepared for such an opportune moment, aimed with his spear at the very heart of the one he had detested all his life. An arrow flew, sealing the Khan's fate and piercing his heart that had shown no mercy. Genghis, the most powerful man to ever set foot upon the earth, rolled off his horse and fell to his death. Despite the summer heat, his followers carried his body back to Mongolia and buried the fallen conquerer near his place of birth. The Mongol warriors decimated Tangut territories as he had ordered right before his death, thus fulfilling his last wish.

With the ascension of Ogodei to power, he proclaimed his desire to construct buildings in Karakorum, a tent city and center of Mongol power, and turn it into a permanent capital. To the nomads, the grasslands that stretched from the Khangai Mountains to the Orkhon River appeared ideally situated for the purpose, but the location was far from the resources needed to sustain their livelihood. Despite this, the regal city thus founded had features that Reyhan considered impressive.

Massive buildings, like those in Persia and China, were erected. Beautiful gardens and lakes, in which migrating birds and waterfowl of every color from swan goose to white-naped crane sought refuge, surrounded the palatial structures. She knew, however, that the poor birds would be hunted by palace guards in their moments of leisure.

Reyhan touched the stone walls of the main palace when examining the premises for the first time and pondered how a nomadic tribe, accustomed by nature to roam the earth, would be content with living in one location. No wonder that they called the city *Karakorum* or "Ebony Prison" in the Mongolian language.

In the southwest corner of the city of Karakorum stood the palace quarters, in the midst of which one could see the Chinese style Amgalan Palace of Ogodei. Two rows of buildings stretched on the two sides of this black and jade-colored structure with four major roads paved in cobblestones leading to tall walls with entry gates in each of the cardinal directions. These walls separated the city from the surrounding areas.

Reyhan walked up the steps that led to the interior of the Amgalan palace. Magnificent works of art hung on its stately walls, but they were not to her taste. Despite the vastness of the structure, she found the enclosure stifling.

Ogodei's coronation took place when the finishing touches were applied to Amgalan. Church bells rang, the Islamic slogan of Allaho Akbar was heard, and the Jews and Buddhists performed their own ceremonies in celebration. The Mongols chanted urra, their slogan of victory, and their voices echoed throughout the empire and in many corners of the world.

Silk shimmered on the back of paupers of yesterday who were once roaming nomads and now masters of the world. Rows of rings bearing precious stones could be seen on every hand. Mongolian men, women, children and even the horses of the Steppes displayed jewelry gained through shedding of foreign blood. Their equestrian way of life remained but took on a royal character. Reyhan saw how they paraded their newer and fancier weapons like whistling arrows, smoke-screen powder, ballistas, and catapults and knew they would be used for extracting the wealth of the rich in every part of the world.

As the Shamans began chanting and praying for the new leader's health, Reyhan felt the burden of guilt upon her shoulders. She was one of them now, queen to the foes of Persia, a destiny she never desired but could not avoid. Subutai arrived late for the coronation, but Ogodei greeted him warmly. The two walked out into an adjacent chamber as soon as the ceremony ended. There, Subutai opened a map drawn on deerskin before the Mongol warlord. He pointed to two countries, namely Hungary and Poland as optimum targets for future invasions. "They have good grazing lands there for our horses and riches waiting to be plundered. Their frozen rivers allow us an easy crossing into Western Europe," he said.

Reyhan who could hear them in the adjacent room shivered. She wondered how she could use her new position to avert further bloodshed. Ogodei would rule his empire in accordance with the civil code set by his father, the Yassa laws. More than fifty nations eventually had to follow these rules, some of which were shaped by the advice of sages. Others were clauses that Genghis had personally considered important. The Yassa laws commenced with praise for the Sole Creator of the human domain and included provisions that exempted Christian priests, Jewish rabbis, Muslim clergy and Buddhist lamas from taxation.

The Founder of the Mongol Empire had proclaimed that adultery must be outlawed and punished. So too must theft, prescribed his Yassa laws, for if thieves were punished, security would prevail to such an extent that merchants could leave their goods unattended, knowing with confidence that no one would touch them. The same laws, however, included clauses that made washing of garb in a river during a thunderstorm, a punishable offense. Thus, one could say they contained some concepts that were acceptable to the scholars of prevalent religions and others that baffled them, but every provision had to be implemented nonetheless.

Reyhan admired the fact that Mongols in general, displayed an unprecedented degree of tolerance towards people of other faiths, although they did so out of convenience rather than a conviction for religious freedom. The coexistence of people of different beliefs, like other decisions by the Mongols rulers, stemmed from a natural, simplistic conclusion, due to a realistic view of circumstances. Ogodei understood the fact that religion had a profound effect on the multitudes, and he said he would utilize that tool to his benefit. "We shall revere the clergy and the priests," he said, "and respect their places of worship. For those who would not fight for bread, riches or honor, would do so in the name of religion. Fires thus started are not easily extinguished."

Although some Mongols had converted to Islam, Christianity or Buddhism, the Mongol belief in Shamanism, as well as their traditions of hunting, war-making, herding, and trade, still formed the fundamental principles by which they lived.

Chapter Thirteen

Revelry

DESPITE OGODEI'S ATTEMPTS TO ADHERE TO HIS FAther's command and accommodate all religious and ethnic groups, he found practicing what the late Khan had preached quite difficult. Ogodei felt like a man who suddenly realized he had fathered too many children. He had to watch the wrangling between the different religious and ethnic groups and felt compelled to act as judge and jury to them all. The Chinese spoke against the Arabs; the Persians vilified the Turks; one religious group would badmouth the other and vice versa. Baseless, illogical accusations flew back and forth. When reason failed, dreams were exhibited as proof positive of the other's wrongdoing.

On one occasion, a man came to claim that he had indeed seen Genghis Khan in his dream. "I had a dream, sire," he said, "of the Great Khan before me in all his majesty, as if he were still alive. He instructed me to inform you, sire, that the adherents to this particular creed should be annihilated."

Flabbergasted, Ogodei scratched his head and looked to Reyhan for advice. His savvy wife whispered, "Ask him in what language the great Mongol Khan spoke in his dream."

Ogodei inquired whether Genghis spoke in his native tongue or another language. The man, dumbfounded, mumbled a bit and replied, "In his . . . in his eloquent native Mongolian tongue, of course."

Ogodei asked, "And can you speak and understand the eloquent Mongolian language?"

The Turkish-speaking man began trembling and said, "I do not Your Majesty."

"Then you have concocted a false tale," thundered the voice of the Khaqan and with the motion of his hand, palace guards dragged the man away.

While Genghis clung to an austere life, Ogodei basked in luxury. Nonetheless, he possessed his father's ambition to expand the Mongol Empire. He managed to quell uprisings in China and Persia, further solidifying his control over those regions. He crushed the Jin Dynasty and gained control over Korea. He also dispatched Subutai farther west into Europe on a reconnaissance mission.

When only fourteen-years-old, Subutai had joined the army of Genghis. He now led the Mongol army as its foremost military strategist. His sharp eyes would peruse a map, and in no time, he would devise an innovative plan of attack. When Subutai spoke, everyone including Ogodei listened, for few of his tactics ever failed.

Ogodei had some of his father's charisma, but he was also an epicurean and wanted to enjoy the fruits of his labor, not just conquer territory. Those fruits included wine and women. With riches pouring in from all quarters of the world, the time had come for the Mongols to revel. He no longer had to rely on the mildly intoxicating effects of fermented milk. Foreign merchants had introduced him to a finer assortment of wines. Ogodei also enjoyed the fulsome praise he received from the envoys of faraway lands as he rested upon the golden throne of the late Shah of Khwarazm transported to Karakorum as a spoil of war.

With a new leader at the helm, Reyhan's position was temporarily elevated, but soon she felt sidelined by the fine-looking women around Ogodei, vying for his attention. Ogodei had managed to charm his way into Reyhan's heart but once he had won her admiration, apparently satisfied with this conquest, he had turned his attention to other women; among them a beauty that he had married at a very young age by the name of Toregene who had lived for some time with her Naiman tribe and returned in time for Ogodei's coronation. There was, of course, more to Toregene than her dark eyes and delicate features. Reyhan soon realized her rival's extreme ambitions and determination. Before long, she captured all of Ogodei's attention and became the favorite of the new warlord.

Envoys and ambassadors from far corners of the world visited the Mongol court and at times had to surrender their wealth and power to the Khaqan. Reyhan knew just what to say and how to say it, to lighten the occasion, and make the Mongols appear superior in stature, in comparison to their foreign counterparts. She added a civilized dimension and a considerable degree of sophistication to their otherwise ordinary settings. Therefore, during diplomatic sessions and in official appearances, it was Reyhan who stood at Ogodei's side; then at midnight revelries, Toregene took precedence.

What had seemed to Reyhan as love at first sight had by this time turned into a nightmare as Ogodei's drinking and womanizing left her alone in her chamber many hours of the day and night. There was a time when domestic tranquility, even within these surroundings and under such unimaginable circumstances, seemed probable. But with Toregene's ascendance in the court, such hopeful aspirations began to seem as doomed as any hope for her country's future.

Neither her beauty nor brilliant mind allowed Reyhan to keep a place in her husband's heart. Her solemn diligence won praise from foreign dignitaries who visited the Mongol court, but Ogodei often said he found her unspoken disapproval unbearable. On the other hand, Reyhan considered Ogodei's propensity to drink, more characteristic of the serf than a ruler.

Her husband's neglect wounded her heart like a spear. The fact that she could not conceive made things worse. *Barren*, that was the word that the court physician had used. *Barren*. How that word in all its implications descended upon her and depleted the essence of her being. She often asked herself how it would have felt if there was another beating heart within her.

I am barren, barren like the desert, a tree without fruit, an existence without offspring. The bitterness of it! My heart feels barren too. A child would have been a source of consolation, someone to love, someone to love me back. I am left without my family, without a husband who cares for me, away from my homeland, in this place that is as barren as I am!

Chapter Fourteen

The Pleading Child

OGODEI CONSIDERED HIMSELF A GENEROUS MAN, BUT he lacked the sagaciousness of his father. After all, he had inherited privilege without having to earn it. Upon ascension to power, he forfeited his right to a considerable portion of the accumulated Mongol wealth and distributed the riches among his officers and guardsmen. Extreme generosity had its demerits, however, for what Genghis had ripped out of the hands of the wealthy, soon began to dwindle.

Unlike his other three brothers, Ogodei had a rather lenient and trusting nature. He occasionally pardoned the condemned or reduced their sentences. Although the Mongols basked in luxury during Ogodei's reign, after the news of his father's death reached him, Ogodei developed the belief that the wealth and possessions of the world, stay in this world when one passes on. He had accepted death as an eventuality from which there was no escape. Thus, his largesse became renowned as he spent his days enjoying wine and music, inviting ambassadors, aristocrats, and nobles from all over the world to pay homage to him.

The additional cost of Karakorum's upkeep further consumed Ogodei's financial assets. After all, his seat of power was located far from sources of agricultural products and other material needed to sustain its economy. Transportation of goods had its own additional expenses, and economizing is always alien to the vocabulary of the neophyte among the wealthy. Therefore, within months of his rise to power, it became necessary to wage more wars, gain more territories, subjugate a greater number of people and enact the insatiable desire of the Mongols to shed blood.

Reyhan approached life with an attitude of anticipating serendipity, always looking forward to what the world would present to her next. And each day ended with utter disappointment in the surprise package fate delivered her. Now and again, communication became less bitter between Reyhan and Ogodei. During those moments she saw him more as a companion than a spouse. She used those occasions to instill in him ideas that would help her nation and the territories where Mongols ruled. In this, she had the aid of an erudite Chinese by the name of Ye Liu Chutsai, who was much respected by the late Khan and had retained his position as an advisor during the reign of Ogodei. Whenever she noticed that the Khaqan found the affairs of the kingdom disconcerting, she would encourage Chutsai to speak truth to power and make Ogodei take a more reasonable path. "Slaughtering people," Chutsai argued, "leaves you with barren lands with no one to cultivate them. Whereas allowing the inhabitants to live, grants you a formidable workforce that enhances the financial resources of your kingdom and increases your stature among the subjects."

The poor savant became the subject of Ogodei's attention at times, and his wrath at others, particularly when his master was inebriated, until he complained one time when he was incarcerated that he could not perform his duties both as an obedient prisoner and a statesman charged with running the affairs of large portions of the world. On days when the pitiable mentor was in prison, Reyhan played the role of advisor.

On one such day, when a sober Ogodei contemplated the idea of turning parts of conquered lands into grazing areas for Mongol horses, Reyhan used the occasion to speak to him.

"The focus of your war efforts has been providing fodder for your animals when indeed the focus has to be installing institutions of governance." She then added, "Many of the inhabitants of the lands you conquered were not happy with their sovereigns. Pains of the war are slowly being forgotten, and realism is giving way to hopes for a future under Mongol rule. With a little effort, you can make these peoples your allies."

"And exactly what would that entail?" he asked, looking impatient.

"You can seek the cooperation of the locals, the learned men among them can run the very municipalities that the Mongols neither have the means nor the manpower, to administer and manage. As the conquered lands begin to prosper, Mongol riches likewise increase."

"I have enough riches to last more than my lifetime," he replied as he reached for a goblet of wine.

"You have frittered away the wealth that your father had accumulated. Your policy of turning a nation of nomadic tribes into a sedentary population has failed miserably. The expense of keeping up Karakorum is draining your wealth. Also, for your information, the purveyors of fine products from the Middle East are overpricing their commodities."

"I am showing them Mongol benevolence," he said.

"You can show benevolence by engaging in fewer wars," she retorted.

"Mongols survive by making war," he said in a tone to imply that the conversation had just ended. "We will continue our advance into Persia and China, and as suggested by Subutai, into Europe. Batu, son of Jochi has agreed to join forces with me in China. He is indeed a brave soul. If our campaign against the Jin Dynasty is successful, I will dispatch him to Kievan Rus and then to Poland and Hungary as suggested by Subutai."

With the passage of time, relations between Reyhan and her husband began to visibly crumble. She kept to her chamber most of the time, and Baako visited her whenever he got a chance, helping her with the chronicles she was recording. One time, in the midst of a deep conversation about the war, they were both shocked to find Ogodei there. He had walked in unexpectedly. Blood drained from Reyhan's face and guilt left its mark on her countenance.

"What are you up to?" Ogodei demanded, looking at her papers from a distance.

In a clear attempt to provide an explanation, Baako risked his life and addressed the Mongol Ruler without being asked first. "Lady Reyhan has just received news from Persia," he exclaimed, "that a dear old friend has indeed died of consumption."

Reyhan felt lucky that Ogodei did not pursue the matter further. He just gave them both a look of utter disgust and left the chamber. The following day, however, he dispatched Baako to the war front as an aid to Tolui's cavalry.

During those days of sheer loneliness with Baako gone, an outwardly insignificant incident changed the course of Reyhan's inescapable destiny. One late summer afternoon when seeking news of Baako at Amgalan Palace, Reyhan found Ogodei and Toregene ready to pass out from drinking, amidst a large group of Mongol and foreign officials.

As soon as the Khaqan's gaze spotted her standing at the entry door, he raised his goblet of wine to her and proclaimed loudly, "Long live the Persian Empire or what is left of it."

Reyhan knew Ogodei was too fuddled to be held accountable for his attitude toward her, but it still hurt her for more than one reason. She walked away from the doorway into the hall. Captivity in the Mongol court, her homeland ravaged by the Mongols, and a husband who had little respect for her, left a gaping hole in her heart that no amount of prayers could fill.

Reyhan felt like a purebred lamb living among wolves. As she walked the candle-lit corridor that led from the auditorium to the main entrance, she heard the wailing of a child whose cries mixed with that of a brewing thunderstorm. The cloudburst rattled the skies, dashing her hopes of venturing outdoors to seek information about Baako from the laborers. Darkness had descended full gloom on the land. She looked for the child and soon found him. He appeared inconsolable, for he had lost his wooden horse.

This pleading child, his hands gripping the sleeve of her dress and hiding his wet face in the folds of her skirt, suddenly presented himself as the very thing that could fill the emptiness in her heart. The child's large brown eyes were filled with tears and his silky dark hair looked disheveled. Reyhan recognized him. He was Kadan, the son of a concubine in the court. She lowered her body and embraced Kadan, breathing in the smell of his hair. It was as if the child's need and hers mingled to fill both hearts with love. How fulfilling it would be to be a mother!

The next day while Reyhan excitedly narrated a story from the Book of Kings to Kadan, she looked up and noticed that Kadan's mother was watching them. In a hurry to explain the intimate conversation with the child, Reyhan said, "I could teach him. I could teach him foreign languages and skills he is going to need when he grows up."

His mother's silence conveyed her consent. After all, she would have had to forgo a great deal of pleasure if she had to take on the full responsibility of raising the child.

Chapter Fifteen

The Lonely Chronicler

FOR REYHAN, TIME PASSED SLOWLY AT KARAKORUM, AND it sped up only when the warriors were departing for a military mission. Two years were spent teaching Kadan, an occupation with attendant pleasures and difficulties. He resisted learning new things, but a few subjects excited his imagination, mostly military adventures and wars of the past. In such cases, he absorbed the material rather quickly; however, he found languages and culture, arts and literature, tedious beyond measure.

Despite Reyhan's efforts, Kadan's brain remained rough and unsophisticated like a pumice stone. Just nine-years-old and he had already developed a patronizing habit of looking at her as if she was someone beneath him. That aggressive sense of superiority which marked the Mongols had lately infected the young lad as well. A Mongol soldier of low rank would feel superior to the most well-known foreign nobles. At the same time, with their authority ripped away from them, the noblemen of subjugated nations shared a sense of camaraderie with their former foes who had become their cellmates.

At first, Toregene tolerated the growing attention that Reyhan was receiving as a teacher but eventually, jealousy began to sprout within her heart. One sunny day, as Reyhan taught her pupil Persian poetry in the garden, Toregene, yanked Kadan off the stone bench where he was sitting and loudly announced, "No Mongol child should learn the language of defeated nations," her nails digging into the poor lad's arm.

As she lectured the boy, an old Chinese gardener was pruning the branches of a nearby birch tree. Toregene turned and kicked the poor man on the shin yelling, "Foreigner!" as she strutted away.

"You are a heartless woman who knows not how to treat others kindly, plus Kadan is not your child," Reyhan cried out.

The bickering had been loud enough to attract the attention of Ogodei and a number of courtiers. Toregene always wanted to avenge Ogodei's earlier attachment to Reyhan, mostly because, on more than one occasion, Ogodei had alluded to Reyhan's unparalleled beauty when he wed her.

Days earlier, another minor incident had almost brought their brewing tension out into the open. It was late in the afternoon. Reyhan was about to take the steps that led to the entrance of Amgalan palace, apparently unaware that Toregene was a few steps behind her. Toregene finding this an opportune moment to assert her superior status, climbed the stairs fast and, sidestepping Reyhan, almost pushed her out of the way to enter the palace first. She was surprised when Reyhan showed no reaction, except blushing.

However, Toregene's resentment had been barely noticeable, until this latest incident. For the first time she had openly confronted Reyhan in a way that everyone noticed, and there was no holding her back. Although hardships had left their marks on Reyhan's once porcelain face, Toregene feared that her rival still retained enough allure to charm her way back into Ogodei's heart.

Reyhan watched as Toregene left the scene looking livid. She knew life in Amgalan Palace would never be the same, and she would now have little to recommend her to the Mongol Khaqan. She would be marginalized, and life within the walls of Amgalan Palace would become nearly impossible.

That very night a tearful Toregene confided in her husband about all that Reyhan had done, and with great animation, she made up a long list of the evil deeds that she attributed to her rival. "Reyhan continuously puts me down in front of other courtiers, she talks behind my back, and the other day she almost pushed me off the railing as I was descending the steps from the upper rooms. Being around her, I have to constantly fear for my life!"

With their tensions laid bare, Ogodei ordered a separate palace to be constructed where Reyhan could "retire" without ever running into Toregene again. Under the circumstances, Reyhan did not mind at all. She only asked that Persian artisans who served at the Mongol court undertake the construction. Ogodei granted her wish. In the meantime, she continued to reside at Amgalan Palace waiting for the new structure to be built.

After the open confrontation with Toregene, almost everyone in the Mongol court avoided Reyhan; acting as if she did not exist. After all, Toregene had Mongol blood in her, and no foreigner had the right to insult her. The isolation had its merits, however, for it gave her a chance to think and to write.

Reyhan looked out the window of her chamber. It was indeed a dreary day. Instead of the glorious colored leaves of shades that put gemstones to shame, autumn in Karakorum had brought with it an unbearable natural phenomenon known as *zud*, a harsh blizzard originating from the frozen lands of the Arctic that was intolerable. A freezing wind blowing outside mercilessly ripped life out of living plants and livestock, turning to ice every blade of grass, and killing the earth upon which it blew.

Reyhan had learned to appreciate solitude when writing became her sole companion. In her journal, her imagination was unleashed, and the world in her mind took shape in a way that was more to her liking, less confused. Yet, she longed for summer days when she could sit with Baako on a bench in an inconspicuous corner of the garden and talk endlessly about Ogodei's foreign adventures. Baako, initially illiterate, had learned the Chinese language from Chaka who had spent her spare time teaching him. He had translated the text of Chaka's chronicles for Reyhan who had in turn begun recording her own observations.

A chambermaid brought Reyhan a small glass of hot tea on a saucer with two bits of hardened sugar broken off a sugar cone. She had been yearning to get back to her writing, and the *zud* had provided that rare opportunity for her to do so fearlessly. She knew she would not be surprised by intruders, her husband being foremost in that category.

She scraped the tip of a tall feather with a small knife, dipped it in a silver inkpot, and began to write.

Entry by Reyhan:

I had a lengthy conversation with Baako when he returned from the front. He tells me that for the Mongols, vengeance is the norm, mercy a luxury they can ill afford. Life is centered on revenge, and getting even with their foes brings meaning to their existence. I for one know that for Ogodei war is like a gamble, a thrill-filled adventure that can lead to one's death or that of one's foe. In Baako's words, what is at stake is life itself and the stars like dice will decide one's fate.

City life dulls the ears of cultured warriors and reduces the keenness of their sight. Their souls have become malleable, and they have soft spots in their hearts even for the enemy, while the hearts of the Mongols are not softened by literature and the intricacy of art. When it comes to killing, they do not think twice before plunging a dagger into the heart of their enemy.

The Mongol army moves at the speed of lightning. They kill with equal zeal all that stand in their way, allowing some of the maimed and injured to flee to nearby towns and villages. By doing so resistance wanes, making the inhabitants easy prey. With each attack or ambush, the Mongol warriors grow in sophistication and discipline. Resistance is futile.

Among the foreigners who are forced to work at the Mongol court, there are some of my countrymen through whom I have learned news of my homeland. The story of the Jackal is of particular interest to me. The Mongols had offered him the position of governor of Otrar, provided that he guides them to Bukhara through the desert of Kyzyl Kum.

Considering the cruel manner in which they killed the former governor, he had decided that his fate would not fare much better. Before reaching the intended destination, though his hands were tied, he managed to roll off the horse on which he was mounted, and slid into a nearby ravine.

They travelled at dusk to avoid the heat of the desert, and the light of the moon was not strong enough for them to see their surroundings clearly. They had no dogs to sniff out the Jackal, and after some fruitless searches, the Mongols decided they would have to find another desert dweller to lead them. Soon afterward, the Jackal escaped toward the south, forming his own group of vigilantes that engaged the Mongols at times and saved targeted communities at others by giving them advance warning.

Reyhan took a sip of her tea and thought about all that had passed. Religious and ethnic minorities lived throughout Khwarazm territories. However, the greatest concentration of them had made Yazd, a hospitable oasis by the desert, their home. The first group that lived there were the Zoroastrians who considered fire holy and always kept a pit of fire lit. Then came the Jews who took pride in being Persian since Ester, a captive in Babylon, was saved by a Persian King and became his queen. Christians as well as Shia Muslims, a minority in the mostly Sunni Persia, formed the other inhabitants of Yazd.

Unlike the many cities and provinces in Persia that the Mongols devastated, Yazd was spared. The governor of Yazd had wisely diverted Mongol attacks against the province by agreeing to pay everything the treasury held to meet the demands of the invading army. Tragically, some remote areas, the first targets of the attack, were trampled upon before any action took place to halt the onslaught.

Reyhan began reminiscing about home, the landscapes, the houses, the people, the children. She brushed off a droplet of tear as she gulped down what was left of her tea. She then decided to think only about those who had survived and reached for her quill to write the following tale.

Entry by Reyhan:

Traces of a Hand

Little Yousef and his family lived in the suburbs of Yazd. Yusef had a favorite tree. Named after Joseph the Prophet, they called him by the Persian phonation "Yousef." He could only climb up the first two bulky branches of the tree but it sufficed for it gave him a panoramic view of the distant mountains. The early morning weather felt a bit cold, but he didn't mind since he was pretending to be king for a day.

The suburbs like other areas of Yazd Province looked like a sea of brown colors; brown mud-brick homes and brown dirt roads surrounded by brown mountains. The turquoise-blue sky contrasted with the terrain. Rivers, lakes, oceans were nowhere to be seen, but patches of flowers added bursts of bright color to the mellow landscape.

The hefty trunks of tall trees rested against fences built with piled-up mud bricks. Their branches appeared black in the early morning light. Yousef climbed onto a branch where he could see the horizon. No snow ever capped those mountains, and they remained as brown as the rest of the landscape throughout the year. But on that morning, there appeared to be a black cloud hovering over the peaks. It was as if ants were crawling down the mountaintops toward the town.

He climbed down and ran to his mother, sitting by the kitchen window. His tongue protruded through his top two missing teeth which made a funny sound when he pronounced certain letters. "Mamma. Mamma. Antz are crawling down the hillz."

"Yousef, it is Easter Sunday, and we are headed to the church, so you better get dressed instead of climbing up trees like a monkey."

"Seven-year-olds have such imagination," Armineh thought. She had to raise her four boys and her daughter by herself since her husband died of consumption four years ealier. Her children, the eldest child Yahya, a boy of nineteen, the twins Malek and Murad, almost thirteen, and the youngest, Ida, two years younger than Yousef, were her treasures.

Armineh rolled up the straw blind and opened the kitchen window. In her small yard, she had planted every imaginable herb and a variety of flowers for medicinal purposes, some already blooming and some past their blooming time. Songs of birds echoed in her ears as a soft breeze blew in her face. Morning dew had settled on the open buds. Hope climbed gently into her heart. One day her children would grow up, and they would no longer need her care. They would get married in the same church where she had said her vows.

How quickly time had passed. Her husband's early death had left her with many cares. Her sole supporter now was her eldest son, who despite his young age, had taken on the responsibility of a small apothecary shop they owned. When still a child, Yahya had memorized the names of all the herbs his father kept in his cabinets. He later persevered in learning their uses from a friend of his father who practiced medicine.

Armineh's gaze lingered as she took a mental inventory of her crop. She would harvest most of the herbs for her son's shop, and some would be left for her to use in the large pickling jars she kept downstairs in the wine cellar.

It was a rather chilly morning. Armineh tried buttoning Yousef's jacket as he stuck out his tummy, a common habit of children that age. She realized that the hand-knit piece was getting a bit small for him. The last button would not close. She decided just to leave it open. She would have to make him a new sweater. "Yarns are expensive," she sighed to herself. She could undo the yarn on this one and remake it into a ruffled little sweater for Ida.

Yousef kept staring at the last button, his cheeks drooping. But the concern she saw in his big brown eyes when he looked up was not about the button. "There are antz crawling down the hillz," he repeated. As he spoke, the pale white light of the early morning sun illuminated his angelic face.

Armineh would have normally dismissed Yousef's comments, thinking maybe ants had crawled up his pants but when she looked, she could not find any on his body. She frowned pensively. Last night she had had a premonition of something terrible happening. She sent her eldest son out to investigate what had troubled the child.

Armineh's family had moved from Yazd's central city, which bore the same name as the province, to the outskirts for a more affordable life. The small church on Shiraz Street, not far from where they lived, made the location of their home somewhat convenient.

Armineh's ancestors had watched their countrymen convert from Zoroastrianism to Islam while they remained Christians. Centuries of coexistence formed human bonds that went beyond religious definitions. Mutual kinships had developed over time, and they had opened their hearts and homes to one another. Naturally, intermarriages had occurred and equally natural, there were funerals in which both sides shared a singular grief within their mud-brick homes.

In Armineh's neighborhood lived many Shia families who took part in an annual mourning ceremony they called "Ashoura." She could little understand the intensity of their religious fervor or the complexity of their rituals, but they were her countrymen, and she wanted to show her support for anything that touched their souls so deeply. Their chanting and chest-beating seemed intense and emotional, and their tears were certainly sincere.

Armineh had committed herself to making a saffron-scented rice pudding each year during Ashoura. She would stand by the side of the street among the devoted and hand out bowls of warm pudding to the mourners. Thus, she had become known as the little Armenian lady who served the best saffron pudding.

Their annual gatherings followed the cycles of the moon, and her religious celebrations followed that of the sun. On that particular year, the ceremony of Ashoura had coincided with Easter. To feed both the celebrants and the mourners, she had to wake up early to make the pudding and bake sweet bread for the church as well. The aroma of fresh-baked bread mingled with the one coming from the pot of saffron pudding, and every once in a while, one of her children would poke a head into the small kitchen to see what concoction was being prepared.

Armineh had heard that if one made a prayer when making the pudding for Ashoura, and traces of a hand formed on the crust, it meant that the pot was blessed, and the prayer would be answered. The hand symbolized the five holy ones, but she wasn't sure which ones. She made a silent orison nonetheless, seeking the protection of all who were holy.

Armineh could hear Yahya run outside the moment she called him. She went to the kitchen window and saw him lifting himself above the first branch or two, shielding his eyes from the piercing rays of the sun. He then ran back in, grabbed Armineh's arm and rounded up his siblings, shouting the dreaded word "Moghoal" to his left and right as he pushed Armineh and the kids down to the wine cellar, the only place in the house almost hidden from view. This sanctuary had other advantages. They kept wine barrels, containers of pickles and honey as well as rolls of cheese there. That would keep them well-fed for as long as it took for the monsters to leave.

Armineh had run in and out a few times to gather what provisions she deemed necessary and was quite out of breath. Hearing the screaming of the neighbors outside, she locked the cellar door for the last time. They sat on the bare floor, overlaid with slabs of gray stone. A layer of brick covered the concave ceiling of the small enclosure built by her late husband. Armineh thanked God that Yousef had his sweater on for it was cold and damp down there. The weak light of a flickering wax taper illuminated the faces of her children, the twins, Yahya and Yousef. Then a sinking feeling, a cold sensation gripped her, where is Ida? "Where is Ida?" she asked barely audible, trembling at the thought.

"Where is Ida?" she suddenly shrieked in horror.

"Ze zlipped out to fetch her doll right before you clozed the door," Yousef said meekly.

Armineh reached for the door, but Yahya's firm hand grabbed hers. "You leave this place, Mother, and God is my witness, I will not let anyone from this household come to rescue you. I hear the shrieks of horror out there, and I know the place has turned into a slaughterhouse."

She was surprised to see such strength in her eldest son. But he did not know what length a mother would go to in order to save her child.

Armineh found Ida in the front yard, entry gate wide open. An alien soldier stood right in front of her. She was staring with wonder at the apparition before her. Ida had never seen a warrior before. This huge man with heavy armor, dismounting a horse must have amazed her. She probably wondered if this was Roestam, the epic warrior of her nighttime stories.

The foreign warrior pulled out his sword, shining, beautiful. He raised it. Ida stared, as if awe-stricken by the gleaming object coming toward her face. Armineh stretched out her arms, her child beyond her reach, her speech silenced by fear, her heart cried out. "Is there anyone out there who can help me?" A mirage, an apparition, approached on horseback. More of them came, with faces covered, like phantoms out of a midnight dream they converged before her. "Who are these men? Angels of heaven or demons out of perdition? Are they the mourners of Ashoura?" But they would not be riding on horses, she realized. She could hear their breathing. Someone pulled Ida's shirt from behind. A head rolled. Not that of her daughter. A sword had beheaded the enemy warrior. Armineh saw the severed head rolling away like a ball. "It is all a game. War is a game!" rang in her thoughts.

Ida ran toward her. "Is this a dream?" Both sobbing now. Two other Mongols who were also at the scene fled. The monsters were gone.

A black-clad man who seemed to be the leader of the horsemen rolled down the bandana that was covering his face. His smile exposed rows of white teeth that contrasted with his sun-darkened skin. Armineh asked tearfully, "To whom do I owe my life and that of my child?"

"Name's Jamsheed, they call me the Jackal. The country is under Mongol invasion. We have formed our own vigilante group. Helping whom we can and warning those that we can't."

"Then you must be the famous thief?"

"Well . . . I have sort of given up the profession . . . for a while now and . . . I am fighting for a cause," replied the smiling former robber, obviously encouraged by the look of approval on Armineh's face.

"I thought the army of the king was pursuing you. Where is the army? Why aren't we being protected?"

"The king's army is in disarray. The Mongols are conquering city after city. The bastards do not fight their wars conventionally. They attack from every corner and every side. The soldiers are panic-stricken."

"And where is the king?"

"The king fled the capital like a terrified hare. The last we heard, our mighty monarch sought refuge in a faraway island of the Caspian Sea. His son, the braver soul among the two, is attempting to regroup the army and fight back. But the news is that they would not last long."

"What brought you here?"

"I heard about the raid in a nearby caravansary."

"I am so glad you did."

"The large group of Mongols that slaughtered your neighbors had already left after receiving a message that the governor of Yazd had laid down his arms. Only a few enemies remained when we arrived here and saw your daughter. I suggest you hide somewhere for now."

As Armineh uttered a prayer, saying softly, "May God bless you, and may the angels protect you," the Jackal and his men vanished as swiftly as they had appeared. She held the crying child tightly, protecting her eyes from the horrors of the scene, as they made their way to the cellar. Lifeless bodies, some clumped on top of the others, lay all over the field. Much loving was needed to placate the poor child.

Before knocking on the cellar door, she noticed the pot of rice pudding still warm on the stove, traces of a hand visible on its crust.

Chapter Sixteen

The Mongol Princess

REYHAN FELT EXTREMELY GRATEFUL FOR THE NEW PALace, built for her by Persian artisans. Her chambermaids rejoiced when they saw it. They went out of their way on that day to serve Reyhan, placing vases full of flowers in every room. For a fleeting moment, Reyhan felt as if she had returned to Persia. Persian architects, unlike their Mongol counterparts, did not see their work as merely propping up walls to shelter people from natural elements, but as works of art that could lift spirits. Glass and mirrored tiles, each minuscule in size, covered vast areas in colorful designs such that closing one's eyes on them took a certain degree of willpower, and melancholy could not survive when so many pieces glimmered and winked.

Although some flowering shrubs and trees were planted in Karakorum and kept alive through the painstaking care given them by captive gardeners, the area surrounding the oasis could not be described as anything more than a stretch of grassland. Despite the location, the new palace suited Reyhan, and she felt at home. Albeit, it seemed to her that her career as a teacher had come to an end until praise for her accomplishments came from an unexpected quarter.

"I have come here with important news that pertains to my lady directly," Baako said one evening when Reyhan permitted him to enter her chamber. Cushioned benches covered in crimson fabric with bits of golden spangle embroidered on them were set up around the circular chamber. Caramel-colored tiles that covered the walls and concave ceiling allowed the rug and furnishings to take center stage. Baako sat on a bench that was nearest to Reyhan and added, "Princess Sorkhokhtani, wife of Tolui Khan is coming over."

Reyhan had met her sister-in-law at her wedding before they left to reside in Inner Mongolia, but that encounter was short, and she could not get to know her better. She had a vague memory of what the Mongol Princess looked like and certainly had no idea of what kind of a person she might be.

"Lady Sorkhokhtani is an incredibly wise woman," Baako continued. "Although illiterate, she looks at knowledge like a miser looks at gold coins. She has heard about your abilities in teaching Kadan and is very much impressed. She hopes that her sons could also benefit from such instructions. They are arriving at Karakorum tomorrow."

"Tomorrow?" Reyhan asked, quite taken by surprise and not knowing what to expect from the newcomers. "I would like to know more about her before we meet."

"Lady Sorkhokhtani is a Nestorian Christian to whom nature has granted the double blessing of beauty and wisdom," Baako said. "She is free of all religious biases. All houses of worship, regardless of their ways, gain equally from her charitable donations. She has realized early on that knowledge is the key to might and fortune. She currently runs the affairs of the lands controlled by Tolui Khan, in the absence of her husband, who is frequently leading Mongol armies into new terrains."

The thought of meeting such a fascinating person revived Reyhan's spirit. As he prepared to leave, Baako added, "Do be careful with the lion cubs, my lady, sometimes they bite off the hand that nourishes them. They are not just children, but future emperors."

She gave him a reassuring smile, as she always did when they were parting, to put his mind at ease.

Early the next morning, as she awaited the arrival of her guests, Reyhan reached for the bejeweled brooch which conjured home for her: the warm embrace of her mother, the stern look on her father's face that she actually admired and considered manly, the sweet scent of smoke rising from dried rue seeds in the incense-burner, and the first moments when she met Ogodei for she was wearing it when he kidnapped her.

Being kidnapped by a handsome prince had seemed romantic at first, but living as a captive in a foreign land had become her curse. She tried not to give in to despair. This was not the time to face the reality of her situation. She had to swim to the surface from its depths and breathe the revitalizing air of optimism. "Not all that you wish for will ever come true, such is the way of the world," her father used to say.

Reyhan opened her bedroom window and looked out at the courtyard. An earlier rainstorm had brought a sense of freshness to the air. A pink glow on the horizon announced the arrival of the sun. Soon its amber rays penetrated the pale blue-gray morning sky, shedding light upon the brown mass of leafless branches. The land enjoyed a few moments of peace after the violent storms of the previous evening. Few clouds still lingered. The same clouds must have passed through the skies of Samarkand, she thought.

Reyhan remembered the sunshine of Samarkand. How the earth sparkled, how the world gleamed. How snow began to melt when tiny green buds appeared upon the branches of trees, foretelling nature's annual renovation. Would she ever see Samarkand again? Would she ever be there among family and friends?

She took a deep breath, and as she did so, she heard the sound of bells, bringing the glad tiding of the approaching royal caravan. But there are no bells for palaces, no knocking on the door. No keys ever lock or unlock the entrance. There are guards outside in uniform, fully armed. There is a receiving line of chambermaids and housekeepers ready to welcome guests anytime they arrive. Reyhan could hear footsteps upon the cobblestone walkway that led to the palace entry and the sweet voices of children downstairs, chirping like newly hatched baby birds.

Enthusiasm surged through her veins. She wanted to run downstairs and greet them. She had done so in the old palace in Samarkand when she was but a child. Her father reprimanded her, "You need to always observe propriety," he told her. He even assigned a maid with the task of walking her up and down the stairs elegantly so that she would observe decorum. Wearing a turquoise-colored damask outfit that signified her Persian taste and contrasted beautifully with her honey-colored eyes, she got ready to welcome her guests.

After the chambermaid announced the arrival of the Mongol Princess, Reyhan slowly descended the marble staircase that led to the palace parlor, weightless as a cloud. By the time she reached the parlor, the maids had removed the fur-lined overcoats of three children, exposing identical glossy brown masses of hair on each head.

Lady Sorkhokhtani greeted Reyhan with the warmest smile. The Mongol Princess had a taller stature than most of her countrymen. Wisdom, maturity, and determination shone upon Sorkhokhtani's beautiful face. Her countenance was fairer than most Mongols, and her features were delicate. She carried herself with the grace of an empress and seemed quite perceptive of her surroundings. The tiny mirrored tiles of the parlor reflected the colors of their clothing.

Sorkhokhtani wore a two-piece yellow garment topped with an elaborately embroidered purple deel. A black cap tied with ribbons under her chin held a tall rimless red hat. A row of tiny strings of pearls covered her forehead like strands of hair. Long tresses of a lighter brown color than most Mongols reached the tightly bound sash of her deel. Her gaze conveyed sincerity and she wore a look of approval as she perused Reyhan's parlor.

Sorkhokhtani introduced her children. Kublai, a stout boy of about eight years of age stood next to Ariq Boke, his youngest brother, who didn't seem to have put more than four springs behind him. He was rather thin by Mongol standards. Hulagu, only a year older, had his mother's features. The little lad reached out and grabbed the Persian Princess's skirt playfully with a big mischievous smile on his face. A burst of naughty laughter followed that made everyone laugh as well. The boy won Reyhan's heart from that moment.

Sorkhokhtani looked admiringly at Reyhan when she bent over the child, gently caressing his soft hair. *Hulagu is going to grow up to be a handsome lad*, Reyhan thought and smiled.

When they got settled in the parlor of the palace, Princess Sorkhokhtani looked around the large enclosure designed in Persian style.

Her gaze moved from tall columns covered in tiny tiles to the ceiling of colored glass from which a rainbow of colors, warmed by the sun, showered their hues upon the marble floor. Miniature drawings of Persian gardens and gilded pieces of calligraphy ornamented the walls. Despite the assortment of colors used in the décor, there was such harmony and congruence in the whole structure that the entire palace looked like one grand piece of art.

Reyhan had added a few drops of rose water to her teapot and the scent filled the air as she offered a glass to Sorkhokhtani. Fresh dates with their pits removed and filled with bits of walnuts were placed on a golden tray. Tiny gold-rimmed glasses that easily fit in the palm of one hand, each supported by a small gold base with handle, served as teacups.

Sorkhokhtani complimented Reyhan's taste and said, "Some of your countrymen work for us now, including this historian by the name of Ata Malek Juvayni that I am sure you will get to meet."

"I have met him already and found him to be quite a learned man. I have even borrowed a book from him about Persian history."

Sorkhokhtani smiled approvingly at Reyhan, who seemed to have noticed the attentive gaze of her guest.

"This palace is Ogodei's gift to me," Reyhan said.

"He must love you very much," Sorkhokhtani commented.

Reyhan frowned. "There is a difference between a gift of love and a gesture of appeasement."

Geraniums of orange and pink color planted in clay pots stood near the large windows of the parlor, and a stream of sunlight warmed their petals as it illuminated the bowl of fruit set on an intricately carved wooden table. It made the grapes displayed in the bowl appear translucent. A bejeweled hookah, among the items looted by the Mongols, stood on a corner table.

"Do you smoke that?" Sorkhokhtani asked.

"Oh, no," Reyhan replied with a laugh. "It serves as decoration for that dark corner of the parlor."

"Have you still retained your attachment to Persia, or do you consider yourself a Mongol Princess now?" was the shrewd mother's next question.

Reyhan, who seemed to be weighing her answer replied, "I must admit that I am still struggling with the notion," and quickly added with a smile, "but I do love Mongol children."

Sorkhokhtani appreciated Reyhan's honesty and integrity but realizing that their positive impression of one another could easily become sullied by this line of conversation, she expressed her admiration for all that Reyhan had done for Kadan and said, "My sons will live in your palace so that they can benefit from your instructions. It is my hope that each of my children learns a different foreign tongue. Hulagu will learn Persian and Ariq Boke, Turkish, for I know you are proficient in both languages. I would like Kublai to receive instructions from the Chinese masters as well. I want him to become a scholar in Confucianism, for the Great Khan wanted Kublai to rule Chinese territories one day, and I myself find the idea rather intriguing. My intention is that they become intelligent noblemen, rather than dim-witted warriors."

Being older than Reyhan and a Mongol gave Sorkhokhtani superiority to Reyhan according to the customs under which they lived. "I like the tranquility of this palace and hope to visit often, both to see the children and learn about their progress. I also see it as an opportunity to engage in conversation with such a learned lady."

Reyhan thanked Sorkhokhtani but kept her eyes on Hulagu for she seemed worried that the naughty boy would touch the hot pot of tea or knock over the tea glasses set on her table.

Before leaving for Ogodei's Palace, Sorkhokhtani asked Reyhan to spend a considerable amount of time each day with her children. She intimated her desire for them to become the next great Khans of the Mongols; for them to become literate, although she herself was not; for them to learn statesmanship and administrative skills that the other Mongols lacked. When Reyhan agreed to assume her duties as a tutor, Sorkhokhtani rejoiced in the idea, and with a warm smile and a kind countenance, conveyed to Reyhan that they could both set formalities aside and just be friends.

Reyhan later met Jochi's son, Batu, a handsome lad of sixteen with black hair and straight, slightly upward slanted eyebrows. He had accompanied the boys. However, he said he would not stay in Karakorum for long. Neither would Mongke, the eldest son of Sorkhokhtani, who was a tall lad of fourteen. The two had arrived separately and were staying at Amgalan Palace. Ogodei had decided to put both Mongke and Batu through intensive training, readying them to take part in military expeditions. The educational plans for the younger children, however, were left mostly to Reyhan.

Chapter Seventeen

A Playmate and Teacher

AFTER SORKHOKHTANI'S DEPARTURE, EDUCATING THE boys became Reyhan's main occupation. She felt like a second mother to them, and although she found Kublai to be quite intelligent and Ariq Boke lovingly tame, her strongest attachment remained with Hulagu.

Kublai received most of his instructions from Chinese scholars, but Reyhan advised him occasionally on rules of good governance. He must have taken after his mother, for he had a gentle nature and absorbed every word that she taught. However, it didn't take long for Reyhan to realize that he craved food as much as he craved knowledge.

Reyhan taught him the importance of adapting one's ways to the culture of the land one ruled. "In honoring men of religion," Reyhan said on one occasion, addressing Kublai alone although all three children were present, "one must distinguish between the pious and the hypocrites. The way to distinguish the two is by knowing that hypocrites are those who are greedy. Religion can be a great tool for those who crave worldly possessions. They will go to any length to present themselves as pious, when in fact they are wolves in the garb of sheep."

In such manner, Reyhan's lessons to Kublai began with Hulagu and Ariq Boke playing with their wooden toys. Occasionally, Hulagu would look up in wonder at the terminology Reyhan was using. He would then mouth the complicated words jestingly to Ariq Boke to the loud giggles of his younger brother.

"Many among the conquered people are farmers," she would say. "If given proper tools, they can produce crops. By providing them with necessities, rather than annihilating them, the ruler can prosper as well."

When left alone with Kublai's younger siblings, Reyhan's tone became more maternal, and she saw them as babies in need of love more than instructions.

"My dear children, alphabets are the basic tools of writing. By learning to place them side by side you can form words and sentences. And then something magical happens. You will be able to speak to people all over the world by sending them the lines you have drawn on paper."

Ariq Boke appeared to be a timid child who did exactly what Reyhan asked him to do. But Hulagu remained quite a spirited one. The boy had a habit of hiding behind a wall and jumping in front of Reyhan, unexpectedly. He would then laugh heartily whenever he saw the surprised expression on Reyhan's face. It appeared to Reyhan that Hulagu saw her more as a playmate than a teacher. This did not reduce her admiration of the boy; however, it only increased it. So often she had to remind herself that he was not hers, that other people's blood, including Genghis Khan's, ran through his veins.

With the weather warming up, Hulagu woke up brimming with enthusiasm every morning, seeking Reyhan and pleading with her to either go to the lake or the flower garden before even having breakfast. She often relented and let the boy have it his way. She would pick up Hulagu and Ariq Boke and place them on top of a large white marble statue of a turtle in the palace garden. Hulagu would then boisterously proclaim that he was the ruler of the world, riding his turtle all the way to Damascus. Reyhan laughed at his childish ways, and he giggled sweetly in return.

Once when Reyhan lifted Hulagu off the stone turtle, she led him to a small pile of mud bricks in a corner of the garden. Siberian pea shrubs were blooming nearby. She asked him to pick up a brick. He did so. She then asked him to hold it with one hand. He tried. Then she asked him to pick up another brick. It was difficult, but the stubborn lad finally managed. His small hands could hardly hold the two bricks together. Finally, he dropped them both. Tears welled up as he stared at her with questioning eyes, wondering what it all meant.

"Never take more than you can handle," she told him as she lifted him and kissed the tears off his cheeks, hoping the hurt would be forgotten and the lesson permanently etched in his memory.

At times, when Hulagu and his brother were away, visiting their Uncle Ogodei's palace, Hulagu would return with an eagerness that warmed Reyhan's heart. She would hold him in a loving embrace, and he would tell her all that had happened in the meanwhile with great emphasis on details.

"Uncle Ogodei has a ring on his finger with a red stone on it as big as my knuckle. He says that he wants to have the mark of the Mongols cut into the stone. So when he sends a command on paper, he can dip it in ink, and the mark will appear on paper. He said he would one day show me how that works."

Reyhan was familiar with the seal. It used to be in a square-shaped ruby with the words "His Holy Majesty in Whose Hands the Sky has Placed Authority and Religion" inscribed in the Mongolian language. Now a geometric design, symbolizing the fact that they were sky worshipers, formed the new Mongol emblem.

At night, Reyhan made sure to be the one to tuck the boys in bed. She refused to leave the task to her chambermaids or palace workers. "Tell me the story of Arash again," Hulagu pleaded almost every night. One night, as summer covered them in a blanket of warmth, Reyhan as usual obliged, beginning the story thus:

"Long ago war was about to break out between the lands of Persia and Transoxiana for they had territorial disputes. The wise king of Persia devised a plan to avoid combat. He asked for a game of archery to determine the boundaries of each land. Arash was a young athlete and had already gained fame for his archery skills."

"I want to learn archery," Hulagu interrupted.

"I am sure that can be arranged," Reyhan responded, adding, "Arash was selected to climb the tallest mountain and from there aim at the disputed frontier, determining the border. As he steadied himself on the mountaintop, he placed all his energy and skill into releasing his arrow. He bent backward to such an extent that although his arrow flew like a bird, soaring through the skies and landing far into the territory of Transoxiana, his own body rolled off the mountain into a ravine below. And thus, he gave his life to ensure his homeland's border."

Hulagu's eyelids had become heavy with sleep. "Mongolia's borders will one day stretch to the ends of the world," the future monarch exclaimed drowsily as he closed his eyes.

"Conquering lands and ignoring the livelihood of its inhabitants seldom profits anyone. By safeguarding such livelihood and allowing the people to thrive, you can actually reap far greater rewards." That last comment she addressed to the child after he had dozed off. However, Reyhan noticed how Kublai was deep in thought as if his young mind processed that insight. Kublai gave Reyhan a meaningful smile. She reciprocated. At least one child understood her perfectly.

Reyhan had learned from Baako about an unsuccessful rebellion in her homeland, brutally crushed by the Mongols. Many had died, among them the Jackal. The news had left her melancholy the entire day. She had never seen the famous thief, yet, in her mind he had become a hero, a legend. After she made sure the children had fallen asleep, and her chambermaids were off to dreamland as well, she sat at her desk.

Reyhan looked out the window. A crescent moon and a lone star serenading it were the only sources of illumination in heaven. The scene reminded her of Arash and his bow.

Entry by Reyhan:

I have found a joy in writing that is indescribable. My tears are shed through the ink that colors the pages of my journal, and my laughter echoes in its words. The journal has become an old friend to me, one that listens to my pains and shares my grief. By returning to my earlier writings, I find myself listening to its side of the story; so by no means would I call this a one-sided communication. It is my sincere hope that one day when I am no longer in this world, a woman in a similar circumstance as I would continue to fill the pages of these chronicles.

Today Baako bore the sad news of the Jackal's death. Although I always thought such an end for him as inevitable, the news of his death saddens me. He had refused to aid the Mongols. His untamable spirit could not bear the responsibilities of governorship. He was a born law-breaker, not one to enforce the law. He saw regulations as something to be laughed at. Standing before crowds to be revered and respected did not appeal to him. He despised politicians and considered some his rivals in thievery. He would never become a stooge of the Mongols.

He had managed to put together enough forces to instigate a rebellion against the invaders. The rebellion was brutally crushed when a member of the Mongol court died in battle. The Mongols carried out a revenge attack, the Jackal being among those who perished. They buried him in the dark in an unmarked grave, fearing that his enemies may show no mercy even to his lifeless body. His memory, however, stays vivid in the minds of those he so gallantly saved.

I must add that the king's mother, Turkan Khatun, is now a servant of a Mongol officer. Even if one knew her in her past life, it would be impossible for one to recognize her altered face now. Hardship and age have left their marks on her face. I have also learned about the fate of the Khwarazm King, my grandfather's foe. The Shah chose an island in the Caspian Sea as his final refuge. Alone, desperate and sick, with only one servant as his companion, void of all the luxuries he once enjoyed, he soon perished; his only legacy being a ruined civilization.

As the waters of the Caspian lapped the shores in their eternal rhythm to rid the sea of the unwanted, the body of the former monarch of Persia was finally carried to its shores wearing the ragged shirt of his servant.

Chapter Eighteen

The Lion Cubs Come of Age

1233 C.E.

REYHAN WATCHED AS SORKHOKHTANI'S BOYS GREW UP into adolescents who saw life as a treat served upon a golden platter. They woke each morning, ready to embrace the adventures of the day. The thrill of youth mixed with the excitement of power and glory pumped new energy into their veins as they entered the prime of life, ready to experience a future yet unknown. They would be the future conquerors of the world, their lives a far cry from the horrors that their grandfather endured as a young lad.

Mongke had grown to be wise and mature, Kublai remained a gentle soul, and Ariq Boke still charmed everyone with his sweet smile. But Hulagu, at fifteen, had grown to be quite different from the vibrant child he had been. At the onset of puberty, Hulagu began to display characteristics that resembled those of his ancestors. He showed little tolerance toward those who vexed him and appeared more aloof.

At times, Reyhan felt that behind a thin veneer of calm, anger boiled within the boy's body. He certainly had inherited his grandfather's fury. She often wondered what would become of him when he grew older, or what would become of the world when he became a powerful chieftain.

Sorkhokhtani's boys spent most of their days training for the battlefield or participating in hunting trips and chasing gazelles to enhance their physical capabilities and alertness; they would put these skills to use when they joined the Mongol cavalry. Their conflicts at times turned into fist fights. Reyhan continued to advise the use of self-restraint, but they refused to listen.

"Humans are malleable beings," Reyhan would say, "they will cooperate with you and join your mission if you give them a chance. Destruction and killing, on the other hand, could leave a population with long-lasting feelings of malice." Her words, effective at times, were as if spoken into the wind at others, for they paid no heed to what they considered Reyhan's constant "moral sermons."

On one occasion when Sorkhokhtani's husband, Tolui, had come to bid the family farewell before leaving for the fronts, Reyhan informed him that Hulagu and his cousin, Guyuk, had gotten into a fight in the middle of a game of knucklebones.

"If I am ever given command of the army," Guyuk said, "I will crush the Persians and put an end, once and for all, to the civilization they are still so boastful of. It would be such a treat to see that miserable Reyhan's face when I accomplish my task."

"Do not speak of Reyhan in such language or I swear to the Mighty Sky that I will put an end to your miserable life," Hulagu snapped. He pounced on Guyuk like a leopard, punching his cousin hard in the nose, causing it to bleed. Tolui intervened and separated the boys. Hulagu turned to Guyuk saying, "Next time you make a remark like that, I will break your neck."

"I was just jesting," Guyuk said.

"Well I do not appreciate your humor," Hulagu replied, furiously.

Tolui advised them to show respect toward one another and then told them of his plans to go to the fronts. In speaking to Reyhan after the incident, Tolui said, "Hulagu is a true grandson of Genghis. He resembles my father in appearance and has taken after him in his ambitions to rule. He seems to have little control over his temper, but I am hoping he will become more understanding as he matures."

Reyhan was at a loss for words, but when Tolui was about to leave, she tried to reassure him with a smile. As the first-born son of Ogodei, Guyuk was groomed by his mother, Toregene, to become the next Khaqan after his father's death, although Ogodei did not favor him.

"I have no doubt Hulagu will change as he matures," she said. "I am not so sure about Guyuk."

Tolui nodded his consent.

"He did it intentionally, Baako, intentionally, with joy sparkling in his eyes," Princess Reyhan said, standing there pale and trembling, tears flowing uncontrollably from her eyes. This was the latest incident, but by no means the first of its kind. Hulagu had just suffocated the newborn lamb Reyhan had given him as a present for his success in completing a course in Persian language.

"Now, now, my lady," Baako spoke gently kneeling by her side, "you have tried to raise a lion cub like a house cat. He is a born hunter, a Mongol, and you cannot change that."

Reyhan looked at Baako through a lace of tears that covered her eyes. Helpless and marginalized in the Mongol court, she felt as if her sense of pride and emotional strength were being drained with every passing day.

When she had first seen Hulagu and his brothers, she had taken them under her wings, nurtured them and tried to bestow upon them knowledge, expose them to the culture and art of the kingdoms their father and grandfather raided.

"I have tried," she said, "the Almighty knows I have tried to raise him properly, but all my efforts seem to have been in vain. I am afraid that Holagu is bound to turn into an irascible monster just like his grandfather."

On the final word of her lament, the sound of thunder quieted her. It tore through the heavens as lightning marred the face of the sky. It randomly targeted winter-dead branches like fiery arrows cast by heaven, permanently charring parts of the landscape. A magnificent downpour ensued. It was as if the skies sympathized with Reyhan and shed tears as well. From the land of nightingales and roses, she had been dragged to where the sound of thunder, or the occasional cries of wolves, shattered the dead silence of the skies.

"I think Hulagu is not as cruel as he appears. It is part of their culture, you see, that considers cruelty as a sign of manliness and strength of character," Baako tried to explain. "He enjoys the approval of others, the fact that the Mongol society admires him means a lot to this young man."

"I don't know if he wants to show off his manliness or he is downright vicious," Reyhan said. "I do not despise him, Baako. How can I? He is like a son to me. But how can I love him when he is just as brutal as the others. Mercy has no place in his heart. Love is just a word he toys with when he is around handsome damsels. He certainly has inherited his grandfather's world-conquering ambitions and thirst for glory."

"It saddens me to see you so distraught, my lady," Baako said, addressing his crestfallen matron. He looked out the window as if thankful for not laboring outdoors at that hour. Fear of thunderstorms, so prevalent among the Mongols, seemed to have affected Baako as well.

"Hulagu's heart never forgives other people's faults and shortcomings," Baako added. "While yours, like the ever-flowing river that stumbles over stones strewn upon its path, carries on pristine, without grudges and thoughts of revenge."

He urged Princess Reyhan to drink the hot, aromatic brew he had made, a concoction of starflower tea with chunks of sugar crystals. The soul-soothing remedy pacified her for a bit.

"My lady, you need not bother yourself about Hulagu so much now. He is almost old enough to join the ranks of the military," Baako said. When she was more composed he added, "Hunting games will commence tomorrow, and it is Arik Boke and Hulagu's turn to prove their status as worthy young warriors."

"That is all they think about, Baako, is it not? How to be better warriors," Reyhan said.

Chapter Nineteen

Fistfuls of Dust

AS PREPARATIONS GOT UNDERWAY FOR THE GAMES, EVEN the animals were excited, as if they could sense the exhilaration in the air. Hulagu and Ariq Boke could hardly breathe. Kublai had no interest in participating, and Mongke, already a seasoned hunter had left to join the Mongol army. No weapons were to be utilized; the hunters had to use their bare hands to trap the beasts.

During the hunt, the participants formed a large ring around a portion of the grassland, leaving most of the beasts—the wild sheep, musk deer, boars, and saiga antelopes as well as smaller animals like hares and corsac foxes—within the circle as they closed ranks to ensure none of them escaped. Then they began to move toward the center of the field, making their circle smaller and smaller and the animals more and more agitated and nervous.

Participating in their first hunt, Hulagu and Ariq Boke each had to tackle a deer. Ariq Boke looked like a coward for he obviously could not bring himself to kill the poor animal staring innocently at him. Hulagu, however, stunned the crowd by smashing the deer's head against a large boulder. He raised the dead animal with both hands above his head to the loud cheer of the other hunters. Reyhan gasped at the spectacle and wondered what else this young man was capable of. It surprised her to find Kublai in a cheerful mood, happy about his brother's success.

"Your efforts have not been in vain," Baako later told Reyhan, "Kublai is displaying the qualities of a great leader. He takes pride in the accomplishments of his brothers rather than trying to achieve everything for himself."

"I have no doubt he will be a just monarch," Reyhan replied.

Baako was right. Kublai had grown to be wise beyond his age, well-read, and fluent in the Chinese language and philosophy. He displayed a mild temperament and was very much fond of a young girl named Chabi whom he intended to marry. He was thoughtful and spoke only after pondering the meaning of what he intended to say.

Kublai often mentioned that he tried to see beyond the spoken words and focus on the speakers' deeds. Therefore, his judgments regarding people were more accurate, and he surpassed his brothers when it came to taking the right stance and making the right decision. He took the most pragmatic path when encountering troublesome situations. He sought the advice of the learned scholars and utilized their expertise. He mentioned more than once that the welfare of his future subjects mattered to him, and he intended to be benevolent toward them. Hulagu, on the other hand, always interpreted Reyhan's words to suit his own way of thinking.

All four sons of Tolui shared their grandfather's ambitions to conquer the world. Kublai wanted to leave a good legacy behind; he cared for the populations that lived under Mongol rule and wanted to set an example of proper management in China. That part of the world fascinated Kublai. Hulagu, however, had other ideas.

"Alas, I am but a wolf cub," Reyhan overheard Hulagu speaking one day to Ariq Boke, "my teeth aren't sharp, and my fangs haven't grown. But the day shall come when I make my enemies repent their deeds. I shall work night and day to form alliances, to gain power, to use the magic of oration and find followers. Our empire shall extend to the ends of the earth and be like none other. The Mongol hawks shall spread their wings and reach for the eternal sky."

Although Reyhan found Hulagu's attitude disturbing, she dismissed it and attributed it to his youth. Despite the prevalence of beautiful women in the Mongol court, Hulagu seemed withdrawn from his immediate circle as if he yearned for a soulmate never to be found. He constantly quoted his father or grandfather, taking pride in what he saw as their achievements and vowing to thread the same path as they had done.

Sorkhokhtani and Reyhan spoke of Hulagu when she visited Karakorum.

"I am afraid Hulagu is growing up to be vengeful like his grandfather. I have tried to instill Christian mercy and forgiveness in him but to no avail. He is a sky-worshiper with a firm belief in retribution," Sorkhokhtani said.

"Well, the appetite for revenge could also be a sign of vulnerability," Reyhan said. "These young men feel quite a burden on their shoulders when they realize they will be ruling large territories of the world. I have tried to teach them to be good to one another and support each other and also be caring toward their subjects."

"Kublai seems to be taking your advice and that of his other teachers to heart, Sorkhokhtani replied, "I'm not so sure about Hulagu."

Tolui's farewell to the boys was his last, and before long news reached Karakorum that he had lost his life. Tolui died, only forty years old, not in war but due to excessive drinking.

When the news of Tolui's death reached Reyhan, she went to meet Sorkhokhtani who was staying at Ogodei's Palace. A dreadful thunderstorm broke, leaving her soaked through to her skin by the time she reached her friend's quarters. Sorkhokhtani greeted Reyhan warmly, offering her a change of clothes.

They sat by the fireplace, drinking tea together. To Reyhan's surprise, Sorkhokhtani looked more determined than mournful. She said that she was heartbroken, but her sense of duty toward her sons surpassed her tendency to grieve for her late spouse. For Hulagu the news proved to be devastating, and Sorkhokhtani expressed concern for him, saying that the boy was beyond consolation.

At his father's gravesite, when only a few well-wishers still lingered, Hulagu, visibly shaken, could barely control himself. He fell on the freshly dug dirt of the grave, grabbed two fistfuls of dust and facing the sky proclaimed loudly, "Death, o' death, how you reign supreme! What little regard you have for the prince or the pauper. Your claws reach deep into human souls and drag them toward the unknown. O' invisible hand of vengeance, I shall defy you, for I know that if I do not dare you and confront you, you will follow me and drag me deep beneath the earth as you did to my father and grandfather."

Chapter Twenty

In the Land of Sunrise

REYHAN'S CHRONICLES DID NOT JUST COVER THE EVENTS in Persia. As the Mongols moved onto new territories, her tales began to incorporate newer and more distant lands. On rainy days, she sought the solace of her chamber. At times, her words lacked depth, and she felt unable to measure up to the task of stating solemn circumstances, and at others the ink flowed onto paper, giving expression to an ocean of feelings.

Not all Seljuk Kings were as benevolent as Reyhan's grandfather. A branch of the dynasty that ruled Anatolia did so by overtaxing and abusing the working class. Anatolia or "The Land of Sunrise," as the formerly Greek-speaking rulers used to call it, could not be branded as a poor country. Being rich and powerful, it had dominance over its neighbors. Yet, the workman's share was nothing but bitterness and despair.

Seljuk conquerors had gradually transformed the culture of the land. Their strict method of taxation, carried out by teams of taxmen called Iqta Units, had left many disenchanted, for the Iqta had the authority to collect money from the oppressed people.

The Iqta would arrive at someone's door, wearing striped robes that distinguished them from the rest of the population. One only had to look upon their severe expressions to know that they intended to collect money or confiscate goods.

Entry by Reyhan:

The Taxman of Anatolia

Ogul tried not to breathe in the cold air; there were ice particles in it. He exhaled into his collar to preserve his body heat. It was almost noon but the sun had somehow managed to fade beyond the clouds and leave the citizens of Anatolia to shiver. He craved some hot, sweet tea but tea leaves and sugar he could ill afford; very little was affordable those days in Anatolia.

Hunger had become Ogul's constant companion. It had placed its ugly mark on the fair faces of his children too. They had five of them by now. His wife Gonul fared no better. They lived on the edge, the precipice where only daily exertions helped them avoid utter destitution. Basic staples had become a luxury they could only afford occasionally.

Ogul was too honest to think about stealing, and as a Christian still retained his faith in God. But attending church had become increasingly difficult and ceased altogether when their appearance and clothing became too unsightly for the holy attendees.

Religion, politics and even culture had no place in a home where poverty ate through every aspect of life and devoured every hope. After the birth of their fifth child, their situation had worsened.

Ogul would have accepted handouts but none were offered, and he was too shy to beg. His wife kept talking about the other suitors she had before falling into his trap; especially one, made-up or real, who supposedly became a wealthy merchant. "Can you imagine the kind of life I could have had?" she kept repeating, her words sawing his overstretched nerves. "As a good-looking lass in my younger days, I could have married anybody. What a pity that I fell for your father," she would say, addressing the children.

Whenever she stressed the word "fell," he would think of the precipice at the edge of which they lived. For Ogul and his wife, love and hate had lost their meanings. They only commiserated.

A light drizzle started which soon turned into an incessant shower. It formed little streams upon the stone-paved roads of richer neighborhoods and turned dirt roads into cesspools of mud in poorer ones.

In the richer parts of Anatolia, rain washed the sweet petals of blue and yellow aconite flowers; it scrubbed their dark green leaves clean and left the brick houses sparkling. Rain sang down drainpipes, slid down happily on the clean surface of methodically wiped windows, it kissed the face of fancy parasols and washed away dust from rooftops.

But in the poor parts of the city, rain only brought mud and misery. It soaked the poor people's single outfits; it deteriorated the already fraying fabric of their ragged attire; it bent their old shoes further out of shape. It lashed against the horse-drawn carriages and their horses. It drenched the faces and blinded the eyes of passersby. Mud crept up the skirts and trousers of pedestrians. Horses pulling carriages behind them became mired saddle-deep in the mud. Puddles of water accumulated in potholes and the earth felt like a sponge that would never dry.

No doubt, many wished they had made it home earlier to settle by the fire and nurse a hot drink. When Ogul reached his humble abode, however, rain had found its way indoors as well. It had saturated the roof and dripped from the ceiling. Pots were placed here and there to keep it from flooding the floors. Ogul sighed deeply as he entered his workshop, the top floor of which they used as their living quarters. Privation was the state of their life, and he could do nothing about it. Fate had condemned them to it, and they could not escape its chains.

His wife sighed too as she recounted the other chances she could have had in life. She was a skin and bone figure of a woman, thinned by dearth and deprivation. Her tongue, however, remained fresh and piercing like a brand-new blade.

In the bare-bone workshop of the aging carpenter, four thin little boys of varying ages stared at their father looking timid. He had removed the banisters of the staircase in hopes of turning them into a piece of furniture for a wealthy customer. His baby daughter, still a suckling infant, would soon learn to crawl and there would be no railings protecting her.

As the weak rays of the sun melted on the horizon, Gonul lit the last piece of taper they had, determined to pray all night for some type of relief. The flickering light of the candle cast Ogul's long shadow upon the wall and the ceiling, making him appear larger than his actual self. For the first time in their long life together, she felt the importance of his presence; as if misery had empowered him and bestowed upon him the glory that shines upon the faces of those who have lived through utter desolation.

"We have something more urgent than food to worry about," Gonul said in a less acrimonious tone. "The taxman will be here tomorrow."

"Taxes, taxes, taxes! Damn the taxman! What do they want? We have nothing to give. How are we going to come up with the money they are asking for? We can barely exist as it is. Don't they see that?" he said with bitterness and fury. The children with fear and hunger written all over their demure faces stood closer to their mother, the less broken of the two parents, the youngest boy pulling on her apron.

"No, they don't see that. They don't see anything," she replied. "The Iqta came by yesterday and threatened to take away our home. We'll have nowhere to stay," she said as she turned toward the small window of the workshop.

"'This is the last warning,' he told me, 'you come up with the money by tomorrow, or you are going to be evicted.' 'But what about my children?' I pleaded earnestly, 'Where would I take them in this cold weather?' He stared at me as if looking at a street dog and said again, 'tomorrow' before leaving."

"If," she said, stressing the last letter as if teaching the children how to pronounce the alphabets, "if I had married one of my wealthier suitors, instead of falling for your father, we would have had a roof over our head that did not leak, an aromatic fire would be lit in our house, and we would have had food . . . warm, delicious food on our table." At this point, her gaze turned toward the empty place where once their table stood.

The next morning, Gonul awaited the dreaded figure of the taxman right outside the door. She was too nervous to wait inside as her husband had done. The blue sky had stripes of dark and white clouds scratched upon it as if it could not decide which one to take on. Only a feeble glow of the sun was visible through the clouds.

A strong wind blew through her clothes, making her thin frame shake all over. Her shoes had become so badly worn that she felt the icy surface of the pavement right through her oft-mended socks, which were threadbare by now and refused further mending. Food for them was a priority, a constant thought that weighed heavy on their mind; clothing for them, an unaffordable luxury. Her body had to befriend nature. Adjust itself to its extremes.

She felt lucky to have given birth by herself without the aid of a midwife, for that would have cost more than they could afford. But the last childbirth had taken its toll on her and drained her body of youthful energy. Yet her spirit remained strong for the sake of her children. That spirit had to continue, like the light of the flickering candle that lit their house last night.

Tears were now a stranger to her face. If she cried, she would cry forever, but she had no strength for that, her energy sucked by the baby from her almost empty bosom. More than the deprivation and hunger, the unfairness of it all bothered her. The lavish life of the rich had to be sustained by taking away every morsel they had to eat. At times, she had the urge to fight back, but how can the empty-handed and weak challenge the powerful?

A dense fog had earlier settled on the land. It had blanketed the city, under the cover of which the Mongolian army had advanced. Dressed in the luxurious attire afforded to them by the looting and pillaging of conquered nations, the mere sight of them left the onlooker in awe of their grandeur.

Their horses, long trained to trot noiselessly, moved in from every direction except the main gate, a well-guarded and protected site. Groups of Mongol horsemen poured into the streets and alleys, stunning the residents, few of which were awake that early in the morning. By the time the news reached the central government, the city was under partial foreign occupation. The Mongols encouraged a number of inhabitants to join them. They informed the citizens that their central government had fallen and that they had no choice but to surrender.

A foreign nobleman riding a stallion, white as spring clouds with a harness of gold, approached the poor carpenter's shop. The taxman stood beside him, but he looked timid and appeared to have walked the distance on foot. Other foreigners accompanied them as well. A crowd of curious men and women began to encircle them, like flies hovering over sweets. The alien aristocrat, a tall young man, introduced himself as Ariq Boke, the grandson of Genghis Khan, and addressed the crowd in flawless Turkish with a barely detectable accent.

He told the Iqta to begin collecting taxes. Color faded from Gonul's face. "What is this mischief? The Iqta never came to our door looking so meek," she thought.

The taxman began trembling.

Ariq Boke repeated, "Go ahead and collect the taxes."

"I'm here to collect taxes," the Iqta said in a barely audible voice. The crowd looked up in awe at the foreigners, not knowing whether to be grateful or fearful.

"Who are you?" Gonul asked.

"We are the Mongols," the nobleman's words echoed. "We are your saviors, here to alleviate the hardships you have endured. Join us, and you will be rewarded."

A tall, thin man of about forty wearing ragged clothes cried, "We will, for there is nothing on earth left to us, the loss of which we would regret later. Most of our earnings go to the treasury of the Sultan, and I don't know to what use they put it, for I don't see any benefits coming from them."

"Well, the Sultan will not remain in power for long," the commanding voice of the newcomer announced. "We are the conquering army, and we respect hard-working laborers in our culture. Artisans, builders, alchemists and even laborers are needed in Mongolia. They will be protected and paid well."

As they rounded up all the men that they found useful to their purpose, Gonul with her mouth left open in astonishment waved goodbye to her husband who had heeded the call of the Mongols.

Before leaving, Ogul assured his wife that they would be well provided for. He also said that he would send them letters from Mongolia so often that they wouldn't even miss him. That last promise he never kept.

Power was about to change hands without Gonul's knowledge, and her entire destiny faced a transformation she could not foresee. Foreigners had come to their land. They had to join their battles, to share their riches, their wealth, their food, and bask in the glory of others when their own country had betrayed them.

Ariq Boke continued, "Those who ruled you have abused you, and we are here to set things right. We shall empower the poor amongst you, if you agree to side with us. To test that power, to feel that power, I ask you to decide what shall be done with the taxman."

"Imprison him," a man shouted. "Hang him," another one declared. Gonul was the first to proclaim, "Long live the Mongols!"

Mongol skirmishes against Anatolia continued for a number of years. The Sultan's forces fought back, but the unsatisfied population showed reluctance in resisting the invaders, and a number of them ended up joining the Mongols.

Book III

At the Gateway of Europe

Chapter One

Kievan Rus

December 1237

THE MIDDLE-AGED PREACHER PLACED BOTH HANDS ON the dark wood pulpit and paused for a moment, "Ryazan is facing a dire situation," he said at last. His tall, ornamented headpiece cast a shadow upon his forehead, and the large golden cross hanging from his neck gleamed against his black robe. "The encroaching wolves from the Far East have invaded our land, leaving us vulnerable."

"As always," he added, "we seek the help of our Savior, Jesus Christ. This cathedral is the sanctuary of the pious. No one will harm us within its walls." As he spoke, people pressed against one another to bring their families inside the church.

"We seek Thy help, Lord," the preacher's voice reverberated against the walls of Ryazan's main cathedral, "from an enemy that threatens our existence." The crowd began to mumble as the church filled to its maximum capacity. Others, who saw men, women, and children congregating, reached the conclusion that maybe the church was the only safe place to be. Many struggled to get inside the old structure.

It became almost suffocating inside. When filled beyond its capacity, people began climbing the outer walls, even the dome up to the cupola filled with desperate individuals. People clambered on top of each other, clinging on to whatever they could. Some rolled and fell off, breaking their backs.

"The roof is caving in!" one man shouted, disrupting the sermon.

The preacher, pale as a ghost, looked up. "Oh Lord," he cried involuntarily. "This is the wrath of God unleashed upon us!" As he spoke, the roof collapsed, crushing part of the congregation under its weight.

"Damn Mongols," an injured man cried as he took his last breath.

The initial report had reached Reyhan through the eunuch on the Mongol invasion of Kievan Rus. More information soon followed, and Reyhan lost no time in recording the unfolding drama. As always, she took the stuff of hearsay and wove these into tales.

Entry by Reyhan:

His Green Eyes

Alexandria, whose customers knew her by the name Shura, was a stout forty-year-old woman who had spent nearly half of her life focused on one thing, her family-owned eatery. The family consisted of herself and her aging husband who didn't play much of a role in the main scheme of her life. Shura's strong arms had carried dish-trays, polished the wide planks of wood that covered the floors, served customers, cooked food, and at times when no help had been available, her hardworking hands had chopped into pieces the freshly slaughtered carcasses of cows and pigs.

They lived in the Principality of Ryazan, near the Oka River. Close to the river, the land descended sharply, creating a protective barrier to the west of Ryazan. Walls were erected in all other directions with broken shards of colored glass inserted in the coping stone like blooming flowers. Brick towers placed at intervals allowed guards to monitor incursions by outsiders. The wooden buildings of the Principality resembled dollhouses, giving a particular charm to the land.

The eatery was located in a corner of the main street. It had gradually become the gathering place of the men in the neighborhood. Smoke from their pipes filled the barely-ventilated enclosure. When the cold wind blew upon the bleached blanket that covered the earth, a big pot of borscht would be boiling in Shura's warm kitchen, smelling of freshly plucked root vegetables. Most of Shura's customers were from among the smerdy, or the peasants. The Rus respected the smerdy as citizens and treated them as equals. Therefore, they would willingly lay down their lives for the protection of the principality.

Shura's small but popular eatery, full of grease and smoke and the laughter of men, was cozy and warm and inviting. At no other time did her place seem more alluring, than in the early days of December. Large particles of snow came down, plucked from the sky like the feathers of ten thousand birds. It settled more than a foot deep on the land, making the roads impassable.

On that cold day in December, the snow had piled up on rooftops, and a thick layer of ice had brought the rippling movement of reflection pools to a halt. Icicles clung to windowsills like curious lads. Snow covered the eyelashes of pedestrians and the mustaches of working men. Water fountains had frozen amid their swirling dance. The cold air penetrated the skin, flesh, and bones of those who dared to leave their homes. But the hot belly of Shura's samovar kept whistling indoors, as the cold wind did so outdoors.

Shura was busy searching the large pot of steaming borscht with her ladle, fishing out at least one piece of stew meat for each man while trying to keep her babushka on her large curly mane. The news of war had made her mundane life appear richer and more cherished now that they faced imminent peril.

Shura often wondered at her life; the fact that she had always lived among men with no women ever for company. Shura's customers had gradually become like an extended family to her. In a sense, she had become a mother to them all. There was Alyosha the farmer, Yakov the zhaleika player, Dmitri the rancher and two men who worked for him, and there was Bronislav the philosopher who didn't have much of an education but liked to philosophize a lot.

Thirty-year-old Alyosha complained loudly that the other principalities were not helping them, and that the Kievan Rus army commanders did not even give them proper weapons. "I've to fight the murder'us heathens with me scythe," he said.

"Word is," said Bronislav, "that the Mongolian warlord has written *a letter to the Prince of Ryazan, demanding a tenth of the treasury and a portion of the citizens to enslave. The Prince has responded by sending a carefully worded diplomatic note, telling the barbarian to eat shi--," laughter prevented him from finishing his sentence.*

"The Mongols are out of their minds," Yakov exclaimed. "Who would want to go to war in this cursed weather? Even the dog is curled up in a warm corner and not chasing the cat."

"Tis ain't happen'd that a foorin army atiks us in the dead o' winter," Dimity the old grave-digger interjected while keeping his head down and surveying the chunks of cabbage swirling in his borscht.

"No one dares to atik these parts in Dicembr, 'cept o' course those who seen worse cold and snow in their own lands," a farmer with a gold tooth proclaimed from the other side of the thick wooden table, carved with the initials of bored customers.

"I have heard the ruffians have crossed the frozen Oka River to get here. How on earth did they do that?" Shura asked, pushing her knuckles into her back, relieved that she had served the last bowl of borscht. Shura's palms were sweaty, and she felt a great sense of trepidation in her heart. They all knew Ryazan didn't have what it took to take on a foreign army and had no way of convincing the other Rus principalities, particularly the powerful men in Kiev, to spare them and find others to fight this war.

"The Mongols skated," Yakov replied, casually.

"Skated?" she almost shouted.

"A merchant friend of mine who travels a lot told me that the Mongolians are famous for scraping bones, rounding their edges and tying them to their shoes. They skate all winter long on the Onon River, and Oka is no different. They are currently almost at our doorsteps," Yakov continued.

The rest of the meal was consumed quietly. Shura cleared the dishes, inwardly thanking God that they had no son to be sent to the war front. When she began pouring hot tea out of her oversized samovar, her husband whom everyone called Uncle Rodion—though he was no one's uncle in particular—began to speak.

Much respected for being the owner of the best borscht place in town, despite the fact that he never lifted a finger to help around the place,

Uncle Rodion lit his pipe pensively and said, "The Grand Prince of Kiev ordered the beheading of the Mongol envoy for he found his message extremely offensive. Now that Kiev itself is being threatened, he has decided to send a regiment to Ryazan to keep the enemies engaged here rather than allowing them a quick advance toward Kiev. He should have dispatched the entire army to confront the invaders if you ask me."

"They cannot rely on locals like us with no military experience to ward off the devils until help arrives," Bronislav said.

Uncle Rodion appeared to be measuring his words for he added encouragingly, "Of course I have no doubt that we can hold off the Mongols until then."

The fact that he liked expressing his views but never helped in the kitchen had annoyed Shura in her younger days, but in her more mature age, his remarks had become her secret source of pleasure.

Dimity the grave-digger, who was assumed to be the most educated among the group when it came to death and dying, asked meditatively, "Do de 'ave any idea of their numbeh? What if tay're in the tousands?" As he said this, he carefully poured some of the contents of his glass of tea into its saucer and holding a sugar cube between his teeth, carried the small saucer to his lips with his fat fingers.

Uncle Rodion cleared his throat and answered, "An informant from the palace in Kiev was at our veche (the local assembly) meeting yesterday. He told us that the inhabitants of the Steppes in their entirety are no greater than the population of one small town in these parts. They are so scattered and divided that the locals should easily overcome them in no time at all. Plus, the palace has reassured us that enforcement is on its way." He blew the smoke out, staring with his large green eyes at the ceiling.

"I wish they allowed women in the veche. I would have had a thing or two to say to that informant," Shura said. Talk of war in recent days made her cling to the sweet memories of the past which floated away like sawdust. Shura reached for the wooden shelves on the wall and pretended to rearrange the ornamental objects displayed there. Among them was a Matryoshka doll, a relic of her childhood. She rubbed its shiny belly with her thumb. "We have no choice," she thought, "we just have no choice."

Several days passed before the well-armed forces from Kiev reached Ryazan. During those days of sporadic attacks by the Mongols, a number of people in Ryazan lost their lives. The volunteer army, made up mostly of local farmers who unsuccessfully turned their farm equipment into weapons of war, was ill-prepared for combat. Having to fight knee deep in slush and snow, they were outwitted by the mounted enemy archers who attacked them with far-reaching arrows. Outnumbered and outsmarted by the Mongols, they did not last long, although they showed unprecedented bravery.

The search began with no hope of finding survivors. Many of the bodies were left supine, eyes open, as if mocking their foes in death. The gruesome task of identifying the dead had left Shura in a state of half-consciousness. How else could she roam in this field of doom, searching for those green eyes? At last, she found him, the smell of pipe still fresh on his stifled breath.

Rodion had not been much help around the eatery, but for her, he was a warm and kind companion and a source of comfort at the end of a long day. Shura tried not to think as she and the grave-digger, ironically being among the few men to survive the short-lived conflict, helped the remaining locals to carry and drop the dead, one by one into a small ravine, using it as one large grave.

Chapter Two

The Female Warrior

IN THE MONGOL ENCAMPMENT, LOCATED IN THE OUTskirts of Ryazan, Batu Khan, son of Jochi, addressed the battalion commanders. He would not share strategic details with the rest of the warriors but spoke to the commanders of each unit of one thousand fighters.

"We wiped out the locals just by sending a rag-tag bunch of our lowest classes of combatants," he announced. "However, the army from Kiev is soon to arrive. Again we will dispatch the same rag-tag bunch and even dress, in old Mongol costumes, some prisoners of war that we have brought with us. The confused enemy will likely attack them, thinking that they are Mongol warriors." Laughter echoed in the large ger. "Victory in Kievan Rus will pave the way for our incursions into Europe," he added, raising his voice.

Soon the Rus regiment from Kiev arrived, setting the stage for a major confrontation. Local men garbed in knee-length tops and colorful trousers stood in awe of the military personnel that had just arrived wearing full armor. Not far from where Batu had addressed his men, the Rus regiment with organized lines prepared for battle. An elderly man in a pointed cap and an embroidered cassock, who looked like a priest among the crowd, welcomed the cavalrymen from Kiev.

The defending army confronted the invaders in a field outside of Ryazan. The few locals who had survived the earlier onslaught stayed behind the impressive-looking Rus officers who held elaborately-designed shields shaped like teardrops. The locals felt more like spectators, admiring the scene. One man spoke out loud saying, "Who can overcome such a graceful display of Rus military grandeur? The Mongols are nothing but a bunch of poorly clad barbarians, their numbers barely reaching one hundred in all. The invaders look defeated already." Those around him nodded in agreement.

The emblem on the yellow flags of Kievan Rus moved with the wind and the metal shields and body armor of the well-equipped Rus fighters, as well as the ornate barding on their horses, reflected the light of the sun. To the defenders of Ryazan, the Mongols appeared terrified, for they fled as soon as the first organized line of Rus cavalrymen advanced. The Mongols even left some military gear and a few unmanned horses on the battlefield.

The heavy snowfall of the previous night had turned the familiar terrain into an alien landscape. In their retreat, the rag-tag unit of Mongols galloped toward nearby hills, crossing the frozen heath with the ease of those riding through fresh green grass. Unsheathing glistening swords, the Kievan Rus regiment charged forward triumphantly, tasting the sweet sensation of victory as they sprinted toward the higher elevations. When they finally caught up with the fleeing Mongols, they realized to their horror that they had merely rushed into a trap set by the invaders.

Atop nearby hills, initially invisible, a superior army fresh and ready for battle awaited the exhausted Rus fighters who had wasted their breath chasing the smaller Mongol unit. The Mongol army stationed on hilltops looked quite different from the small wild-looking unit dispatched earlier to the front to mislead them. These warriors numbering in the thousands had fur-lined leather attire embellished with gold, a match for the heavy armor of Rus cavalrymen.

One hundred Mongol standard-bearers mounted on horses began a fantastic show of flag-waving, as their drum beaters commenced a rhythmic call for death. The Rus were stunned by the grandeur; the harmony and the order among the so-called barbarians. Well-rested, proficient and determined, the invaders began their onslaught.

The Mongol archers took position as the first among enemy ranks to initiate the battle. Stationed strategically above ground, they could target their enemies with ease. With every Mongol drumbeat, a larger number of Rus fighters fell.

One Rus officer braved the arrows raining down on him to reach a Mongol warrior on horseback who had shown great alacrity in combat. When he came close, the helmet of the warrior who had moved quickly to avoid being targeted fell, exposing the long black braids of a woman. Shocked at what he was witnessing, the Rus officer hesitated for a moment or two, giving the female warrior the chance to shoot her arrow first.

"Charge," the Rus Commander shouted, as he saw the officer fall. Reluctantly at first and then with great zeal, they began ferociously attacking the Mongols who were descending upon them in a dark avalanche. With their backs to the Oka River, the Rus fighters had no venue for retreat. The field turned into a slaughterhouse.

Kievan Rus, like many parts of the world in those days, anticipated a Mongol invasion, but never one of such devastating magnitude. Snow turned to slush and slush mixed with blood, leaving the earth a crimson color. The horse-mounted aristocrats of Kievan Rus, watching their men perish against the Mongols' relentless attacks, attempted to flee the scene. Their heavy armor prevented a speedy flight, and they soon succumbed to their agile foes.

Chapter Three

Poland

1240 C.E.

THERE ARE MOMENTS IN EARLY SPRING WHEN THE clouds above reach out to the earth like a translucent fog, enrich the air with moisture in blissful ecstasy, and give the world the glad tiding that renewal is near. At such moments, even those harboring the greatest pains in their hearts over a recent calamity would feel the weight of despair being lifted off their shoulders if only they step outdoors.

For Princess Krisztina, blessed with more good fortunes than she could count, the sense of renewal felt almost unbearable. She had never had so much joy in her entire life; her veins pulsed with exhilaration as if she was about to burst out of the shell that formed her body. Lounging upon a settee in a room with a balcony facing the garden in the royal castle of Silesia, Krisztina at seventeen believed she had the demeanor and beauty that could make any fairytale come to life.

Still wearing the silk gown she had worn during the welcome ceremony for the Grand Duke of Kiev's cousin, she got up and walked toward the balcony to take in the fresh air. Krisztina was the niece of Henry II known as Henry the Pious, the High Duke of Poland and Silesia. The Duke's brother had died some years ago, leaving Krisztina and her younger sister, Zofia, under his care.

Krisztina playfully twirled on her toes, reaching for the skies with her arms. The hem of her long pink dress swirled around her feet. A gentle spring zephyr, full of nothing but goodness embraced her. She inhaled the soft breeze and smiled. Her fingers combed away unruly strands at both temples. Even the horses sounded rather cheerful to her ears. She could hear them whinnying, as they carried away the tired guests of the castle, most importantly the cousin of the Grand Duke of Kiev, one Mstislav.

The birdlike sound of a whistle had lured her away from the reception to the balcony overlooking the garden. Agile as a dove, she tiptoed her way to the edge and peered over the balcony. The garden was lit by a bright moon that night. She looked around to see where he was hiding this time. "He," was Wiktor, the son of the castle woodworker who had grown to be an officer in the army but with little prospect of advancement.

Wiktor, now eighteen, had lived with his family on the castle grounds and had been a playmate of Krisztina since childhood. One sunny day last Michaelmas, he had told her that he loved her as they stood gazing through the window of an apothecary shop after their morning stroll. Her positive reaction to his declaration had surprised him, but she had been expecting it.

Krisztina recalled the scene, one of many encounters, when they had felt as one soul in two bodies. Both being too young and inexperienced, they had allowed rumors to follow them wherever they went.

As children, they had roamed freely on the rolling grasslands that surrounded the main castle. Their childish admiration of one another was seen as training for Krisztina, for thus she would grow to appreciate those beneath her. But years had passed, and they never outgrew one another. Quite the contrary, their attachment rose beyond their own expectations, as they experienced the prime of youth together. They were repeatedly forbidden by her uncle from meeting again, threatened at times and admonished at others. Yet, they disobeyed. When the royals engaged in entertaining dignitaries or meeting with public officials, Krisztina would sneak out of the castle to find Wiktor in the yard by the wisteria trees.

Leaves of a nearby branch covered Wiktor's face in the highest boughs of a tree where he had perched, waiting for Krisztina. The air had become chilly. As soon as he saw her, he tried to pull himself closer to the balcony, but before reaching for the balusters, he slipped and fell with a thud on the moist soil. Krisztina's golden locks got in the way as she bent down to reach for him. It was a futile gesture, for there was no way to save him from the fall. Laughter surged through her lungs as she struggled to swallow the overpowering sensation, fearing that someone might hear her. The look of satisfaction on her face must have annoyed Wiktor who looked embarrassed.

"You enjoy my suffering, don't you?" he said rather loud. "I love you, you know, with all my heart, with all my soul." His curly blond hair shone in the moonlight.

Her cheeks felt hot. His open declaration of love was almost too much for her to bear. As she playfully calculated the best response, she turned around, meeting the stern eyes of the sovereign. Color left her face. His towering height and his stooped shoulders made him look like a predator.

"I will see you in my chamber," the monarch said coldly, reminding Krisztina of the extent of his authority, and without further words, he retreated.

She joined him a few minutes later, disheveled and teary-eyed.

"Have a seat," he said, looking her straight in the face, while she tried to avoid his furious gaze. "You are a member of royalty, and there are duties enshrined in that status." Each word gained in volume and intensity as he spoke. "By continuing this path, you will be disinherited and cast off." He paused then added, "He is the son of our woodworker for God's sake."

The Duke continued in a frostier tone, "You are probably contemplating marrying this . . . this fool, who used to play with pigs and cleaned up after horses. In that case, you would have to live in hunger and poverty, and you will not be very happy once this infatuation gives way to bitter reality. Living in hardship means that you will lose your beauty, and he will no longer be interested in you."

As her lips began to quiver and her eyes became flooded with tears, he added in a kinder tone, "Members of the royal family are like peacocks, there is a mystique to them from afar. They are beautiful when seen from a distance and ordinary up close. You cannot mingle with the masses, and you cannot allow this infatuation to go on much longer. Call it love or what have you. But it cannot be."

Krisztina became pensive. In her heart, she still felt defiant, although there seemed to be some sort of logic to what her uncle was saying.

"Mstislav, the cousin of the Grand Duke of Kiev has asked for your hand in marriage," the monarch added in a formal tone as if discussing a matter of policy with his ministers. "He seeks our support in defeating the barbarians responsible for the devastation his homeland has faced. This is a difficult time for Europe. We are in danger of an imminent attack by the same hordes. Kiev is now our ally. I highly recommend that you accept Mstislav's offer. Otherwise, I will be forced to disinherit you and place you in a position that no woman of nobility should suffer. Mstislav is a man of royal upbringing and would be a suitable husband for you. He could preserve the honor of our family, and the marriage will also seal the alliance."

"But uncle," she protested meekly, "he seemed so cold and unapproachable at the banquet. He hardly said a word to me and kept staring at his shoes as if he found them more interesting. I doubt the existence of any affection towards me on his part."

"Affection or no affection; that is the end of my argument," he stated somberly. "Pray tell me your decision by tomorrow, but know that you will have to bear the consequences."

After a sleepless night, Krisztina went out for a walk down the stone path that encircled the castle, the very path she took with Wiktor whenever they had a chance to meet. She brushed past the wisteria trees that used to conceal them from curious eyes watching from castle windows. Dark clouds foretold of rain, but only a tiny droplet or two touched her face. Her temples throbbed. Her eyes burned with yet unshed tears. She blamed herself, she did not know why. How could she blame her uncle who was like a father to her? She had to obey and respect his decisions as the ruler of Poland.

The sky knitted a row of thunderstorms. In her desperation to leave the palace to get some fresh air, she had not brought a shawl along to wrap around her shoulders. A cold shower ensued, pounding her under-dressed body. The piercing needle-like droplets stung her skin. Despite the cold and her wet clothes, she was still steaming inside. Her cheeks burned from the frosty raindrops that mixed with her unceasing tears. Destiny's cruel turn had divided them forever, and they could not go back to the blissful ways of the past.

Krisztina returned crestfallen to her chamber and found it filled with flowers with a note in an unfamiliar hand.

May I have the honor of a private meeting with my lady?

Signed, Mstislav.

She recalled the words of her uncle as she stared at her wet, wild-looking reflection in the mirror. What if poverty destroyed her looks? What if Wiktor's love for her ceased now and forever? She imagined herself running away with him and forgoing the luxuries that ensured her beauty, her status, her charm.

She thought about Wiktor. Their love like a fire engulfing a white field of cotton had taken over their lives unexpectedly, infusing their souls together. Yet, she knew deep in her heart that this passion would not last. She began to believe that Wiktor's love could turn into a slippery slope. Her sister Zofia was too young for her to share her misfortunes with; therefore, sadness weighed heavy on her heart when she found no one that would understand her grief. Yet, she knew her uncle had spoken the truth; this had to end.

The monarch had allowed them a last farewell. Krisztina knew harsh bluntness would be the only way to get her message across to Wiktor, without both falling to pieces. That afternoon she chose the shadow of the wisteria trees for their meeting, hoping that the lavender blossoms surrounding them would soften the blow.

"I am to marry Prince Mstislav of Kiev. My uncle will not have it any other way."

"But we are promised to one another. You gave me your word."

"Promise or no promise; you are the son of a woodworker, and I am a member of the royal family."

"I am an officer in your father's army, now in charge of my own unit."

"Yes; a petty officer."

"How can you speak to me so?"

"It is you who need to learn how to address me as your superior," she said, hiding her trembling fingers behind her back. Oh, how hard it was for her to utter such words to one she loved so tenderly! But the dagger had to be forced to kill what he felt for her, or his suffering would multiply with false hope. "I am betrothed now to the cousin of the Grand Duke of Kiev, and it will not be long before I move to Kievan Rus."

"Does he love you as I do?" was his only reply.

Wiktor's face looked like rigid stone, but her eyes felt like a tumultuous sea. She could barely restrain herself from sobbing. "Such love should be forbidden as sin," she said, "for in due course it will turn passion into loathing and hate. I will be shunned by the nobles if I marry you, and grief at the turn of fortune will turn any love into aversion eventually." Sorrow welled up in her heart as she spoke these words. Tears were choking her, yet she managed to keep them from flowing down her cheeks. She bit her quivering lips and struggled to focus, landing her gaze on a lifeless object, the dead branch of a nearby flowering tree that had failed to bloom.

Wiktor was furious that she did not wait to hear his thoughts. His feelings did not matter. When he returned to the barracks and his lonely chamber, his tears gushed out in agony. He felt broken, abused and betrayed.

Finding not a soul around understanding enough to share his grief, he kept the pain to himself. What a fool he had been to give his heart to such an unworthy creature. Unworthy? He wished she had been unworthy. Had he a thousand hearts multiplied tenfold, he would have gladly sacrificed each and every one of them before her feet. He was the one unworthy of her. But she had not expressed remorse.

Anger turned into bitterness in his heart. Oh, the pain of remembering those eyes pleading with him, knowing full well that she remained beyond his reach. She belonged to another, and he had been a fool who had lost her. Could he turn back the hands of time? How could he recover from a love that he had nurtured since childhood and now its roots reached deep within his soul?

"Oh, cursed fate," he cried, "you have ripped out my heart, and yet I live. What life is this; to breathe, to eat, to drink, to sleep, to sustain oneself for what? Death, blessed death would only end this pain, this dreadful agony. The cool earth of the grave will soothe this burning heart."

He stared out at the wet road, visible from the window of his chamber. It was as if the life that he had imagined for the two of them crumbled like an ice palace before his eyes, and the remnants were rinsed out with the ensuing rain.

Chapter Four

The Fake Ambassador

THE FOLLOWING DAY, A FRENCH AMBASSADOR ARRIVED to meet the High Duke of Poland on matters of security. The man who presented himself, however, was none other than Bolad, a Mongol spy dressed to look like a French dignitary. Only one fully familiar with the language could have detected his slight accent.

Bolad's aquiline nose, light skin, and dark brown hair that formed large curls around his slender face made him look European. Therefore, he was chosen by the Mongols to gather information on Europe. His father was an officer in Genghis's army and his mother a captive brought to Karakorum from Georgia. If one paid close attention, one could detect his Mongolian heritage in his features, like the slight slant of the eyelids, the thin eyebrows, and the protruding cheeks. He appeared shrewd and observant. When he narrowed his dark brown eyes, it was as if he could see the depths of people's souls.

Bolad had received training since early childhood to speak several languages including English, Persian, Chinese, and French, and at times served as an interpreter to Mongol officials. At other times, he became their eyes and ears as a former Persian King used to call his scouts.

"As you are aware," the emissary spoke in French knowing that the Polish Monarch understood the language, "there have been disturbances—to put it mildly—occurring in different parts of Rus territories caused by the barbarians of the Steppes. Among the subjects of attack are fortresses, castles, and palaces. I have been sent on a mission by the Government of France to ensure the safety of the royalty in Europe. Being an expert on security matters, I can give you advice as to what additional fortifications are needed to ensure your safety in case of a surprise attack."

The fact that a small entourage did not accompany the French envoy, a norm in such diplomatic missions, must have struck his hosts as a rather curious matter. But the ambassador's regal attire, embroidered with threads of gold, appeared to have ensured the Polish Royals that he indeed represented the French Court.

During the course of dinner, the eyes of the ambassador rolled in every direction, taking in every nook and cranny of the castle. After dinner, his hosts led him on a tour of the other quarters in the castle. In the end, he asked if there were any other routes for escape. The High Duke assured him that no others existed.

Henry the Pious stepped out into the garden at dusk to escape the unbearable environment of the castle. He could still hear Krisztina crying in her room. Three days had passed since he had told her to end her relationship with Wiktor. A thick fog slumbered lazily. The first row of tall birch trees obscured a fence beyond which lay the road to the castle. If an intruder climbed over the fence, guards standing ten feet away from that spot would not be able to discern him. The monarch frowned at the idea.

The High Duke returned inside to join his wife for supper in the private dining hall of the castle. Deep in thought, he kept his eyes on the blood-red wine offered to him in a golden chalice. He had not removed his crimson cape and gold crown that he had earlier donned for a formal meeting with the army commanders. He knew the white fur edge of his bejeweled crown covered the furrowed lines on his forehead, but could not hide the concern on his face.

Europe had fallen into a state of disarray that it had never known before. Feudalism had turned the continent of green pastures and abundant orchards into a divided region. News of the Mongol invasion of Kievan Rus had slowly reached the other parts of Europe, and the Mongols' ambition of establishing the Golden Horde in the vicinity of

Poland felt like the realization of Henry's worst nightmare.

His wife, Anne of Bohemia, appeared concerned. A brewing storm from the Far East was threatening Christendom. "Who are these Mongols?" she asked.

"They are nomads of the East, hoping to conquer the West. I have learned from the Grand Duke of Kiev that each Mongol warrior carries two or three horses along. When in need of nourishment, they slaughter them, consuming their raw flesh and drinking their blood. Thus, they retain full mobility during raids, for they need not set up fires and cook food for their cavalry."

He stared for a moment at the complicated design of the Persian carpet spread on the floor and added, "They never take the beaten tracks, but always find new means of approaching their destinations. They have already defeated the Jin Dynasty, devastated Persia and Transoxiana, attacked Kievan Rus, and now they are threatening Hungary and Poland. Magnificent civilizations of the East showed little resistance. It is as if they panicked and succumbed to the Mongols."

"What is the secret to their military success?" she asked.

"The Mongols are viciously patient as they await their prey like packs of hyenas outside the walls of a city which they have placed under siege, driving the inhabitants within to the border of starvation. They force the captured craftsmen from more sophisticated civilizations to build siege engines and other instruments of warfare on location. No merchant dares to enter or exit the city, knowing that they will be ruthlessly killed. Then they light their fires and wait there for weeks, setting up camp by the border walls. They do so with the patience of the hunter. And as they wait, the targeted city runs out of supplies, and the starving men and women inside lose their will to fight."

"I am concerned for Krisztina's safety. Is it wise to send her off to Kiev under these circumstances?" the queen asked. "I saw her speak with Mstislav, and I am not sure if she has any tender feelings for him. I suspect she agreed to the marriage out of a sense of duty. Even Mstislav seems more interested in an alliance with Poland than love or admiration for her."

"She will fare no better if she stays here. That woodworker's lad is likely to lure her into an unfortunate marriage or elopement which could be disastrous, not only for our reputation but her own prospects as well," he replied, pushing aside the goblet of red wine that he suddenly found distasteful.

"Is there any way that this confrontation can be avoided?" the queen asked. "From what you have told me, the Mongols already rule large parts of the world. Maybe through meeting some of their demands, we can avoid an all-out war."

Her husband moved toward her, caressed a few strands of her golden hair out of place and said, "There is a reason why women should stay out of politics."

The queen frowned but ignored the slight and asked, "There is something else bothering you. What is it?"

"Walking past the cathedral this morning, a stone rolled off the cupola and hit me hard on the head. What do you think it means?"

The queen, who looked concerned, opened her mouth to say something, but decided otherwise.

Chapter Five

The Raid

SUBUTAI BAHADUR HAD THE STATURE OF A BIRD OF PREY with long nails and sharp teeth. His voice sounded as if it came from the depths of the grave, husky but strangely feminine, like metal being sawed against its grain. He had piercing eyes, and his nose resembled a large beak. One could easily imagine him wearing feathers on his back and made to look like a vulture. Genghis Khan had entrusted Subutai with the strategies of war when he was young, and he now continued to plot invasions under the command of Genghis's progeny.

From his thin lips that at times opened to a ghastly wide grin, he uttered words that made others shiver. "To conquer Hungary," he said, addressing the Mongol commanders in their encampment, "we need to first subjugate Poland. Bulgaria as well will get to feel the sharp claws of the Mongols. The expeditionary force dispatched to Europe has brought back a treasure chest of information."

Strands of white hair stood out of his pointed helmet, the only sign that he was nearly sixty. "Our spies have been monitoring the Europeans. We know of their manners of fighting, their heavy armor, and their superstitious beliefs. They believe in magic, and magic is what we will bring to them in the form of smoke. We shall use gunpowder for that purpose and create a smoke barrier that would shield one army from another. If they succeed in joining forces against us, then we will use the smoke screen."

The Mongols had already crossed the Danube, sliding their way across the thick layer of ice on the river that had yet to melt. The traces on the ice rewrote human history as the warriors arrived at the gates of Europe.

The commanders were dead silent. Subutai's voice resonated within the ger. "To conquer the kingdom of Hungary, we must ensure that the Poles do not come to their aid. That would mean that we would have to divide the Mongol forces. One army would be sent to keep the Poles engaged during our attack against Pest." He moved to a map rolled out on a table, his armor screeched.

Subutai placed his forefinger where the lower reaches of Poland lay to show where the venue of attack should be. "Here is where we begin." He paused for a moment, turned toward the chief officers and added, "Europe is a land where division rules. Neither Poles nor the Bulgars nor the Germans nor the Hungarians get along. There is even division between the Papacy and the Roman Emperor, a rift that threatens to become an all-out war."

"Such news is music to my ears," Batu Khan, Jochi'powerful son and heir, replied. He intended to take part in the invasion of Hungary and had assigned to his older brother, Orda Khan, the task of conquering Poland.

Batu had a rather pleasing countenance. Just as ambitious as Subutai, he considered himself entitled to the wealth bestowed upon his father by Genghis. By annexing portions of Kievan Rus, Batu could now pursue his dream of establishing the Golden Horde, his own kingdom. The enmity that once existed between his father and Genghis's other sons had now infected him and his cousins. He had gone to Europe to prove his mettle, to show the world his worth in hopes of attaining the Mongol throne as the next Khaqan. Subutai, on the other hand, being a calculative, cunning strategist in this gamble called war, refused to take risks.

Although Ogodei had dispatched some Mongol princes to Europe, the Khaqan prioritized war with the Song Dynasty in China. Batu had thanked him for his lukewarm support but he kept the Mongol princes engaged at the borders of Rus, away from the main arena of war, so they would not get much credit for any victory.

"There are lush green lands to the west and north of Europe. Farther up, we can reach the Atlantic Ocean," Subutai said as the others stared at the unfamiliar terrain. The words he used sounded just as unfamiliar to the group that had gathered around the outstretched map. They did not know much about Europe or all the strange-sounding names Subutai uttered. They only trusted him as the war planner who had led so many missions victoriously.

"What is an Atlantic Ocean?" one of the officers asked.

"It is water as far as the eye can see and beyond it, the world ends," Subutai replied.

The imminence of war got Wiktor thinking in a new direction just days after Krisztina's rejection. The fog of pain and confusion in his mind was clearing up enough to renew his will to fight. He would probably mourn his loss for the rest of his life, but at least the intensity of pain would gradually subside. Wiktor began to think about the enemy, and he found the thought comforting. *What is the weakness of this group of very determined warriors? The Mongols have come from a cold climate, like that of Europe. They are fewer in number, but they have greater mobility and resolve.* With that thought, he closed his eyes for much-needed rest after many sleepless nights.

At midnight, he woke up with a jolt. "Rise, rise," his commander shouted. "The castle is under attack."

With fierce determination, Wiktor donned his suit of armor that consisted of a tunic and leggings of chain mail, as well as iron plates. He put a surcoat on top. Before wearing his head and neck gear, he wiped from his mind earlier thoughts of eternal unhappiness, drinking the potion of vengeance instead. Routing out the savages could become his salvation. It felt good to think about the Mongols, about the enemy. Maybe they too had loved ones who had cheated them. Maybe that's why they had come, fighting against tangible forces rather than dealing with complicated, intangible ones.

He would take his rage, unfulfilled hopes, fury at his dire destiny to his foes. He may have lost the love of his life, but they would not take away his beloved homeland. No man, no devil from another world would see their dream of ruling Poland come true. Rage gave him superhuman zeal, frustration strengthened his determination, the pain he had suffered made him feel immune to all ills and injustices, and thus he took part in the battle to save the castle. His audacity and gallantry strengthened the resolve of his compatriots. Once in full gear, they charged toward the castle, like an impenetrable wall of steel.

The faces and appearances of the Mongol warriors with their straight raven-black hair, large front teeth, wide nostrils, long mustaches that reached beyond their chins, and rough leather garments were unlike anything the Poles had seen before. The rumors were true: here indeed stood the army of Satan. Wiktor advanced firm and fearless.

From a safe distance, the Mongols propelled boulders at the castle after drenching them in naphtha and setting them on fire. Boulders smashed into the stone walls, and soon the entire structure was engulfed in flames. Occupants of the castle, aristocrats and laborers alike, fled to the farthest corners of a cellar down below. This route the High Duke had not disclosed to the fake ambassador. As they fled, they locked the multiple doors that were put in place long ago for their protection.

"The devils have brought dragons with them that spew fire and smoke from their mouths." A Teutonic knight spoke amid the crowd rushing toward the cellar, "Using that cover of smoke, they attacked us blindly, but knowing where each soldier stood prior to the dragon exhaling the fumes, they knew exactly where to hit and whence to dodge, but we knew not where they stood or when the dragon would strike us."

"May the devil strike them with infernal fire," another knight of the order of Templars spoke, making all heads turn in the direction of his voice. The two knights stood on top of a staircase protecting those seeking shelter down below. "I have found one of their bows. They bend their bows against its natural grain, giving it far superior strength than that of ours."

Wiktor's words put out the flames of superstition as he declared out loud, "There are no dragons. They have learned the art of these incendiaries from God knows where." Then whispered to himself, *the Mongols will regret this,* as they climbed from the back entrance of the castle, hidden from view, to reach the upper levels. He asked his comrades to bring as many pails of water as they could carry to put out the flames.

The Mongol warriors had entered the unknown territories as if blindfolded. They had to rely on their instincts to lead the way. At times, they were hindered by the thickening fog as they went on fighting in inclement weather, during a snowstorm or in torrential rain. However, only the fear of thunderstorms made every Mongol warrior tremble.

Earlier that day, Dark clouds like large gray whales had come together in the frenzy of a thunderstorm. In a sudden strike of lightning that the Europeans attributed to a blessing from heaven, and the Mongols to a sign that the spirit world was against them, the sky lit in jagged streaks of light and a roaring thunder announced a much-needed downpour. The incessant showers that followed put out the flames in no time.

A Mongol arrow targeted the heart of the Polish Commander. He fell several stories down and hit the stone pavement motionless. Wiktor instinctively took charge. He believed they had enough men to outnumber the cold-hearted and senseless enemy. He decided that they would open the gates of the castle and attack them head-on, realizing that in a long-distance confrontation, the Polish fighters were sure to be defeated. He led the men outdoors, leaving a small number to fight the remaining flames. In a twist to the conventional ways of war-making, he ordered his men to surround the enemy and attack from every angle. His chivalry urged the reluctant warriors to hold their ground.

His horse, wearing the cold, heavy armor, moved far slower than the agile steeds of the enemy. A metal shield covered the horse's face and a single metal horn placed between his ears made it look like a unicorn. Wiktor imagined it to be so. His steed could fly and strike such fears in the hearts of the barbarians that they would regret ever having set foot upon their land. He also imagined the man who had challenged him in love before him, and he fought like life didn't matter to him, and it didn't. He rushed into the enemy lines like a madman. He screamed at his foes, his voice loud, his determination unfaltering.

"This is my land," he cried, "and I will not tolerate invaders." As if saying, *this is my woman and no one else can have her.*

Colors blurred before his eyes as the glitter of shiny metals met leather, flesh, and bones. The combat so close, Mongols and Poles breathed the same air, both sides young, flags separating them as enemies, brave heart against brave heart.

Chapter Six

The Pond

AS THE RAIN SUBSIDED, A BLINDING SMOKE ROSE OVER the field. The scene disappeared in the mist. Here and there an arrow would pierce the thickening cloud, or a sword would slash a limb. Screams of pain followed, but to charge against the enemy was futile. The Mongols, on the other hand, knowing full well the location of each knight, attacked despite the fumes; their leather attire remaining almost unseen while that of their enemies glittered.

"All we have to do now is push them toward the Pond to achieve victory," Wiktor's voice rose. His men congregated around him upon hearing his voice, though they could not see him.

When the castle was constructed a century earlier, a thin layer of soil was spread on an unstable wooden surface that covered a neck ditch. The castle guards called this area, covered with grass, "The Pond." Everyone familiar with the environs of the castle knew to avoid it.

When a few of the Mongols attacking from the left flank staggered and fell into the ditch, the others realized a trap was set for them. The resumption of the lightning and thunder they feared more than anything signaled the warriors to retreat. A few of their bravest men remained fighting the Poles as the others fled.

Droplets of blood had splattered on Wiktor's shield. A lance had wounded the leg of his horse. War had taken its toll on his foes, but somehow, he did not feel victorious. With the battle over and the flames of the castle put out, Wiktor realized that the flames within him had not subsided. Victory against the foreign enemy had distracted him for a while but had not brought relief. The thirst for vengeance had prompted him to fight the Mongols with every ounce of his power. And now that the enemy had retreated, he had no other goals to pursue. He could not take revenge upon Krisztina, for he loved her too much, and the fact that she had betrayed him had not changed his devotion to her.

That evening Wiktor received Poland's greatest honor, and he was knighted. But there was no smile on his lips, no pride in his eyes, no gratification in his heart. Young, beautiful damsels in robe-like attires of imported Chinese silk, wearing the jewels of India and Persian perfumes, smiled at him, suggestively. But did he care? How could he ever trust a woman again? All he hoped for was to extricate himself from the castle. The monarch too regretted what he had done, for the lad he had belittled had now become the greatest hero in Poland.

Just like the night when the castle received the dignitaries from Kievan Rus, Krisztina played the lyre. Wiktor used to like the sound of her instrument. But that night, as she softly strummed the keys, it pained him to watch her fingers. She played beautifully as if pouring her emotions into every note. The guests at the reception were transfixed by the tantalizing melody. No one spoke or made a move until she struck the last chord. A few clapped. Then all rose in unison to give her a standing ovation.

When she looked up from her instrument, he gazed at her for only a moment then turned away, keeping his focus on the words of the High Duke. Wiktor noticed the tears in her eyes, yet he knew there was no turning back. They had lost each other forever. At the end of the royal speech in his honor, he left that intolerable scene for the chilly outdoors.

"I have abided by the rules of religion and chivalry," he cried out loud when he found himself alone upon the road that led away from the castle. "I have risked my life to save Christendom, but neither faith nor destiny have saved me from the bottomless pit into which I have fallen. We kill those who profess other faiths, even though their conviction in theirs is no less than our devotion to ours. Now that my hour of trial has come, I see more sympathy in my enemy's eyes than I do in the eyes that I have cherished more than my own life. My beloved has chosen another man for a mate, and thus my fate is sealed. My days have turned into nights, my nights into endless grief. I pick up my sword to slaughter the heathens, but I know not why. I sometimes wonder if they have a loved one who awaits their return, while I have no one to return to."

News of the Mongols' defeat spread like wildfire, and the following day a group gathered in the main square. Music and laughter could be heard for miles around. Town criers pronounced victory throughout the land and sounded special horns known as cornu as the glad tiding of triumph at war. The evil ones had fled. Poland was safe. Celebrations ensued. Strangers hugged one another like long lost relatives. People totally unrelated to each other danced together in joy.

"We have been spared," a man shouted. "The Horsemen of the Apocalypse have decided to return to their derelict homeland," shouted another man. A woman giggled as she tapped her feet on the floor, enticing the others to dance. A man dressed himself in Mongol costume, darkened his face with brown ink and riding a fake horse, took his bizarre act to the main square. The crowd stood gaping at the spectacle. People laughed and shouted obscenities at him, showering the fake foe with insults and ridicule.

Soon the sounds of jubilation turned into chants of victory as if Poland had won ultimate triumph over the Mongols. Instead of preparing for the forthcoming battles, crowds of people danced merrily, joyfully pirouetting to rhythmic tunes. They held hands and sang melodies that filled their hearts with pride and pleasure. In the midst of the ongoing revelry, people remained unaware that only a small contingent of the vast Mongol army had been deployed to wreak havoc at the castle, and the larger forces were approaching Legnica.

The white flags of Poland bearing large red crosses waved happily in the wind upon every rooftop. But one man remained aloof; one man to whom Poland owed its temporary triumph. Wiktor, returned with a heavy heart to his lonely abode, a small cottage not far from the castle. Krisztina's eyes haunted him still, her voice remained in his ears, and his heart ached for her even more so when he saw others rejoicing in the streets. As bells tolled victory in Poland, Krisztina was carried off by Prince Mstislav to a land under siege by the Mongols.

Chapter Seven

The Prisoner

AS REYHAN REACHED FOR HER QUILL PEN, SHE HEARD A knock. "Come in," she said without turning, expecting one of her chambermaids. It surprised her to see Baako at the door. He was now an old man, and the snow of age had settled upon his once black curls.

"I need to speak with you, my lady," he said as he entered, and Reyhan offered him a seat. "There is a woman among the prisoners of war brought here from Europe. Her hair is the color of autumn leaves drenched in the rays of the sun and her eyes like a cloudless morning sky."

Long familiar with the flowery language of Baako, Reyhan asked, "Do you know where exactly in Europe she came from?"

"No, but her clothing of silk and hand-woven lace, the color of ripe persimmons, is stained in parts and torn in others, yet; the quality of her attire bespeaks her royal lineage. Her appearance shows marks of the treacherous treatment she has suffered during her journey, and they have placed her in chains."

"Were you able to talk to her to learn more about her circumstances?"

"No, my lady, I do not know her language, and neither does she mine, though she knows that I am a slave as she is now. I asked the woman from the territories of the Rus... what is her name, the one who said she owned an eatery there and is now a cook in the Mongol court?"

"You mean Shura?" Reyhan asked.

"Yes. She was able to speak with her, for the poor girl is partially familiar with that tongue."

"I will ask Hulagu to release her from bondage. He is the only one among us whose words the prison guards abide by. Oh, and bring Shura here. I need to speak with her."

Baako lingered by the door. When Reyhan looked at him inquiringly, he said, "I am afraid there is another unfortunate matter, my lady. The Grand Duke of Kiev and his companions were killed by the Mongols in a bloodless fashion, supposedly honoring their rank in society. The victorious Mongols placed the wooden door of the castle over the handcuffed noblemen and crushed them to death as the Mongol officers feasted upon the door, using it as a makeshift table. Sometimes one wishes for a bloody death."

Unable to hear more, Reyhan raised her hand in a gesture to stop Baako from providing further details. Baako left but quickly returned accompanied by Shura who lost no time in explaining the condition of the prisoner.

"Her name is Krisztina, Madam. She asked me where *the hell*, pardon my language, Madam, I am just quoting, *where the hell is this place they have brought me to*. I told her it was Mongolia and that she should be very respectful when referring to that name. I also reminded her that she needs to bow before Mongol officers and dignitaries. And what does she do? She gave me the dirtiest look that anyone ever gave me."

"Did she say anything about her family or where she came from?"

"Yes, indeed the girl is the niece of some king in Poland betrothed to Prince Mas . . . Mastis . . . Mstislav of Kiev. As she left Poland for Kievan Rus, sitting next to her betrothed in a carriage with her younger sister accompanying them, a unit of Mongol cavalrymen attacked them, taking her prisoner." Shura added that she had learned the particulars of Krisztina's abduction from Mongol warriors returning from the fronts.

"Mongols attempted to steal away the girl's younger sister as well, who was but a child of no more than thirteen," Shura continued," but the valiant Kievan Prince, as is the tradition among all men from my part of the world, drew his sword to save the child."

Shura seemed too overwhelmed to concentrate.

"*Did* he save the child?" Reyhan asked.

"O' Madam, they ended up killing the Kievan Prince, and unfortunately the young girl got killed during the scuffle. The older sister, meaning the prisoner, did not see the fight for she was carried away before it happened."

"Have you disclosed anything to Krisztina about the fate of her sister and her betrothed?" Reyhan asked, some part of her reliving how she herself was ripped away from her family.

"No, Madam; I was not sure whether I should tell her in her state of distress."

"Please do inform her that Prince Mstislav no longer lives but spare her the gruesome details. Also, do keep the news of her sister's death from her. It is too much at once. Anyway, that matter can be brought to her attention when she is stronger and can bear the sad news." She paused. "Tell her that her younger sister had a chance to flee the scene."

Reyhan spared not a moment after her conversation with Shura. She wrapped a shawl around her shoulders and hurried toward Hulagu's residence. The Mongol Prince, surprised to see Reyhan flustered, asked her the cause.

"There is a young European woman among the prisoners," Reyhan explained. "I implore you to seek her release immediately. God knows what will happen to her if you don't. I fear she would be abused by the guards if there is a delay in setting her free. She has been fettered but appears to be from a royal court in Europe. It is easy to identify her among the other Rus captives. There is also an elderly woman brought here from the territories of Rus by the name of Shura who has been employed as a cook. She can be of assistance as a translator."

Krisztina's heart began to pound when one of the guards pointed to her and gestured that she should accompany him. During the journey, it had occurred to her to begin loud, repetitious recitations of this verse from the Bible in Latin, "Be strong and courageous. Do not be afraid or terrified because of them, for the Lord your God goes with you; He will never leave you nor forsake you." The Mongols must have assumed the words to be a witch's spell. Therefore, probably fearing that she might turn them into rodents, they let her be.

Krisztina's wrists and ankles were in pain from the shackles placed on them. Her mouth felt dry. Ringlets of hair stuck to her sweat-drenched forehead. She could barely stand and didn't know how much longer she would be able to bear her captivity. She had had little water to drink, and the food was almost unbearable. So, she had gone mostly without for many days since her capture. A thought that she was too young to die kept her alive during this time of great ordeal. She had no idea what became of Prince Mstislav or her poor sister. She had a feeling that Mstislav was killed, but she kept assuring herself that somehow her sister survived. She could not bear the thought of something bad happening to little Zofia.

The guard led her to an opening where a high-ranking Mongol, whom she thought was possibly a prince, judging from his attire, stood. He looked handsome with rather delicate features compared to the other Mongol warriors she had seen thus far, his brown hair visible under the feathered metal helmet he wore, his eyes kind and respectful. He smiled at her for a moment before he began to issue orders in a tongue unfamiliar to Krisztina. Immediately the guards unchained her. The stout Rus woman Krisztina had spoken with earlier was by his side and assured her that she would be safe.

"This is Prince Hulagu," the woman said, "grandson of Genghis Khan." Krisztina had heard that name before, but the image she had in her mind was that of a barbarian, not the handsome man standing in the deportment of royalty before her. She gestured to Krisztina to bow before the Prince. Hulagu waved the curtsy to be unnecessary and moved toward her, holding out his hand instead. The kindness he showed toward her, the strength that emanated from him, and the sense of safety after the long journey melted all of Krisztina's resolve, and she fainted into his arms.

When she finally opened her eyes, she found herself on a soft bed in a palatial chamber. Two eyes, the color of honey, were watching over her. She could not understand the language of the middle-aged woman who was addressing her, but through Shura, she learned that those eyes belonged to a Persian Princess by the name of Reyhan.

Reyhan had a beauty that age could not erase, and one could see that her charms had no rival in her younger days. Through Shura, Reyhan informed Krisztina that until her full recovery she would remain under her care. Krisztina smiled politely to acknowledge her appreciation, but soon tears began to fill her eyes. Choking on her words, she asked about her companions, mostly her sister.

"Prince Mstislav fought bravely to save your sister and during the battle with the Mongols, unfortunately, he lost his life. Your sister, from what we have learned, ran away during the skirmish—that is as much as we know," Reyhan said and Shura translated.

"I knew it. My little sister, my beautiful Zofia is alive," Krisztina said tearfully.

Reyhan noticed that Krisztina did not mention the late Prince to whom she had been betrothed and did not appear to lament his loss. She asked Shura to bring them some tea, then sat beside Krisztina and held her hand.

Chapter Eight

"The World" Comes to the Mongol Court

EARLY THE NEXT MORNING KRISZTINA WOKE UP TO THE sound of Mongols chasing after their horses to feed them and harness them. The goats and sheep were bleating, which mingled with the strange tongue the Mongols spoke. She heard the neighing of a horse and rose to look out the window. How strange, she thought, even their horses look different. They were rather short and stocky with large heads and long, thick tails and manes. This was such a different world, and she knew adapting to it would not be easy. Shura helped her bathe and gave her fresh clothing. The Rus woman had also prepared some borscht that she ate with great appetite.

Krisztina felt like driftwood carried by the waves of the sea to an unknown shore, yet, she believed that somehow the angels looked after her. How else could she have survived the ordeal of being taken as a prisoner of war? And that prince, Hulagu, would she see him again? Would it be inappropriate to ask Reyhan about him? It was almost a miracle that she was placed under Reyhan's care. Shura had explained how Reyhan had been abducted from Persia and brought to the Mongol court which made them both victims of conquest. So much sincerity and wisdom shone in Reyhan's eyes, and she displayed such a caring attitude that almost from the moment they met, Krisztina felt that she could trust Reyhan.

The following morning, Krisztina had recovered enough to go for a walk in the garden and see the other palaces as well. Magnificent works of art hung on their stately walls, but they were not to her taste. Trophies from different parts of the world were mounted together and lacked coherence. Different paintings and ornamental objects from Chinese calligraphy to Persian works of miniature were juxtaposed randomly as if by people who could not make up their minds which art they liked best. Despite the vastness of the palatial structures occupied by different Mongol dignitaries, Krisztina found their enclosures claustrophobic.

In the center of Karakorum, she was surprised to see a church, a mosque and a number of Buddhist temples standing in close proximity near the marketplace. She returned to Reyhan's palace, excitedly describing to her friend, with Shura's help, the existence of a church in Karakorum. She added that she was shocked to see a mosque right next to it.

"Here in Mongol territories, all are free to worship as they please so long as they abide by Yasa laws."

"What are they?"

"They are rules devised by the late Genghis Khan. There are aspects to them that make sense and others that make no sense at all, but we have to abide by them nonetheless. I will explain them to you one of these days."

Unlike the other palaces Krisztina had visited on that day, Reyhan's was well-lit and inviting, filled with the scent of roses. They both enjoyed engaging in conversations during which Shura acted as translator. They all laughed when she struggled with words she could not clearly pronounce. One time, Reyhan explained her interest in the Mohammaden flower known by the Crusaders who had carried it from Asia to Europe as the Damask Rose.

"Mohama . . . Mohamma . . ." Shura murmured but could get no further.

Reyhan intervened, saying, "Gole Mohammadi." She also took a stem of the heavenly scented pink flower out of a vase for Krisztina to inhale its aroma.

On another occasion, Reyhan brought five rolls of fine silk in yellow, red, blue, green and purple, and Shura tried to explain that tailors at the court could make them into dresses for Krisztina in any design.

"The Persians call the fabric Abrish," Shura said, looking lost.

"Abrisham," Reyhan corrected her, holding the blue one next to the European Princess's face, and expressed her surprise at how the color of Krisztina's eyes almost instantaneously turned darker like the fabric.

"Abrisham," Krisztina repeated in flawless Persian to the delight of Reyhan.

Within a few weeks, Krisztina and Reyhan no longer needed Shura to be present as they learned to communicate with each other in Persian, first clumsily and then more comfortably. The Mongols, in general, did not speak the language, and that gave them greater freedom in their discourse.

Hulagu began visiting Krisztina almost every day. He brought gifts of food and pastry. When she went for walks in the garden, he asked to accompany her.

Festive events took place at the Mongol court on a regular basis, honoring outstanding warriors, celebrating victories in distant lands, or displaying Mongol wealth to foreign dignitaries. The Mongols could now afford to wear a different color of silk for each event. Krisztina could choose from all the silk fabrics her heart desired and choose she did, but her gowns were made in the European style.

Everywhere she went, Kirsztina could sense Hulagu watching her. Every time she turned, he would be behind her, or a few feet away. He seemed conscious of her movements, of the way she spoke, of the way she laughed and particularly of the way she looked at him. Although the Mongol women of the court were extremely beautiful, Krisztina looked exotic. Seeing Hulagu looking so timidly at her, considering his status as one of the most powerful men on earth, excited her imagination. Every time their eyes met, she blushed.

One morning when the two of them were out on a leisurely walk, Hulagu told Krisztina that he was very much in love with her and expressed his desire to marry her.

Krisztina wanted Reyhan to be the first person to hear the news of Hulagu's proposal but said that she was more anxious than happy.

"I don't know if it is destiny that leads me or my own obstinate soul, but I find myself always led to the edge of the cliff that separates what is stable and clear from that which is elusive and unpredictable," Krisztina confided.

"What exactly do you mean?" Reyhan asked, perplexed.

"Oh, Reyhan so much has happened in so short a time. The tumultuous winds that carry me from one part of the world to another leave me confused."

She told Reyhan the story of Wiktor and how they were parted. Then added, "I was led away by Mstislav, a man I hardly knew and little cared for, toward Kiev when he was killed so tragically. Here I am now facing the prospect of marrying the grandson of Genghis Khan, and I fear that even this path will not lead to the green pasture of bliss."

"There are aspects of life that are ordained by Providence, your destiny, you cannot change or alter. But there is also the willpower granted to you as a human being that allows you to resist what you see as wrong and embrace that which is proper and right," Reyhan said.

"I left Wiktor because my uncle would have otherwise disinterited me, leaving me in poverty and misery, and now it is as if I am marrying Hulagu for riches and status, but that is not really the case."

"I think you are obsessing too much about matters that are completely out of your hands. Come now! Let us see what type of gown you would like to wear on the day of your wedding ceremony."

"Can I tell you a secret that I wish you never repeat upon all that is holy to you?" Krisztina asked.

"Of course you can trust me as I have trusted you from the moment Hulagu brought you to my palace."

"O' Reyhan, I like Hulagu... but he has such an overpowering personality that at times... how can I say this? I fear him."

Reyhan walked up to her and tied the ribbon under Krisztina's bonnet that had come loose and said, "Mongols do create such a sensation. No wonder the world has succumbed to their audacity and power so easily. Look at it this way, by being his wife and soulmate you will be sharing that power."

With the arrival of summer, Reyhan wrote a note to Sorkhokhtani inviting her to Karakorum. She worried that the news of Hulagu's growing attachment to Krisztina would reach Sorkhokhtani before she had a chance to explain the circumstances. Although it seemed prudent for Hulagu's mother to be informed of his romantic interest as soon as possible, Reyhan felt a bit nervous for being the undesignated match-maker. She had been struggling for days with the idea of how to present the facts to Sorkhokhtani, without exposing herself and Krisztina to the wrath of the powerful Mongol Queen.

When Sorkhokhtani arrived, Reyhan's nervousness rose to a fever pitch. Hulagu's mother straightened her skirt as Reyhan poured tea out of a china pot for two. Reyhan's hands shook a little as she tried to use the right words, convincing the Mongol Queen that her meddling in her son's life was justified.

"There was a woman of regal stature among the prisoners of war brought here from Europe," Reyhan said as soon as they both sat, facing each other in her parlor. "Everything about her indicated her royal birth, and we later learned that she is indeed the niece of Henry the Pious of Poland who recently died in the Battle of Legnica. Of course, we have kept that information from her and will disclose it in due time, when she is stronger."

She paused and then continued, "When I first met her, her constitution revealed the hardships she had endured. She possesses a beauty that is rare in these parts with hair the color of gold, and eyes the color of the sky. I asked Hulagu to release the princess from captivity and allow her to stay at my palace."

"Well, it probably did not take long for my sky-worshiping son to fall in love with those blue eyes," the shrewd Mongol Queen replied as if she had read Reyhan's mind.

"O, Khatun," Reyhan said, addressing her apologetically and using the Mongol epithet for my lady, "I am afraid that has been the case. Her name is Krisztina, but Shura calls her by the Rus name, Dounia.

I love that name for it means "the world" in my language. We all call her Princess Dounia now. She is quite young and impressionable. She does share your faith in Christianity, and I am sure she will learn the customs of the Mongols by your grace," she said, hoping those words would erase the lines of doubt from Sorkhokhtani's face.

"From what you tell me it appears that Dounia is here against her own will, launched into a totally different culture, and left with no choice but to marry a man she hardly knows. Hulagu, we both know, can be a difficult person to get along with."

"Well, as a female prisoner of war, Dounia could either marry a Mongol prince or wrestle with the serfs over who should be doing the laundry," Reyhan remarked with more sarcasm than she intended, and then reminded herself that Sorkhokhtani had nothing to do with the misfortunes that plagued her own marriage to Ogodei. She then added, "Hulagu is tough on the serfs and on prisoners of war, but he has never been disrespectful to any of us," Reyhan said in Hulagu's defense.

"Remember the time when I thought I had lost the turquoise talisman that belonged to Hulagu's great grandmother. He acted like the world had come to an end. Storming out of my chamber, he went riding on his stallion with such fury that I thought he would never return to Karakorum. Moments later, I found the necklace tucked under a cushion. It had fallen when I had dozed off. I think I will give it to Dounia as a gift, to connect with his ancestry."

Reyhan took that remark as her consent and smiled.

"What do you know about Dounia's background?" Sorkhokhtani asked in a challenging tone.

"The Polish Princess was betrothed for a short period of time to a cousin of the Grand Duke of Kiev before he was killed, and she was brought here," Reyhan said matter-of-factly, knowing the futility of hiding anything from the Mongol royals.

"How does she feel about Hulagu?" Sorkhokhtani asked, still looking concerned.

"She has consented to the marriage, although I am not sure about her true feelings. Hulagu professes that he loves her. I told him to respect and honor her. He said Dounia is a Christian *just like my mother.*

I asked him whether *he* is a Christian. He said he is a mere politician without religious binds."

Sorkhokhtani laughed at that remark and said, "Well my other politician son, Kublai, seems to have completely lost his mind. He cuts up paper in different sizes, places his stamp upon them, calling them paper money. He even says, and he could be just jesting, that he would put to death anyone who claims that this is not the real thing.

"Oh, and there is this Roman who has come to the court of Kublai," Sorkhokhtani added as if she suddenly recalled the name, "calls himself Marco Polo. He is neither a warrior nor a merchant and insists that he just likes to journey the world to *see* things. Can you imagine that!"

With Sorkhokhtani's blessing, a date was set for Hulagu and Dounia to be married. The wedding took place at Amgalan Palace with rows of flowers greeting the guests. Hulagu and Dounia recited their vows before a Christian priest and a shaman blessed them as well. A teary-eyed Reyhan and an equally teary-eyed Sorkhokhtani were among the witnesses. Too overjoyed to express any other emotion, Reyhan and Sorkhokhtani kept wiping their eyes as they watched Hulagu's union with Dounia.

A tiara of flowers sat instead of a bejeweled crown on the beautiful bride's lace covered head. She was wearing the turquoise necklace Sorkhokhtani had given her. Dressed in white silk because she had refused to wear the traditional Mongolian bridal gown, Dounia looked teary-eyed too. She may have been overwhelmed by the beauty of the ceremony or she may have been thinking of Wiktor and how she had lost him. She never spoke of it, not even to Reyhan.

Hulagu kissed Dounia on both cheeks as a sign of his devotion to her. The newlyweds then mounted a flower-strewn carriage in front of an ululating crowd of admirers. Reyhan tossed sugar-covered bits of almonds and rose petals at them in accordance with Persian tradition, and they rode away to their designated bridal ger in the Mongol landscape.

Chapter Nine

The Runaway

KRISZTINA HAD READILY ACCEPTED HER NEW NAME. SHE knew Reyhan loved calling her Dounia, yet, in her heart, she could not easily forgo her Christian name and promised herself to use the name Krisztina if she ever got a chance to write letters. She considered Hulagu's attempts to charm his way into her heart as temporary relief for her troubled mind, for she still saw herself as a captive. She felt trapped by an unfamiliar, alien culture; a culture that did not understand her or her beliefs. She appreciated the fact that Hulagu had rescued her from a far more degrading course, but still could not bring herself to adapt to Mongol ways. She felt homesick and doomed to bondage, married or not.

With the consummation of their marriage, Hulagu seemed for a time fulfilled, but Dounia was left in utter confusion, playing the role of a Mongol Princess and wife to Genghis Khan's grandson without a sense of belonging. The only moments of respite came when she was riding her horse in the grasslands; the vast prairie surrounding their palace calling her to run away. It was like a living being, a creature of God. How foolish she had been to have left Wiktor, her true knight, cowed by her uncle's command: By that one act, her destiny had formed in ways totally incomprehensible.

The almost always blue, cloudless Mongolian sky felt like a painted prison ceiling to her. She missed the fog of Europe, the misty weather, the mild temperatures, the grape-shaped flowers of the wisteria trees planted along the stone wall of her uncle's castle. They were the envy of other European royals when they bloomed in spring. Most of all, she missed Zofia. Homesickness and the rough environment of the Steppes finally got the better of her, and she found herself utterly wretched.

It had barely been three months since the wedding ceremony that united Dounia and Hulagu when she burst into Reyhan's Palace one afternoon, declaring openly, "Confound this life . . ."

Reyhan quickly looked around to see if there were any chambermaids present. When assured that there were none, she put a hand over Dounia's mouth and urged her to come into her private chamber. Hulagu had left for the fronts, but if he learned of such an outburst, his own temper could flare.

"Such language," Reyhan said, "could cost you your life."

"I miss home," Dounia uttered before she could stop herself. She told Reyhan of the chess games she used to play with her uncle on days without event—she had not even these at her disposal now. "I don't dislike Hulagu. He has been kind to me. But now my existence is like the chessboard, and I feel like life has checkmated me. Whichever way I turn, there is a roadblock, an emotional trap, no answer. I can't live like this Reyhan. How do you bear it? How can you act like nothing has happened? We are virtually enslaved by these Mongols."

She walked toward the window to look outside, and then abruptly turned, adding, "The other day, I asked Hulagu to accompany him when he travels to Transoxiana to meet the local administrators there. He refused. My opinions don't count, and my needs do not matter to him. I was too fearful to pursue the matter further, so I let it go."

Reyhan sighed. "Living with the Mongols is like living on the edge of a cliff," she said sympathetically. "One never knows when one will become the subject of their wrath. Patience and prudence are the keys to your survival. And isn't that what life is all about, to face and overcome the challenges of this world?"

"I find the Mongol court insufferable," Dounia uttered with frustration. "Their customs, their lifestyle, their language and their habits are all anomalies to me."

"But what exactly do you propose we do? Their destructive forces have been unleashed upon mankind, and there is no escaping for anyone. Persia and Transoxiana are under Mongol control as are the Chinese territories of Jin and Song Dynasties. Life is not easy for the inhabitants of those lands, but at least here we are considered royals. We want for nothing."

"I miss home, Reyhan, I miss my family. I cannot say that I resent Hulagu in any way, but the idea of living in the confines of Mongol palaces is an agony," she pleaded.

"And what are you going to do about it?" Reyhan asked.

"I don't know about you, but I plan to run away. Even nature is unbearable here. Storms rip through the skies, threatening the earth with bolts of lightning; that awful cold wind that blows once in a while freezes your bones, and hail pummels the lands. You saw how the lightning almost killed us when we went for a walk yesterday. And then there is the attitude of superiority of the female courtiers. They pass me by without acknowledging me as if I am inferior to them. I miss home."

"The world is not the same as before. It is the domain of the Mongols. Their rule stretches across the civilized nations from Korea to Kiev," Reyhan said.

"Hulagu has been kind and compassionate toward me, but he never is and never will be my soulmate. The best Hulagu could do for me is to treat me like a pet, like a dove kept for the sole entertainment of the master. I was left with no choice but to accept him and before him, Mstislav. Had I not accepted Mstislav and decided instead to marry my first suitor, Wiktor, my uncle would have disowned me."

Dounia had throughout her young life upheld the Polish court view that commoners are commoners and royals are royals. But it had been different with Wiktor. Wiktor was a friend she had grown up and fallen in love with. He overlooked her shortcomings and ignored her tantrums when she could not deal with matters that contradicted her wishes. Now she had other vexations. The fact that Mongol courtiers considered themselves superior to her annoyed her, as did Hulagu's constant engagements abroad, fighting one war or another.

Reyhan ordered tea and used soothing words, but Dounia still felt uneasy when she finally departed to return to her quarters. As she walked away from Reyhan's Palace toward Hulagu's, she stared at the nearly endless stretch of grassland and the distant hills before her. How it would have felt to run away to the wilderness where no one could find her, to live like the primitive people had lived, and to feed upon the fruits of the earth?

Although the night was soon to cast its dark shadow, she decided to take her horse for a ride. At dusk, Karakorum was almost picturesque. Dounia took note of the candles that were lit upon every alcove and recess in its stone walls. The streets were illuminated in a way that reminded her of Poland. The air was a bit cold, but she didn't mind. The horses were agitated and kept neighing in distress, a sign that a storm was brewing. She ignored them as if in a trance and walked toward the barn that held her favorite mare, a palomino not unlike the Konik horses of Poland. Mounting it, she felt more powerful, more determined than ever to leave the Steppes.

Dounia still tried to calculate her days according to the Gregorian calendar. The Chinese calendar used by the Mongols, which associated animals with different years, continued to be alien to her. For Dounia, this was another day in September; she didn't know exactly which one. The tall larch trees planted in Karakorum swayed right and left as the wind swept their branches in one direction or another. She recalled the earlier warning by Mongol shepherds that a violent windstorm was brewing, but she was too depressed to worry about it.

At the bend of the river, when Dounia's mind was fully absorbed by the ever-flowing motion of the water, her horse stumbled on a small boulder and fell over, toppling its rider to the ground. She knew the moment she fell off the horse that the poor animal had broken a leg. The mare moaned gently and fell unconscious. Her own hair tangled in a thistle bush, one foot under the weight of the horse and her skirt caught in some thorny web, it took her a while to free herself and be able to stand up. She felt for the horse's pulse; it was still alive. By the time she realized this, the cold winds had begun to blow so fiercely that forward movement became impossible. The cold combined with the fear of the peril she now faced, forced her to start thinking of a way out.

The high chorus of crickets began to grow louder and more ominous as the clouds became denser and darker. In due course, the night also placed its heavy lid of obscurity on the land, quelling all hopes of a rescue. With lagging steps, she threaded the prairie for a while, dazed by what happened. She rested her back against the bulky trunk of a nearby tree in utter misery and dropped to the ground in exhaustion, thinking that she would surely become prey to some wild animal.

Showers of hail began to beat against her body as the skies bombarded the earth with pebble-sized balls of ice. Heavy rainfall followed with its frozen droplets as cold as the earlier downpour. Before succumbing to the shock of the incident and the bone-chilling cold, she heard herself scream, shattering the silence of the night.

Chapter Ten

Black Leeches

BAAKO HEARD AN UNEARTHLY CRY FROM THE GRAY plains beyond Karakorum.

"Ogul, wake up, we have to go." Baako anxiously watched the Turkish man turn over in his sleep.

Ogul, the carpenter that the Mongols had brought with them from Anatolia, shared a small ger with Baako. A large piece of felt cloth kept their two chambers separated. In addition to a pillow and a blanket, they each had a mattress stuffed with sheep's wool that they treasured. The ger was set up on the outskirts of Karakorum. The carpenter's family still lived in Anatolia, and he sent them money with the caravans that headed that way, but he seldom talked about them, and never showed any signs that he actually missed them. He kept to himself most of the time and the two ger-mates rarely communicated with each other. On that fateful night, Ogul was deep in sleep.

"I can hear it again. Its a woman's cry," Baako said. "Grab a lantern."

"It sounds like a wounded doe," Ogul said, reluctant to rise up.

"It's a woman. I am sure of it. Grab a lantern. We have to hurry before it's too late and the wolves get to her first."

After walking about two thousand paces, they located the injured horse, and not far from where the poor animal lay, they found the unconscious woman. By the time they brought her to Reyhan's quarters, Dounia's frail body was shaking uncontrollably.

"She must have been trying to escape," Ogul said, "for no one would go for a ride at night in the midst of a storm." They had woken up Reyhan and were all gathered in her parlor.

Reyhan gave Ogul a stern, meaningful look. "Not a word of this to anyone. Baako, you spread the news that Dounia has come down with consumption and will remain under my care."

Although the Mongols had constructed a more sedentary station in Karakorum, their nomadic spirit still yearned for the cozy comfort of gers. Therefore, in addition to palatial structures that could house all, members of the Mongol nobility, including Sorkhokhtani, had their private gers.

Fearing that Dounia might speak of her desire to leave to Hulagu's servants, Reyhan nursed Dounia in Sorkhokhtani's ger. Sorkhokhtani was staying in Amgalan Palace and did not mind at all. Her ger held every bit of creature comfort a woman in those days desired. In addition to a large bed, it contained a Chinese black lacquered table with a mirror. On it stood a container of talcum powder and scented oils as well as kohl in a tiny silver jar that could be used as eyeliner. There were several combs and brushes, robes of silk to be worn over cotton nightgowns hung on a rope in a corner, and a number of soft fur-lined house shoes were placed right underneath.

The following evening, Reyhan found Dounia in a fit of high fever. She rushed to the clay pot of water they kept nearby with her handkerchief, soaked and placed it on the patient's forehead. Dounia spoke incoherently of seeing silhouettes of horses galloping toward Europe, crushing everything under their hooves. She kept asking for her parents, her sister and for the people that she had left behind. Reyhan hugged her fever-stricken head, patting her wet hair that had turned the color of molten gold from excessive sweat. "My dear, my dear Dounia, you cannot leave us now."

Fearful that her ward might not have long to live, Reyhan rushed out to a nearby ger, alerting the occupants and requesting the court physician. She then returned breathless to her nursing duties.

"It is consumption." The Chinese physician who had hurried to the ger, still in his house robe, looked grim. "I only have one remedy to try." He then reached for a jar of leeches in his timeworn medical bag. Dounia looked up at Reyhan with lusterless eyes while the latter stared with horror as the physician placed black leeches on Dounia's pale skin.

With the nature of Dounia's illness established, the physician left an herbal potion with Reyhan to bring both the patient's fever down and allow her to sleep. As he had directed, she mixed the potion with hot water and allowed it to seep for several minutes, then poured the concoction into a glass teacup. The smell of medicinal herbs filled the ger.

Dounia kept tossing and turning every which way in her delirium, but once the fever subsided, Reyhan was able to put a spoon of the brew to her pale lips. Dounia took a sip and said it tasted bitter and sweet at the same time, and she had to force herself to swallow the medicine. Yet, her eyes that remained fixed on Reyhan's concerned countenance showed her appreciation.

Dounia soon fell asleep, her head resting on soft pillows. Reyhan turned with a sigh to find Sorkhokhtani at the entry to the ger. "We need to speak," she said. The two women stepped away from the ger and walked a few paces on the stone pathway that led to the Amgalan Palace.

"Dounia will die if she is not reunited with her relatives in Poland," Reyhan said.

"Why do you say that?" Sorkhokhtani asked.

"Dounia's constitution is not fit for this environment. Is there any way we can arrange for her safe return to her homeland?" Reyhan pleaded.

"But she is Hulagu's wife," Sorkhokhtani objected.

"She will be a wife to no one but the Angel of Death if her illness persists," Reyhan replied. "They have captured the girl and brought her to this land, little heeding the fact that humans are perishable beings."

"I am afraid no one can enter the European continent at this time," Sorkhokhtani said with compassion in her eyes, "for the black plague has spread among the inhabitants. People are dying in droves. Her return to Europe would spell her death as well; no one is immune."

Reyhan saw no other means but to personally go to the kitchen each day to supervise and ensure the quality and cleanliness of the food being prepared for the invalid. Herbs and vegetables had to be thoroughly washed and meats cooked for hours.

When Reyhan was not fussing about food and tea, she ordered Dounia's cotton sheets and clothing to be frequently changed. She took time to braid Dounia's golden tresses after Shura washed her hair. Reyhan's loving care and tireless efforts were not in vain, for Dounia's health began to improve within a fortnight. Her pale cheeks turned pink, and the old glimmer returned to her eyes.

Hulagu learned of his wife's illness and subsequent recovery halfway through his journey back from the fronts. He ordered an assortment of teas from China, honey from Transoxiana, and pistachios and almonds from Persia to be brought to Karakorum via the Silk Road. Under Reyhan's supervision, the almonds were then double peeled and laid in fresh jasmine flowers for days to absorb the magnificent aroma. Extracts of rosewater, fresh pistachios, and fragrant saffron were then added as ingredients to make dainty Persian cookies. A magnificent tea was thus prepared and carried to Dounia's chamber.

On warmer days, Reyhan had a chair set up in the garden where she covered Dounia with blankets and told her stories from the "*Book of Kings*." Before long Dounia was on horseback again, galloping as she used to do in nearby fields, riding her favorite mare whose leg had healed. With Dounia's recovery, however, her longing for her homeland returned.

It was a beautiful afternoon in early spring. The fields were covered in an array of purple, blue and yellow wildflowers. Fresh grass had grown where the earth had been frozen before. The sun melted among chunks of clouds. On that morning Dounia sat on her bed, sipping her tea. Reyhan waited with her for Hulagu's arrival from the fronts.

"I appreciate all you and Hulagu have done for me. Yet, I would be deceiving myself if I said my life had a purpose here. I am aware only of stagnancy."

Reyhan remained silent, inwardly impressed at Dounia's philosophizing after what she had been through. She only said, "I understand how you feel."

"There are those of us who live and those of us who just wait." Dounia complained, "Wait for opportunities. Wait for change. We go about our daily routines. We try to engage with others. We laugh when others laugh and cry when they do. But we are always waiting, never really living. Some like us are captives. Some enslaved in other ways; by their own souls, by their own lack of confidence, and by their own fears."

"Overcoming those fears and facing challenges is our lot as women," Reyhan replied. And then finding this an opportune moment she added, "Running away or defying the Mongols will not help at this time. Chaka tried the same thing, and it cost her, her life."

"Who is Chaka?" Dounia asked, her eyes brightening with curiosity.

"She was the first princess to be brought to the Mongol Court through an arranged marriage. She became Genghis's advisor and remained devoted to him until he killed her with his dagger. One mistake on her part led to her death."

"What was that mistake?'

"She maintained her ties to her family despite strict orders by Genghis not to do so."

"How do you know all of this? Did you meet her?"

"There is a secret manuscript which is now in my possession. Chaka recorded the events of her time like a historian and kept it hidden from the Mongols."

Dounia looked amazed. "Where is this record?"

"I have tried to continue that tradition; not even Sorkhokhtani is aware of this endeavor. The manuscript is to remain hidden until future generations discover it and learn from its lessons."

"Can I see it?" Dounia asked.

"I am aging Dounia, and the hardships I have endured throughout the years have taken their toll on me. From the moment I stepped foot in Mongolia, I searched for a cause that would give meaning to my life. I did not want to spend my time with fruitless thoughts and reminiscences. When I came across this manuscript, I knew I had found that purpose, that mission. I entrust you with it, and I beg you to do your utmost in its safekeeping. The only person other than myself and now you who is aware of its existence is Baako. He was the one who brought information from the war fronts to me."

Noticing that Dounia's mind was working in a new direction, Reyhan added, "Oh, and there is another thing I want you to keep in mind. Wealth and fortune have their privileges, and you happen to be married to one of the wealthiest men on earth. Like the alchemist, whatever Hulagu touches turn into gold."

Entry by Krisztina:

> *I am holding a manuscript in my hand that contains the secrets of the women who were brought to the Mongol court before me. Its leather cover is a bit worn out, and the pages are turning dark yellow around the edges. I find it quite intriguing that I am given an opportunity to convey my side of the story. It was almost instant relief from that dark sense of melancholy and lack of purpose that had plagued me for almost a year. This manuscript and the idea of sharing my life story with others have uplifted my spirit, and so I begin my entries.*
>
> *The people of the Steppes live in their stretch of grassland occasionally interrupted by mountain ranges and barriers of hills, isolated from many other nations. Rivers snake through this grassland and rocks cover the Gobi Desert in the south. As the Mongols conquered more lands, they came across the intricate fabrics and fancy metals turned into jewels, as well as delicate women that the other civilizations had. Their desire for such possessions only increased their appetite for more war. They now control large portions of the world, and as Hulagu's wife, I share the Mongol wealth and power laced with a constant sense of guilt. For they have conquered Poland as well.*
>
> *I must admit that my feelings toward Hulagu are beginning to change. After all, he has saved me from a life of subjugation and virtual slavery. He has shown kindness and admiration in every possible way. My resistance melts a little each time in the warmth of our nightly embrace.*

When Mstislav sat next to me on that fateful journey to Kiev, I felt his cold presence, and I knew I could never be happy living with him. Fate brought me here. Hulagu may not be the ideal husband for me, but at least he is warm, he is alive, full of feeling. Overwhelmed by the news of my illness, he ordered ingredients to be brought from far corners of the world to be made into sweets for me. Yet, I have seen how violent he can be at times.

I know Hulagu has a temper. His actions may be read in the eyes of the prisoners of war. I keep telling myself that the path I am treading is not one chosen by me and that I have no choice but to adjust to my new circumstances. His wishes, whether a demand that I be present for a certain celebration or absent on other occasions, have to be fulfilled. Sometimes I fear what would happen if he loses his love and fondness for me.

Hulagu's attempts at winning my affections are sometimes clumsy. When he showed me the freshly planted flowers in the garden, he began to boast about the fantastic maneuvers of Mongol warriors in Europe. He only stopped when I coldly responded by saying that it depends on one's perspective.

Intimacy at times turns into attachment between two people, especially if one is an entrapped, downtrodden princess and the other the rescuing prince. Such has been the case between Hulagu and me. I do feel safe in Hulagu's arms though, and I am beginning to learn to love him, although I am not sure if the feeling is brought about by admiration on his part or my total sense of helplessness that makes me feel like a victim of drowning, clinging to anything that would bring me to the surface of the water.

Gradually my new identity feels more familiar. I am now known as Princess Dounia. Although, in my heart, I shall always remain Krisztina and retain the love of Poland, but to the Mongol court I am Dounia, a symbol of a once proud world that is now a mere captive.

Chapter Eleven

The Good Omen

THE SCENT OF MOUNTAIN CEDAR AND SANDALWOOD filled the air as the Shaman burnt incense and blessed each and every fighter heading toward Europe. But when he reached Bolad the Spy, his smile withered.

"Be careful, son," he said, "take an amulet with you that would protect thee from harm; an item not soiled but innocent, pure in its nature and its purpose."

No Mongol warrior would take such a warning lightly. Bolad left the temple where the ceremony took place immediately after the services to ransack his ger, hoping to find something. He did. It was his father's pendant. The old man had been dead for many years, but by no accounts would he have been considered innocent. The item was not quite what the Shaman had prescribed; however, left with no other option, he placed the pendant in his pocket and left.

"What is it that you are holding?" Bolad asked a trembling girl of no more than eight who stood in front of a rather large ger. The girl, who shook with fear, was hiding something behind her back. She held out a handmade doll with the tip of two fingers as if to minimize the connection between herself and the subject of her guilt. Her auburn hair, disheveled, curled around her face and a threadbare gown barely covered her thin, white shoulders. A slave.

"I am going to . . . to return it," she said as tears welled up in her eyes.

The enormous size of the warrior standing before her made her shudder. She stared at the hilt of the sword tied to Bolad's belt.

"Whose servant are you?"

"My lady," she replied barely audible.

"And which lady is that?" Bolad asked, laughing at the reply. The girl shrugged in response. "Why did you take the doll?"

"I once owned one when I had a family," she said, a teardrop escaping and rolling down her pale cheek. She probably had come from a region where people shared her pale color and reddish hair. Bolad snatched the doll, happy to have found his amulet and the girl exhaled audibly in relief when he left.

When Bolad arrived at the Mongol camp near the region of Mohi, Batu Khan, commander of the forces of invasion, summoned him for a top-secret meeting. Batu spared not a moment in commencing the discourse with his trusted spy.

"I need victory in Europe to ensure my ascension as the new Mongol Khaqan," Batu said. "You have been my ally, and you can guarantee this victory. Before the warmth of spring thaws the ice-covered rivers, we will ready our horses for the incursion."

Batu was ambitious but level-headed; he knew when to strike the enemy and when to withdraw his forces to avoid unnecessary casualties. To overcome the remaining forces in Europe, he had to deploy the best of his archers, those with the greatest physical fortitude and mental tenacity at the point their enemies began to flag. After the Mongol victory in Legnica against the Poles and prior to subduing the Hungarians, a Tumen unit, ten thousand in number, led by Batu had arrived near the region of Mohi.

They stared for a moment or two at an outstretched map. Unlike Batu, whose motions were meticulous and calculated, Bolad's gestures were quick, bordering on nervous.

"The Teutonic Knights have joined them. So have the Knights Hospitaller," Bolad said.

"Put it to me plainly, Bolad." Batu looked up and exhaled deeply toward the smoke-darkened felt ceiling of the ger. It was clear that Batu did not quite understand the complexity of European military hierarchies. All he wanted to know were the flaws of his foes.

"They are special forces with strong religious convictions, mostly Germans and Slavs. They are some of the fiercest fighters in Europe and have been fighting the Muslims for centuries over the control of Jerusalem. I would say, they are quite experienced in all forms of warfare."

"We kill people to attain wealth," Batu said. "They slaughter each other to become more pious."

They both laughed. A lifetime of shared memories made the bond of their friendship unbreakable; they were like brothers. Thus, despite differences in status, they did away with formalities and addressed each other on a first name basis when conversing in private.

"Setting all other elements aside, number-wise, can we overcome them?" Batu asked.

"I doubt it. They have already taken position on the other side of this bridge; their numbers are too numerous to count. This conquest will be tougher than fighting the Poles. I am sorry Batu. I wish I had better news."

"Don't look so disheartened. We are destined to rule the earth as my grandfather used to say, one way or another."

Chapter Twelve

The Recurring Nightmare

MARIA LASKARINA RAN TO HER HUSBAND'S BEDCHAMBER, where he was tossing and turning in agony. She began to shake him. "Wake up! Wake up! You are having another nightmare."

King Bela IV, leader of Hungary and Croatia, opened his swollen lids that always made him appear tired and sleepy even at midday, his face soaked in sweat. Maria wiped his face with her handkerchief. She reached for the goblet of water by his bed.

"Drink," she insisted. "It will help."

"Nothing helps," the king replied. "It is the same damn nightmare."

"Your mother again?" Maria was not only Bela's wife but his companion, friend, and soul-mate since childhood.

"How can I wipe that cursed vision from my memory?" Bela asked. "I was no more than seven when those monsters killed my mother right before my eyes."

Maria had heard this story countless times but always listened, wanting to soothe her husband. Bela's mother had gone for a ride in the very forest where he had roamed one morning, chasing after his dog. The barons pursued her, forcing her deeper into the woodland while Bela's father was away. As landowners and noblemen, the barons, who were mostly children of European knights, were exempted from paying taxes and enjoyed political influence within the royal courts. Many had castles and palaces of their own and had jointly formed an establishment similar to a parliament known as "Diet."

"A spearhead wounded the leg of my mother's horse, and she fell rolling on the green grass," Bela added after swallowing some water. "They congregated around her, forcing their spears into her young flesh. Blood gushed from every corner of her body, turning the green meadow crimson red, as I stood at a distance watching the gruesome scene."

"And what does your father do? Instead of punishing the corrupt barons responsible for her murder, he ignores the entire tragedy and simply remarries as if nothing of significance has occurred," Maria said sympathetically. "It is all behind you now. Your father is deceased, and you ordered all the chairs in the Assembly burnt so that as punishment the newly appointed barons would have to stand up during the entire time they convene," she said smiling, hoping her sarcasm would pacify the monarch.

Indeed, King Bela had a troubled childhood. His father, Andrew II never let the poor traumatized child out of his sight and kept reprimanding him over the slightest shortcoming. Bela's German mother, before being murdered, had placed her own family members in positions of power in Hungary, thus bringing upon herself the wrath of the barons who were excluded from the decision-making circles.

The death of King Bela's father had not put an end to his nightmares. However, it had allowed Bela to pursue much-needed reform. He returned the lands confiscated by the undeserving barons to the people and opened Hungary's doors to immigrants. Those immigrants, known as the Cumans had been defeated by the Mongols in earlier skirmishes and had sought refuge in Hungary. Thus, Bela had come to be known as the "King of the Cumans."

The following morning, King Bela addressed the March session of the Diet. "The Mongols have already devastated Kievan Rus and Poland. Their threat to Hungary is imminent," he said. "The Cumans consider Hungary their home, and they can help defend our homeland, acting as a buffer against outside aggression."

The powerful barons of Hungary, although sidelined, remained defiant. They continued to show resistance to Bela's strategy for defense. King Bela argued for hours, trying to convince them that the

Cuman immigrants were actually an asset for the country as the Mongols carved their way deeper into Europe.

"We Hungarians can easily push our enemies back to where they came from without any help from the Cumans," one baron proclaimed loudly.

"You cannot push the Mongol genie back into the bottle," Bela replied, frustrated, "until all its wishes are fulfilled." Realizing he had the attention of the full House, he added after a pause, "The Cumans are a powerful fighting force, and they will not allow foreign enemies to invade their backyards."

"That is if they do not succumb to the temptation of serving as spies for the Mongols. I have heard that espionage is quite a lucrative trade," another baron sarcastically declared.

"They are different from us!" yet another one objected. "They eat different foods; they dress differently; they are foreigners. We should not have allowed them entry into Hungary in the first place."

"No Hungarian lass feels safe around these Cuman vultures," an old baron raised his voice.

"Kick them out!" A couple of the younger Hungarian aristocrats shouted from the back of the assembly room.

"We cannot stand here arguing over insignificant matters when the Horsemen of Apocalypse are upon us!" King Bela snapped as he rubbed his temples in frustration. As always, the meeting with the barons adjourned without reaching any conclusive decision.

The infighting among the political elite had created discord among the ranks of the Hungarian military as well, weakening their fortitude and resolve. The troops were paralyzed by indecision and therefore lacked the tenacity necessary to wage war.

King Bela had requested help, but most European leaders had let him down. That, the Mongols knew. For they never invaded any land before running reconnaissance missions and gaining enough information about the social, political, and military conditions of the target country.

The Mongols, aware of Bela's adamant position regarding the Cumans, used this very group to place him under pressure, leaving him with no choice but to fight. When Bela returned to his chamber, an emissary of Batu Khan delivered a letter to him, requesting that he hand over the Cuman subjects of Hungary so that the Mongols could punish them for their atrocities in earlier confrontations.

Karakorum had woken up to the news of another military engagement. Krisztina sat at her desk to write the following account of an incident that was brought to her attention by Baako. This time she decided to follow Reyhan's example and write her findings in the format of a tale, albeit in Polish.

Entry by Krisztina:

Sadness in Sunset Street

Easter brought with it a solar eclipse the likes of which had not been seen in many years in Hungary. The Magyars perceived the covering of the sun as an omen portending the horrors that would lie ahead. Overnight a layer of ice had sugarcoated the otherwise dirt roads and alleys of Napnyugta or Sunset Street. Candles were lit in the houses and cottages as the pale sun began to melt on the horizon.

The imminent war was on everyone's mind. Not a war in some distant land, but right where it threatened the tranquility of Napnyugta. It crept its way into conversations, it cast a shadow of gloom on otherwise happy faces, and it made well-prepared meals distasteful. The inhabitants could smell the stench of the dreaded six-letter word haboru (war) in every corner of their country that seemed to be shrinking in size with the passage of each day, as the shadow of the invading aliens loomed larger.

"Stop crying for God's sake. You are spoiling our dinner. It is a sin to be ungrateful before God's bounty. We have food on our table, a roof over our heads, and a fire burning in the hearth to keep us warm," the man said, frustrated.

It was too late, however; the mother's contagious tears had already afflicted little Natalia and droplets of it were forming pools by her plate of goulash.

"I cannot help it," her mother said looking utterly miserable. "Aurelian is our only son. He is old enough to be married and to have a family of his own, not to be dragged to that slaughterhouse."

"It's not a slaughterhouse. It's the war front, and he has a duty toward his country," the man countered.

"Well, the country hasn't done enough for me to repay it with my son's blood," the mother retorted like a tigress protecting her young.

"Calm down, my pet. Why do you always assume the worst? Not all who go to war get killed or injured. He could return a hero and marry a girl of his . . . or your dreams," he said, apparently unable to hold back the sarcasm.

He then added more gently, "You remember when at barely twelve he came down with a bad case of pox. You were about to lose your mind over the matter. But he survived with only a few pockmarks on his skin which to me makes him more handsome than ever."

His reassuring talk brought a faint smile to her lips, but the trepidation lingered on her face.

The defeat of the Polish army in the Battle of Legnica had had its effect on the psyche of the Hungarians. The rhythmic sounds of approaching Mongol hordes and their victory chants of urra sent waves of terror throughout the Continent.

Inhabitants of cities subconsciously realized that like a deadly game of chance there would be those who would be spared and those who would suffer. When looking at one another's faces, the Magyars wondered who was marked to die by the hands of destiny and who was to be spared the pangs of death. It appeared as if everyone felt watched, bared, void of protection, vulnerable like slugs unable to find their shells. Under such circumstances, no one can dream of a future; minds become stagnant, ideas wither; souls feel empty, social life becomes extinct.

Terror not yet materialized shattered nerves, paralyzed otherwise fighting men and brought daily activities to a halt. Agriculture suffered, industry stood still, craftsmen no longer cared to pursue their trade, men were inclined to remain indoors, trust among them vanished, culture languished, and religion became the rope to which people clung for solace in hopes of an intervention by Providence.

Chapter Thirteen

The Bridge over Sajo River

RUGGED YELLOWISH-BROWN STONES PAVED THE BRIDGE over Sajo River and masked its arched masonry beneath the deck as well. The bridge rose like a giant sea serpent out of the blue-gray fog of the night. The waters of Sajo exhaled a mist that engulfed the entire arena in gloom. Sea-smoke covered stone formed islands here and there across the length of the river.

Mongol horses had splashed through shallow waters and waded through rivers; they had climbed perilous mountains, descended narrow valleys and slid over frozen lakes carrying their riders to destinations from which they could not afford but to return victorious.

Batu and Subutai had reached the embankment, a bridge away from their foes who had camped there days in advance, so great in number that their silhouettes could be seen as specks on the distant horizon.

"Things don't look so good. They have formed a solid wall with their shields, yet they can attack us with their arrows as we cross the bridge," Batu said.

"I will take a portion of the army downstream to find shallow waters that are easy to cross. This way my unit can take them by surprise." Subutai replied. "You do your best to fend them off in a frontal assault."

"Are you sure this is going to work?" Batu asked, looking concerned.

"I joined your grandfather's men when I was but a lad of fourteen, and since then my mind has been focused on only one thing: a strategy to win wars," Subutai responded and then asked, "Are you as determined as I am to win this one?"

Batu looked at him fiercely, "I have the determination of a hungry dog picking a bone to bite on. Tonight, we shall drink to victory."

"Bolad will remain with you, Baidar and Kadan will accompany me," Subutai said as he signaled his men to prepare for departure.

With Subutai gone, the number of Batu's men appeared too scant in the confrontation that was about to ensue. Bolad must have noticed the concern on Batu's face as the commanders gathered in the main ger for the last time before crossing over to the other side.

"I have a solution that would put our minds at ease and strike fear in the hearts of our foes," Bolad said lifting the handmade cloth doll above his head as he spoke. "Imagine this doll lifesize!" He paused and looked triumphantly at his comrades in arm who seemed awestruck by the suggestion. He then continued, "From a distance, the lifesize effigies would appear real. Now imagine many such dolls mounted on wooden frames as a backdrop to our operation. Our foes would think that the small army unit being dispatched to the front is merely an advanced guard, and a major attack is yet to occur."

"We could use the fabric and wood from our gers for the purpose," Batu replied thoughtfully, lines of concern that had earlier formed deep furrows upon his forehead began to melt. "We will ask each of our warriors to assemble at least five such figures within the hour."

Mongol warriors knew the basics of stitching and frequently mended their own clothes torn in combat. Many complained, however, finding the undertaking tedious and unnecessary. The task being accomplished to the satisfaction of Batu, they made their first attempt to confront the enemy. As they reached the halfway mark on the bridge, the flags of the Knights, as well as that of the Hungarian army, became visible. The sheer number of foes struck fear in the hearts of the Mongols. The knowledge, however, that Subutai's forces were racing to reach the battlefield and would soon arrive, gave them courage.

Meanwhile, Mongol horses under Subutai's command slid upon the algae strewn embankment. Steam rose when the ice-cold raindrops hit the warm earth as they made their way down toward the shallower waters of the Sajo River. The wind blew their moistened manes and tails as they trotted bravely forward upon the now glistening land. Their leather armor slapped against their muscular frames.

Chunks of ice formed a slushy surface on the river. Baidar lashed out, not addressing Subutai directly but with his face toward the thawing river. "Now what, are we to walk on water?"

"We will if we have to," Subutai replied coldly.

"How on earth are we going to do that?" Kadan retorted without thinking and instantly seemed to have regretted his harsh tone toward Subutai.

"I see some boats nearby. We will tie them together and form a floating bridge," Subutai said, repeating the suggestion of a Chinese engineer who had accompanied them.

The stunt allowed for a quick, albeit inconvenient means of crossing the river. The boats were attached side-by-side forming a rather lengthy but unstable bridge upon which they encouraged their horses to cross after dismounting and leading them one by one.

Rust-colored weeds had grown on the banks, giving the scene an ethereal beauty. The warriors had no time to enjoy the serene landscape as they hopped like hooded amphibians from one boat to another. It was a cumbersome attempt that only the persistent, desperate Mongol horsemen would obediently undertake. Finally, they reached the shore under the cover of a moonlit night and quietly approached the arena of war.

Banners of every color, like linen hung on ropes to dry, made flapping noises in the breeze. The noise sounded louder than normal as silence descended on the battlefield. The Mongols under Batu's command had earlier advanced with their horses galloping at full speed. They suddenly came to a halt before reaching the organized lines of their foes. The Mongol drums began to beat in a threatening, menacing way. The two armies stood at a visible distance of about thirty paces from one another. Flags signaled the initiation of the battle, and the commander of the European forces cried, "Charge!" As he did so, the Mongols rushed senseless toward their foes.

Unlike the stunning display of military prowess seen earlier by the Mongols in Kievan Rus and Legnica, this time Batu's unit appeared disorganized, incoherent and ill-prepared. The Mongol horsemen trudged forward as if driven by invisible forces. They knew that turning back was punishable by death and going forward was the only way to survive.

From a distance, it appeared as if celestial bodies were engaged in a night of merrymaking. Fiery arrows flew against the night sky like shooting stars aiming for hearts too young to die. Sparks from the arrows set ablaze the fake army earlier constructed, unveiling the ruse. Under a deluge of spears and javelins that were thrown at them from every angle, Batu was able to cross the bridge, as some of his men perished right before his eyes. Although the Mongols cared little for the lives of their foes, the soul of a Mongol warrior was too precious to lose. The more courageous among them fell into the river, swam to the shore despite being wounded, and attempted to fight the enemy to the last breath.

Batu began to lose hope, for Subutai's men were nowhere to be seen. All the careful planning and the precision they used in their earlier confrontations were of no use, and defeat seemed inevitable. The Hungarians, confident as forces are who are defending home territory, were ready to annihilate the Mongols.

A line of sweat formed on Batu's forehead. His men were few, certainly not sufficient to fight against the powerful Hungarian warriors and their allies. Arrows rained on Batu's forces, as Bela's army, sure of victory, moved forward in a clear attempt to make the final kill.

Centuries of coexistence under the harshest conditions had tied the Mongol souls to one another such that they could almost sense each other's presence from afar. That sensation brought hope back to their hearts; the sensation that their comrades were near and coming to their rescue.

King Bela turned to one of his officers and smiled. "The Battle of Mohi will be one to be remembered and celebrated throughout history," he commented. He lifted his lance, ready to charge toward Batu when roars rose from behind him. Subutai's army had finally made it.

With the speed of an avalanche, they descended upon the Hungarians who were shocked and bewildered as they found themselves encircled by the Mongols.

Drenched with their leather suits weighing cold and heavy upon their bodies, Subutai's men had ridden fast toward the arena of war where Batu desperately awaited their arrival. With the freshly arrived units forming organized lines, the Hungarians realized the tenacity of their implacable enemies.

Subutai came to rescue Batu and his men when they were exhausted and vulnerable. Age had not deteriorated Subutai's resoluteness, and failure remained unacceptable as he unleashed a wave of Mongol horsemen against the European cavalry. Caught between the forces of Batu and Subutai, the Hungarians and the knights fought with all their might. Both sides were young, both sides eager to fulfill the aspirations of the banners they held. With one side accustomed to conventional ways of fighting, the other resorting to every ploy imaginable, victory lay in the hands of those who could surprise their enemy.

The ceremonious movement of the European warriors was in sharp contrast to the bewildering motions of their enemies who seemed to be acting upon no strategy except their own impulses, thus adding to the confusion of the battlefield. The tactics of Subutai's men, although unconventional and irregular, were well-planned and executed. They tore their way toward the enemy like an unstoppable instrument of doom. Their maddening maneuvers appeared to be straight out of the guidebook of Satan indeed, for no particular method governed their actions. If it hadn't been for the determination of the knights to subdue the attackers, fear of the possible supernatural powers of the Mongols would have deterred some from engaging their foe, tempting the less experienced fighters to flee the scene.

Cries of the battle-hardened could be heard for miles, as well as the whimpering of the dying. Breastplates and gauntlets tore to shreds and hoods fell off as heads were severed. No armor could protect man from the brutality of other men. Within hours since the commencement of the battle, the Hungarians endured so many casualties that the continuation of the battle became impossible.

Pieces of cloth mingled with human flesh were scattered throughout the field of battle like rose petals thrown at the feet of a newlywed bride. But here, the bride was none other than the Angel of Death and her bouquet, the souls of young men whose bodies littered the arena. Silver swords slashed sanguine skies, raining blood and pestilence upon the earth. For those who died didn't simply perish, the blood that had spilled would spread disease among the living.

Fear had gripped the throats of otherwise courageous men so tightly that even those with broken limbs and broken souls did not dare to cry. Blood had mingled with dust, making the air difficult to breathe. The choking sensation and the dark realization that their country was now conquered, paralyzed even the most courageous of Hungarian warriors.

The weary eyes of Bela's men beckoned him to come to their rescue. But the situation had rendered him powerless. He felt as if the earth was pulled from under him like an unwanted piece of rug. The eyes staring at him weighed heavy upon his conscience, pulling him under just like heavy chains pull in a drowning man deep into the bosom of the sea. He had to confront the enemy like a hero, but his strength did not match that of his mighty foes.

Entrapped within a circle of fire with only one escape route remaining, the Hungarians began to flee, clearly forced by the natural need to preserve their lives. The Mongols intentionally left them this passageway. The Europeans retreated through it in disarray, seeing it as a miraculous intervention and not a deathtrap. The warriors of the Steppes descended upon their petrified foes like hungry vultures, killing the senior officers and allowing the low-ranking men to flee.

As bodies of the young defenders of Hungary lay in the fields in tens of thousands, and their steeds left unburdened fled the scene of carnage in every direction, a foot soldier pushed his way into Bela's tent.

"Who are you? What is your name and rank, and what brings you here?" Bela demanded.

"Sir, a matter of high urgency is the reason for my intrusion," the young soldier being addressed replied. He was none other than Aurelian of Sunset Street, standing tall with his light brown hair forming sweat drenched ringlets around his handsome face.

"You have not stated your name," Bela said, alarmed.

"My name is Aurelian, and I am a new recruit, a petty but proud foot soldier in your army, sir."

"Why haven't you fled with the others?"

"It is you, sir," he said almost breathless, "it is your life that I fear for. For mine is that of a worthless soldier and you . . . you are a sovereign. It's a slaughterhouse out there. The Mongols are killing and mutilating our men. Only petty foot soldiers have managed to escape, for the Mongols are focused on killing the commanders and senior officers."

"You still haven't told me why you are here," Bela said.

"They cannot tell us apart, sir, the prince and the pauper, save for the clothing we wear, and if we were to exchange those clothes, you have a chance of escaping," Aurelian said.

"I have no fear of death," Bela replied, sternly.

"I know that sir and neither do I," Aurelian replied. "But I am just a foot soldier while you are the hope of Hungary. You cannot stand there in your fine regalia recognizable by the enemy. We need to switch places now. I do not intend to return to my family as a defeated soldier. I would rather lay my life for the land where I have been born and to which I belong."

"And so do I. I prefer death to defeat," Bela replied.

"Your demise would mean the death of hope for the people of Hungary. Do not put me in a position, sir, that I force you to abide by the will of a common soldier. I came to lay down my life, and I will not take back what I had intended to give. But if you die, Hungary's aspirations for a future will die with you."

Bela, seeing no other option, reluctantly removed his white cape bearing the embroidered red cross that signified him as a nobleman and donned the torn surcoat of the foot soldier on top of his metal armor.

Chapter Fourteen

The Seal of Hungary

AS DAWN BROKE, A THICK FOG DESCENDED UPON THE treetops. The weak rays of the sun were not powerful enough to penetrate the grayish clouds that covered the sky. A suffocating weight had descended upon the land, one so evil and so injurious that even nature sensed its presence.

The sky wore a veil of gray on that mournful day. Raindrops like tears slowly dripped on the wretched earth, as nature bemoaned the fate of man. Tree branches reached for the sky, as if pleading for help for no human had the strength to do so. The yellow daffodils that once adorned the roadsides were trampled upon, turning them into a nauseating spectacle next to the blood-drenched streets.

As towns and principalities of Hungary were crushed one after the other, security became more precious than the air one breathes. There was an urge to run, to flee but one knew not where. Deep forests, dark jungles, burrowed holes in the ground, abandoned wastelands became far better sanctuaries than populated cities, but even fleeing to such places had its risks.

Those who hoped to be spared could not help but visualize the possibility of imminent death and the pain of suffering through a gruesome butchery. People in Kievan Rus and Poland who were taken as prisoners of war and were already assigned humiliating tasks fared better than Hungarians who were in abject abeyance awaiting the inevitable end.

For those who did not dare venture out, food became scarce, rotten bodies left on the streets became infested, and disease spread. The young and the elderly easily perished with few shedding a tear or two. The enormity of the horror experienced left no room for mourning. Death almost became a sanctuary in itself, for in death there is no terror, no suffering. The interred seemed to be the ones who were spared, for the living faced a far darker future.

Ultimately the dust settled, and rain washed away the stench of blood. The Mongol storm had left its devastating mark on the country's history, and they now ruled the nation by the power of the sword. There was no chance of defiance. For the defiant would be uprooted instantly.

With the battle over, the Mongol officers congregated in the main camp, but despite the fact that they had reached overwhelming victory against the Europeans, Batu was in a state of great fury. He snapped at Subutai in front of all the other officers.

"You were late! They would have annihilated us if you had arrived any later than you did." Batu's voice echoed through the ger that was speedily assembled for the meeting of Mongol commanders. The fire burning in its midst needed more time to warm up the entire enclosure. Clouds formed out of his mouth as he spoke, yet his voice remained steady and powerful. Few people could speak to Subutai as Batu did. He was a true grandson of Genghis and had inherited his ego.

"We needed you as reinforcement," he said, his voice trembling with anger. "Many of my men perished, and a large number were badly injured. We stood on the precipice of annihilation when Your Excellency dragged your reluctant forces into the arena."

"No Mongol warrior is ever dragged to the arena, they go voluntarily, and they give their lives for the Khaqan gladly," Subutai spoke, recoiling. He spoke calmly, although his temples were visibly throbbing. "We charged our way through freezing waters," he continued unabated. "The terrain was impassable. We had to tie up some boats and create a makeshift bridge to cross it."

Batu calmed down a bit when he heard that. He lifted a silver chalice filled with the brew concocted in a nearby vineyard and drinking to Subutai's honor pronounced aloud, "You have done so much for the Mongols that no man dares to question your integrity. I blame myself for jumping to conclusions too fast. It is just that we were placed in a very difficult predicament last night."

Subutai, looking undaunted, raised his chalice to Batu's health and the atmosphere of jubilation returned to the camp.

Among the items looted from the defeated army during the Battle of Mohi was a precious piece of round metal with a wooden handle attached. The coin-shaped piece, made of gold, was the official seal of Hungary. Two rows of Latin writing surrounded the embossed image of the Hungarian King, seated upon the royal throne, wearing his cloak and crown. Subutai kept playing with it and appeared deep in thought when Bolad asked, "How do we keep the Hungarians from remobilizing against us?"

"What if King Bela himself urged his countrymen not to mobilize because... doing so would jeopardize his plans to negotiate with the Mongols?" he replied, smiling his sinister smile while flashing the metal piece before the eyes of his confused men. "Anything bearing the imprint of this seal is as good as the words coming right out of His Majesty's mouth."

He then ordered for a very convincing announcement by the King of Hungary to be drafted by Bolad and firmly pressed the ink-covered seal upon it. In the dark hours of late evening that day, Bolad placed the announcement on the door of the main courthouse.

The Mongol invasion left a large portion of the Hungarian army as well as many civilians dead. Many more were wounded and maimed. After all, what are aunts and uncles, siblings and family; what are collective joy, continuity and love, mutual happiness and shared pain to those who seek gold and silver.

Words could not describe the horror they had witnessed. Therefore, they sought refuge in silence. A nauseating feeling of loss, of being powerless, of vulnerability, compounded their grief. "Why do they hate us so?" they bemoaned without uttering a word. "We shall overcome," they cried in silence without shedding a tear.

As the Mongol forces approached the gates of Vienna, Subutai asked to see Batu, stating that he had an urgent message just delivered to him.

"We need to return to Mongolia," Subutai declared upon entering Batu's ger.

"We are at the borders of Vienna after all that we have suffered. We cannot just retreat." Batu replied, frustrated with the suggestion.

"Ogodei has died. A Khuriltai is taking place in which you need to be participating."

"Who will replace Ogodei?" Batu asked, shocked.

"Toregene has struggled long and hard to ensure the succession of her son Guyuk, although he was no favorite of Ogodei. Indeed, Guyuk is so unpopular that the Khuriltai is reluctant to acknowledge him as Khaqan. Word is that Toregene will serve as a regent until a final decision is made."

Batu turned away from Subutai as if to ponder the developments. "That will be the end of Karakorum. I am not returning. I have struggled long and hard too, and I do not intend to become a subject of Guyuk or any other Mongol Khaqan. I want to rule my own territories."

"Rebelling against him will have consequences," Subutai replied, looking concerned.

"Not if he cannot reach me," Batu said.

"What exactly do you mean?"

"I will be staying in the lands adjacent to the Volga River, establishing, I assure you, an empire of my own."

"You are not serious, are you?" Subutai said, frowning.

"Just look at the loads of silver and gold that we have looted out of Europe. Do you expect me, Subutai, as intelligent and experienced as you are, to hand all this over to my rival, Guyuk, and pay homage to him? What mindless creature would I be to submit to defeat without waging war, to hand over the reins to my opponent before the match even begins? I almost perished over the bridge that crossed the Sajo River."

"Will your men stay with you?" Subutai asked.

"My men no longer see me as an inexperienced commander but a Mongol hero. I possess the wealth, the glory, the name, the lineage and the reputation needed to establish my own empire."

"And engage in continuous combat with Guyuk and his men. That is exactly what Genghis Khan feared; for if you fight among yourselves, you will be too weak to confront your external enemies." Subutai warned.

"My intention is not to fight Guyuk, Subutai, but to live beyond his reach."

"I would have to return to Mongolia to report on the change of circumstances," Subutai said matter-of-factly.

"Take those nine huge sacks of human ears we cut off from fallen Hungarian soldiers as proof of our victory."

Not long after Subutai's return, news reached Batu that Guyuk was indeed chosen as the next Khaqan. Guyuk's coronation took place in August 1246, and by April 1248 as he made an attempt to attack Batu, he died on the way. The death was attributed to his poor health, and the matter quickly dismissed. Yet, suspicions lingered. Some believed that he was actually poisoned. Guyuk's death gave an opportunity to Princess Sorkhokhtani who had groomed her four sons for the position of Khaqan over the years.

Back in Karakorum, Krisztina wrote the following.

Entry by Krisztina:

> *It is difficult to write when paper is so scarce. I have to be careful writing, careful with the ink; careful no one walks in on me. But what a poor captive like me can do. It was not a surprise to me that the Mongols won the Battle of Mohi. They seem to be winning every war they engage in, regardless of who their enemy is. The escapades of the Mongols at times take on a lurid hue, giving me nightmares. Seeing the devastation in Hungary, Bulgaria submitted to Mongol rule without resistance. That was wise! God knows how many lives were spared. Some in Hungary hid their treasures and burnt down their homes and farms to leave nothing for their foes. But the Mongols caught those who were known to be*

among the rich and bound them above simmering fires until they confessed, and the treasures were disclosed. I feel pity for them. They are my brethren in religion, but war knows no mercy. Batu had ordered that out of every fallen Hungarian soldier they cut off an ear. They brought back sacks full of them. First, I thought it was rotten animal flesh. I swooned when I realized these were their "trophies." I turned so pale that those about me assumed that I had died.

Chapter Fifteen

Captive and Captivated

WITH THE PASSAGE OF MONTHS, DOUNIA'S COUNTE-nance fell. Hulagu was away most of the time engaging in battles, smothering uprisings of the subjugated and mitigating skirmishes among Mongol rivals. Reyhan had noticed how utterly homesick Dounia appeared. Early in winter, however, when the Mongol men prepared for their annual hunt, excitement returned to Karakorum.

The Mongolian winter games were meant to keep the cavalry occupied and in shape. They commenced when the rivers froze, but before snow accumulations reached a level that would drive the animals, mostly wild sheep, ibex, saiga and black-tailed gazelle as well as larger animals like wild boars to their shelters. The challenge was to attack the animals—whether rodent, fowl or mammal—in an open field without the use of weapons. Thus men displayed their strength and courage. On such occasions, women participated as spectators.

On a chilly day in The Year of the Tiger, rows of huntsmen took their positions as they began to slowly converge, tightening the circumference of the entrapped animals who became more agitated with the constriction of their habitat. The hunters could not kill the animals until flags were raised to indicate the culmination of the hunt. At this early stage, they only had to contain the beasts in the ring.

The excitement and thrill of the game brought both Dounia and Reyhan out of their lodgings. The recent news of Baako's death had left Reyhan quite despondent. Therefore, she saw this as a much-needed opportunity to overcome her grief. Baako had died of bloody flux as he accompanied Hulagu in one of his military ventures. For Reyhan, he had been a friend, a companion and a shoulder to cry on. Without his caring support, she feared she would not be able to handle issues with a calm composure as before. Yet, she knew life had to go on.

The two ladies had wrapped themselves in fur-lined overcoats in the chilly morning and holding glasses of warm goat's milk, cheered their favorite hunters. When a row of spears rose in the air at the start of the ceremony, Reyhan looked at Dounia's face. The spear-like shadows of her long eyelashes formed lines upon her pale cheeks as she looked down bashfully. *How many hearts might those lash-spears break!* She saw that one of the Kashiks (imperial guards) took particular notice of Dounia and feared that her restless young ward would fall prey to the sentry's advances. Torn between her love of Poland and her new life and attachments in Mongolia, the European Princess appeared vulnerable, and Reyhan worried that she could easily be swayed by a young, ambitious warrior. She kept a close eye on her ward as a result.

The fine-looking Kashik, with his eyes focused on Dounia, almost allowed a hare to escape, but quickly dismounted and chased after the animal. He slid through the dirt field and to the awe of the spectators, grabbed the hare. He looked up, his hands and outfit muddied during the struggle, and smiled at Dounia who was clearly beside herself with excitement. She was cheering and laughing gaily to the verge of losing her honorary place among the royalty until Reyhan gave her a stern look of disapproval that warned her about overstepping acceptable boundaries.

The entrapment of the animals continued for several hours with the apparently self-composed Dounia casting a glance in Reyhan's direction every so often to meet her guardian's approval. As the sun went down, the weather became too chilly for outdoor activity. Reyhan, using the drop in temperatures as an excuse, gently led Dounia away.

Sorkhokhtani was the only woman in the court, other than Reyhan, who fully supported Dounia, after all, the girl had brought so much joy to her son's life. The other women were more cordial than kind to the young princess, and some displayed outright animosity.

As they walked side-by-side, Dounia complained to Reyhan about the pettiness of some Mongol women. "Arrogance seems to be a virtue in their culture. They feel superior when they can belittle you."

"There are all types of people among the inhabitants of every land. When you confront indecency or outright evil, leave such people to their own devices and pay no attention to them. Soon they will leave you alone."

A recent storm had left their path strewn with debris. Heads down, skirts slightly lifted, they watched for any obstacles along their way. Reyhan stopped. They had reached a crossroad where the two paths leading to their respective abodes diverged. She then looked her young companion straight in the eyes and said, "I noticed that sentry paying particular attention to you. I can tell you horror stories about women who crossed the line when their Mongol husbands were away." Reyhan had heard things, mostly through palace gossip, about instances where unfaithful women were summarily executed or exiled into the wilderness.

"I was just laughing at the spectacle," Dounia said, defensively.

"You are but a child. Your mouth still smells of your mother's milk. I see you frolicking among horses and goats and cannot but wonder that you may have found a greater degree of freedom here in the Steppes than you had ever enjoyed in the confines of a European castle. But you must learn your limits which may not seem defined to you at this time.

"I am sorry that my behavior met your disapproval. In fact, there seem to be very few ladies who approve of anything that I do here. Of all people, Reyhan, you must have sympathy for me. Life for me has been a fairytale turned into a nightmare."

"Things could have been a lot worse had not Hulagu rescued you."

"He rescued me all right, but then left me months at a time while he went pursuing God knows what in remote parts of the world," Dounia said as tears welled up in her eyes.

Reyhan knew better than to pursue the matter further. They parted with Reyhan returning to her palace to join Sorkhokhtani for tea.

Sorkhokhtani was staying with Reyhan for the duration of winter. Halfway through their conversation, Reyhan brought up her concerns over Dounia. They both seemed to have noticed that the young European Princess was beginning to adapt to her new life, but there were matters about which they both worried.

"Dounia wants to follow the old pattern set by her family in Europe, although somehow unsure of the righteousness of their ways. At the same time, she seems to enjoy the sort of freedom from the rules and restrictions of the Europeans courts that her new environment offers, and for which she feels a sense of guilt," Reyhan said.

"I believe there are elements of Mongolian culture and way of life that Dounia finds very much enticing. Mongol women have opportunities few in other parts of the world enjoy. Some lead their own clans; some take part in the army; others like me rule their own territories. Of course, she is not inclined to admit this," Sorkhokhtani said.

"I know. I dare not mention this to Dounia, but she seems to be both captive and captivated, for she is now exposed to so many new ideas and new ways of thinking," Reyhan said, smiling.

"She plays that instrument of hers she calls a lyre beautifully, the one our artisans built for her. The sound mesmerizes the listeners, and Hulagu is almost in a trance when she plays." Sorkhokhtani said, sipping her tea.

"I was watching Dounia today, taking great interest in the annual hunt." She stopped without mentioning the sentry.

"She is still young," Sorkhokhtani said.

"Dounia, true to her name, represents the current state of the world. I get the feeling that the transformation she is undergoing is what awaits the world in the near future," Reyhan said.

Although Dounia felt as if the life she coveted was beyond her reach, she began to appreciate the Mongol style of clothing, particularly their fur-lined overcoats that she had her tailor fashion into a cape. Of course, there were also aspects of her European culture that in turn impressed the Mongol ladies. Dounia braided her hair in a way that was unusual, wrapping her tresses around her head and tying in at the nape of her neck as if a serpent had bit its own tail circling past her temples. The hair-do made her look quite handsome. Soon the Mongol women began imitating Dounia's style to the sardonic reaction of their husbands who only laughed.

One morning, Dounia walked in to speak with Reyhan and found Sorkhokhtani instead. She caught the older woman making an awkward attempt at braiding her hair in the European style. The latter blushed deeply and tried to quickly undo what she had already done.

"You like my hairstyle, don't you?" Dounia asked, smiling openly. "There is a trick to it. Let me show you."

Sorkhokhtani smiled back and seemed only slightly embarrassed now that she saw her daughter-in-law's genuine interest in her hairstyle.

"It's actually quite simple. You divide your hair in three and fold the two sides over the middle part, just like that. Here, hold this mirror."

As Dounia handed over the mirror to Sorkhokhtani, she noticed her own reflection in it. She tried to quickly wipe away the frown that gave her a gloomy expression, but she was not quick enough for Sorkhokhtani's searching look.

"Is Hulagu treating you well?" Sorkhokhtani asked.

"Oh, yes," Dounia replied, a bit too abruptly to sound believable.

"Is there anything that bothers you?" Sorkhokhtani insisted, rephrasing.

"No, everything is fine," Dounia said, forcing a smile.

"I raised Hulagu. I have taught him to be patient with others. I do not deny the fact that he sometimes shows little mercy toward his subjects, but deep down there is a sense of decency in him. Try to delve into that decency and be good to each other."

"I will," Dounia replied meekly.

"He does intend to travel to Kievan Rus to visit his cousin Batu. I can suggest that you accompany him. I think the journey would do you both good."

Dounia smiled and embraced Sorkhokhtani for making the suggestion.

Chapter Sixteen

The Enchanted Fountain

DOUNIA WAS SHOCKED TO SEE HULAGU CARRYING A dead deer into their bedchamber. "You know how I hate the carcass of dead animals."

Hulagu ignored her comment and placed the still bleeding animal on her dresser.

"I heard you and Reyhan participated as spectators at the annual hunt," he said

"Yes. What about it?" she asked, a bit defensive.

"I see that the maneuvers of some of the sentries impress you."

"Nothing impresses me more than seeing my husband more often."

"I am a warrior first and foremost as I have mentioned so many times. And wars require that I stay away from Karakorum for months at a time. During those months, I expect my wife to be at her best behavior. Your conduct as a member of the Mongol court matters."

"I have been at my best behavior and always will be," she replied firmly. "Now pray take that bloody thing out of my chamber or I will ride my mare all the way back to Poland, and you see if you can stop me."

She had managed to make him laugh, and all was well again, for now. Dounia knew Mongol spies among the spectators must have informed Hulagu. However, she could not help noticing that her mother-in-law kept asking questions about her married life in a way that began to make her paranoid.

"Did you disclose anything about my troubles with Hulagu to my mother-in-law?" Dounia asked, barging into Reyhan's chamber unannounced later that evening.

There was no need for any such disclosure. Sorkhokhtani being a very smart woman could easily see the telltale signs in Dounia's face. At the same time, Reyhan knew there was no point in arguing with Dounia. She would believe what she wanted to believe.

Reyhan made an attempt to change the subject and putting a smile on her face said, "I just received the news that Mongke is chosen by the Khuriltai to be the next Khaqan, and he intends to make your husband the commander of Mongol Forces."

"Pray tell me before my confidence in our friendship shatters. Did you or did you not speak to Sorkhokhtani about my troubles?" Dounia repeated her questioning, clearly unfazed by the news.

Cornered by the comment, Reyhan found no other refuge but to disclose a secret. Hulagu was building a palace for Dounia and intended to surprise her with the finished structure, prior to leaving for Kievan Rus.

The major renovations at Karakorum were Reyhan's idea. She had suggested changing an old structure at the far end of the premises that resembled a Chinese pavilion into a European style palatial edifice. She had shared her plans for the project with Hulagu and recommended redoing the palace, hoping to pacify Dounia. Hulagu had ordered the renovations during Dounia's illness, using the help of craftsmen from different parts of Europe who were now at the Mongol leader's command.

"I told Sorkhokhtani that you missed the place where you grew up. Hulagu intends to give you as a present, a palace almost exactly like the one you had in Europe; including gardens and a pond with swans imported from Hungary."

Dounia's large sky-blue eyes grew even larger at Reyhan's disclosure.

"Oh, and there's more. An artisan from a faraway land called Paris has built this incredible silver fountain there."

"Paris," Dounia repeated, apparently entranced by the idea. French dignitaries frequented the Polish court where Dounia grew up, and she had traveled to France as a young child on one occasion, accompanied by her family.

"The bejeweled tree that forms the body of the fountain is taller than the height of four men with branches reaching the top windows of the palace. Four golden dragons hang from its boughs, out of the mouths of which flow all manners of wine. An angel stands on top of the tree, and like magic, the trumpet she holds makes a noise, and bells ring when a certain lever is activated."

Dounia, speechless with excitement, nodded for Reyhan to continue.

"Pears covered with pearls and apples covered with rubies hang from the tree. Four golden lions with sapphire eyes stand at its base as if guarding the fountain."

"Hulagu has done all that . . . for me?" Dounia asked.

"I have been told the garden will be breathtakingly beautiful in spring with wisteria trees blooming in it."

"I have got to see it now and cannot wait," Dounia said.

"We would have to disguise ourselves if you want to venture near those premises."

"Oh, that would be such an adventure," Dounia said, her excitement visible in her expression.

"We cannot go there dressed as princesses," Reyhan said, laughing. "I will ask Shura to help us out with this scheme."

That same evening, Dounia and Reyhan, camouflaged in the garbs of washerwomen, left their chambers to visit the new structure, about three thousand paces from Reyhan's Palace. Obscurity had its merits, for one's self-consciousness does not cloud one's mind. The two women, unchained from all ceremonial obligations, frolicked and laughed like children on their way to Dounia's new abode.

An earlier drizzle had layered the dry grounds, releasing an earthy scent. Here and there a torch was burning, lighting their way and filling their hearts with anticipation. The sight, when they finally arrived, exceeded their loftiest expectations. Tall and majestic, cream-colored marble covered the exterior of the palace with its Gothic spires embellished with gray stones. Marble statues of soldiers and maidens stood at intervals, carved onto the building's facade.

The fantastic fountain installed by a French artisan sprang from the center of the garden. Dounia accidentally touched the lever, and four drinks of different colors began pouring out of the mouths of the dragons. The sound of the trumpet rose as several bells installed on top of the contraption began ringing. It woke up the temporary occupants, including Hulagu who had returned from the fronts unannounced. He had been spending the night in the newly built structure to make his final inspection in the morning. He ran outside to see what the matter was, only to find Dounia there with Reyhan, dressed like the poorest of his servants. Moments later, when he discovered their ruse, the look of concern faded from his face, and he began to boom with laughter. He then offered to lead the two ladies on a tour of the palace.

"Do you think this will keep our little European dove's mind preoccupied while I am away?" Hulagu whispered to Reyhan in one of the rooms when Dounia was busy examining the wall paintings in another.

"Maybe for a while; having a baby might be another," Reyhan said, laughing.

Dounia who must have heard their laughter joined them. "What is all the mirth about?" she asked.

"Following my grandfather's footsteps in reaching out to allies, I intend to visit my cousin Batu who now leads the Golden Horde," Hulagu said. "It is my wish that you accompany me on this formal visit to Kievan Rus."

"Oh, I would love to. When will this be?" Dounia asked.

"At the onset of autumn, we shall depart. There are issues that I must tend to first, so you have plenty of time to prepare for the journey."

Chapter Seventeen

Golden Ringlets

A DARK SHADOW OF GLOOM FELL UPON KARAKORUM AS news reached Hulagu that his ailing mother had passed away. Sorkhokhtani had been ill with consumption for months while visiting Kublai with her health deteriorating further each day. Her funeral was held in the main cathedral of the Chinese region of Gansu, and she was buried in the grounds of that church.

The sorrow was short-lived though, with the excitement of the journey ahead to Kievan Rus pacifying Hulagu and drying up Dounia's tears. Reyhan was not so easily consoled and continued to mourn the loss of her friend.

Early one morning, Dounia found Reyhan in a serious mood when she was about to leave for the stables and ride her favorite mare. Although Reyhan had been melancholy since the death of her friend, her expression showed irritation instead of sadness. When Dounia asked what bothered her she said, "You should not have a haughty attitude toward the poor and destitute or those that you call commoners. Remember how Sorkhokhtani used to care for the poor. A simple turn of events or an unfortunate happening may lead one to become one of them. Their poverty is no fault of their own and no indication of the baseness of their character."

Reyhan was referring to an episode she had witnessed the previous day with Dounia demanding that her seamstress should redo an outfit which needed minor repair. Dounia understood what Reyhan was referring to and blushed.

"Haughtiness is no virtue Dounia, you need to reach out to those who are beneath you, and you will find loving hearts and caring souls," Reyhan said as she rolled a sheet of paper into a cone and placed some cookies in it for Dounia to munch on as she headed for the stables.

On her way there, Dounia suddenly noticed a small boy of about seven, quite thin in stature and with golden hair! At first, she thought it was the reflection of the sun on the boy's head that made his brown ringlets look golden, but she was not mistaken. She walked toward him and asked where he was from while speaking Mongolian. He gave no response.

"Jak ci na imie?" she tried asking for his name in Polish. No answer. She tried Russian. Again. No answer. Persian, "Esmet chieh?" No luck. The boy just stared and smiled, exposing two missing front teeth.

Probably a slave, Dounia thought and offered him the paper cone filled with cookies. The boy's grin widened, and after gratefully accepting the token with soot-covered hands, he ran to show off his goodies to other children.

Days later, when Dounia came to the stable to fetch her horse, the same little boy approached her. There was something in the boy's movement as he stood on the tips of his toes like a butterfly, opening his hands like wings. He handed over to Dounia a bunch of wildflowers he had gathered with flowering weeds tucked in between. The look in his eyes, his smile, touched Dounia to the core. She bent down and embraced the poor child.

Entry by Krisztina:

> *We are soon to depart for Kievan Rus. I look forward to the journey ahead. Sorkhokhtani's passing away was such a blow, particularly for Reyhan who seems to have aged since she heard the news. The excitement of the upcoming journey, however, allows me to focus on more pleasant things than death which reaps souls in greater numbers than any other time in history.*
>
> *Hulagu did not mourn his mother's death the way he did his father's. Although I was not present at the time, Reyhan told me how devastated*

he was when Touli Khan died. I wonder what he would have thought of me as his daughter-in-law if he were alive.

My attitude toward commoners and subjects of the Mongols has changed since Reyhan spoke to me about them, and I found this young boy with blond hair among the slaves. He reminded me of Wiktor when he was a child. I still cannot stand the idea of living a life of poverty but feel for them and understand how difficult their lives are. I also feel sorry for their children who are likely to lead lives of poverty as well. I miss my own childhood too. What a carefree and delightful era it was and how soon it came to an end.

Chapter Eighteen

Sarai Batu

[The Home of Batu]

A SHEER LAYER OF GOLD REFLECTED OFF THE WINGS OF a group of sparrows soaring toward the sky. Leaves had begun to imitate the different shades of fire, and the smell of birch wood burning in fireplaces filled the air. Autumn had arrived in all its abundance in Sarai Batu, the Mongol capital in Kievan Rus territories. Fruits were harvested and made into pies, and candles were lit early in the afternoon, as the sun began to set quite soon at the end of the day. Trees with heavy trunks clawed their roots deeper into the ground as their leaves formed colorful skirts upon the earth. Apple trees, the cheeks of their offspring having ripened for the season, had their produce harvested and carried to the markets of the town. Maidens filled jam jars and readied pickles for the long winter ahead. Smoke from the chimneys rose to greet the light fog of autumn.

Nature remained the only unchanged aspect of life in that part of the world. Every other aspect was transformed by the Mongol invasion. The cold winds ushered in the news of Princess Krisztina, once betrothed to Prince Mstislav, arriving at her adopted homeland of Kievan Rus. The idea of a former Kievan royal visiting the territories, even as a member of the Mongol court, brought a surge of hope to the hearts of the devastated inhabitants. After all, she symbolized the return of their long-lost honor. Although now allied to the Mongols, Dounia still symbolized Kievan Rus in all its beauty and grandeur, standing tall and proud like the queen that she was and would always be.

Strands of Dounia's golden hair caressed the fur lining of her cap as the wind blew in her face. Her thick braid cascaded down one shoulder. Wearing a fur-lined leather coat dyed scarlet, she disembarked along with the other members of the entourage and entered a platform upon which a group of Mongolian and Rus dignitaries awaited them, carrying gifts of different sorts for the visiting royals. Not all spectators looked happy. Upon arrival, some openly frowned at the sight of a former Rus Princess standing by the side of a Mongol Emperor and visiting like a foreigner with no ties to the country. But most people greeted Dounia with smiles. Dounia, in turn, tried to appear unaffected by the frowns and smiled back affectionately at those who were pleased to see her.

Batu welcomed Hulagu, the latter looked quite impressed by the Mongol rule that Batu had established in that part of the world. Batu embraced his cousin warmly and appeared equally impressed by Dounia's beauty and elegance. The inhabitants, in general, had adapted well to the new circumstances, although Dounia later heard that they considered living under foreign rule as the Mongol yoke.

Dounia decided to step away from the rest of the delegation and reached beyond the braided barrier rope to shake hands with the spectators. It was as if this sweet, humble gesture melted the hearts of the reluctant ones as well, instantly turning the entire crowd into her admirers. Nosegays of flowers were offered to her, and many reached out to shake hands with her. They chanted her name as they pushed one another to get closer to their princess.

The streets of Sarai Batu were paved in wood, something Dounia had never laid eyes on before. The land was unique in its splendor and charm. Seeing it for the first time thrilled Dounia. War damages had mostly been repaired, and newly built structures could be seen here and there. Colorful domes stood like turbans on top of cylindrical buildings. Flowerpots adorned the front yards and eyes peeped from beyond upper floor windows, for all were curious to see the newly arrived delegation.

The surviving Rus aristocrats appeared ostensibly humbled. Gone were the days of luxurious attire and extravagant parties described to Dounia in detail by Mstislav. As she soon learned, except for the segments occupied by the new Mongol rulers, old palaces and other institutions of governance had become run-down. With their sources of wealth and prestige depleted, the former Rus nobles had lost their popular base. Citizens paid tributes directly to the new rulers, and the former politicians and decision-makers that had yielded to the Mongols were sidelined. Only occasionally, and mostly during visits by foreign dignitaries, did the old Rus aristocracy appear on the scene as part of the background to prove Mongol benevolence toward former members of the court.

Batu had allowed some Rus officials, who had accepted the Mongol rule and had agreed to pay tribute on a regular basis to the Golden Horde, to hold municipal positions. These old aristocrats looked subdued and avoided wearing the gold-embroidered outfits they once owned. Instead, they were at times indistinguishable from low-ranking clerks. Few retained the role of advisor to the new rulers. Among them was a man by the name of Arseni of whom Mstislav had spoken at length, telling Dounia that he had little trust in the man and always eyed him with suspicion.

Dounia immediately associated the name with the description when they were introduced and knew he was the one Mstislav had warned her about. Arseni was a tall man with dark hair and a sinister smile. He used to work as a high-ranking counselor to the court of the Rus Prince. Dounia could envision him accommodating every Mongol's wish in order to retain his status.

As she followed Hulagu and Batu, she tried to take in the splendor of the corridors of the palace through which they walked. Magnificent painted ceilings arched above her head, and life-size portraits of former Rus aristocrats hung from the walls, reminders of an era that had come to an abrupt end half a decade earlier. Apparently, the new rulers were so impressed by the richly painted works of art that they did not discard them.

The delegation moved toward a set of stairs by the side of which

Dounia could see Mstislav's private chamber. She was certain of that fact for his name, although faded with the passage of time, still remained carved upon the door. Before the war, the room was used for private meetings and high-level discussions.

Mstislav had told her before he died that special paddings were used between the layered walls of this particular chamber so that conversations were not heard by outsiders. Mongols apparently did not know about its soundproof quality and considered it a storage room for unwanted items, for it was made to appear as such.

Deeply impressed by the portraits hung on the walls, Dounia had fallen a few steps behind the other dignitaries. With a swift motion, Arseni grabbed Dounia's elbow. The urgency of the matter he seemed to have in mind, flashed in his eyes as he said, "I need to speak with you privately, now." He then pushed her toward the chamber, placing a firm grip upon her mouth to prevent her from screaming.

Once inside, Arseni locked the door and released his grip on her. Carved furniture of rosewood, covered in dust, stood on a time-worn Persian rug. There were no windows to the room, and no paintings or decorations could be seen except a veneer of mahogany wood that covered the walls from corner to corner.

"What manner of greeting a guest is this?" Dounia asked, shocked and resentful.

"Listen to me," he demanded, "that is if you care about your sister."

"My sister?"

"Your younger sister Zofia is alive and well but will be killed if you do not cooperate with me."

"Where is she? Can I see her?" Dounia's heartbeat quickened when she heard the name.

"That is not possible yet. However, if you play your part to my satisfaction, such a meeting can be arranged in the near future."

"What am I supposed to do?"

"Encourage your husband, and his brother the emperor, to attack Baghdad and Damascus rather than Christendom." He stared at her for a moment or two with his black eyes and gripped her arm more tightly.

"Don't forget I am a Mongol royal now. God help you if you harm my sister in any way," Dounia hissed as he let go of her.

"Sleeping with the enemy must have its privileges. If you betray me or disobey my order, not even the Mongols can come to your sister's rescue," Arseni replied.

He abruptly opened the door, allowing Dounia to exit while giving her a meaningful smile and pointing to the main dining hall where she was to join Hulagu.

Shaken by the incident, Dounia entered the hall to sit at the elegant table set for the guests. The Rus aristocrats weren't the only ones that had undergone change. Batu had changed too since the last time Dounia and Hulagu had seen him. Rus cultural influences could be seen everywhere in his court. Even the food served, although still consisting mostly of animal meat, bore the Rus signature decorations with which Dounia was familiar. Whole cooked lambs and fowls with floral designs drawn on them with creams and jams had their eye-sockets filled with fruit. They took center stage on the elaborately carved surface of a long table of walnut wood.

An attendant carried a fabulous bouquet of chrysanthemums for the reception with such pomp as if the arrangement ornamented him. He placed it in the middle of the long table. Batu politely acknowledged Dounia with a smile as she sat next to her husband and congratulated Hulagu for his brother Mongke's ascension to power.

"Mongke has granted me the position of the commander of the Mongol Army," Hulagu proudly announced.

"Well. Congratulations on that account as well," Batu replied, smiling.

"He is of the belief," Hulagu continued, "that Mongol territories need further expansion. Therefore, wars are imminent."

"What part of the world does he have in mind?" Batu asked.

"He is considering putting an end to the Song Dynasty in China. Another exertion into Europe is also being contemplated."

"I hope they leave the territories of the Golden Horde alone," Batu said, looking a bit concerned.

"I am certain they will," Hulagu replied, his tone reassuring.

When Europe was mentioned, Dounia moved slightly in her chair, feeling oppressed. From that moment on, every sound became a blur. She could not hear or comprehend the conversation taking place around her and began thinking about what Arseni had asked of her. If she refused his demand, her beloved sister would die. *What horrific choices!* In her panic, she knew she had to push the campaign away from Europe and toward Muslim lands, saving her sister's life in the process.

She had completely lost her appetite as she stared absentmindedly at the amber-colored handle of a tray before her. It reminded her of the color of Reyhan's eyes as if her eyes haunted her even before she found out about her scheme. How could she betray her so?

Chapter Nineteen

The Assassins

MONGKE SUMMONED HULAGU UPON HIS RETURN FROM Kievan Rus for a private exchange. The scent of cardamom filled the air as an attendant poured a brew in a small cup with gold minaret designs. Mongke, the new Khaqan took a sip out of the small, handleless cup, frowned and quickly placed it back onto its saucer. He then cleared his throat, smiled and said, "The palace chef has brought this brew from Yemen that he calls *Arabic coffee*. It's a bit strong for my taste but helps revive one's senses."

The meeting had convened in Mongke's private ger in Karakorum. Its exterior appeared ordinary and indistinguishable from the gers of low-ranking officers in his army in order to ensure his safety and prevent it from being easily targeted in an ambush. The interior, however, revealed the luxurious life of Mongol rulers. A layer of thick silver-colored satin screened the entire space. A multicolored Chinese rug, with geometric designs woven in gold thread, covered the floor. Rows of narrow white marble tables with gold bases stood against the walls. The brothers sat face to face upon intricately carved white marble chairs with silk cushions. Hulagu turned the ring on his finger so that the large ruby set upon it was right side up.

"I am sure you did not summon me here to discuss the Arabic brew. Skip the preliminaries, for I am eager to know what you have in mind," he said in his usual matter-of-fact way.

"The reason why I invited you here," Mongke replied, "is because the only formidable force remaining before us is the powerful Caliphate in Baghdad. You are now the commander of the Mongol Army. Therefore, I leave the strategy and tactics to you and your men."

The two brothers exchanged meaningful glances. They considered each other comrades now on a mission to rule the world. They knew they would not leave any stone unturned, or any challenge circumvented in this quest. The stage appeared set. They had all the means they needed at their disposal, and most of all, they had the will and the tenacity to carry out their wishes. Caliph Al-Mustasim, the brother of the man that once Reyhan was to marry had it not been for the turn of events that brought her to the Mongol court, now ruled Baghdad.

"What intelligence do we have on the Caliph?" Hulagu asked, after a pause.

"Al-Mustasim is not what you would call a popular leader. He lives lavishly, hoarding treasure while his subjects are suffering. His governors are refusing to pay him taxes, so he has threatened to march over with his army and collect the sums by force. Oh, and there is also division within the court," Mongke added.

"Any internal division of that sort can be exploited to our advantage," Hulagu suggested. "We can encourage such a rift to our purposes."

"I have heard Ibn Alqami, his perfidious grand vizier, is secretly plotting against him, undermining his rule from within. Ibn Alqami may be willing to cooperate with us," Mongke said.

"I never trust a traitor. Their loyalties shift like sand dunes in a desert," Hulagu said.

"The Caliph is greedily holding on to the wealth he has accumulated, so much so that he has foolishly abstained from providing his army commander with the resources he needs to defend the capital," Mongke stated, smiling.

"Even though their army has been weakened, Baghdad is the heart of the Muslim world. To succeed we need to form the largest assault force to date. I will also use our latest siege engines as well as catapults to break into the city walls and crush their resolve to fight," Hulagu said.

"I urge you to visit Persia to ensure that our subjects in that region remain subdued, lest they are tempted to help their brethren in faith in Baghdad. There is also a growing cult branched out of the Ismaeli sect in Persia that is known as the 'Assassins.'"

"Oh, yes. I have heard about their supposedly impenetrable mountain fortifications—the Alamut," Hulagu interjected excitedly.

"The cult lives and worships beneath a veil of secrecy, resorting to political pressure when they can and when they fail, to assassination, in order to gain power. In fact, they sent us an envoy with a message of peace who later had the audacity to make an attempt on my life. I had his skull crushed and sent back with a warning to them not to ever mess with the Mongols again."

"I have heard they use hallucinating drugs, engage in all types of debauchery and gain power by assassinating opponents in nightly raids, slithering unseen throughout the land, dagger in hand, dressed in black garb with their faces covered," Mongke said.

"The people of Persia are terrified of them. They have succeeded in instigating so much fear among the inhabitants that no one dares to oppose them," Hulagu said, taking a sip of his coffee.

"They have gained strength over the years while we were occupied in China and elsewhere, taking over the central and eastern parts of the country and managing to build their extensive fortifications and numerous citadels. We have engaged them before in battle and overcame some of their smaller strongholds, but the main citadel high up in the mountain is quite difficult to reach."

"I understand the importance of conquering Baghdad, but victory over the Assassins will give me the needed clout to overcome that metropolis with little resistance and few casualties among the Mongols," Hulagu suggested.

"It's about time we put an end to the Assassins, but people say they are invincible," Mongke stated pensively.

"Only the Mongols are invincible," Hulagu said, but then both brothers burst into laughter. Power had changed them both and left them more confident of victory than ever before.

An attendant walked in to announce the arrival of a Chinese Prince who was bearing gifts for the Khaqan. Mongke made a gesture of consent to Hulagu and then to the attendant he said, "Guide him to the guest quarters."

Before leaving, Hulagu turned to Mongke and asked, "If I return victorious from these wars, what prize will be awaiting me?"

"You can form your own empire in Western Asia. Remember that we will own the nations we conquer, and we will be ruling them eventually."

Chapter Twenty

The Encounter

AT THE MONGOL BARRACKS, ROARS OF LAUGHTER FOLlowed two young warriors who had rolled onto the floor, wrestling as if to death, kicking each other, and knocking over benches and other furniture.

"Get up, both of you," Hulagu, who had just walked in on them, shouted. "What is this all about?" he demanded. The two men fighting got up and paid their respect while still fuming with anger.

"He owes me five gold coins, sir," the taller of the two uttered.

"Whatever for?" Hulagu asked.

"We were betting on the debate last night, and he cheated," the other warrior said.

"I did not. It was a fair game, and I won," the taller one yelled.

"You are talking about the debate between the prisoners?" Hulagu asked.

"He served them some wine," the shorter warrior replied, "knowing that the Christians would be the only ones who would partake of it, and the Muslims would refrain. The Christians won the religious debate last time, so my bet was on them."

"But the Christians were too drunk to talk, let alone engage in inter-religious discourse," Hulagu said laughing, then immediately frowned as he faced the taller warrior. "Did you not know that serving alcoholic drinks to the prisoners is against the rules?"

The warrior's face turned gray.

"I am interested in hearing their arguments," Hulagu said lowering his voice. "How are the Buddhists prisoners doing in these debates?"

"They lose every time, sir. The two other groups gang up against them," the shorter warrior replied, adding, "It's more fun than the wrestling match, sir."

"Our shamans can beat them all in any debate, sir. But it is beneath the shamans to engage with the captives," the taller warrior said, hoping to regain his ground.

"I don't want to have to repeat this. No more airaq for the prisoners," Hulagu said, sternly. "We need to keep them under control."

"They are under control, all right. Their only weapons are their tongues," the tall warrior said.

Hulagu gave the two an intimidating look, then addressed the men regarding the missions ahead.

A year ago, Reyhan had asked Baako to remove one of the stone tiles in the atrium adjacent to Dounia's Palace, making a compartment to hide the manuscript. As Dounia returned the manuscript to its secret location at dusk, she heard footsteps behind her. Quickly she got up, removed her ring and held it one hand while dusting her skirt with the other. As she had feared, it was Hulagu.

"I dropped my wedding ring," she said, showing the large blue diamond mounted on a gold ring as she replaced it upon her finger. She then ran toward Hulagu to embrace him, hoping he would not inspect the area. A lit lantern was a few paces away from where she stood, leaving the freshly dug up tile in the dark.

"My two favorite women, just the people I hoped to see before I leave," Hulagu announced with open arms and a broad smile as he entered Reyhan's parlor with Dounia at his side.

"Leave?" Dounia asked, alarmed.

Dounia pouted. "You are leaving me again," she whispered barely audible.

"I am a warrior. Have you forgotten that? And warriors go to war. My men are awaiting me outside, and I have not much time to bid you farewell," Hulagu said.

"Where to this time?" Reyhan asked.

"I am to confront the Assassins," Hulagu replied. "What do you know about them, Reyhan?"

"They are a relatively small group, but deadly in their tactics. Their founder was actually a religious man. But then as the group gained strength and formed its own structure of governance, it came to be seen as a threat to the Seljuk Dynasty. The Seljuk tried to subdue them through military force but failed in their attempts, mostly because of the sharp incline of the mountainside where their fortifications stand."

"I see. Anything else?" Hulagu asked.

"When the group felt threatened, they resorted to unusual tactics to overcome their powerful enemies. They are quite well-trained and swift in their stealthy maneuvers. They crawl like snakes at night, provoking a fear far greater than their actual strength."

"You mean the powerful Seljuk army could not defeat them?" Hulagu asked, looking perplexed.

"They are stationed atop a treacherous mountain beyond the reach of a regular army. Plus, their clandestine ways of waging war are unnerving. My grandfather held a meeting with his army commanders to combat the Assassins. The next morning, he rose to find a dagger launched deep into his pillow close to his head, pinning a note of warning."

"What was the warning?" Hulagu asked.

"LEAVE US ALONE. THE NEXT TIME THE DAGGER WON'T MISS."

"Well, the Mongols haven't missed their targets thus far either. My next target after conquering the Alamut is Baghdad." Hulagu paused for a moment in an obvious attempt to see the effect of his words.

"You have everything you need right here," Reyhan said, clearly shaken by his last abrupt pronouncement. "The woman you love, a country to be proud of which is at the peak of its power and glory. You have fame, you have wealth, and you can have happiness. What is it that drives you to shed more blood? To achieve what? Let those people be."

"It is not your place to determine what I should or should not do. It had been a dream of my grandfather, nay his vision, that the Mongols should rule the earth. That aspiration is in my blood, for I am a true progeny of his," Hulagu proclaimed with a harsh tone that he had never used before in addressing Reyhan.

"Sometimes vulnerability is hidden beneath a veneer of audacity," Reyhan said, with bitterness in her voice.

Hulagu looked angry, but there was a sublime gravity to Dounia's appearance that made Hulagu look at her instead and pause before leaving.

"Something is clouding your mind. What is it?" he asked.

"Spare the Christians," Dounia uttered involuntarily, but she immediately bit her lip as soon as she faced Reyhan who had turned pale as a ghost.

Dounia shuddered inwardly. She had just stumbled awkwardly into the arena of international affairs and military strategy; a merciless arena of which she had little knowledge, for she had never seen the results of a campaign up close. Before she could collect herself or think of something to say to soften the blow, Hulagu left.

Dounia's religious views stemmed from her desire to uphold the general perceptions of the European courts, rather than genuine faith. Eventually, the prejudices of the court became her prejudices, and the longing for a better hereafter became her motive to attend church regularly. She did so, however, as long as their views and inclinations did not contradict with her desire to live fully and happily in this world.

"In that short phrase, you have created an ocean that drifts us apart," Reyhan said. "You could have asked him to spare the lives of the women and children regardless of their faith, to let the civilians be, to have mercy upon the defeated. Why didn't you?"

Dounia turned toward the door as if to stop Hulagu, although she knew he had left already. Considering the absurdity of her reaction, she then turned to take a more quarrelsome posture in an attempt to justify her earlier statement. She knew she had done wrong, but she also knew that any attempt to show her remorse now would be futile.

"What kind of a religion sanctions divorce?" Dounia said, in a clear reference to Islam.

"An enlightened one that understands human nature," Reyhan retorted, looking livid. "Did you by any chance encourage Hulagu in his ambition to conquer Baghdad? I thought we had reached some understanding between us, setting aside religious hatred and keeping our minds and hearts open."

"There is no understanding we can have. Muslims and Christians have been killing each other and will probably continue to do so till the end of time," Dounia replied, further angering her interlocutor. She had stumbled inadvertently and continued to fall further away from Reyhan with every statement she made.

"Krisztina," Reyhan said, calling her by her Christian name rather than the beloved name of Dounia, "What have you done! Why do you think Heavens subjected our civilizations to such severe punishments? We slaughtered one another in the name of God before the Mongols were unleashed on earth. I haven't found any major differences between what each of these religions prescribe. The only difference seems to be in the ambitions of those who falsely profess to be religious and then commit all types of atrocities to gain power."

She paused and looked around as if to find something, some way of convincing Dounia before adding, "Don't you see what is happening? There are debates continuing well into the night between Muslim and Christian prisoners of the Mongols. If only they had had such communication before."

"Yes," Dounia replied, realizing that she was only adding injury to affront. "The Mongols see it as a game, and they bet on who wins the debate."

"It is said that 'to smother a fire; a greater conflagration must be lit.' Maybe the inferno ignited by the Mongols in Christendom and Muslim lands alike was necessary to bring both sides to their senses," Reyhan said.

Dounia's resolve to stay on the defensive melted, as she broke into a crying fit. "They threatened to kill my sister, Reyhan."

"Who did? Oh, let me guess... During your journey to Batu's territories, right?"

"This Rus advisor who now serves in the court of Batu Khan told me my sister, Zofia, would be killed if I refused to encourage the change in Mongol military strategy."

A dark shadow of gloom fell upon Reyhan's face. "O' Dounia," she said, "I have to tell you what I have up to now refused to disclose about your sister."

"You knew about her all along?" Dounia asked.

"Your sister was killed prior to your arrival at Karakorum."

Dounia began to tremble uncontrollably, and tears rolled down her cheeks. Reyhan helped her to a seat. She poured rosewater into a goblet of cold water and gave it to Dounia to drink in order to soothe her. They had no option now but to wait for news from the warfront.

Chapter Twenty-One

The Eagle's Nest

IGNORING THE WINDS OF EARLY WINTER THAT PORtended a difficult season, Hulagu stationed his forces around the rock mountain that housed the main citadel of Alamut. The Mongols had crossed many mountains as they left their imprints on faraway lands, but the sight of the Eagle's Nest fortifications was a scene they had never encountered before. The giant rock mountain of deep gray color rose among the steep gorges through which clear water flowed.

The Mongols repeatedly struggled to reach the summit, failing in every attempt. The mountain was simply too steep and treacherous. During one such attempt, horses slipped, and riders fell; screams were heard, but the Mongol cavalry continued its forward progression. Finally, as they approached the gates of the main citadel, cauldrons of hot oil greeted the first few who had dared to reach the gates. For every Mongol soul that was lost, Hulagu's anger rose until it reached a fever pitch.

"They shall pay for putting us through this," he hissed and found no other way but to retreat.

Finally, Hulagu resorted to the age-old Mongol tactic of waiting out the enemy. He decided to surround the fortifications and wait through the duration of winter until the residents of the citadel ran out of food. As days turned into weeks, life became unbearable for those perched high up on the mountain. The Mongols feasted on slain beasts that they roasted over fires. The wind carried the smell of cooked food to the hungry men and women within the rocky fortifications.

"I have been sent down here to speak with you, sir," a thin man with a turban of striped black and white cotton finally came down to meet Hulagu. "I have urged the residents of the citadel to surrender themselves, for I understand the power and the resolve of the Mongols, something they do not seem to recognize. Now it appears as though they have agreed to abide by my advice."

"Who are you to address me directly and so fearlessly?" Hulagu asked.

"I have lived my life sir, and the few remaining years of it are not much to cause fear of death within me," the man said, his white hair and beard attesting to the credibility of his statement.

"Wisely spoken," Hulagu said, "but you are yet to introduce yourself."

"I am a scholar from the city of Tus. They know me by the name of Khajeh Naseer or in short, Tusi. I beg you to hear me out. Spilling the blood of the innocent will only bring you infamy. If you seek glory, spare the lives of women and children, the innocents, who are trapped in the compound."

"Tusi," Hulagu repeated, "I like that name but are you not one of them?" he asked, pointing upward at the mountain fortifications.

"No, I am a mere captive of theirs, kept like a bird in a cage under conditions that truly suppress my soul," Tusi said, his eyes shining. "When the City of Neyshabur was placed under siege during the early years of Mongol reign, my wife and I were given refuge here. What enticed me initially were the numerous manuscripts held at the Alamut's magnificent library. I realized too late that leaving the fortifications was not as easy as entering it."

"Why is it that they have sent you as an emissary?" Hulagu asked.

"Under siege, the Grand Master of the fortress saw no alternative but to seek my aid. He knew I would return to him, for my wife is still held there. I told him, sir, that we are facing an inferno that would spare no one as it passes through the walls of the citadel. I also added that I had spent my life in austerity to gain wisdom, and that wisdom tells me that under the circumstances that we are in today, the only way would be to submit to the rule of this superior army."

"How would I know that you speak the truth?" Hulagu asked.

"I studied the science of my time in the city of Neyshabur, and I am well-known for my capabilities there. The Hashishins or as you say, 'the Assassins' lured me into their citadel, and I have been held captive by them ever since. I feel no sorrow for my captors, but there are a number of women and children living within the structure. I understand, sir, your intentions to subdue the Assassins, but I implore you to spare the lives of the innocents who are there at no will or design of their own."

The man's plea impressed Hulagu, but he tried not to show it. The scholar had gentle manners, spoke wise words, and had a noble countenance. "How can we reach our objective with minimum loss of life?" he asked.

"Allow me, sir, if you will. Maybe I can convince the powerful men within the compound to surrender."

"All I need is for the Grand Master to surrender himself. Tell him I will spare his life and that of his family if he does so before the sun sets. I will allow the women and children to leave, but those who have and continue to resist us or have Mongol blood on their hands will receive the most severe punishment," Hulagu stated sternly.

After hours of back and forth negotiations with the old man climbing the mountain and descending it with the last of his strength, the Grand Master yielded. The men remaining within the fortifications were forced to surrender as well. The Mongols triumphantly crossed the threshold of the citadel, facing little resistance. They swiftly cut down the few who chose to resist by taking part in hand-to-hand combat with their powerful, well-trained foes. Tusi remained in his chamber during the battle and looked surprised to find the great Mongol warrior at his very door.

"Do you drink this brew?" Hulagu asked as he sniffed a container that smelled like wine.

"They are for my scientific experiments," Tusi replied, smiling.

Hulagu walked around Tusi's chamber, picked up one of his books and looking at the strange drawings asked, "What is this that you write? It is not in any language that I have ever seen before."

"It is a branch of mathematics that is called Trigonometry."

"Does Trigonometry have military applications?" Hulagu asked.

"Trigonometry affects every aspect of life."

"And what type of contraption is this?" the Mongol Commander asked, looking at a large metal device.

"It is an instrument through which I observe the stars," the scholar replied.

"Can you read the signs from the stars for the most auspicious times for attacks?" Hulagu asked.

"I am no soothsayer, sir," Tusi replied, "but I can demonstrate to you the importance of science in practice and what knowledge can do for mankind." He then picked up a glass jar from a nearby shelf and dropped it in front of them, shattering it. Hulagu just watched, obviously wondering what the old man was trying to prove.

"You are not startled, sir, for you are aware of my action, and you are confident that it is a harmless move. Had this same act happened in the dark, taking you off guard, it would have surely alarmed you. Science is light. It illuminates our path, allowing us to see what is otherwise obscure."

Hulagu touched the long metal tube tilted toward the sky. He moved his finger across the round glass piece at the tip of the tube.

"We do share the love of the eternal sky," Hulagu said, as if talking to himself.

"But we see it in two different ways," Tusi said. "You see it as a supernatural being to be worshiped, and I see it as an open space to be explored. My contributions are to all humanity, and my struggles are for the promotion of science." Tusi looked around his chamber, and as if realizing for the first time that he was no longer a prisoner to the Assassins, he added, "I have suffered long and hard during over two decades of virtual captivity within these fortifications, sitting like a jewel upon a ring of despair."

"You are a jewel indeed," Hulagu smiled in admiration, "and you can be of great assistance to me. I have found you, Tusi, quite an intelligent man." Hulagu then looked straight at the scientist and added, "I would like you to serve me as an advisor at my palace or accompany me during my missions."

"Do I have a choice to refuse the offer?" Tusi asked, looking nervous.

"My decisions are not subject to the will of others. Consider it an order," Hulagu replied sternly.

"I suppose it is not difficult for one to leave one form of captivity for another," Tusi said, looking crestfallen.

"No one dares to address me in such a way. But I have to admit, I admire your audacity, and your honesty and integrity have had a bearing on my decision to retain you as an advisor as I move against Baghdad."

"You are a world conqueror, sir," Tusi replied, "and I am not a man of war, nor a schemer of strategy and concocter of tactics needed to achieve victory. I know my opinions will have no bearing on your ambition to conquer the world. Of all the things that God has created, what interests me most is the vast sky. At night, I look through my instruments at planetary rotations, the stellar formations, and the wonders of the universe. All I want is access to scientific manuscripts, and a means to observe the stars, an observatory."

"And all I want from you is that you provide me with the clarity you speak of, at times when matters become obscure. You will have access to all the amenities that you seek in order to monitor the stars. I will build an observatory that will not only house your current instruments but any future ones that our engineers can build for you. I intend to bring scientists and men of knowledge from every part of the world to assist you in your endeavors. In addition, all the manuscripts containing scientific information that are held within the compound's libraries will be at your disposal. But before you gain access to them, you have to learn to obey my command."

"Yes sir, I understand," the genius replied. "I also know that at one point wars will end, and humanity would need the light of knowledge to continue. I can help you when the day comes that you would need to administer the conquered lands and oversee the welfare of the inhabitants."

When Hulagu left, Tusi's wife, Narges Khanoom, who said she had heard their exchanges from her small bedroom chamber, objected. Age hadn't erased traces of beauty from her face. Her long braids, white as that of her husband's beard, embellished her floral house-gown.

"Are you going to collaborate with those Mongols against the Caliph of Baghdad? Are you not a man of piety who seeks wisdom through living austerely? Do you now seek to use such wisdom against Providence?"

"It is not Providence," Tusi replied, "that is bringing Baghdad to its knees. It is the Caliph's vanity, his false notion of invincibility, and his want of wisdom that is soon to unleash the Mongol tidal wave. Let the detractors say what they may. The observatory is my hermitage where I can find solace and focus on the future because it is my hope that through my discoveries and contributions, the world will one day witness an age of enlightenment."

"Are you telling me that you condone this war?"

"Far from it," Tusi replied resolutely. "It is just not within my power to prevent it. I see the matter as inevitable, for large parts of Europe are already devastated by the Mongols. China is under their rule, so is Persia, and Baghdad is the only remaining power. The Mongols will not rest until they conquer it. My only hope is to prevent a large number of casualties and mitigate the intensity of the war."

"This is just so hard for me to accept," she said, looking miserable.

"I am wise enough to distinguish between that which is inevitable and that which can be changed. I know there will be those who will belie me and even blame me for the actions of Hulagu and the invasion of Baghdad. But in acceptance of this responsibility, I was not given a choice. It is not that I value my life more than my human obligation. But I do know that the loss of my life will not change Hulagu's mind about what he is determined to do. It will merely deprive the world of any scientific contributions I am able to make during my lifetime and take away any chance I may have at mitigating crises."

His wife just looked at him with concern and sympathy in her eyes.

Lifting his finger as if reading the mind of the woman who had shared his joys and sorrows for decades he said, "I will use whatever power that is vested in me to dissuade Hulagu from carrying out his most brutal missions, and to promote the proper administration of conquered lands to preserve as many lives as possible."

Chapter Twenty-Two

The Siege of Baghdad

1258 C.E.

LA ELAHA ELALLAH, THE FAMILIAR CHANT OF "THERE IS no God but One God" was heard as the funeral procession carried the body of a deceased man in mid-afternoon through the main streets and alleys of Baghdad. What would have normally attracted some attention received little notice, however, since a greater calamity would soon befall the inhabitants of the city. News of the impending war had already spread from mouth to mouth and from town to town.

The mourners carried the body, shrouded in white, stopping only when they reached the door of the Grand Mosque. The pallbearers had wrapped keffiyeh around their heads, covering their faces save for their eyes.

One man slipped away and placed a note which everyone assumed to be the location of the funeral service on the door of Baghdad's main prayer hall. People ignored the writing for they were bound to see it during evening prayers.

One of the mourners chanted the names of God and prayers for the dead in fluent Arabic. But as the wind blew aside his shawl, he displayed features not seen in those parts. Lucky for him, only one street vendor seemed to have noticed this when he looked up and stared at him for a moment or two, but the matter was so subtle that it was quickly overshadowed by the incredible news of war on the horizon.

As the sound of Adhan called for evening prayers and people flocked to the main prayer hall, a handful got close enough to read the posted message:

To the people of Baghdad:

After sending several delegations, communicating our desire that the Caliph must pay regular tributes to the Mongols, and each offer being flatly rejected, this final missive is dispatched by Hulagu Khan to the Caliph and the inhabitants of Baghdad. Resistance will be futile. Any assemblage to confront the Mongols will be crushed. Therefore, I urge all citizens to refrain from any attempt to gather with the intention of warding off the newcomers or resisting their command. In due time, provided the inhabitants fully submit to Mongol wishes, Baghdad will be allowed partial autonomy.

Signed –Hulagu, Commander of the Mongol Forces

Despite the numerous territories conquered by the Mongols, Hulagu had remained unsatisfied, his grandfather's task being left unfinished. He wanted the Mongol banner raised in every capital of the world, and his craving for revenge against those who had defied him remained unfulfilled. He had found the idea of a European invasion quite tempting, yet, the riches of the Muslim world had prompted him to look eastward toward Persia and Baghdad.

Hulagu was heir to an empire and like the child of the practitioner of medicine who strives to be like his father or the offspring of a sailor who grows up dreaming of becoming the captain of a ship, Hulagu envisioned expanding the territories that his grandfather, Genghis, had conquered.

As he stood under a burning torch in the Mongol encampment outside of Baghdad, it appeared as if flames were bursting from his head and his crown was on fire. He addressed the most prominent members of his inner circle in his husky voice.

"There are those who claim that the Mongol Empire is on the decline. I shall teach them that my grandfather's reign is not over yet, and the Mongols are alive and well. I will watch with pleasure when the day comes that I defeat my foes. I will pull the rug from underneath them so hard that they will fall and break their crowns," he proclaimed loud enough for the large crowd congregated around him to hear.

He paused as if enjoying the sound of silence as all held their breath not to miss a single word of their commander's speech. He then added, triumphantly, "We shall empower the minorities in order to sow discord among the inhabitants. The Christians who live there have been devoted to their homeland and many of their young men may be inclined to join forces with the Caliph. But there are disgruntled ones among them, and we shall be able to create division within the ranks of the defenders. We will enter Baghdad as liberators of the Christian minority."

Trepidation cast its shadow upon the Caliph's land as the war commenced. On the 29th of January 1258, to the sound of drums, the Mongols proceeded toward the gates of the city. Siege engines stood tall at the barrier walls, allowing the Mongols access to their enemies. With their scouts and spies informing them ahead of time regarding the Caliph army's capabilities and weaknesses, they moved fast and ferocious, inflicting irreparable damage on their foes at the onset of war. The defenders of Baghdad who lacked the resources they had repeatedly requested from the Caliph and were denied, found themselves facing a well-trained, sophisticated army.

A reddish hue had formed on the horizon. Ashen clouds sprinkled with a mixture of copper rays from the sun, lazily rolled from one side to the other, little heeding the calamity that was taking place below as if tired of the atrocities of men against men. It was another bloody chapter in human history that nature had no desire to witness. No animal, no natural disaster could do unto man what he could do unto his own.

Each side pitched their standard. The Mongols lifted their sulde ornamented with yak tails, and the defending army displayed red flags bearing a black crescent and star. Each side saw the other as the personification of the fiend or some evil omen. Steam rose from the dilated nostrils of Mongol war horses as their front hooves rose at the command of their riders. Their eyes bulged, but their hind legs remained firmly on the ground, ready to take on the Caliph's army. The Mongols had meandered through the hills and valleys of the land like wild waters. With stealthy moves unprecedented in the history of the region until that time, they crept up to enemy lines. They broke embankments, flooding the land behind the army of the Caliph.

Hatchets beheaded fallen warriors who were wounded by the sword. Flames destroyed what swords could not. A great civilization was brought to its knees, its wealth stolen, its dignity crushed. Grazing lands and forests were set afire as the Caliph's Empire turned to dust.

The scent of gunpowder filled the air, mixed with the bitter aroma of burning trees and bushes. Mongol rage like a wave rose to the surface, and surged, crushing souls in its wake, ripping out the beating heart of the land. Dark silhouettes of Mongol warriors seemed like specters from another world as they plunged their hands into sacred chambers of human life, stealing away forbidden fruits: a father's gold tooth who had laid down his life to protect his family, the gold chain around the neck of a young girl whose body was mutilated by the Mongols, a tiny knife with an ivory handle used by the young girl's brother who now lay dead as he rushed to her defense. Similar scenes repeated throughout the land leaving a treasury of confiscated goods in the hand of the usurpers.

Commodities of greater value in the eyes of the Mongols, such as gold and silver, coins and jewels, were carried to the camp of the Khan. The truly precious possessions, the intangible, obscure ones like the happiness of a young girl, a father's love, a mother's tears, were allowed to wither away.

Trembling maidens shied away from windows and hid in dark corners. More than ever they felt defenseless. Mercy had packed its bundle of cares and left the land. The wealthy envied the mud-dwellings of the poor for they appeared safer, and the poor wished their dwellings were subterraneous.

Further deterioration of the crisis was unimaginable, but the Mongols managed to wreak such havoc in Baghdad that the few who escaped the carnage ended up telling horror stories to nearby towns and villages. Thus, the will to fight began to wane, and courage frittered away even before the Mongols reached them. Baghdad fell within forty days.

There was no rain for many days, and from the festering bodies there oozed a Pandora's box of pestilence that haunted the survivors. Neglected for being too many to inter, the petrifying bodies were left unburied, turning into a fertile ground for disease. Finally, the rain came in the form of a nighttime drizzle. The cold night air turned its droplets into a thin layer of ice, glistening upon the blood-drenched soil as if mocking the horrid landscape.

There appeared to be no end to the nightmarish scenes that continued from street to street and from alley to alley. The vivid expressions on the faces of the dead melted like features carved on ice statues under the hot sun. There was a sarcastic irony to all of this if ever one was inclined to laugh at such a gruesome display of horror. A butcher lay on his back upon a table where he used to chop up meat, the very knife of his trade poked deep into his throat. A shopkeeper lay dead upon the floor with his remaining trinkets of coin splattered all over his body. A donkey had fallen on top of his rider as if asking that they each take turns in giving rides. Little hope remained in the hearts of the survivors. The future was nowhere to be seen. The past had slipped away noiselessly, dragging away with it all traces of normalcy.

In time, the rising sun shone upon the land, and nature healed what no other means could. The emotional wounds remained, however, time like a remedial ointment worked its way through months and years. Eventually, hope, like an ever-sprouting plant, began to take root again.

Baghdad was still reeling from the intensity of Mongol attacks when Al-Mustasim was sacked, and the inhabitants realized they had foregone the brutality of one ruler only to become subject to another. The Ayyubid Dynasty in Damascus was also subdued. Hulagu's triumphant entry into Damascus, and the kindness he showed toward the Christian minority there was celebrated in Europe as a victory against the Saracens; although Hulagu himself could hardly distinguish one religion from the other. He sought military conquest and used internal division as a mere tactic to ensure success.

Entry by Reyhan:

As Batu had crushed parts of Christendom, Hulagu wreaked havoc in Baghdad, the heart and center of the Muslim world. Thousands upon thousands were slaughtered as the Mongols showed no mercy. Baghdad's Darol-Hikmat, the greatest library in existence was destroyed. Millions of hand-written manuscripts were thrown into the Euphrates, turning its water black with their ink as the streets of Baghdad were paved in red blood.

The Mongols threw the Caliph into a cell with all his accumulated gold but refused to give him food in order to punish him for hoarding the wealth of a nation while his army starved. He was then rolled into an expensive carpet, among the many he had amassed and was trampled to death. Thus, his own wealth became the instrument of his death. The Caliph had enough gold stored in his treasury to provide every means necessary for the success of his army but somehow greed and the false hope that maybe the Mongols would spare Baghdad, made him withhold his support for his warriors. In an attempt to promote the Christians and subjugate the Muslim inhabitants of the metropolis, Hulagu destroyed and plundered the mosques and spared the churches.

Initially, I blamed Dounia and then myself for Hulagu's course of action, but as of late I have realized that it is part of Mongol scheme to sow discord among the otherwise harmonious populations. To add salt to the wounds of the subjugated, Hulagu left most positions of power in the hands of Christians. He did the same in Damascus. In this, he differs from his grandfather, Genghis, who promoted harmony among all people of faith. It is indeed a bitter seed that Hulagu has sown. The enmity he creates is likely to last for generations.

Famed Persian scientist Tusi believed that the conquest of Baghdad by the Mongols, considering their long-term strategy, was inevitable. Although Tusi witnessed the realization of his dream observatory, he could do little to prevent the carnage that ensued in Baghdad, nor could he save his ailing wife from the fangs of death not long after the fall of that great civilization. While living in Baghdad, the Angel of Death claimed his soul as well.

Chapter Twenty-Three

A Tawny Afternoon

1259 C.E.

A LUSH, GREEN, FRUITFUL SUMMER HAD ARRIVED THAT year, and Maragheh, in the northern stretches of Persia, never looked more enticing. Its cooler temperatures suited the Mongol taste, and its greenery provided enough fodder for their animals. As a light drizzle caressed the carriage carrying Hulagu Khan, he asked the driver to stop near the bank of Sufi Chay River. There, he settled down to study the terrain over the next fortnight.

The Mongol chariots of war had continued their rampage in far corners of the world during the reign of the sons of Tolui. Their intent, however, had changed from mere plunder to the administration of the affairs of conquered territories. Kublai struggled to become the first emperor of a united China and have all three former territories of the Jin and Song Dynasties, as well as the Tangut people, under his rule. Hulagu, who had reached the age of one and forty, chose Persia to establish the Ilkanate Dynasty, considering Maragheh, the birthplace of Reyhan, as his capital.

Hulagu had intentionally arrived at the end of the summer season to assess how bearable Maragheh would be in its hottest months. The vast green prairies and hills that bordered the city contrasted with the open skies that stretched above. Hulagu gazed at the uninterrupted horizon. The sun appeared brighter than ever on that afternoon as he walked out of the ger set up for his temporary stay. Pure, blissful, tantalizing summer air surrounded him. The sun made him giddy. It recklessly splashed its rays all over the plains, showering the surrounding meadows with sequins of light. It was a yellow afternoon, amber yellow as if the entire scene was drenched in a tawny brew. Even the stone embankment glittered like glass. Beyond the advantages of the idyll, Maragheh teemed with vineyards, enough to satisfy the thirst of his army.

The locals, having heard that the Great Khan of the Mongols was moving there, greeted him with bowls of apples, walnuts, almonds, and grapes. They brought saplings of roses to be planted in the future palace garden and peacocks to roam that garden when in bloom. They even brought along a tamed tiger cub on a golden leash trained to be kept as a pet. Celebrations ensued, and everyone cheered, either out of joy or out of fear, when Hulagu announced Maragheh the capital of his territory in Persia.

Hulagu's joy proved to be short-lived, however. When the cooler winds began to blow, news reached him that Berke, Batu's brother, had revolted against him, announcing his intention to wage war. Not all Mongols had remained sky worshipers. Some had converted to Buddhism, others to Islam or Christianity. Berke, a convert to Islam had begun attacking Hulagu's territories to avenge the destruction of Baghdad, an Islamic capital. Hulagu had no choice but to move his forces to the Caucuses. Thus, the first sparks of Mongol civil wars were ignited as winter commenced.

Hulagu's men carried swords and axes, as well as their famous Mongol bows and arrows and shields of leather, stretched over tightly-wound lightweight wicker. Long accustomed to transporting their provisions while sitting on top of their saddles, the warriors never considered their loads too heavy.

The unusually warm season in the Caucuses had turned knee-deep snow into slush. A bridge of ropes enticed Hulagu to cross the half-frozen river to speed up the movement of his cavalry toward Berke's encampment; a moment's decision that proved fatal.

Seventeen hundred miles away at Karakorum, Dounia was the bearer of a heartwarming secret that she could not wait to disclose to Hulagu. She imagined the look of surprise on his face, how delighted he would be to hear that they were expecting a child. Three months into her pregnancy, she had already set up in her chamber a golden bassinet, looted during the early days of Genghis's rule.

The world smiled at Dounia, spreading before her a golden path to happiness and contentment, now that she had recovered from the news of her sister's death. She was too young to know how this deceptive world, this bride of a thousand grooms, could playfully lay the path to one's destruction in the colorful hues of joy. She put on her new dress that instantly deepened the blue color of her eyes.

Dounia had remained in Reyhan's Palace for the duration of her pregnancy. She placed a few drops of jasmine water on her neck and wore the talisman of turquoise that once belonged to Chaka, for the blue in it matched her gown, its torn leather rope replaced long ago. Before going down to Reyhan's parlor, she wrote the following note in the manuscript.

Entry by Krisztina:

> *In Karakorum the lake is frozen solid, so it must be December in Europe. Hulagu left for the front again after making a short stop here, leaving me under Reyhan's care. Reyhan has forgiven me for my terrible blunder amidst the trickery of Arseni. Now she treats me like a spoiled daughter, does everything to please me, especially considering my condition. She even had a caravan bring me pomegranates from Persia. I tried them, and they were a bit too tart for my taste—they are not a fruit I am used to. The last message that came from the front indicated that Hulagu should be home soon. I cannot wait to share with him the news of our first child and to let him know how much I have missed him. I have had a dark blue dress made just for the occasion.*

Chapter Twenty-Four

The Sweet Song of His Hawk

DOUNIA WALKED INTO REYHAN'S PARLOR, TOO EXCITED to wait for her husband in her chamber. Bright sunshine illuminated portions of the parlor. Through the stained glass window, Dounia followed the rainbow-colored Mongolian ducks, the most beautiful of their species, as they sauntered about the pond oblivious to the cold. She too looked as if she belonged to the same tribe; her movements being an imitation of theirs.

Dounia had earlier braided her hair into a crown upon her head with a blue ribbon interwoven into her golden strands. She thought of the moment she would break the news of her pregnancy to Hulagu and what his initial reaction would be to another royal child being born among the Mongol clan. She smiled at the idea. *Who would have thought that she would one day be the mother of a Mongol Khan or a Mongol Queen? Who could have even imagined such a fate?*

When Dounia heard the sound of a trotting horse, she felt the hour had finally arrived for Hulagu and her to be united again. The sound of the approaching rider mixed with the sweet song of his hawk. She rushed to greet her husband, but when she reached the front door, what she saw was Hulagu's horse. Another warrior was riding it with Hulagu's bird tethered to his wrist.

Reyhan, who had heard the commotion, came rushing to see the newcomer. She got there in time to catch Dounia as she swooned at the news that the stranger carried. If Reyhan hadn't been there to support her, Dounia would have certainly collapsed on the hard stone pavement.

"My God, what is it?" Reyhan asked as she helped Dounia to a seat.

"Hulagu is seriously ill," Dounia who had regained consciousness replied, sobbing.

"How bad is it?" she asked looking at the messenger.

"The cavalry was crossing a bridge of ropes connecting the two sides of the river in the Caucuses. The ropes that formed the shaky structure appeared worn and ready to tear. We did not know when the rupture would occur and who would be the unlucky one to fall into the half-frozen river below. We had almost reached the other side when the bridge caved in, and some of Hulagu Khan's men drowned. When our leader fell in, the others pulled him out from under a sheet of ice, but he developed a fever afterward. His condition, I am afraid, is deteriorating as we speak," the man said.

"I can't endure it Reyhan," Dounia pleaded. "Now that I have learned to love him, now that I am bearing our first child, he cannot die . . . Lord, he cannot die. I have to go to him now."

"You are in no condition to leave. I will go to him," Reyhan replied.

Sorkhokhtani's old chambermaid, who occasionally visited Karakorum and happened to be there at that inauspicious moment, suddenly appeared at the door. She must have heard the messenger for she looked pale and shaken. Dounia reached out to Reyhan and fell into her arms.

"If there is any way," Reyhan said, "that Hulagu's health could be restored, I will do my utmost to bring that outcome."

"I beg of you to go to him and help him out," Dounia said. "You are the only one who can." With pleading eyes, she looked at Reyhan. "I leave my heart and soul in your care. Come back to me bearing the glad tiding of his health, for I cannot stand this news."

"How can I travel as a woman alone through all these territories?" Reyhan asked, looking helplessly at Sorkhokhtani's chambermaid who had served the late Mongol Queen for decades.

"Mongol territories are safe," the woman said. "All you have to do is wear this." She removed a metal object that she had tied around her neck with a ribbon. "No one throughout the territories ruled by the Mongols would dare harm the bearer of this. You will be considered a subject of the Mongol Khaqan, and whoever touches you will bring the wrath of our people upon his entire nation."

"What is this? A talisman?" Reyhan asked, taking the iron amulet with the Mongol insignia on it.

"It is called a passport," the woman replied. "It can perform miracles as far as crossing borders are concerned, for no one will be hindering you. A few Mongol cavalrymen, as well as a coachman, can accompany you on this journey."

Before leaving, Reyhan walked into the kitchen, a separate building situated outside the palaces made of rough stone inside and out. It had a tall concave ceiling and small windows inserted into the walls to allow the smoke and smell of food to exit. It almost resembled a prison, except for the fact that dried herbs and bunches of garlic adorned one side of the wall while the stove stood at the other. At a long wooden table in the middle of the kitchen, Shura was cutting up a large onion. Her hair still covered in an old babushka had turned white, and her face had wrinkled considerably since she was first brought to Mongolia. She quickly wiped her hands on her greasy apron as soon as she saw Princess Reyhan.

"You have to help me," Reyhan said as she grabbed Shura's arm. "I am leaving for the fronts. Hulagu is bedridden, and I need to be by his side. I leave Dounia under your care, for I am not sure when my return will be."

"Fear not my lady," Shura assured her, "I will see to it that all goes well for her and the baby when the time comes."

Chapter Twenty-Five

The Nighttime Journey

DARKNESS DESCENDED HEAVY UPON THE EARTH. REY-han and her companions traveled a road strewn with boulders and rocks toward the Caucuses. The horses stumbled at times as they made their way to where the injured patient lay.

They had chosen the night time for traveling, because it was safer and their presence less visible to highwaymen and robbers. Reyhan wore a long, black cloak, made according to Dounia's instructions to cover her identity as well as her gender. She tried to keep her ears open, and her eyes did not dare to shut, not even for a moment, since the path was treacherous. Ironically, her hope lay in the power of her former captors, the Mongols. She knew that any harm coming her way would be brutally avenged. Therefore, she openly displayed the medal that ensured her safe passage through the cities and towns. Earlier she had seen the stone tablets placed near roads and highways that warned those who disobeyed the Yassa of the punishment that awaited them.

Reyhan looked at the fast-moving grayish clouds above. Cool air blew against her face. She patted the head of a camel that strode by her. The humpbacked creature could travel for miles without the need for water or nourishment, while its milk ensured fresh food for the small caravan. In its slow, graceful movements she could feel the forward motion of time. Memories of days gone by moved like watercolor images before her mind's eyes. She remembered Hulagu as a child, their first meeting, and the attachment that almost instantly formed between them. How he had reached out and playfully grabbed her skirt when he was a mere five-year-old; and that mischievous smile that had melted her heart.

At the break of dawn, the mountainous terrain appeared like folds of a brown silk gown as pearly clouds formed a necklace of white on each peak of a skirt. Reyhan recalled how she used to wear silk gowns and pearls to receive foreign dignitaries at Ogodei's court. She touched her face with the tips of her fingers. The dew of youth had dried upon her skin. Her head ached, and she could feel the wrinkles on her face cutting deeper into her flesh. Her heart was aging too, but her soul had remained defiant, always embracing the early years of youth. With the instinct of a mother about to visit a long-lost child, she reached out for a silver mirror in her sack and grabbed a small bottle of almond oil to refresh her face. She did not want Hulagu to see her looking so worn-out.

They had been traveling for more than three weeks. When the first rays of the sun became visible, they stopped at a caravansary to rest and replenish. Reyhan ordered the few horsemen accompanying her to take turns resting and guarding the chamber where she stayed. One of them hurried to fetch her some refreshments before she fell asleep.

At dusk, they got back on the road, speedily moving toward their destination. She could hear the howling of wolves in the distance. Soon a large pack of them approached the small caravan. These predators did not recognize the authority of the Mongols, and they did not abide by Yassa laws. Hunger and instinct had drawn them toward the travelers. The few dogs accompanying them barked at the wolves, but they were no match for the superior beasts. The wolves and dogs tore at each other's flesh, and two of the horses came under attack as well.

One of the horses pulling Reyhan's carriage fell to the wolves. The carriage began to sway, and it was about to fall over. But in a daring move, one Mongol horseman approached and quickly cut loose the dying horse, replacing it with his own steed while continuing to ride at the same speed as the caravan. The bloody confrontation left them with only three dogs. They lost two horses and sadly the camel as well.

In the rush to make it quickly to Hulagu's bedside, it had not occurred to them to bring sharpshooters along. But the travelers were left intact and for that, Reyhan was grateful. Although shaken by the event, she had known that the journey would be treacherous and now it seemed that they had gotten through the worst part of it. She tried to steady herself in the carriage and gathered some blankets around her to stop her body from trembling. The last thing she needed was to become ill herself.

Upon arrival at the Mongol encampment, Reyhan found Hulagu in a dire condition. She had not forgiven Hulagu for the attack on Baghdad. However, today he laid on a sick bed a broken man, and for Dounia's sake, she had to reach out to him. She tried to remember Hulagu not as he was now, the bloody conqueror of Baghdad and tormentor of Damascus, but as a child she once embraced and learned to love. She had blamed herself for days for his upbringing but then concluded that he was the true grandson of Genghis regardless of the impact she or anyone else could have had on him. He remained remorseless to the end.

Physicians from China and Persia were at Hulagu's bedside, but Reyhan felt that maybe her presence, the kindness and love she had shown toward him since childhood, would provide a better remedy in helping him recover. That assumption proved to be correct.

Hulagu recuperated for a while; color returned to his pale face and indrawn cheeks. The wild look of his countenance brought on by fever changed to one of recognition and composure. But soon he fell feeble and weak back onto his pillow, moaning through deliriums and nightmares. One day he rose with the sun, eyes blood-shot, shirt drenched in a night sweat. He asked for a quill and a roll of paper to write his last will, instructing the Mongol army regarding the affairs he had in mind.

As he coughed, a drop of blood dripped from his lips and rolled down the page upon which he had written his instructions. It mixed with the black ink on the white paper which he crumbled and tossed across the room in extreme agony. Reyhan gave him a fresh sheet, and when this second attempt at writing ended, he fell back onto his pillow again and collapsed from the exertion.

Reyhan's presence and motherly care revived the invalid temporarily. Yet, despite her efforts, Hulagu had become too weak, reducing his chances of survival. Realizing that he might soon leave this world, and with no clergy or minister being available, Reyhan felt that she must act as one. She built up the courage finally when she found him barely awake. "Do you believe in God, Hulagu?"

"Although I had converted to Christianity, in this final moment of my life it is Buddhism that I embrace. I have seen the impact of its teachings on my brother, Kublai. The people of China admire him, but I am despised in the lands that I have conquered."

He looked into Reyhan's face for a moment or two before adding, "Take care of Dounia and our baby for me."

"You know I will," Reyhan replied.

"Oh' Reyhan, death is the final victor. No one is able to defeat it. Have them carry me and bury me in Maragheh, near the Sufi Chay River where you were born. My soul shall know your presence there, and I shall rest in peace," he uttered with difficulty and permanently closed his eyes to the world.

Before Hulagu could truly fulfill his desire for greater conquests, destiny had ruled him out, and the Angel of Death claimed his soul. The wealth he had plundered, the lands he had conquered, the women he had captured, all were left to others. Wearing simple military attire, he was buried deep within the earth, leaving behind a bloody legacy. However, to those like Dounia, to whom he was not a world conqueror but a loving companion, his death dealt a heavy blow.

Chapter Twenty-Six

The Withering Rose

DOUNIA LOOKED UP. A LONE VULTURE CIRCLED THE SKY, casting its dark shadow upon her body. She had stepped outdoors to take in the fresh air. The sight of the bird of prey brought a frown to her face, and she decided to go inside. She felt such trepidation in her heart, the like of which she had never felt before, a premonition that a calamity was soon to befall her. A sinking sensation in her gut told her things would not remain the same, and soon she would reach a precipice beyond which life would lose its meaning.

Dounia's charitable activities that included reaching out to the poor had kept her busy during the few months that Reyhan was away. Her vocation had increased her popularity among the downtrodden people. The ladies of the court, however, considered her actions degrading to a member of the royal family.

Again and again, Dounia tried to imagine the moment of Hulagu's triumphant arrival, a fennec fur cap on his head, standing tall before her, smiling at her. He had been a rock-solid mountain upon whom she had relied. But with Reyhan's return, her hopes were crushed.

"I am sorry my dear, his doctors did all they could, and he revived for a short while under my constant care but . . ." she could not finish her sentence as tears rolled down her cheeks.

Color left Dounia's face. Voices echoed in the room, words rumbled back and forth among the crowd that had gathered around her, but she could only hear her own screams that moved like a wave within her head. Reality had struck her a blow that shattered her hopes and dreams.

Messages of sympathy poured from dignitaries and officials all across the world, but none could soothe Dounia's aching heart. *Is God punishing me?* she lamented. *Is there no one to lift me out of the abyss into which I have fallen?*

Dounia insisted on being left alone after assuring Reyhan that she would sleep. But she stayed up all night in her chamber. She lit a taper by the dark window. Eclipsed by the light of the moon, the candle's light looked dim. The branches had woven their tentacles around the aging building as if ready to devour its innards. Dark green foliage covered parts of the windowpane, concealing her view. Her heart felt suppressed by despair. She had lost her loved ones and family in Poland, and now the only man who could have sustained her away from her homeland was gone. Life's riches had turned into dust but little souvenirs of days gone by remained to torment her longing soul.

Dounia had long suspected that Reyhan also suffered privately, that she swallowed her anguish and silenced her cries, putting on a mask of tranquil dignity to ward off inquiring stares. At times, when she entered her chamber, an incessant stream of tears washed over Reyhan's aging face, as if the dark sensation of guilt for involuntarily being an accomplice to the Mongols loosened its chokehold on her. Only when feeling absolutely wretched, did those secret expressions of grief, about the losses Persia had endured, turned into sobs barely audible to outsiders.

Their mutual pain drew the two women closer. They spent many afternoons having tea together in the garden. And when the weather became inclement, they sat in the parlor and chatted for long hours about the countries they had left behind, the loved ones they missed, and their mutual concerns for the future of the world.

Entry by Reyhan:

> *Hulagu's death and witnessing Dounia's dire situation has been a blow to me from which I believe I will not recover. I have experienced a withering autumn in life, and a cold winter has followed it, sapping away the spring of youth and the fruitful summer of middle age. Therefore, this may very well be my last entry.*

Kublai has set the stage for the formation of a unified Chinese nation. Ariq Boke took charge in Mongolia but then fell out of Kublai's favor. Hulagu, my troubled ward, grew up to induce both fear and admiration in many hearts. He established his kingdom in Persia and was well received by the inhabitants of the land who were too wise to confront the Mongols at the peak of their power.

It has been many years now that I have been cooped up in this palace that is also my jail. I live with a lie each day that I am a Mongol Royal, when in fact my true identity was stolen from me. What gives me solace and ebbs the intensity of my grief is the writing that I do. When I first began to write the chronicles, I took the horrific tales of the war front that Baako related to me, poor soul, and turned them into stories that sounded more like fiction than reality. But that reality is not lost on me, nor to the readers of these pages.

Dounia was troubled to find Reyhan one day in the hallway of her palace looking lost and dazed. She had known for a while that something was troubling her friend and companion. Dounia noticed how much Reyhan had aged since her journey to find Hulagu. She looked worn and withered. The woman who stood before Dounia was only a faded picture of the Reyhan she knew. She looked as if she felt the weight of the world upon her feeble shoulders. Her ashen face spoke not only of her old age but of her ill health. Reyhan's hair had grown long and gray, her face long depleted of the cheerful pink that signifies a youthful complexion. Even her honey-colored eyes had lost their luster and no longer looked vibrant. Dounia feared that she would lose her. Maybe she already had.

"Come have some tea with me," she said, but Reyhan refused, complaining that she was too tired. Her constitution appeared weak, yet she stood erect and proud like a condemned prisoner insisting on her innocence.

"There is something I need to tell you, Dounia. I may not be around much longer," Reyhan said.

Dounia held out her hand. Reluctant at first, Reyhan took it, and instantly her expression changed. Color rose in her cheeks in a feverish way as she was led to a seat.

"I fear that my death is imminent, Dounia. My soul can no longer bear it," she choked on her words and bit her lips to stop herself from crying.

"Oh Reyhan, do not speak of death. With Hulagu gone, I cannot live life without you."

"The manuscript will become your refuge, your companion in your darkest days," Reyhan said. "You will pour your heart onto its pages, and like an old friend, it will listen to you. The book will be your means of communicating with those who will come long after you have parted with this world. So, do consider it a means of reaching out to those who would understand."

Dounia knelt beside her, but Reyhan insisted that she sit by her side, for she could harm the baby she was carrying. Tears filled Dounia's eyes as she tried to contradict Reyhan, to give her hope, to revive her. But she knew it would be of no use.

As Reyhan closed her eyes, she felt the most intense pain she had ever felt in her life. But it soon washed over her like a wave, and she found herself in the bathhouse of Samarkand as a bride being readied for a bath. The pool had no water, however, it was filled with rose petals instead, and she began to float above it as petals in the palest color of pink fell upon her weightless body like soft rain.

One could say Reyhan embraced death. Her life had been suspended between the moment that she was kidnapped by Ogodei till the time that she learned to live again in a world beyond the reach of the Mongols.

Her tomb was never visited by future generations, her presence never acknowledged by history, but she left her mark upon it anyway.

Chapter Twenty-Seven

The Sprouting Seedling

IT WAS A RAINLESS, SUNLESS, CLOUDY DAY IN JUNE OR July. Dounia did not know which. Lazily she opened her window and yawned. Baby leaves of pale green from the early days of spring had by now matured and grown dark. The air felt hazy and misty as if the earth had enjoyed the pleasures of a hookah and blown its smoke all over the treetops.

During summer, Mongol women busied themselves with chores that had to be accomplished before the onset of winter. Felt fabrics had to get washed and readied. Warm clothing had to be shaken out of their summer slumber and packed away; boots had to be polished. Everyone seemed occupied except Dounia who had no choice but to sit idly by watching her chambermaids run around the palace.

Being in her last month of pregnancy and too heavy for any activity, even walking, she spent her days embroidering a scene of a mother and child on canvas. The project was going forward slowly, and she wondered if she would ever finish. Inexperienced in motherhood, she could not even let her tired mind dwell on the prospect of an infant. It remained her only source of hope, though, and she wondered at times if it would be a boy just like Hulagu or a little girl.

Light reflected off the silver tray and the hot china pot that Shura had placed on a nearby table. The pot had a floral design, and a row of little roses in hues of amber and white covered its red porcelain face. It was too beautiful to be used as a contraption for holding scalding hot water. Dounia picked up a glass teacup and stared at its shiny surface which mimicked the colors of the pot. The white leaves drawn on it became more pronounced and as she poured into it, the tea brewed to a deep maroon color.

She wondered what type of brew fate prepared for her on that day. She felt melancholy in every hour now that Reyhan had left this world. Dounia hoped her friend would find freedom from bondage in the next. With Hulagu gone, Dounia had lost her only attachment to the Mongol way of life, save for the child she bore. The idea of returning to Europe had turned into an elusive dream. Years after her abduction from that continent and forbidden from maintaining contact with anyone there, she had no idea if her return to her homeland would ever be possible, or if given such an opportunity she would not be devastated to learn that the remaining members of her family had also perished.

The only thing keeping her feet on the ground and her mind somewhat at ease was the responsibility of rearing the child of Hulagu who could very well become the next Khagan or a Mongol Queen. The idea both thrilled and overwhelmed her. Without Reyhan's motherly advice, she only had Shura's congenial companionship to look forward to at the end of each day, and that, only after the latter was done with her daily chores. She would ask Shura to tell her tales from Kievan Rus. Heartwarming stories of bogatyrs or Rus knights who served in the court of Vladimir I of Kiev and sweet narratives of a faraway land that were not unlike the stories from her own place of birth.

She reached for the pot to pour herself more tea, but a sharp pain in her abdomen stopped her. *Its time* she cried out, and at that very moment, Shura who happened to have forgotten to take away the used sheets returned to her chamber.

"My Dear, oh . . . have no fear . . . I will get help . . . just wait . . . you just," she said before running down the stairs as fast as she could to reach the other chambermaids and call for help.

Soon Dounia was carried to a special ger by three Mongol women assigned to the task, where a Chinese physician stood ready to help her with the delivery. The scene appeared to be too much for poor Shura, who went outside where she could not hear the painful cries of the lonely mother. Shura had told Dounia that she had never known motherhood and the sensations associated with it. But she understood how mothers suffered through childbirth and beyond.

It was late at night when an eerie silence replaced Dounia's constant and heart-wrenching cries. Shura ran toward the ger, only to find the physician's sad face as he held out the body of a stillborn male child.

Empty words, lifeless stares, and faded smiles greeted Dounia, but none could soothe the burning pain of her loss; a loss that left a gaping hole within her soul, never to be filled again. The child of their love, the fruit of their passion, the proof of her devotion to a husband lost, was no more.

Dounia remained inconsolable. She stared at the colorful silk threads of her embroidery and found a depressing sight in what used to be a gratifying object to behold. Reyhan's death, right after Hulagu's demise was a blow Dounia could barely sustain. The child had become the only thing that kept her clinging to life. With the baby being stillborn, that connection was cut.

The redundancy of life at Karakorum had worn her down. Without Reyhan or Sorkhokhtani being there to look after her or supervise the servants, they had slowly become negligent in preparing her food and catering to her needs. The deep down disdain the Mongols had for Dounia soon became overt. Any respect they had previously displayed because of her marriage to Hulagu, their hero, began to wane. Without him, they started to show disregard and sometimes outright negligence. They treated her as a former queen, an appendage to the royalty. If she had given birth to a healthy child, things would have been different. She would have been the mother of the next heir to the throne, but now she had lost her place in the Mongol society.

Dounia began to notice a series of slight changes that increasingly became impossible for her to bear. Ladies of the court would not show their disapproval outright, but instead paid no attention to her. Their expressions were not blunt enough for one to realize the reason for their disapproval or how it could be rectified, leaving their victim out of balance at all times. What troubled her most was their lack of reaction; ignoring her as she addressed them; the tilt of the head, the eyes that rolled in another direction and delicate gestures like a barely noticeable mouth grimace. Such attitudes worked as daggers that destroyed her character and social standing.

Dounia knew of detractors among them, but she also understood that confronting them would be of no avail, for she would only end up hurting her reputation further. The very people that she considered inferior and looked down upon, she now longed to befriend. But even Shura avoided her company, although for an entirely different reason. The birth of the stillborn child affected her deeply, giving her nightmares, and Dounia was a constant reminder of that tragedy.

With the scourge of loneliness being combined with dejection, the spider of unhealthy thoughts began to chew away at Dounia's mind. A different kind of fire from the one burning in the hearth began to simmer within her, a slow-burning fire that consumed her soul. A pain no longer acute, but mild and malignant, progressively devoured her livelihood.

Lack of human interaction began to take its effect. Her mind started to play tricks on her. She feared the shadows on the walls when the maids lit the candles at night. Her nights were restless, her days dreary. The slightest sound alarmed her, and a sense of foreboding constantly haunted her. Images of devastation in her homeland became vivid before her eyes, images of death and destruction everywhere.

Days began to lay heavy on her mind, and it took hours for minutes to pass. Seasons became excruciatingly long. Spring brought with it reminders of the happy days that no longer existed. In the summer, she felt dreadfully lonely. Fall lacked the colorful leaves and the intoxicating scents she used to enjoy in her homeland, like the scent of potpourri and birch wood burning in the fireplace. By winter she knew her soul could no longer endure it.

The final blow did not come in a subtle form. She was not invited to the Annual Feast, an important occasion that in the past would have meant being cast out by the tribe. And although she did not anticipate such a dramatic outcome, Dounia was deeply hurt. She felt abandoned by the world, like the sole survivor of a shipwreck washed off on an empty shore, carried by a giant wave to utter desolation; an orphan with no hope of being restored to her family.

That evening an idea began to take shape in her mind.

Twilight brought with it an unbearable sense of loneliness. A profound sense of despair overtook her. It felt as if her burden of sorrows became heavier by the minute; love, laughter, and happiness washed out of her life in the torrential rains of gloom. She felt defeated. How could she overcome so many calamities; a husband who never returned from the war, a friend who perished in despair, and a child stillborn were just too much for her to shoulder.

That night when spring appeared years away, she wrapped a knitted shawl around her thin frame and filled the pockets of her dress with stones; a dress once covered in embroidered red blossoms that now looked faded like dirty flakes of snow.

She walked aimlessly and hopelessly toward the very river by which she had contemplated escape many years ago. Walking on the embankment, she stared with lifeless eyes at the rhythmic flow of water. Tranquility had left her life long ago, and in its stead, constant rapture and turbulence in a harsh environment had taken hold of her. Sweet childhood memories rolled before her eyes, the voice of her mother singing lullabies in her ears, her father reading her a bedtime story. She remembered her uncle who most probably was dead by now as were her other family members. War and pestilence left little hope in the hearts of those who witnessed Europe's deteriorating circumstances from afar.

She waited till the moon rose, casting its light like a lasso around the neck of the river. Dark was the night, dark as the soul of an unremorseful criminal. She could see her image in the water, and it looked shattered like an image reflected in a broken mirror. She felt powerless as the strong hands of fate crumbled the story of her life to toss it among the burnt ashes of history. She would be forgotten as if she never existed. The air felt cold, and she felt colder inside, shuddering when she thought of all that she had lost. She had come from afar, from the land of springtime daffodils, summertime orchards, colorful harvests of autumn and snowy winters. How she had withered away in this harsh environment. The stones she had filled her pockets with, weighed down her gown.

Dounia stared at the moonlight's broken traces upon the black waters of the river. She had an urge to join it, to drown herself in its cold embrace, for her body to disappear within its black folds and for life to be drained out of her by its breathless waves. And thus, to free herself from pain, from the chains that held her still to Mongol lands. She sat by the bank of the river, allowing the soles of her feet to touch the surface of the water.

Droplets of rain began to fall, mixing with her tears. She lifted her face toward the dark sky and closed her eyes, allowing the cold drizzle to wash her face. It had a numbing effect on her and the longer she remained in that position, the more hopeful she became that the rain would put out the burning fire within her. She placed her hands on the cold slabs of stone that formed the embankment. There she felt the delicate foliage of a sprouting seedling that had broken through the rough surface.

Dounia lifted herself off the embankment with what little energy she retained, determined to survive. If a seedling could do it, so could she. Her chamber that she had earlier deserted with disgust, she saw as a caravansary, a temporary place to stay till she got her thoughts together. Determination and the yearning to survive gave her a new surge of energy. She wrote a letter to Kublai Khan begging him to allow her to return to Poland now that her husband no longer lived.

Kublai Khan agreed, and arrangements were made for her safe journey. Although when she returned to her homeland, she could hardly recognize Poland, so much destruction had taken place. The castle of her uncle lay in ruin. Through an old guard who still lived on the premises, she sought information about Wiktor. He informed her that her uncle was killed in the Battle of Legnica, and every member of the royal family had also perished. But Wiktor, her once dear Wiktor, was alive, injured in battle, broken in spirit with a missing leg.

She left her suitcases with the guard and ran toward the small cottage where he still lived. He was temperamental and lived like a hermit. But Krisztina brought with her memories of far better days.

Wiktor liked her new name and kept calling her *My Dounia*.

They married without ceremony, and she nursed and cared for him until the day he died. It had been a decade of dedicated, dutiful commitment by Dounia, and she was grateful for the chance. Dounia continued to live in her country of birth for a few years after Wiktor's death, receiving a government stipend as a former member of the royal family. She did visit Karakorum one last time, and there she added a note about the wars and about herself to the manuscript she had shared with Reyhan and Chaka. She then hid the writings behind the stone slab.

Last entry by Krisztina:

> *I am writing the final segment of this manuscript on a visit in my old age to Karakorum. I had to visit it one last time before my days in this world ended. My palace looks abandoned, and no curious eyes watched me as I removed the manuscript hidden beneath a slab of stone. Well, the truth is that I have so many memories in this place. There are only a few chambers that are still usable in my palace, and I am actually sitting in my old bedroom as I write this.*
>
> *My return to Europe, I can describe as mostly uneventful and rather depressing, considering that I had lost most of my family members. I did meet Wiktor, however, as broken as we both had become, and we agreed to live together in the suburbs of Silesia. He had never married and had always retained the hope that I would one day return to him. Our shared memories of the past kept us entertained while he was alive. He had lost a leg in the war and appreciated my caring presence near him in his old age.*
>
> *The Mongol wars eventually took an unanticipated turn. After Kublai's army was defeated in 1260 by the Egyptian Mamluk, the second severe blow to the Mongols came a decade later when a storm at sea sank the Mongol flotilla near the coast of Japan. Wave upon wave crashed their ships, and the Mongol armada sank to the bottom of the sea in what the Japanese attributed to Divine Vengeance. I must add that the Mongol rule, however, brought with it unprecedented exchanges among civilizations. Europe is undergoing a transformation not seen in*

a long time. Greater compassion is being shown toward people of other faiths, and greater opportunities will be given to women. Exposure to other civilizations has had its impact. I end this writing in hopes that one day someone, maybe a woman in my own situation, will discover this manuscript and act upon it.

Book IV

The Mirror

Chapter One

The Hakeem

1398 C.E. (100 Years Later)

IN SAMARKAND, THE CAPITAL OF KING SHAHROKH, SON of Tamerlane, summer had settled down as if intending to stay for a long time. The sun's warmth crept under the earth's skin. Its iridescent footprint pirouetted on the grassy meadows surrounding the castle grounds, and the velvet green earth cover sparkled in its rays. Ponds looked like desert mirages as light reflected off their surfaces. Colors of flowers and clothing alike had come to life. Eyes were cast down though, and at times a parasol, a book, or a mere hand protected the eyes of passersby from the glare.

The old street beggar, panhandling with the meticulous promptness of a bank clerk, being there each day at the same spot from dawn to dusk, smiled cheerfully, jeopardizing his trade, for only by looking sad he could gain a coin or two from sympathetic bystanders. The birds sang their gratitude for the glorious morning, ululating. Two tomcats that had been fighting all night over a female feline dosed off like old friends next to each other on a street corner.

The fortification that formed the body of the castle built by Tamerlane prior to his departure from this world and ascension to power of his son, Shahrokh, stretched to the skies like a mountain. A sloping track of steps encircled it with numerous minarets topped with golden domes serving as guard posts for the sentries. The warm weather had enticed the flowering trees planted along this cascading mansion to bloom before their time.

Rays of the sun like divine bliss nourished the spirit of earth-dwellers below. Smiles grew spontaneously upon lips. Joy was inevitable on such a beautiful day. But the sun's glow did not reach the dark chamber of the queen who was quite unhappy.

After returning from Karakorum, she had the manuscript they found there translated. For several days now she had been reading the writings of Chaka, Reyhan, and Krisztina. The brutalities committed by the Mongols made her feel as if her limbs could no longer carry her frail body. Listless, she dragged herself to bed. All the carnages she read about in the hand-written manuscript were now her inheritance through a dynasty into which she had married, her name drenched in the bloodshed of the Mongols. Days of restlessness and nights of feverish hallucinations ensued when she finished reading the manuscript.

Members of the court, as well as King Shahrokh, who had just returned from a journey to the coastal towns of the Persian Gulf, became alarmed. Her utterances were heard at times by chambermaids who related them to the king.

"She calls herself a hypocrite," an older maid reported.

"She cries all night," said another, "even in her sleep that looks more like a fainting spell."

"She barely eats," a young maid said shyly, encouraged by the words of the other two. "Sometimes I do not see her eat a morsel for two days in a row. She looks so frail."

Of course, that fact was so ostensible that few had failed to notice.

"Shall I send for the Hakeem?" the first one asked.

"Yes. I am afraid that will be necessary," the king replied.

The Hakeem's apothecary shop stood in the farthest corner of the Grand Bazaar of Samarkand, now an old structure that still retained some of the charms of its early days. The evening was fast approaching, and the Hakeem had to hurry before the bazaar closed. He measured some powders to make a healing concoction for a patient and looked up to find a woman of no more than five and twenty staring at him pleadingly.

"What ails you, Madam?" he asked.

"It is not me who is ill, but one of the finest ladies ever borne in this land," she replied.

"Who are you speaking of?"

The woman brought her head slightly closer to the Hakeem. Holding her pink floral chador in a way that no one could read her lips even from a distance, she whispered, "Her Majesty, the queen."

The Hakeem, whose profession extended beyond that of running an apothecary shop and included functioning as a physician, shrugged his shoulders. "I have never treated members of the royalty before," he said. "You might want to seek the help of a physician more proficient than I."

"There are none, sir, or I would not have come hither. People speak of miracles that you have performed and dying patients that you have saved," the girl said, demurely.

"Well, one should never rely on rumors. There is hardly ever anything truthful in them."

"I beseech you, honorable physician, for I have nowhere else to go. You sec," she lowered her voice even further, "my lady's ailment is not of the kind that affects the body. It is her spirit and mind that is ailing."

The Hakeem's curiosity piqued. He set aside his spectacles as if the aid they provided to his vision impeded his hearing, and listened with greater attention to the girl's comments.

"Before reading this manuscript that the royals found in the ruins of Karakorum, she used to be as happy as a nightingale sitting upon a rosebush," the pretty girl who had introduced herself somewhere in the middle of her conversation as Raana, lady-in-waiting to the queen, added, "but now my lady is melancholy all the time. She cries for no reason at all. Her husband, the king, is a loving man and cares for her like no other. He is concerned that she might die of sadness."

"Why is it that he has sent you rather than one of his guards or an advisor?" the physician asked.

"I am my lady's trusted chambermaid, and His Majesty has found it necessary to keep this entire matter secret. I beseech you to visit my lady and use all your proficiency to find her a cure."

"Does she realize she is ill?" he asked.

"I am afraid not, sir. She just asks to be left alone, shedding tears over this manuscript. Day in and day out she reads its pages and cries."

"Do you know what is written in it?"

"She told me it was written by women who lived during the reign of Genghis Khan and his progeny and chronicled the wars."

"Well, the matter could be quite distressing to her."

"It is more than that, sir. The manuscript has triggered something within her. It is that she feels guilty for all that was done; not only of the massacre of so many people by the Mongols but what her own father-in-law, Tamerlane, as the last Mongol conqueror committed, cutting down large populations in order to expand his territories."

"Well, Tamerlane took pride in the fact that he was a Mongol ruler although many dispute that claim." The Hakeem said, and added as if thinking out loud, "He was one of the most brutal conquerors ever to rule this land."

The girl glanced over her shoulder to her right and to her left and said, "I beg of you, sir, not to use such language in reference to the late king."

"Well, nothing that happened was the queen's ... Lady Gohar-shad's fault," the Hakeem said.

"Yes, but my lady has taken it all upon herself. She has confided in me that she feels as if the guilt of all that others had done is now firmly placed on her frail shoulders. She has lost her appetite. She barely eats anything and stays up most of the night."

"I shall see what I can do. When shall I see her?"

"Directly sir! Pray, follow me."

The Hakeem put away the last ingredient of his concoction and packed his instruments of healing, then followed the girl to the castle.

"My dear daughter," the physician, being a sagacious man, kept stressing as he followed the girl through the length of the bazaar, in an attempt to convey to the shoppers and passersby that his intentions were entirely paternal toward that beautiful creature. For those who knew him and had never seen him walk with a young woman before would otherwise get the wrong idea.

They walked out of the bazaar together, but no carriage or guards waited to take them to the castle.

"We shall walk, sir, if you don't mind. It is less conspicuous this way," Raana said, apologetically.

Unused to exertions even as mild as walking, the stout Hakeem was quite out of breath by the time they reached the gates of the castle, two thousand paces from the bazaar. The girl then led him to the queen's chamber.

"You do not seem impressed by the majesty of the castle," the girl said.

"These marble floors, the ornate walls, and the fantastic ceiling make me wonder about the impact this ornamented cage has on the soul of a young woman. Does the empress ever travel . . . outside of this city?" he asked.

"Yes sir, my lady travels quite a bit . . . with her husband," Raana replied and left as soon as the physician was let into the chamber of the queen.

In the middle of a chamber lit by a candelabrum, stood the empress dressed in such a deep shade of ultramarine that the beholder wondered if a piece of the night sky had fallen to cloak her. Embroideries in gold mimicked the tiara she had upon her head. A veil of fine violet silk cloth covered her dark tresses, except for a few strands that had curled unintended onto her forehead. Her long lashes accentuated a face that appeared cut out of pure white marble. Black eyebrows shaded deep brown irises too large for her delicate features, making her look both beautiful and majestic.

The Hakeem, who realized he had stood in awe of the queen's beauty longer than was deemed appropriate, gave a slight cough. He forced himself back to his professional demeanor and asked, "Can I be of help, Your Grace, regarding anything that might be ailing you?"

"Where do you run when you are thine own enemy?" the queen asked.

"Why would my lady think that she is her own foe?"

"I have asked about you. Your late father, also a great physician, disagreed with what Tamerlane did, and I do know you share his views. Your father's life was spared by Tamerlane because he never expressed his views in a way to arouse public anger against the monarchy. Therefore, I know that I can speak with you openly. I feel doomed because my name is mired in the blood that was shed by others. Is there no solace for one who has unwittingly joined hands with those who have transgressed?" She then showed the manuscript to the Hakeem and explained its content.

"This is no fault of yours," the physician said.

"I was raised in a household of wealth and privilege, and I have married into royalty. My father was a very rich man, and my husband rules an empire. But reading this . . . reading what these women wrote has allowed me to feel what it is like to be hungry and to live in fear. I can now sense the horror of losing loved ones in war. I won't be able to live with myself if I don't do anything about it."

She pointed with her delicate fingers to a tree in the distance that was visible from the window. "One-fifth of the world's population was cut down by Tamerlane alone, pruned as if they were limbs of trees. This murderous campaign started with the Mongols, and then my father-in-law." She paused, "We," she looked down at her hands, "I have seen the suffering of the people. I know that the wealth we possess, the power that our family has gained and my children will one day inherit, stems from a great amount of injustice. I have become the unfortunate inheritor of this bloody legacy which must end. People need to heal; their dignity must be restored, their lives mended, their places of worship repaired."

"These all seem like noble undertakings," the Hakeem said, sympathetically.

"People think that I have gone mad, but the truth is that days and weeks of contemplation have opened my eyes. I have cried day and night, and as the tears were shed, my soul revived. I have a new sense of purpose; my determination is strong. My vision was blurred but now is cleared. I shall restore what lies in ruin, and I shall bring hope back to the hearts of the people. Mongols will be remembered well when I am done with what I undertake to do. As God is my witness, I will reach out to the despondent, to the afflicted."

The Hakeem left the room deep in thought. When the king approached him and asked about the condition of his wife, he replied that she is of sound mind and suffers no physical ailment.

Shahrokh did not seem satisfied with that answer, and the question lingered upon his face. The king appeared to be an intelligent monarch but unsure of himself and uncertain about the correctness of his decisions. He was a rather thin man with handsome features who did not look much older than Lady Goharshad. He paced back and forth nervously as if contemplating a subject of great importance.

"Speak plainly. Is my wife suffering from the illness of the mind?" The king asked, looking seriously at the physician. "Let me be forthright with you. The mentally ill are shunned by society, and their continued presence in a royal court would be difficult to justify."

"Sir, she is wiser than any man that I know," the Hakeem replied in a sly reference to the king.

"Why is it then that she keeps crying day and night over this manuscript we found in the ruins of Karakorum?"

"It is not the manuscript itself, sir, it is the atrocities that were recorded in it. Atrocities committed by generations of Mongols that unfortunately, your father with all due respect, condoned and continued. She feels the burden of guilt on her shoulders and feels as if her name and that of her progeny has been mired in blood because of what they had done." The Hakeem realized too late that his remarks were completely out of line and apologized hurriedly for being too upfront.

"My father . . . was a world conqueror. Be careful not to disrespect him," Shahrokh replied looking irate.

"My intention is not to disrespect anyone but to simply state the facts about your wife's health. My lady, the queen, has a benevolent soul and a compassionate heart."

"Under any other circumstances, I could have had you beheaded. But desperate as I am to save my wife, I am bearing this," the king said.

The Hakeem repeated his apology.

"My ancestors were warriors. They were conquerors in wars that they engaged in and naturally people died. That is no concern of hers. But it seems as if she has taken it upon herself to set things right, for she believes that she is responsible for their deeds," the king said more calmly but with concern visible in his countenance.

"Why?" the Hakeem asked.

"Because she is married to me, and I have inherited the legacy of the Mongols for better or for worse," he replied. "For days she spoke to no one, abstained from eating throughout the day, breaking her fast on a meager meal at night. She spends her nights crying, holding prayer vigils."

"There is another side to this coin," the Hakeem replied. "What may seem to others as ailment could be an indication of the transformation taking place within her soul."

"I do not understand, sir," the king said. "All I know is that my wife has lost interest in life, and takes no pleasure in anything that my vast kingdom has to offer."

"Well, she may soon find a different source of fulfillment, one that will give her a strong sense of purpose."

Shahrokh, who appeared unconvinced, politely thanked the Hakeem for his services and rewarded him graciously. However, the shadow of concern upon his face did not disappear.

Chapter Two

The Transformation

LADY GOHARSHAD FELT A BURNING LUMP IN HER THROAT when the Hakeem left as if finding an understanding soul allowed her to drop her burdens. Tears rushed to her eyes and flowed down her delicate skin; the pain had been unbearable. Her body weakened by days of fasting, her mind, her soul, her resolve strengthened. Life took on a new meaning, a new urgency.

Tamerlane, who considered himself the last of the Mongols, had conquered vast territories that his son now ruled. The chance still existed for them to establish a good name for the Mongols. She could reach out to the devastated, revive hope among the destitute, help rebuild what lay in ruin, and in doing so allow her husband's dynasty to be remembered as a benevolent one. There was no room for negligence, for procrastination and for losing chances and opportunities to do good.

One day, instead of strolling around the garden, she decided to visit the city, but soon realized that her regal attire attracted too much attention. She went again to the city on another day and wore a black silk chador to obscure her identity. Her strolls took her to neighborhoods of the poor and the sick. She reached out to the pregnant mother who had lost her husband to consumption and had no source of income, and she tended to the needs of an elderly couple with no children to care for them. She spread her wings of kindness over children who had not known compassion throughout their young lives; her basket always filled with treats.

As days went by, the king became concerned when on certain afternoons he could not find his wife. He worried about her drifting again, and saw these exertions as misguided—another sign of a fall in mental health. He summoned the Hakeem. Judging by his balding and graying hair, fleshy and wrinkled face and bushy eyebrows, one could say that the physician was in his mid-fifties. The king lost no time in expressing his concerns when the Hakeem arrived.

"I have listened to your advice, but now my wife roams the streets during the day, hiding her identity in order to see what truly goes on in the lives of the people left under our care. This is her way of seeking atonement, I suppose," the king said.

"Well sir, the only thing that I can tell you is that many men complain that their wives engage in that which is forbidden religiously," the Hakeem said in an obvious reference to adultery. So, maybe you should be thankful that she has taken such a path." The physician then took a sip of the black tea offered to him earlier on a silver tray. His countenance showed his full confidence in his work and in his patient's health.

"You don't understand, sir, she is a queen to an empire so grand that the world has not seen the likes of it. Yet, she acts like a commoner, a charitable patron, but still beneath the dignity of royalty," the king confided.

"She is a very intelligent woman. I believe she could be a great advisor to you," the Hakeem said with a sugar cube in his mouth slurring his speech.

The conversation with the Hakeem, who appeared not to have a care in the world, left Shahrokh as dejected as before.

The king decided to address the matter at dinner that night. "Your outings have become a source of concern for me," he said as his wife sat down to eat.

"I feel blessed with a great sense of purpose," Lady Goharshad said. "A physical change is taking place within me. I now have a mission, an incredible desire to improve the lives of the people. And in helping others, I do no harm to us. In fact, I may have saved your life."

"What exactly do you mean?" the king asked, alarmed.

Lady Goharshad moved the tray of food away from her husband before he could reach for it. "Have you hired a new chef?" she asked.

"Yes, in fact, we have," her husband replied.

"This dinner of roasted quail, do not partake of it. The chef is innocent and unaware, so you can let the poor man go, but he has been set up to poison you on this very night. We need a food taster in the castle like your father used to have."

"Pray tell me," Shahrokh asked, frowning, "where did you obtain that information from?"

"You know how I roam the streets at times to learn the circumstances of the poor and destitute."

"And?"

"I helped a shoemaker that had injured his hand and had been out of work for weeks. He saw the regal bracelet on my hand, bearing the insignia of the Mongols, and confided in me."

"What did he say?"

"He begged that I do not disclose his name and spare him for divulging his secret. But a woman in their neighborhood who had intended to poison you, in hopes that the blame would be placed on her former husband, concocted this scheme. The shoemaker learned of the matter when he passed by a window of her house and overheard her confiding in her sister."

"Who is the husband?"

"Your new chef is her former husband. Recently, he left her for a younger woman. She gave him a pouch filled with poison instead of the spice he had requested of her, hoping he would be accused of murder and executed."

"We shall see how true that is," he mumbled in disbelief.

Shahrokh stared, stunned at his wife for a moment or two, then summoned the chef. The poor soul, trembling head to foot, obviously fearing that he had aroused the king's wrath, admitted that a new spice was indeed given to him by his former wife to improve the taste of poultry and allow him the opportunity to put his culinary skills on display.

Shahrokh then dismissed the chef without further comment

and summoned the guards to arrest the woman who had plotted the scheme, the real culprit.

When the chef left the room, Lady Goharshad said, "Retain him, for hence he would be your most trusted man in the Kitchen Tower."

The next morning at breakfast, Shahrokh asked his wife what she thought of the new plan he had in mind for the city.

"I am considering further renovations in Samarkand and Herat," Shahrokh said. "I thought you might like to see the sketches, once they are drafted."

"Why not extend such renovations to other cities as well?" the queen asked. "Can you imagine what it would mean to the people if we rebuild and refurbish what was ruined? Think of what that could do for the morale of the inhabitants."

"Well, first of all, we need to fortify defenses in each city in the event of outside aggression," the king said. "Local tribes challenging our governance in neighboring countries are turning into formidable foes, and one always needs to be on guard."

"Then, that would be the perfect place to begin. We would also need hospitals, charitable foundations, schools and institutions of higher learning, libraries, and of course beautiful monuments, orchards and gardens, and fountains. You will be remembered as the king who brought life back to the people of Persia and Transoxiana."

As buildings were being erected, hospitals, schools and libraries built, and orchards planted, Lady Goharshad decided to visit Samarkand's old bazaar, wearing her black chador over her gown. The bazaar, once known as the Grand Bazaar of Samarkand and now only referred to as the old bazaar, no longer retained the charm and glory of its original construction. Pieces of the stone pavement could be seen here and there under the dirt-covered floor. The fire pits had been replaced with oil lamps that lit the way, but they were not uniform in shape, placed here and there haphazardly. Shops still displayed their goods of fabric, spices, and jewelry to advantage; however, the presence of thieves threatened the safety of shoppers.

Lady Goharshad watched as a poor man dragged his tired feet toward the grocers. The shop was a rather large one, and the shopkeeper had placed bins in full view of his customers. Each bin contained a heap of a different kind of vegetable: large white turnips, purple beets, and greens glistened like gems.

The poor man offered the grocer a black dirham, saying that he hoped to purchase something for dinner. The shop owner looked condescendingly at the meager offering and handed the man some withering potatoes upon which mold was beginning to grow.

"That's all?" the man asked. "I have a family to feed."

"That's all your money will buy," was the ice-cold reply.

"A black dirham for a bag of rotten potatoes, that is an unheard-of price," Lady Goharshad who could no longer restrain herself uttered. "What you are offering this poor man is not fit for human consumption, yet you charge the price of the best grocery."

"I am the only grocer in these parts and have every right to set the price as I wish. Don't like it; settle for plain bread."

Frustrated over her encounter with the overcharging grocer, Lady Goharshad, who considered such trade nothing less than thievery, returned to the castle. There were numerous pieces of jewelry stored in a large room; most of them war booties plundered by Tamerlane.

Lady Goharshad cared little for them. She refused to wear a lot of jewelry and did not consider the items plundered as righteously earned. One piece, an heirloom necklace that once belonged to her mother, she did treasure and wore occasionally. Its large emeralds and diamonds set in gold were unique, and it held memories dear to her heart. She reached for the box that contained them. Feeling vexed, she knew the sight of them would soothe her. When she unlocked and opened the rosewood box, however, she noticed they were missing.

She asked Raana about it, and the young woman said that a butler cleaned it earlier. Lady Goharshad asked that they immediately summon the man.

"Where is my necklace?" she asked the butler, a man of more than seventy years of age.

"Khanoom, I beg of you, I replaced it as soon as I finished polishing your necklace. I have worked honestly in this castle most of my life."

Lady Goharshad lost control of her temper. Fuming, she said, "I have no tolerance for thievery. Take the man to the dungeon until he confesses."

The old man began shaking in distress, and as the guards attempted to carry him to the prison, he lost consciousness. At that very moment, Lady Goharshad recalled that she had hung the necklace with the outfit she planned on wearing for a formal occasion the following night.

"Leave him be," she said, embarrassed at her own temper.

During dinner that evening, Lady Goharshad sat frowning as her husband excitedly informed her about the progress of the reconstruction crew.

"What is the matter? I thought you would be pleased with these new developments," he finally said.

"I am concerned about the state of the old bazaar which has fallen into decay. People are grateful that a new one will soon be erected, but the old one is still considered by many of the poorer citizens as a marketplace where goods could be purchased at a lower cost. However, vandalism has recently become rampant, and the enclosure has all but turned into a meeting place for gangsters and robbers. Order needs to be established, and the surrounding neighborhoods as well need to be improved for they are quite dilapidated and also subject to break-ins and theft."

"And there is another thing," she added after a pause. "If the lone grocer at the old bazaar owes as much as a single black coin in taxes to the Treasury, I would make sure that that black coin is confiscated from him."

Chapter Three

The Broken Vase

LADY GOHARSHAD BECAME BOLDER ABOUT VISITING poverty-stricken parts of town near the old bazaar. She no longer hesitated before donning a ragged black chador on top of her silky attire. She headed toward the said location, little heeding the fact that it was insecure and infested with criminals and disreputable characters.

Shahrokh found his wife in a beggar's chador at the entrance hall of the castle, headed for the streets again.

"Where are you off to this time?"

"I will not be long, I assure you. It is just a short trip from here."

"You cannot be leaving the castle, dressed in a beggar's outfit. You are the queen of the land."

"Yes. But I am also a servant of God. Please. Allow me to reach out to your less fortunate subjects. I cannot walk among them looking like a queen."

"But why would *you* have to go? I can send others."

"It will not do. I have had many sleepless nights, and I have one particular neighborhood in my mind."

"You have kept away from all social gatherings for months now. Dignitaries from Europe to China have visited, weddings and celebrations have taken place, and all the time you have kept to yourself."

"What I have undertaken is of far greater importance to me than all those social gatherings."

Although Shahrokh reluctantly conceded to her departure as she took a public stagecoach to reach her destination, he immediately sent three of his best cavalrymen to pursue her without her knowledge. He then summoned the Hakeem.

"My wife dresses as a beggar and walks the streets of the capital to find the needy," Shahrokh stated, looking dejected.

"That is the most compassionate act that I have ever heard of, sir," the Hakeem calmly replied.

"How can I allow her to continue this path? I am the king, the heir to the throne of Tamerlane."

"And she is a pure-hearted human being, reaching out to others who are in need. She is going to bring a good name to your dynasty."

Shahrokh was at a loss for words. When he tried to repay the Hakeem with numerous coins, the physician refused to accept it.

"It has been my greatest honor to have served my lady. She is among the most unique women that ever walked upon this earth. Our nation is proud to have such a munificent sovereign."

Lady Goharshad asked the coachman to stop when she reached her destination. As she dismounted, she noticed a woman, dressed in rags, standing in the middle of the main alley that led to the old bazaar. She intended to reach out to the poor thing on that day, for she had heard from her neighbors that the woman faced eviction.

The cold, damp, slippery pavement must have sent chills up the young woman's bare feet. The wind blew through the torn layers of rags that covered her body. Her thin lips had turned crimson, and the tip of her nose was red. So too were her cheeks. It was not the healthy, rosy glow of youth, but the feverish redness of illness and affliction. The woman looked like she could no longer maintain her balance and collapsed on the stone pavement.

A crowd began to hover around the unconscious woman who had hit her head on the curb when she fell. People stood around, but no one made an effort to prevent the fall. When Lady Goharshad reached her, she noticed that the woman's skull was broken like a fragile vase. Blood began to gush out of the fracture as color drained from her face, leaving her brown eyes the opaque blue-green color of a slaughtered lamb.

Her children began wailing hysterically, clearly without understanding what had happened to their only protector. Lady Goharshad watched the scene with horror. She knew the mother was beyond help. Her three tiny girls had huddled together, sobbing for a loss their little hearts could not bear. Their mother looked like a broken doll that could never be fixed.

The youngest girl with light brown curls and big brown eyes was a mere toddler. Her face was dirty, and she was clothed in rags that must have belonged to earlier generations for she was not old enough to have worn them to shreds. She was sucking her tiny thumb. The other two, not much older, wailed and cried. The landlady of the deceased woman discretely went inside her hovel, leaving the poor lasses to the mercy of the streets. Lady Goharshad stared at her with contempt before she closed her door.

As if willpower and wisdom had left her head simultaneously, Lady Goharshad dropped to her knees and gently brought the three sobbing cherubs into her loving embrace. She had learned of their mother's predicament and had every intention of reaching out to her before the eviction, but she had not arrived in time.

The children began tugging at her worn rag of a chador like victims of a shipwreck clinging to driftwood, causing her chador to slip off her head. Before she could collect herself, her regal attire became exposed, leaving all who had gathered around her in awe. Although fully clothed in an emerald green dress and veil, her damask outfit and particularly her bracelet, a wedding gift from her husband, shone like a thousand stars. Covered with bits of diamonds; at the center of the bracelet lay the famous Mongol emblem. The spectators, whose number had grown by the minute, turned their attention from the dead mother to the beautiful noblewoman before them.

"Now what do we have here?" a stout, sinister-looking man in his fifties said who looked like a butcher in dirty clothes and a blood-stained faded apron. A few other fellows began to move closer to her.

Just at that moment, she heard the sounds of hooves fast approaching. The captain of the special guards, his sword slashing the skies, appeared as in a dream. Lady Goharshad rose, thanking the captain, knowing without having to ask that he was sent by her husband to shadow her movements. He bowed and then to the great amazement of everyone, including the fat butcher, lifted her like a feather by her belt, mounting her in one incredibly swift motion on a spare white horse he had brought with him.

"No," she begged, "I cannot leave them," pointing to the three children who had stopped crying, looking stunned by all that was happening. Obviously realizing that this was no place for an argument, the captain asked two breathless cavalrymen who had just caught up with him on horseback, to carry the children to the castle as well.

The landlady, as if suddenly aware of the opportunity of a lifetime passing her by, flung open the door of her hovel from which she had evicted her tenants. She then loudly announced that those children were the light of her eyes, and that for a small payment—bracelets would certainly be acceptable—she would care for them all her life. All Lady Goharshad had to do was point to her ragged chador for the landlady to recall that she had been a witness to her earlier attempt to desert the children.

The king had yet to see the three girls, but their arrival in the royal court had occupied his mind since the previous evening when he heard the news. He broached the subject as soon as his queen sat down at the breakfast table.

"We have two sons of our own who are now eight and ten years of age," Shahrokh said. "The idea of adopting three children straight from the ghettos into the castle baffles me."

Lady Goharshad remained silent, so her husband went on with his argument, which sounded more and more convincing to him with the passage of time. He finally gave up and smiled when the three little girls came to sit at the family breakfast table, all washed up and dressed, looking as if they always belonged to the royal family.

"Do you even know their names?" he asked, addressing his wife in a much kinder tone.

"No," she replied as she swallowed a gulp of tea, the enormity of the task she had undertaken obvious from her expression. "The eldest looks about four years old and says her name is *Soo Soo* which is a sound, not a name," she whispered. She then looked up after examining her saucer as if she had seen it for the first time and said, "Let us name them after celestial bodies; how about Soraya meaning 'sky', Setareh meaning 'star', and . . . Sahar 'dawn.'"

Shahrokh laughed at the suggestion and recalled the days when the Mongols worshiped such astronomical forms. Unlike his father, he detested bloodshed and dismissed some of his predecessor's beliefs and practices as mere superstition. "Let us have a celebration in honor of our extended family and familiarize the girls with their new environment."

Chapter Four

The Mosque

AUTUMN ARRIVED, GRACING THE WORLD WITH RUFFLES of silver, gray and blue visible against the sky. At the fabric shop in the old bazaar, a middle-aged woman chose a floral cotton fabric that suited her best for a chador. The shopkeeper held one end of the fabric on the left side of his prodigious nose and stretched it out from there to the tip of his extended right hand's thumb to roughly measure one length. Measuring four such stretches of fabric, he assured the woman that the amount would be more than sufficient for a chador and maybe there would be enough left to make a small veil out of it too. The price, however, was more than the woman could afford, so the disappointed customer left the shop complaining about the high prices of commodities. The shop owner, equally disappointed, loudly complained that his kids did not consume fabric for food, and he had to pay the same high price for their daily bread.

That particular shop had attracted Lady Goharshad's attention, for she noticed a woman leaving in a hurry looking as if she was about to burst into tears. "Why did she leave so distraught?" Lady Goharshad asked the shopkeeper as soon as she walked in.

"Well, she was hoping to purchase some fabric at a discount, but even at that reduced price, she could not afford the material."

Lady Goharshad looked at the fabrics stacked in rolls on the store's numerous shelves. Most of them were cotton prints of varying colors, beautiful yellows, and blues, and pinks. "You do like a bargain, do you not?" she asked as she placed a black velvet pouch upon the counter and opened its silk ribbon tie, disclosing numerous dinars. "If you can manage to find her and give her that roll of fabric free of charge, I will purchase the entire inventory of your store."

"Upon my eyes, madam!" The man who had been staring at the precious coins finally spoke.

"Run," she said and watched as he sprinted out of the shop, dragging the roll of fabric with him.

He returned breathless, apparently not just from the exertion; the presence of such a wealthy customer in his humble shop must have been enough to send his heart racing.

"How will you carry them, Your Eminence?" he asked, words stumbling out of his mouth.

"I will not," she replied, stressing the first-person pronoun. "You will be carrying them in camel loads to the castle tomorrow morning, and the guards will reward you for your services."

The king had spent the day in utter agony. The Treasury had informed him during their weekly session at noon that the Beyt-ul-Mal or the House of Wealth, a depository of public funds—from collected taxes to income from trade—was virtually empty. The Treasurer placed the blame for the shortage of funds entirely on the queen and her extensive, or as he described it "never-ending" renovations, throughout the kingdom.

"To put it simply, these projects, as benevolent as they may seem, just cannot go on," the Treasurer, who was known for his long white beard and bald head, had said while looking up from his papers with his beady eyes securely resting above his hooked nose.

Shahrokh tried to drink his tea but had a hard time erasing the self-righteous expression of the Treasurer from his mind. The sun was about to set over the minarets when Lady Goharshad finally came in.

"Where were you?" Shahrokh asked with irritation.

"I spent the day at a Shia mausoleum. The place barely accommodates the many who visit the site on a regular basis to pay their respect. There needs to be a structure, a mosque erected right next to the burial grounds, and I intend to build a magnificent one."

"This idea of building a structure next to some sort of sacred site for our Shia subjects perplexes me when our dynasty is a Sunni one," her husband interjected.

"And how much more pertinent that makes it," she replied.

"My dear wife, you have a generous heart, and I have learned to appreciate your caring attitude toward our subjects. But the Treasury's wealth has its limit, and that limit has already been reached in the re-building projects you advocated and moving the capital from Samar-kand to Herat."

She looked up, lifted her hand and placed it upon her neck where an elaborate necklace of diamonds and emeralds shone. "I will sell this," she replied as the King stared at her in disbelief.

Chapter Five

The Sun Descending

"COME ON DEARIES!" THE OLD LADY SAID AS SHE CRUMbled a piece of bread and spread it for the doves that frequented her house. "This fresh bread was meant for you because you got here first. Otherwise, I would have finished it before you came." The birds chirped as if thanking her for the delicious morsels, the pitter-patter of their feet breaking the silence on the sundrenched mud-brick windowsill.

"Go on. Eat them all up. The stale bread would do for me. You are special birds, aren't you? You have the honor of flying over the dome of the mausoleum, never dirtying it. Always clean, always clean."

She turned from her window to look at the mature white-as-snow housecat purring behind her. "Don't you go chasing after my beauties," she said. The tomcat was too chubby and too well-fed to bother chasing after the birds. He seemed to have his eyes on a tiny mouse, though, that showed up once in a while in the kitchen, but even it appeared to require more than he could muster for the chase.

The old lady had been living in that house for more than a decade since her husband died; her devoted spouse was a believer who had spent all his life saving to buy the house closest to the mausoleum. Every brick in that odd-shaped two-story building held cherished memories of days gone by. The wider upper floor, where two bedrooms were located, seemed to have been placed on top of the lower one by a very clumsy builder, for the two levels had little in common. It stood like an oversized hat on top of the lower floor, which contained a small kitchen and family room and had a much smaller window next to a very narrow entry door. Offers were made to her to purchase the place at a high price because of its location, but she had always refused.

"How on earth would they expect me to sell this little piece of heaven?" she said, thinking of her wedding that took place so long ago in the very same building but addressing the doves pecking on the morsels as if nodding their approval. "They say it is odd-shaped, but not for me. It is perfect, and my birds love it too. Here I lay safe every night knowing that I am on blessed soil, close to the Sacred One. Here no one will harm me."

She tried to push away the dark shadows of concern that had lately been bothering her. *This one man keeps pestering me, saying that he is here on behalf of the king or somebody important, insisting that I must sell the place because they are building something here. He says that his words are as good as his master's, and it cannot be refused. He offers me these ridiculous sums, but what am I to do with all that money? I have everything I need right here. My life is like the sun that descends along the rooftop, but I intend to live here to my last breath.*

Noticing that the pecking of the birds had stopped, she crumbled the last piece of fresh bread for them. "This is where I want to live, near the Blessed One," she said, wrapping an old shawl tight around her shoulders, "for here no one will harm me, and I can sleep at night knowing that I will be safe and looked after."

Although Lady Goharshad benevolently auctioned her heirloom necklace to a wealthy merchant from her hometown to benefit the construction of the mosque, such sacrifice proved to be unnecessary. Soon people from all corners of the world, even as far away as China, flocked to see for themselves the magnificent kingdom of the son of Tamerlane. The land had enjoyed the tranquility of peace since Shahrokh came to power, and the revenue stemming from such visits and the trades that ensued filled the coffers of the king in no time.

The fabrics Lady Goharshad had ordered were brought to the castle and laid on sofas outside the chamber of the queen. She intended to have them made into different size outfits to be distributed among orphanages throughout the country, a present from an unknown donor.

Lady Goharshad began to move the fabrics around thoughtfully, juxtaposing them, and putting contrasting and matching colors in the vicinity of one another. As she played around with the fabrics, an idea began to take shape in her head. *What if*, she thought as a chambermaid announced the arrival of the Architect.

"About the design of the interior, my lady, what are your suggestions?" the Architect abruptly said as he entered. The forty-year-old stout man with curly black hair seemed nearly out of patience and humor after waiting a full hour to see Lady Goharshad. "We are at your service, Madam. We have artisans who have ideas about how it should be designed, and maybe you can look at some of their outstanding sketches."

Lady Goharshad gave no answer. After a pause he added, "The structure is being built according to schedule, and we have installed the multiple vaulted ceiling as you requested, but we don't know what type of tilework to use for the interior."

"I think I have an idea for that," she said, smiling and turning her face toward the fabrics. "How is that for a design," she pointed to the fabrics laid on top of one another in a geometric pattern.

The Architect stared for a moment, then said, "that is the most beautiful idea. The design will be unique. Could we have the fabrics, Madam?"

"No, they belong to others, but you are welcome to have a painter depict them on paper before the fabrics are made into outfits."

"We have other issues," he added before leaving. "There is an old lady that absolutely refuses to sell her odd-shaped house which is within the expanded plan of the structure we are constructing."

"Well then make it less expanded. Let the poor woman be."

"Your Majesty, you don't understand. Avoiding that area, meaning the home of the old lady, would be tantamount to redesigning the entire structure in a way that would not appear balanced and proportioned."

"No sir, *you* don't understand. My purpose is to refrain from exploitation. You are working on sacred land. The structure cannot be built on oppression and abuse. I intend to visit the lady, not to force her off her property—far from it. I would like to see if there is anything I could do to assist her."

Chapter Six

The Bricklayer

KAVEH, THE OLD MAN ASSIGNED TO BRINGING DONKEY-loads of mud bricks to the construction site, repeatedly took out his frustrations on his scrawny donkey, his only means of living. Kaveh considered the poor animal a lazy good-for-nothing creature that needed to be constantly reminded of its chore. He was never in a good mood, but today he felt particularly sour. He had quarreled with his wife and tripped on the crooked stone stairs in front of his shabby house, leaving him limping and exasperated.

Kaveh's braided leather belt that he used as a whip was at least a decade old. It looked cracked and tattered in a number of places, but he could still use it to vent frustration at opportunities lost, opportunities that could have saved him from a lifetime of poverty. He did not use the whip on his wife when she complained of hunger, but he did slap her occasionally to put her in her place and show her that despite the misery in which they lived, he still ruled his own house.

The donkey was horribly slow, its load being unusually heavy on that day. As the man hobbled, grabbing his aching leg, he lifted the whip furiously to either break the animal's back or make it go faster. At that very moment, a hand covered in a white silk glove grabbed the whip in midair. As the whip coiled around the delicate wrist, the diamond bracelet of the owner of the gloved hand caught the man's eyes. Kaveh recognized the Mongol emblem in a geometric design that had stoked fear in the hearts of the people of the world for centuries.

Although he had never laid eyes on it before, he had heard about the owner of the fine piece.

"The Mongol Queen!" he uttered, embarrassed by his own impudence. "Your Majesty," he said as he knelt before Lady Goharshad, grabbing his aching leg.

"How much do you get paid to bring in the bricks each day?" she asked as she gestured him to stand up.

As she spoke, she began removing the bricks one by one, lightening the load placed on the animal, her gloves covered in dust. The man swiftly got up and tried to help out.

"How much?" she asked, looking frail as if overcome by the strength of her own emotions. "How much do you get paid for each load the donkey carries?"

"I am paid five black dirhams, Madam," he replied meekly.

"I will double your pay provided that you stop beating and mistreating the poor animal," she said, giving the man a stern look. "Lighten its burdens and feed it well. I want to see it gain weight."

As Lady Goharshad spoke, a group of workers gathered around her. She used the occasion to instruct them as well. "I want everyone to refrain from the use of foul language while working on the premises and avoid back-biting, fighting among each other or any action that would desecrate the holy grounds you are working on." She paused, looked at the donkey and added, "I don't want a single animal hurt, injured or even overburdened during the construction. Feed the animals you use for transporting material and quench their thirst frequently, placing light loads upon them." For that, she assured them, she would double their pay.

While speaking, wind swept aside her silk chador, exposing her features. She noticed the lingering gaze of a young bricklayer who almost fell off a half-finished wall. His gaze remained on her as she collected herself and left the scene.

From then on, she began to notice the same bricklayer every time she visited the site. He would stand in a corner, staring at her like a lost boy as she gave orders to the Architect and engineers about the construction of the building. She considered it a childish crush that the young man would quickly get over and tried to ignore his presence, but the unwanted attention did not cease.

Every time Lady Goharshad stopped by to check the progress of the work, she felt the heavy gaze of the young man that seemed to penetrate the thin fabric of her chador. His attentions irritated her. The extraordinary sense of discernment that she often used in settling arguments failed her when she tried to figure out his intentions. She blamed herself for being the means of such infatuation in a young lad who probably was several years her junior. She began to wear a face veil of white lace that partially covered her face in addition to her black chador. She even reduced the number of her visits to the site, despite her initial intention to oversee every step of the process in order to ensure structural perfection.

One day, to her relief, the bricklayer failed to show up and was nowhere to be seen the following day. On the third day, the Architect addressed the issue and insisted that he needed to find a replacement for the missing worker. To this suggestion, Lady Goharshad most happily agreed.

A few days later, Lady Goharshad's carriage stopped by the construction site. The cold of winter had still not set in. The rain showers of late fall had begun to pound the earth intermittently, and the touch of the sun barely warmed the air. Lady Goharshad raised her head toward the sky, grateful that the rain shower of the previous night had ended. She had a few instructions to share with the Architect and intended to leave the nearly completed construction site rather quickly to return home in time for midday prayer and lunch.

"Oh Khanoom, I beg of you . . . he is my only son, and he is about to perish," an old woman, dressed in shabby clothing that looked like a villager approached Lady Goharshad. "He has not eaten in days and is on his deathbed. He says he is in love with you. What can I do?" She grabbed Lady Goharshad's chador, kneeled and made her proclamation before the gathering crowd of workers.

"I have told him I could go ask a girl in our own neighborhood for her hand in marriage, but he absolutely refuses. I beg of you, what am I to do? I am a poor mother, my husband died years ago, and I have no other child," she said, crying and pleading before the astonished audience.

"Madam, I am a happily married woman," Lady Goharshad said as she tried to free her chador. She could no longer bear the presence of the supplicant before her.

The incident became exceedingly embarrassing as the woman continued to plead on behalf of her son, repeating his claim of love as the workers began to chuckle and chortle at the ridiculous scene.

An attendant was about to drag the woman violently out of her sight when Lady Goharshad cried out, "Leave her be! She fears for her son's life, and it is only natural for her to react in such a way."

Distraught, Lady Goharshad returned to the castle to reflect on how to proceed.

Chapter Seven

The Trial

THE INCIDENT LEFT LADY GOHARSHAD SHAKEN AND publicly embarrassed. She could not blame the old woman. Somehow, she couldn't blame the lad either, a young bricklayer with few prospects for marriage. She did blame herself, however, thinking that maybe if she wasn't so excited over the donkey and had left lecturing the workers to the Architect, this would not have happened. This turn being the outcome of her stepping out of her station.

No matter how graciously the lady had behaved, this infatuation was not considered a trivial matter that the imperial court could sweep under the rug. The news would likely be overblown and turned into ugly gossip, spreading like wildfire throughout the kingdom and beyond, challenging the dignity of the throne.

Lady Goharshad did not even feel like facing her husband and explaining the situation, although she knew that she should. She convinced herself that he would understand. That evening at dinner, she shared the incident and without waiting to see his reaction, left the dining room.

The matter did not end there. As she had feared, the winds of gossip turned this small spark into a magnificent conflagration involving the court. Those who had earlier complained of her exertion of influence and overspending saw this as an opportunity to put her in her place. A judge ruled that the bricklayer had to express remorse or face the noose, for disrespecting the royals was not a trivial matter. But the lad adamantly refused to renounce his proclamation of love.

Lady Goharshad buried herself in her chamber, refusing to see or talk to anyone for several days. "Oh, Allah," she lamented, "what is this trial that you have subjected me to? Oh why" she asked, "was I put through such a difficult morass from which I see no escape but through utter failure, in the loss of human life or the disgrace of a kingdom? What evil had I done to bring such calamity on a family so poor?"

Finding no answers in solitude, she decided to visit the Hakeem.

The Hakeem was surprised to find Lady Goharshad in his place of business. It had been several months since he had seen her in her chamber. "Can I be of assistance to you?" he asked.

A thin veil covered part of Lady Goharshad's face, yet, the lines around her eyes showed more care than they had before.

"I need to speak with you privately," she said, appearing uncharacteristically shy and looking down at her pointed toe shoes as she spoke.

"This is a public place in the bazaar," he said.

"Sometimes a public venue such as this renders greater privacy than a chamber in a castle where people can overhear you."

"I have heard of your latest concerns. So, there is no need to allude to them, for I do have a recommendation to make," the wise Hakeem said.

"It is not that I am in the prime of youth. I am two and thirty years of age which is considered old by many standards," Lady Goharshad said, her misery evident in her voice.

"Well, maybe it is your benevolent soul that the young lad has fallen in love with," the Hakeem said with a smile.

"This is not a matter for jesting. My honor, our nation's honor, is at stake and so is that of a young man's life whom I hate to see hanged for undermining my dignity," she said. "You know I am happily married. My husband adores me, and I love him with all my heart. He is the most understanding man, and I have come to appreciate his open-mindedness, but I am afraid this horrific predicament is going to pull us apart."

"Well, this incident has certainly humbled you, my lady," the Hakeem said. "What is the decision of the king?"

"My husband accepted a judge's decree who had ordered that the lad renounce his public proclamation that he was in love with me, or prepare to die. The problem is that the young man adamantly refuses to do so."

"Does the lad know he has fallen in love with the queen, the wife of King Shahrokh?"

"Yes, indeed he does. But it seems as if he has no comprehension of the gravity of the situation and does not understand my position as queen, or my status as a married woman."

"What is his name?"

"They call him Jamal. He is the son of a construction worker who died years ago."

"Have you tried to convince this Jamal, maybe by offering money, opportunities and the like for him to give up on this misguided notion?"

"'I would rather die a thousand deaths than to renounce my love for one so worthy,' he says."

"He realizes that his *love* is not being reciprocated, so it is quite selfish of him to obstinately insist upon this public declaration, even to his own detriment and his poor mother's devastation," the Hakeem said.

Tears began rolling down Lady Goharshad's chin, mixing with the kohl that lined her eyes and seeping through the lace that covered her face. The Hakeem felt sorry for her.

"The young man staring at me made me feel quite awkward but that does not mean that I wish him ill, and certainly I do not want to see this poor young man hanged for something he had no control over. What will help me overcome this quandary? Why has this happened to me when my intention was to build a mosque in all pureness on sacred soil for a mistreated minority?" she said.

"A structure pure and sacred, in this you may find your answer," the sagacious man said. "You see our surroundings, the homes where we live and the establishments where we work, affect us. Imagine an elderly grandmother lovingly serving food to her grandchildren. You can almost breathe in the tenderness in her home even when no one is there. Now consider the atmosphere of a disreputable neighborhood."

The Hakeem coughed and continued, "Not that you have been to one, but you can imagine a place where foulness and filth have devoured the souls of men. In such places, in the morning, even if all have left the premises after a night of debauchery, one can still sense its vileness."

"What are you suggesting?" Lady Goharshad asked.

"Well, the mosque was built by sinless hands on sacred soil. Will it be a wonder if by staying there a while the lad will experience some sort of transformation? There are aspects to the human soul that are little understood, for most men of medicine place their focus on understanding the physical body, and so much attention is paid to our corporeal needs that the human spirit is often ignored."

"So, are you suggesting that if I confine him within that structure, he is likely to change his mind and renounce his declaration of love, to avoid being thrown into a dungeon or get publicly hanged?"

"Exactly. I suggest you allow him to dwell within the mosque for a period of forty days."

"What if he does not agree to the confinement?" she asked.

"You can convey to him through a messenger that this is your condition for uniting with him in marriage. He must spend forty days and forty nights in prayer and supplication in that holy place, and that you will then divorce your husband and marry him at the culmination of this period without delay."

"I will?" she asked, her eyes widening at the outrageous suggestion so incongruous with the norms of society. "Do you think my husband would agree to such a bizarre arrangement even if this plan of yours works?"

"He certainly has agreed to all that you have asked for so far."

"What if it doesn't work?"

"Tell the king that you will submit to any decision by him or by the judge at the culmination of the forty days."

Chapter Eight

The Rumors

LADY GOHARSHAD LEFT THE HAKEEM AT THE BAZAAR TO have her awkward discussion with her husband. When she arrived at the castle and brought up the subject, she found Shahrokh quite indignant. Her suggestion that the lad be allowed forty days of contemplation in the mosque appeared to have made this generally even-tempered man furious.

"I understand the misery of a peasant woman pleading for the life of her son, but I have little understanding for her son's refusal to apologize and renounce her words. I have sent my guards to arrest and put him to death if he refuses to recant his proclamation of sinful love. But you are telling me to wait some forty days, allowing him a chance to repent? My father beheaded people with no feeling of remorse over minor indiscretions. Why is the life of this one young man so important to you?" Shahrokh asked, looking her straight in the eye. "Do you love him?"

"Of course not," she replied, choking on her own words. "His advances have been absolutely disturbing to me, and you *know* that. But I have committed myself to rectifying the wrong, to healing the wounds, not opening new ones. I beg of you to allow him to hold his vigil for forty days."

"And then what happens? Pray tell me," the king asked, frustration clear in his voice. "You will seek divorce and marry him as you have promised. Why, one needs to keep one's promises, don't they? It matters not if my reign becomes a subject of mockery and ridicule the world over."

"This bothers me far more than it bothers you," Lady Goharshad said. "It is as if a forbidden, sinful, lustful air has surrounded my being. Yet, I have foresworn the shedding of blood or taking the lives of men. Even if we settle for imprisoning him, I fear his poor old mother will die of sadness."

"I have granted you everything a woman might wish for," he said, his voice shaking with anger. "I have fulfilled your commands even though at times I have doubted their prudence. You have sought the company of the indigent and orphaned, and I have been patient. You have roamed the streets in a beggar's garb, and I have put up with it. And you consider this wise Madam for me to allow an insane man forty days to think about whether he wants to marry my wife or not?"

"He is a young man, and I hope this period of solitude will be a chance to liberate his soul from this infatuation and thus allow him to go free. I will be beholden to you for life if you would only spare him for now and give him but this one chance. He cannot die on my account without such opportunity for penance," Lady Goharshad pleaded.

"Why am I being put through this?"

"There is a reason why your father chose you, his youngest son, as the heir to the throne before he died rather than your three older brothers," she said.

"Oh, and how I wish it were those three who were facing this incredibly excruciating trial."

"It is a trial, is it not? A trial by Providence," she said, seizing on the opportunity his words provided. "And I am certain our love shall overcome it, and we shall prevail at the end."

Shahrokh gave no answer and left in apparent frustration to see his advisors who were awaiting his final decision.

When the king insisted that the lad be spared the noose for now, the counselors did not look amused about how this whole situation was unfolding.

"What is your verdict, sir, regarding the culprit?" one advisor asked.

"My wife, the queen, has requested that we wait for forty days," Shahrokh replied coldly.

"Do you mean the queen does not give her consent to such a punishment for a man who has overstepped all bounds of ethics and attempted to defame Her Royal Highness? As her legitimate husband, you have every right to take action regardless of what her wishes may be."

"I intend to heed her request. She has never disappointed me before. I have not forgotten how every one of you reacted regarding the extensive renovations undertaken in response to her suggestions. We now see the prosperity that it has brought to our kingdom. The fact that she reaches out to the poor left everyone in this room, including myself, with raised eyebrows and lines of concern on our foreheads. Yet, her benevolence, and by extension, our rule, has become legendary."

"But this is different, sir, we are talking about the honor of your wife."

"We are also talking about a poor man's life."

"What mockery is this?" an old advisor who was too angry to keep his opinion to himself exclaimed. "You are the son of Tamerlane, for heaven's sake, and must have some degree of his audacity and determination in your blood. Drag the man out. Execute him publicly before he dies of this misconceived infatuation. Make an example of him for the world to see."

"I will do so when the queen consents to such action," the king said, resolutely.

A small number of people in the court of the King expressed their sympathy with Lady Goharshad, yet even those few wondered out loud why she was so adamantly protecting this young man's life and placing not only her own reputation but the entire country's honor in jeopardy.

Rumors began to follow the royals like birds of prey circling a dying man. They ranged in breadth and depth and included outrageous notions such as, "the queen being a sorcerer has placed a spell on the king that has deprived him of his wits and ability to make decisions."

Lady Goharshad could hardly leave the castle. Everywhere she looked there were mouths that talked and eyes that rolled in disapproval. *She is ruining her husband's character*, they said. *He must be a great man to endure it. She is older than the young man who has fallen for her, therefore wiser, and must know better. She is risking the empire's status over a childish infatuation. They say she is the one who seduced the poor boy. Now she has asked him to pray in the new mosque. What mockery of religion is that?*

Rumors ebbed and flowed like a restless torrent, threatening the foundation of Shahrokh's Timurid Dynasty and feeding the imagination of idle minds with no other care or concern except counting their riches and finding faults in others. Shahrokh was a tolerant man, but even Lady Goharshad's empathizing husband had his limits. He said that he still supported her decision, but rumors had reached him, and his advisors insisted that he take action.

"Divorce the queen!" the more brazen of the advisors said. "You can have any other woman on the face of the earth," he added. "Why allow this to get out of hand," the others insisted, "when the answer is so simple."

This was not a simple matter for the royal family. Invitations to participate in events began to drop, and foreign dignitaries reduced the frequency of their attendance. After all, royals without a good reputation were as unwanted as bankrupted men of trade. Rumors grew to a tidal wave and carried the message of trouble in the land of Tamerlane to the far corners of the world. Enemies of the kingdom began to see this as a sign of weakness, and plots began to take root to overthrow Shahrokh.

Lady Goharshad opened the door to her chamber in the castle with a new surge of determination. "Summon the old woman who approached me regarding her son," she demanded from an aide. "I have an urgent message to convey through her."

The old woman came and seemed quite happy to carry the news of the queen's plan to her son. Color returned to the young man's face as soon as he heard Lady Goharshad's decision.

"She would be yours, of course, there is no doubt," his mother assured him.

"I promise," he said, "I shall do as she has requested. I will hold this vigil for forty days or forty years if I have to for her hand in marriage."

Chapter Nine

The Reflection

WORKERS AT THE CONSTRUCTION SITE HAD ACCESS TO A mirror mounted on a wall at the entry to the mosque. During the forty days of Jamal's confinement, however, the other workers received their wages but could not enter the premises. Construction ceased, and the usual sounds of renovation became silent.

After praying for a full five hours with his mind wandering in all directions and mostly asking God for a chance to be united with his beloved, the lad settled for a meager meal of bread and cheese and some hot tea, provided to him twice daily. He then started walking around the nearly finished mosque and stopped at the entry where the hexagonal mirror reflected his image.

The mirror, crooked around the edges and chipped at corners, was mounted to reflect the average height. A very tall man had to bend his knees to see a full reflection of himself in it. Jamal's height, however, allowed him a good view without having to raise himself or bend his knees to lengthen or shorten his stature.

A beam of light streaming through the transom window bounced off the mirror. Jamal stared for a moment or two at his own reflection. He certainly looked handsome. His brown hair curled onto his sunburnt skin, making the whiteness of his eyes appear like ivory encasing brown irises. If the date written on the cover of his mother's Quran was correct, he was now exactly one and twenty years of age. His feet ached; no, when he thought of the queen they burned as if he had walked through a field of fire.

His mind was young, vivacious and unyielding, ready to explore the treasures of the world. He had embraced the altar of worship rather than the gallows, for his choices were clear when on one side stood the Angel of Death and on the other, a chance to be united with the queen. The mere idea of the grand prize before him brought a surge of happiness to his veins.

He knew his youth would eventually wither like petals of cut flowers, and only dullness of old age would remain. All that he wanted to attain, all that meant anything to him, all his hopes and dreams were bundled up and left beyond his reach. What meaning did his life have without her in it? The moment he had laid eyes on her, her majesty, her beauty, her grace, captured his heart. She embodied perfection. It mattered not if they plucked him like a fresh bloom, as long as he could proclaim to the world the love that had engulfed him and by doing so unburden his aching heart.

He may have lacked education and wisdom, but he was never deficient when it came to yearning, a sensation he had lived with all his life; yearning for the luxuries he could never have, yearning for a life that would never be his, and now yearning for a woman who would never accept him. But no, he adamantly refused to allow yearning to become his constant companion in life.

Splotches of gray marred the surface of the looking glass. Staring at himself in the mirror made him a bit uncomfortable. Something about his reflection bothered him. He felt as if he was staring at a hypocrite.

That very afternoon, his prayers had a note of sincerity to them, and he tried to shed some tears. But when he returned at dusk to where the mirror stood, cracks here and there made the image distorted, particularly with a taper lit on a nearby alcove. He looked into the mirror, and all he could see was hypocrisy. *Why? What has become of me? Am I a fraud, insincere in what I profess as love?*

As days turned into nights and nights into days, he maintained the same routine. Praying and worshiping for five hours, eating his meal, walking to the mirror and staring at himself. And each time he looked into the mirror, the image became more and more distorted.

Was it the mirror or what he perceived in the mirror that had become distorted? He knew not. The bizarre image looking back at him irritated him, yet he had a hard time looking away from it. The polished surface stoked the greatest fears in him. Or was it that he had come to know his true self now that he had had a chance to contemplate his life, in solitude? *How could he have desecrated the name of such a virtuous woman with his vile attempts, knowing full well that he could never fulfill such a desire?*

The mirror reflected the deep recesses of his mind. It was not him but a vile reflection of him as if a sadistic painter had made a bizarre depiction of his face. The reflection reproached him, mocked and ridiculed him. The image haunted him, even after he slept. The repugnant face took center stage in all his nightmares. He wanted to rip off and throw away all that defiled his soul. He felt infested, diseased, an impurity that no scrubbing could wash away covered his heart and mingled with his soul; the extent of the damage done by his misconceived passions overwhelmed him. He had brought ill repute to a kingdom that stretched to the horizon in vastness and reached the skies in grandeur.

"What right had he to her?" the image in the mirror seemed to ask.

He began to despise the mirror, hate his own reflection. Yet like a magnet, he was drawn to it, every morning and every evening as he performed the same ritual. He came to believe that an invisible hand altered the image, for each time he peered into the mirror, the expression on his face looked scarier. Each time he returned to the altar, his supplications became more profound, his tears more sincere. Through prayer, he sought relief for his tormented soul, a lifting of the burden of guilt that he now felt upon his shoulders.

How hideous he had been beneath the veneer he wore as a face, a mere façade to fool others. Was it love, truly love, that he felt for the fine woman or was it vanity, his desire to own what could not be his? She embodied everything he lacked: beauty, wealth, power and majesty. He understood that very well now. She had not reciprocated his love but recoiled from it. Were it not for her forgiving, benevolent soul, he would not have been given even this short respite, and they would have surely taken him to the gallows. He envisioned his body swaying on a noose for all to see, his soul descending into the eternal fire. He shuddered at the thought. The noose was still there, waiting for him.

He shed tears as he contemplated his wrongs for thirty days and thirty nights. He wore himself thin. His face turned pale. Tears became the holy water that washed away the impurities of his soul. He refrained from looking at the mirror, the instrument of his torment, but rather sought the light within his remorseful heart as his supplications continued.

In the lonely corner of the mosque where rays of light coming from a window of multi-colored glass illuminated the sacred niche, the young man kept vigil until the blue thread of his prayer beads tore, and its green globules rolled all over his prayer rug wet with tears of piety. For more than a month now, he had shed tears of repentance, cried in defiance, and bowed in submission, until his heart filled with the love of the Creator, displacing his obsession with the queen.

He felt pure as the day he was born. The light that filled the enclosure was not from an external source but from within his soul. He felt the ecstasy of innocence and the joy of rejuvenation. He felt as if he had a far keener sense of his surroundings.

Hours turned into days until the forty days were up. On the last night of his seclusion, he stayed up all night and fell asleep right after his morning prayers, exhausted from entreaty before the Almighty. When he woke up, the sun illuminated his chamber. As he opened his eyes, the most incredible sensation of serenity filled his entire being. A feeling of innocence, of being loved by a higher power who cared for him. "Is this God?" he wondered aloud.

As he wiped away his last tears with his wet hands, an overwhelming, overpowering feeling of lightness and warmth, of kindness and purity overcame him. He felt one with the universe, each minuscule part of his being, the exact identical copy of all living and non-living things around him. They all spoke the same language; a language he now understood. He could sing in that language, raise his voice and join the chorus of life. He fell to his knees before the King of Hearts, the King of Souls.

He stared at the staircase that led to the immaculate structure that held the sacred body. The door above it was kept locked, preventing him from entering the mausoleum. The stairs weren't built right. He began imagining how he would redo them, and a wonderful sense of relief came over him. His occupation would become his salvation.

Finally, a knock at the door to his place of confinement announced the culmination of the forty days. When the door opened, a middle-aged man with spectacles entered who introduced himself as the Hakeem.

Jamal had such an unearthly countenance that the Hakeem wondered whether the young man was human or fay. When he asked Jamal if he was mortal, a smile more beautiful than the early rays of the sun illuminated his face, and he replied that he was indeed. But now that he considered himself at the service of the Almighty, he realized that he had been the cause of misfortune for the venerable Lady and that he had to ask for her forgiveness.

"I have done wrong. She does not love me, and I have no right to her. I wish to apologize to my lady, the queen," Jamal said.

"What caused such a transformation?" the sagacious Hakeem asked, already knowing the answer but wanting to hear it from the lad's mouth.

"I have gone down to the depths of a dark ocean in which I could have drowned, and I have found something, sensed something that has penetrated every aspect of my life. I am free from want, from anger, and from hate. Like water contained in a vase, I have now joined the ocean. My life is enriched, my feet firmly grounded in the soils of earthly living, but my soul like a tree reaches up to the heavens. Oh' what bliss this is, what overwhelming joy; I have been an embarrassment to our people. From now on, I shall mind my ways."

The story of Jamal's incredible transformation and his efforts aimed at improving the structure of the mosque spread as speedily as the earlier rumors had done, and what was a means of castigation and condemnation became a source of commendation and awe. For Lady Goharshad and her family there was nothing but words of praise as tranquility returned to the Kingdom.

Epilogue

IN A CORNER OF THE CASTLE GARDEN, SAT THREE haughty young ladies. Soraya, the eldest of the three, had grown to be quite a beauty. She was struggling with a painting of a rose bush, and being too proud to be making a mistake, was quite vexed by the fact that her governess was keeping a close eye on her sketch. The other two girls, Setareh and Sahar were sitting on a nearby bench, learning calligraphy from another governess. No one could tell that the well-brought-up young ladies had one day faced imminent peril as their mother lay dead in the slums.

King Shahrokh found Lady Goharshad enjoying the serene scene. As he joined her, partaking of some grapes, he laughingly said, "To think that I almost lost you." He noticed that she was reading the manuscript again and asked, "So, what were Chaka's final words?"

"You should read this yourself," she replied laughing.

"I never have time. But I am curious, read it to me."

Last Entry by Chaka:

In history lies a lesson for the future, and those who ignore it are condemned to repeat the mistakes of the past. Therefore, I consider it a duty toward future generations to share with them what has passed within the confines of these walls, and within the mind of a conqueror, the world may never see the likes of again. The gray twilight of ignorance and hate and the dark night of war and plunder will ultimately end, and a dawn of enlightenment will break one day. The bloodletting will cease. And the world will see a better day tomorrow.

Recommended Resources

Chambers, James. *The Devil's Horsemen: The Mongol Invasion of Europe.* New York: Atheneum, 1985.

Charles River Editors. *Karakorum: The History and Legacy of the Mongol Empire's Capital.* California: CreateSpace Publishing, 2017.

Hay, Timothy. *The Mongol Art of War.* Pennsylvania: Casemate Publishers, 2007.

Grousset, Rene. *The Empire of the Steppes: A History of Central Asia.* Translated by Naomi Walford. New Jersey: Rutgers University Press, 1970.

Rossabi, Morris. *Mongol and Global History.* New York: W.W. Norton, 2011.

———. *The Mongols: A Very Short Introduction.* Oxford: Oxford University Press, 2012.

Saunders, John Joseph. *The History of Mongol Conquests.* Pennsylvania: Penn Press, 2001.

Weatherford, Jack. *Genghis Khan and the Making of the Modern World.* New York: Crown Publishers, 2004.

Weatherford, Jack. *The Secret History of the Mongol Queens: How the Daughters of Genghis Khan Rescued His Empire.* New York: Broadway Paperbacks, 2011.

Acknowledgments

THIS JOURNEY BEGAN WITH THE THOUGHTFUL INPUT and support of the faculty and students of Johns Hopkins University as well as the talented members of the La Madeleine Writers Group: Natasha Tynes (author of They Called Me Wyatt), Chelsea Henderson, Wendra Chambers, Sahar Siddiqui, Gina Wilkinson (author of When the Apricots Bloom), Abiola Johnson, Maura O'Brien-Ali, Ruth Hupart, Maria Said, and Nancy Strickland Hawkins were all there for guidance and support. Among the challenges I faced in writing about the 13th Century was avoiding modern terminology in order to retain the flavor of the era. To this end, I had the privilege of working with my editor, Dr. Nicole Miller, former editor of Harvard Review, who is well-versed in classic literature. I am also indebted to the insight and attention to detail of my publisher, Colin Mustful, who helped me during the final stages of editing.

Author's Biography

F.M. DEEMYAD WAS BORN IN KERMANSHAH, IRAN. SHE grew up in the capital, Tehran, attending bilingual schools run by Christian and Jewish minorities. Her father, born and raised in India, had come to Iran when he was in his late twenties. Being the son of a linguist who had taught English Literature in India for a number of years, he exposed the author in her preschool years to the English language, and she learned to love classic literature under her father's instructions. She received a Master's degree in Writing from Johns Hopkins University in 2016. She currently resides with her husband in Maryland.

CPSIA information can be obtained
at www.ICGtesting.com
Printed in the USA
BVHW081300030921
615648BV00001B/3